The Cruelty

The Cruelty

SCOTT BERGSTROM

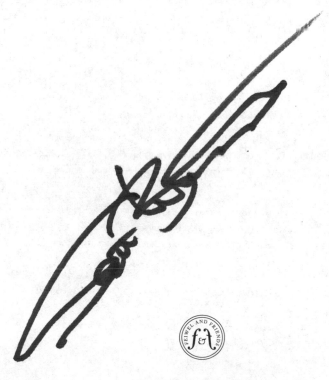

FEIWEL AND FRIENDS
NEW YORK

A Feiwel and Friends Book
An imprint of Macmillan Publishing Group, LLC

The Cruelty. Copyright © 2017 by Scott Bergstrom. All rights reserved.
Printed in the United States of America by LSC Communications US, LLC (Lakeside Classic),
Harrisonburg, Virginia. For information, address Feiwel and Friends,
175 Fifth Avenue, New York, N.Y. 10010.

Our books may be purchased in bulk for promotional, educational, or business use. Please contact
your local bookseller or the Macmillan Corporate and Premium Sales Department at (800) 221-7945
ext. 5442 or by e-mail at MacmillanSpecialMarkets@macmillan.com.

Library of Congress Cataloging-in-Publication Data is available.

ISBN 978-1-250-10818-0 (hardcover) / ISBN 978-1-250-10817-3 (ebook)

Book design by Vikki Sheatsley

Feiwel and Friends logo designed by Filomena Tuosto

First Edition—2017

1 3 5 7 9 10 8 6 4 2

fiercereads.com

For Jana,
the fearless one

"Part of the reason for the ugliness of adults, in a child's eyes, is that the child is usually looking upwards, and few faces are at their best when seen from below."

GEORGE ORWELL

One

The boys are waiting for the beheading. They sit raptly, like impatient jackals, waiting for the blade to fall. But if they'd bothered to read the book, they'd know it wasn't coming. The book just sort of ends. Like a movie clicked off before the last scene. Or like life, really. You almost never see the blade coming, the one that gets you.

Our teacher, Mr. Lawrence, reads the words slowly, stroking that awful little patch of beard under his lower lip as he paces. The soft drumbeat of his footsteps on the linoleum floor—heel-toe, heel-toe—makes it sound like he's trying to come up on the words from behind. *"As if that blind rage had washed me clean, rid me of hope; for the first time, in that night alive with signs and stars, I laid my heart open to the benign indifference of the world."*

The footsteps stop when Mr. Lawrence arrives at Luke Bontemp's desk, and he taps the spine of the book on the kid's head. Luke is texting someone on his phone and trying to hide it beneath his jacket.

"Put it away or I take it away," Mr. Lawrence says.

The phone disappears into Luke's pocket.

"What do you think Camus is talking about there?"

Luke smiles with that smile that has gotten him out of everything his entire life. Poor Luke, I think. Beautiful, useless, stupid Luke. I heard his great-great-grandfather made a fortune selling oil to the Germans and steel to the British during World War I and no one in his family has had to work since. He won't have to, either, so what's the use of reading Camus?

"'Benign indifference of the world,'" Mr. Lawrence repeats. "What is that, you think?"

Luke sucks air into his lungs. I can almost hear the hamster wheel of his brain squeaking away beneath his excellent hair.

"Benign," Luke says. "A tumor or whatever can be benign. Maybe Camus is, you know, saying the world is a tumor."

Twenty-eight of the twenty-nine kids in the class laugh, including Luke. I'm the only one who doesn't. I read this book, *The Stranger*, when I was fourteen. But I read it in the original French, and when Mr. Lawrence assigned an English translation of it for our World Literature class, I didn't feel like reading it again. It's about a guy named Meursault whose mother dies. Then he kills an Arab man and gets sentenced to death, to have his head cut off in public. Then it ends. Camus never gives us the actual beheading.

I turn back to the window, where rain is still pattering, the rhythm of it pulling everyone in the room deeper into some kind of sleepy trance. Beyond the window I can see the outlines of buildings down Sixty-Third Street, their edges all smeared and formless through the water beading against the glass, more like the memory of buildings than the real thing.

Though we're discussing the last part of *The Stranger*, it's the opening lines of the book that always stuck with me. *Aujourd'hui, maman est morte. Ou peut-être hier, je ne sais pas.* It means: Today, Mother died. Or maybe yesterday, I don't know.

But I do know. I know exactly when Mother died. It was ten years ago today. I was only seven at the time, and I was there when it happened. The memory of it comes to me now and then in little sketches and vignettes, individual moments. I hardly ever play back the whole memory start to finish. The psychologist I used to see said that was normal, and that it would get easier with time. It didn't.

"What's your take, Gwendolyn?" Mr. Lawrence asks.

I hear his voice. I even understand the question. But my mind is too far away to answer. I'm in the backseat of the old Honda, my eyes barely open, my head against the cool glass of the window. The rhythm of the car as it bounces down the dirt track on the outskirts of Algiers is pulling me toward sleep. Then I feel the thrum of the tires over the road slow and hear my mother gasp. I open my eyes, look out the windshield, and see fire.

"Gwendolyn Bloom! Paging Gwendolyn Bloom!"

I snap back to the present and turn to Mr. Lawrence. He holds his hands cupped around his mouth like a megaphone. "Paging Gwendolyn Bloom!" he says again.

"Can you tell us what Camus means by 'benign indifference of the world'?"

Though part of my mind is still back in the Honda, I begin speaking anyway. It's a long answer, and a good one, I think. But Mr. Lawrence is looking at me with a little smirk. It's only after I'm speaking for about twenty seconds that I hear everyone laughing.

"In English, please," Mr. Lawrence says, arching an eyebrow and looking at the rest of the class.

"I'm sorry," I say quietly, fidgeting with my uniform skirt and tucking a strand of my fire-engine-red hair behind my ear. "What?"

"You were speaking French, Gwendolyn," Mr. Lawrence says.

"Sorry. I must have been—thinking of something else."

"You're supposed to be thinking about the benign indifference of the world," he says.

One of the girls behind me says, "Jesus, what a pretentious snob."

I turn and see it's Astrid Foogle. She's also seventeen, but she looks at least twenty-one. Her dad owns an airline.

"Enough, Astrid," Mr. Lawrence says.

But I'm staring at her now, drilling into her with my eyes. Astrid Foogle—whose earrings are more valuable than everything in my apartment—is calling me a pretentious snob?

Astrid continues. "I mean, she drops in here the beginning of the year from wherever and thinks she's all superior, and now, oh, look, she's talking in French, not like us dumb Americans. Just *look* how sophisticated she is. Queen of the trailer park."

Mr. Lawrence cuts her off. "Stop it, Astrid. Now."

A few of the kids are nodding in agreement with Astrid; a few others are laughing. I can feel myself trembling, and my face is turning hot. Every synapse in my brain is trying to force the reaction away, but I can't. Why does anger have to look so much like humiliation?

The guy sitting next to Astrid, Connor Monroe, leans back in his seat and grins. "Check it. She's crying."

Which isn't true, but now that he said it, it's as good as reality in the minds of the other kids. *lolololol gwenny bloom lost her shit and cried in wrld lit #pretentioussnob #212justice*

The school bell in the hallway rings and, like a Pavlovian trigger, sends everyone scrambling for the door. Mr. Lawrence holds his book up in the air in a sad little attempt to keep order, shouting, "We begin again tomorrow, same place." Then he turns to me. "And you'll be up first, Bloom. You have all night to meditate on the benign indifference of the world, so come up with something good. And in English, *por favor.*"

I nod that I will and gather up my stuff. Outside the classroom, Astrid Foogle is at her locker, surrounded, as always, by her disciples. She's doing an imitation of me, a monologue in fake French, her shoulders hunched, nose squashed with her index finger.

My eyes down with the proper beta deference, I slide by her and her friends on my way to my own locker. But Astrid spots me; I can tell because she and her friends go silent and I hear the heels of their shoes—*they're Prada pumps, you little sow*—accelerate toward me, her friends just a pace behind.

"Hey, Gwenny," she starts up. "Translation question for you. How do you say 'suicide is never the answer' in French?"

I ignore her and keep walking, hoping for a sudden fatal stroke—hers or mine, doesn't matter. The heat radiates off my face, anger becoming rage becoming whatever's stronger than rage. I can only imagine what it looks like. I fold my shaking arms over my chest.

"Seriously," Astrid continues. "Because someone like you has to have thought of suicide from time to time. I mean, why wouldn't you, right? So, *s'il vous plaît,* how do you say it, Gwenny? *En français?*"

I spin around, and the words come bursting from my mouth. "*Va te faire foutre.*"

Astrid stops, and for a half second—no, less than that—fear snaps across her face. But then she realizes where she is, in her kingdom surrounded by acolytes, and the real Astrid returns. She arches her beautifully pruned eyebrows.

One of her friends, Chelsea Bunchman, smiles. "Astrid, she just told you to go fuck yourself."

Astrid's mouth opens into an O and I hear a little gasp sneak out. "You little piece of trash," she says, and takes a step closer.

I see the slap while it's still in midair. I see it, but even so, I don't do anything to stop it. Instead, I cringe, shrinking my head down into my neck and my neck down into my shoulders. It's a hard slap—Astrid really means it—and my head twists to the side under its force. The nail of one of her fingers catches my skin and stings my cheek.

A crowd is forming. I see the grinning faces of Luke Bontemp and Connor Monroe and maybe a dozen other students staring wide-eyed, less in shock at what they've seen than in glee. They're standing around Astrid and me in a semicircle, as if in an arena. This is entertainment, I realize, a time-honored kind. I take note that Astrid didn't punch me, didn't kick me, didn't pull my hair. She very calmly, very deliberately, slapped my face. It was the uppercase-*L* Lady slapping the lowercase-*m* maid.

Instead of slapping her back—and, who am I kidding, Gwendolyn Bloom would never slap back—I close my eyes, the humiliation like the winds I remember from the Sahara, hot and hard and lasting for days. An adult voice orders everyone to move along, and when I open my eyes, there's a middle-aged teacher whose name I don't know standing there with his hands in the pockets of his khakis. His eyes travel from Astrid to me and back again.

"What happened?" he asks Astrid.

"She told me to—I can't say the word. It was a curse word, *f* myself." Her voice is demure and wounded.

"Is this true?" he says, looking to me.

I open my mouth, about to rat her out for slapping me. "It is," I say instead.

L'Étranger, the title of the book we're studying in World Lit, is usually translated into English as *The Stranger*. But it could also mean *The Outsider* or *The Foreigner*. That's me, all of it—stranger, outsider, foreigner. I'm technically an American. That's what my passport says. But I wasn't born here and, until the start of junior year this past

September, I had lived in the United States for only eighteen months, right after my mother was killed. We—my dad and I—came to New York so he could take up a post at the United Nations, which isn't too far from my school, Danton Academy.

There's no way in hell my dad could have afforded a place like Danton on his own. But my father is a diplomat with the Department of State, and private school for us diplobrats is sometimes one of the benefits. Depending on which country you're in, that private school might be the only good school for a thousand miles and you're sitting in class with the son or daughter of the country's president or king or awful dictator. That happened to me once. The asshole son of an asshole president sat next to me in my math class. He wore shoes that were made specially for him in Vienna and cost five thousand dollars a pair, while kids were starving in the streets just beyond the school's stucco walls.

Not that it's so different at Danton. The kids here are the children of presidents and kings and dictators, too—just of companies instead of countries. Most of my classmates have always been rich. Usually, the only poor person they ever meet is the foreign kid who delivers their groceries for them or brings over the dry cleaning. My dad makes what would be a decent living anywhere else in the world, but to the kids at Danton we're poor as dirt.

Sitting on the bench outside the assistant director's office, I fuss with my uniform skirt—God, I hate skirts—pulling at the hem so that it falls lower on my black tights, flattening out the little pleats. The uniforms are an attempt to equalize us, I suppose, but there are no restrictions about shoes. Thus, wealth and tribal loyalties are displayed with the feet: Prada pumps and Gucci loafers for old money versus Louboutin flats and Miu Miu sneakers for new money. I'm one of the irrelevant two-member Doc Martens tribe. Mine are red and beat-up, but the other member, a quiet artist's kid from downtown who's tolerated by the others insofar as he's a reliable source of Adderall, goes with polished black.

Not that if I suddenly showed up in Prada it would make a difference. I don't look like Astrid Foogle, or any of them, really. I'm too tall, too thick-waisted. Nose too rectangular, mouth too wide. Everything some kind of too. My dad and my doctor say I'm just fine the way I am—say it's hormones, or muscle from all my years of gymnastics. Everyone's built differently, don't accept anyone else's definition of beauty, et cetera, ad nauseam. But it's their job to say things like that. So I color my hair at home with the very finest CVS store-brand dye, lace up my Doc Martens, and pretend not to care.

When the assistant director finally steps out of her office, she's all patronizing smiles and fake concern. Mrs. Wasserman is her name, and she's forever wearing a cloud of perfume and sugary joy, as if any second she expects a cartoon bluebird to fly out of the sky and land on her finger.

"How are we today?" she asks as we go into her office.

"Amazing," I say, sinking down into a chair upholstered in blood-colored leather. "Just perfect."

Mrs. Wasserman steeples her fingers in front of her as a signal we're getting down to business. "I'm told that you're facing some interpersonal challenges with one of your classmates."

It's all I can do to not roll my eyes at her euphemistic, bullshit tone. The thing is, 95 percent of this school is made up of kids who are very rich and very WASPy. The 5 percent who aren't are either here on scholarship or because their parents work at the UN. The others don't like us Five-Percenters, as we're known, but we help people like Mrs. Wasserman pretend Danton Academy is something other than an elitist bitch factory.

Mrs. Wasserman consults a file folder. "Do you go by Gwen or Gwendolyn, dear?"

"Gwendolyn," I say. "Only my dad calls me Gwen."

"Gwendolyn it is, then," Mrs. Wasserman says with a cookie-sweet smile. "And is what it says here correct, Gwendolyn—you tested out of the AP exams in, my goodness, five foreign languages?"

I shrug. "We move a lot."

"I see that. Moscow. Dubai. Still—quite a talent." She runs her finger along a line in the file. "Must be tough, having a stepfather in the State Department. New city every couple of years. New country."

"You can just say 'father.'"

"Sorry?"

"He's not my stepfather. He adopted me when he married my mom. I was two."

"Father, yes. If you like." Mrs. Wasserman shakes her head as she makes a note on the paper in front of her. "Now to why you're here: Danton is a safe space, Gwendolyn, and we have a zero-tolerance policy on emotionally abusive behavior."

"Right. Just like the handbook says."

"That includes cursing at faculty or students, which means when you swore at another girl in French, you were in violation."

"Astrid didn't understand a word of what I said until Chelsea Bunchman translated it."

"The point is you said something hurtful, Gwendolyn. Whether you said it in French or Swahili it doesn't matter."

"It matters if she didn't understand it."

"That's just semantics," she says. "Do you know that word, 'semantics'?"

"The study of what words mean. Which would seem to apply."

I see the muscles in her face tighten. She picks up a pen and holds it so tightly I think it might break. "I understand it's the anniversary of your mother's passing. I'm sorry to hear about that," Mrs. Wasserman says gently. I can see the idea of it makes her uncomfortable, makes

9

her wonder what to do with me. Punish the girl because of her *interpersonal challenges* on the anniversary of her mother's *passing*?

Mrs. Wasserman coughs into her hand and continues. "The normal consequence for swearing at another student is a day's suspension. But under the circumstances, I'm willing to forgo that if you issue a written apology to Miss Foogle."

"You want me to apologize to Astrid?"

"Yes, dear."

It's an easy out and the obvious choice. I lean back in the chair and try to smile. "No thanks," I say. "I'll take the suspension."

It's still raining, the cold kind that might turn to snow later. March is bad this year, no sunshine at all and not even a hint of spring. Just skies the color of steel and the stink of New York's own garbage soup running through the gutters. Black SUVs are lined up at the curb, Danton Academy's version of school buses. The very richest kids use these—private mini limos that pick them up at the end of the day so they don't have to suffer the indignity of walking home or taking the subway.

I'm headed for the station a few blocks away. I don't have an umbrella, so I pull up the hood of my old army jacket. It used to be my mom's from when she was a lieutenant way before I was born. When my dad and I were moving a few years ago—Dubai to Moscow, maybe, our two most recent posts—I found it in a box. My dad got teary when I put it on, so I started to take it off. Then he said it looked good on me, told me I could have it if I wanted.

My mom. I'd been avoiding the subject all day and mostly succeeded until World Lit. Hard not to think about it when you spend an hour talking about Algerian justice.

The rain patters against my face, and it makes me calm. A guy with a black-and-green kaffiyeh around his neck shelters beneath the awning of his gyro cart on Lexington just outside the subway station. I order my food in Arabic—a gyro with everything, I tell him, and don't be cheap with the lamb.

He squints at me with a surprised smile, and I wonder if he understood me. My Arabic is rusty as hell, and the formal kind no one really speaks except on TV.

"You Egyptian?" he says as he takes a pair of tongs and starts arranging pieces of lamb on a pita.

"No," I answer. "I'm—from here."

I get variations of that *are you x?* question a lot, though. My eyes are umber brown, while my skin is a pale, translucent sheath pulled over something else—brass under tracing paper, a stoned boy on the Moscow subway told me once. What *x* is, though, I have no idea. My mom's not around to ask, and the dad I call dad, because he is my dad legally and in every sense but one, says he doesn't know. My bio father's name isn't even listed on my original birth certificate from Landstuhl, the American military hospital in Germany where I was born.

"Special for Cleopatra," the man says, tossing on some onions and smothering the whole mess with the bitter white sauce that I love so much I would drink it by the gallon if I could.

On the subway platform, I devour the gyro. I hadn't realized how hungry I was. Maybe getting slapped like a peasant does that to you. I'm waiting for the N or Q out to Queens. I wish a train would come already. I wish it would come so that I could put some physical distance between me and this island and the memories Camus dredged up.

Just then, as if I'd willed it to come, the Q train screeches mournfully to a stop in front of me. I shoot the soggy tinfoil-and-paper wrapping of the gyro into a trash can and climb on board.

Most people hate the subway, but not me. It's a strange, wonderful thing to be alone among the hundred or so other people in the car. I pull a book out of my backpack and lean against the door as the train shoots through the tunnel under the river toward Queens. It's a novel with a teenage heroine set in a dystopian future. Which novel in particular doesn't matter because they're all the same. Poor teenage heroine, having to march off to war when all she really wants to do is run away with that beautiful boy and live off wild berries and love. Paper worlds where heroes are real.

But as the train screeches and scrapes along in the dark, rocking back and forth as if any moment it might fly off the rails, I find myself suddenly unable to follow the story or even translate the symbols on the page into words. The memories just aren't going to let me get away this time. They demand to be recognized, insistent as Astrid's slap.

Today's my dad's birthday. The worst possible day for a birthday. Or rather, the worst possible day *because* it's his birthday. That's how it happened, ten years ago today. Coming back from the birthday dinner his work friends were throwing for him at a restaurant in Algiers.

I have to think about it, right? It makes you sick if you press it down inside, right? Okay. No more fighting it off. Go back there, I tell myself. Live it again, I tell myself. Be brave for once. Ten years ago today.

My mother gasps as we round a corner; the sound of it wakes seven-year-old me from sleep. I look out the windshield and see fire. I make out the faces illuminated in the light of a burning police truck. They're men, a dozen, twenty. Mostly bearded, mostly young, their skin orange in the glow of the flames. We've stumbled across something that doesn't concern us. A beef with the military police that's gone in the mob's favor. But the men are made curious by us newcomers, and they peer into the windows of our car, trying to make out the nationalities of the faces inside.

My mother yells at my dad to back up. He shifts into reverse and looks over his shoulder and guns the engine. For a second, the Honda shoots backward but then jerks to a stop. There are people back there, my dad shouts. Run them over, my mom shouts back.

But he won't. Or maybe he will, but he doesn't have time. He doesn't have time because a glass bottle shatters on the roof and liquid fire cascades down the window on the driver's side of the car. A Molotov cocktail is what it's called, a bottle of gasoline with a burning rag jammed in its mouth. The poor man's hand grenade.

The rule taught to diplomats about what to do if a Molotov cocktail breaks over your car is to keep driving, as far and as fast as possible, until you're out of danger. A car doesn't really burn like it does in the movies. It doesn't explode right away. It takes time. And time is what you need if you want to stay breathing.

But the crowd gets closer and something happens, something that makes the car stall out. My dad tries to restart the engine, but it just turns over and over and over, the ignition never quite catching. My mother's door opens, and she yells at the man outside who opened it. She doesn't scream; she yells. Yells like starting her car on fire and yanking open her door was very rude and, by God, she'd like to speak to whoever's in charge.

I don't see what happens next because my dad is reaching over the seat and unbuckling my seat belt. He pulls me like a rag doll into the front with him. I remember how rough he was being, how much it hurt when he yanked me between the front seats. He clutches me to his chest like he's giving me a big hug and leaves through the same door as my mom, the door that's not on fire.

Blows from clubs and bats rain down on him. I feel the force of the blows traveling all the way through his body. He's taking them for me, or most of them. Three or four strikes land on my legs, which are sticking out in the open from beneath my dad's arm. I try to scream in pain but can't because my dad is pressing me into his chest so hard.

My dad doesn't stop running until he's away from the mob, and I'm dangling over his shoulder and he's turning around for some reason, turning around and running backward. Then I go deaf because the pistol he's firing is so loud. It's like the end of the world is happening two feet from my head. He fires again and again and again and again. My vision narrows to almost nothing, then disappears altogether as I black out.

Fourteen stab wounds to the chest and neck. That's the official cause of my mother's death. That's what the report from the autopsy says, and that's what my dad told me when I was old enough to ask him about it. I was nine years old, or maybe ten, when I asked. But there was more, of course. Stuff that happened to her in the time after she was pulled from the car but before she was stabbed. Stuff my dad said he'd tell me about when I got older. I never did ask him about the other stuff, though, and he never brings it up. It's probably easier on him if he doesn't have to say it, and it's probably easier on me if I never have to hear it.

We're in Queens now, and the subway rockets out of the tunnel and into open air. It lurches around a corner, the wheels screaming like demons, so loud I can barely hear my own thoughts. I squeeze the bar above my head tighter so I don't fall over. My body bends with the momentum of the train. Then it slows and its wheels shriek on the wet tracks as we come up on Queensboro Plaza, all gray industrial buildings and new apartment towers and brightly lit shops with windows advertising lottery tickets and cigarettes and beer.

I hoist my backpack on my shoulder as the train stops and bolt out onto the platform, leaving the memories to slouch and hobble after me. I take the stairs two at a time, then three at a time, a race to the bottom. When I reach level ground, I needle and veer through the slow

14

and old taking their sweet time until I push through the turnstile. Guys out on the sidewalk in front of the shops whistle and catcall after me.

I start running and keep running. I bolt across a street and a yellow cab swerves and honks. I run until my lungs burn and I'm soaked with rain and sweat. I run until the blind rage has washed me clean, rid me of hope. And for the first time, on this afternoon alive with neon signs and stars, I lay my heart open to the benign indifference of the world.

Two

And for a fraction of a second, I'm arcing through the air above the earth, apart from it, an arrow neither in the bow nor yet in its target. I wish I could stay like this, free of the earth, floating.

But gravity won't hear of it. Gravity pulls me down from my back handspring, bluntly, unskillfully, like the big dumb magnet it is. I'm too fast for it, though, and I won't let it wreck me. My hands touch down on the surface of the balance beam. It's a thin layer of suede over wood, and it'll break your neck if you're not careful. Then my legs arc back up, over my body, one, two.

When you're standing on your hands, the center of gravity is the thing. The balance beam is ten centimeters wide, so you don't have much room to play with. Even being off by a centimeter or two is too much. A centimeter or two is the difference between a gold medal at the Olympics and driving your spine into the ground like a javelin with the force of your entire body weight. Gravity doesn't much care. Gravity is benignly indifferent.

I cartwheel to the side, back to my feet, then pause just long enough to catch a single breath. Bracing my hands on the edge of the suede and wood of the beam, I push back, then up into a handstand. I waver for a moment, my left leg thrashing out as I feel myself begin to fall. So then I right myself, balance restored, no problem.

But a wave of uncertainty that begins in my arms rolls up through my chest and tips me forward. I rock my hips back to correct it, but I overcompensate and now my legs tip too far in the other direction. My right arm quakes, and I see the world around me bend and tilt. I try to kick my legs around to break the fall, but it's too late. I smash into the mat chest first and my rib cage slams into my lungs, blasting all the air inside me out through my mouth.

A boy who was practicing on the rings—a Ukrainian kid from Brooklyn I've seen a few times—drops to the ground and scrambles over to me. "You hurt maybe? Handstand maybe too much hard." He helps me to my feet, hands me a towel. I close my eyes and breathe into it. "Is okay," he says, and places a hand on my trembling shoulder.

I thank him and stagger away like a drunk. My body is spent and it feels like someone has injected Drano into my muscles. When I get to the locker room, I throw a towel over my head and collapse onto a bench, elbows on knees, breathing so ragged the air whistles when it goes in and out, leaving a faint taste of blood on my tongue. It sounds strange, but I like this—the pain, the ragged breathing, the little taste of blood. It reminds me I have a body, that I am a body. That I'm something real, instead of just the thoughts in my head.

I drop the towel to the floor and strip out of my leotard. When I reach the showers, it takes a minute for the water to come out hot, but I stand under the cold rain anyway. It's harsh water that smells like chlorine and rust, and it comes out hard. It beats against my skin, billions of little stinging needles.

. . .

17

I started gymnastics after my mom was killed. I was seven years old, and for a month or two afterward, all I did was lie in bed rolled up in a ball, rolled up inside myself, screaming as loud as I could into a pillow saturated with tears and snot. My dad would hold me, of course, but then he would cry, too. We fed off each other like this for a while until we both dried out. That was right after moving from Algiers to Washington.

One Saturday, we drove to an electronics store because my dad knocked his cell phone into the sink while he was shaving and he needed a new one. Next to the store was a gymnastics studio. We stood there at the window watching a boy on a pommel horse, swinging around like gravity didn't apply to him, like he had been exempted from the rule that eventually everything goes crashing down to the ground. A teacher came out, an Asian woman. I thought she was going to tell us to go away, but instead she asked if we wanted to come inside and take a look.

The addiction was born, and when we left for our next post, I discovered that most countries have Olympic training centers in their capital cities, where my dad would be stationed with the embassy. The best coaches were always willing to take on a new American student, especially if the new American student paid in American dollars.

No one ever pretended I was Olympics material. Too tall, too big, they all said, and no grace at all. I was all gangly raw power, like a thick chain instead of a whip. But getting to the Olympics, or even competing at all, wasn't why I started and it wasn't why I continued. I chased those bits of seconds spent in the air, those moments cheating gravity, for the drug called freedom. So what if the high of not having to think about anything else only lasted a tenth of a second? So what if the bullies and the loneliness and the memories were waiting for me on the ground? I could always get back on the beam.

· · ·

Back in the city, the rain has stopped, and in the dark of early evening, the streets feel clean. Surfaces glimmer, and Manhattan smells of cold, clean water instead of garbage and gasoline for the first time in months. I make my way across Third Avenue and down to Second, where I turn left. My first stop is the bakery on the corner, where I take ten minutes to choose just two cupcakes: one chocolate with red icing, the other lemon with pink icing. The shopkeeper wraps them up in a little box.

A few doors down, the lights are still on inside Atzmon's Stationers. I press the doorbell and see a figure shuffling slowly at the back of the shop. Then the door buzzes for me to enter.

"*Guten Abend, Rotschuhe!*" says Bela Atzmon loudly from the back of the shop. Good evening, Red Shoes, is how he greets me because of my red boots. He's Hungarian by birth, but spoke German in school.

I make my way through the dark wood shelves lined with stacks and stacks of writing paper in every possible color and texture. Brass lamps with green shades cast everything in a warm, old-fashioned kind of light, as if the store had been here, unchanged, for a hundred years. I hope this place never has to close, but who writes letters anymore?

At the front of the shop is a glass display cabinet full of pens, and it's here that Bela meets me, peering at me over the top of his glasses.

He's somewhere north of eighty, maybe even ninety, but he's still thick and strong. He was a farm boy, he told me once, from a little village far from anything anyone would call a big city. "Is today the day, Red Shoes?" he asks, his accent thick as peanut butter.

In addition to the stationery store, Bela and his wife, Lili, own the apartments above it. My dad and I live on the fourth floor, and the Atzmons on the fifth. We became friends with them almost as soon as we moved in, and we go to their apartment at least twice a week for dinner. Afterward, Bela always forces a Hungarian fruit brandy called palinka on my dad, and the four of us sit and talk. Politics. Religion. The lives they'd led—first in Hungary, then in Israel, where they'd made their home for thirty years before coming to the States. Bela waves his fourth or fifth or sixth brandy of the night around like a conductor's baton as the stories get darker. Then Lili scolds him and he stops. After a while, I usually go downstairs to do my homework, and as I leave, Bela and Lili always squeeze my hand and give me a little kiss on the cheek. It's the kind of thing I imagine grandparents do. Always looking at me like I'm treasure.

It takes me a minute to dig through the pockets of my jacket and find the thin envelope I put there this morning. I take it out and remove the contents—ten twenty-dollar bills—and spread them out on the counter.

Bela clicks his tongue and shakes his head. "Too much, little one. Didn't you see the sign in the window? Today only, fifty percent discount for any young woman wearing red shoes."

"That's not fair to you."

Bela takes up the money and gives me back half. "If the world were fair to me, I'd be driving a Bentley home to a mansion in Beverly Hills." From a drawer beneath the counter he removes a slender plastic box. "But then I would be in California and you'd be here, paying full price."

He sets the box down on a little velvet mat and opens it. The fountain pen—piano black with the words *To Dad, Love G* engraved in script down the side—actually glistens as if it were wet. I pick it up and remove the cap, rotating the pen in my hand, watching the silver nib at the end catch the light like the blade of a scalpel.

I climb the three flights of stairs to our apartment. There's only one apartment per floor, each running from the front of the building all the way to the back. I enter and hear Miles Davis playing softly, an elegantly melancholy piece, a trumpet alone in a dark room, talking to itself: *It's not so bad, no, not so bad*. My dad says it lifts his spirits to think someone at some time could handle sadness with such grace.

I kick off my boots and pass through the kitchen, where on the small table in the corner there are take-out boxes from the Indian restaurant we like.

"Dad?" I call. "What's with the Indian food? Spaghetti a la Gwendolyn, remember?" Every year since I was eight I made spaghetti for him on his birthday. He was too sad to go out that first year after my mom was killed, and it just sort of became a tradition after that.

He's lying on the couch, almost flat except for his neck, which is bent a little so he can see the screen of the laptop resting on his chest. This is how he is most of the time when he gets home from work: worn out, ground down after a day of heroically battling memos and reports. His title is political officer, which sounds interesting, but he says all he does is shuffle papers and go to meetings. They're top secret papers, or so he tells me, and the meetings sometimes have him leaving for Nairobi or Singapore on a day's notice. But they're papers and meetings nonetheless, and how interesting can that be?

"Hey, kiddo." He smiles, the laptop's screen reflecting in the lenses of his glasses. He's been losing weight lately, and his face is long and narrow. *Stress*, he answered me last week when I told him I was concerned. *Stress is the key to staying thin.*

I drop to the floor next to the couch. "Happy birthday, old man."

He looks down at me over his glasses with a dorky expression of confusion on his face as if he had no idea today is his birthday, just like he's done every birthday. He reaches over and rubs my head. "Sorry about the Indian food. I was just tired of spaghetti. I thought we'd try something new tonight."

"Indian isn't new."

"So—kale soup from the vegan-hipster place? Fine with me."

I smile, pull his hand away from my hair. On the laptop screen is small type I can't quite make out and a picture of a fat man with a shaved head, eyes open, a black dot the size of a dime near the center of his forehead. It takes me a second to recognize that the black dot is a bullet hole. "Ew," I say. "What the hell is that?"

My dad closes the laptop. "Viktor Zoric. Shot by a cop two days ago at his home in Belgrade," he says as he stands. "It'll be in the paper tomorrow. *Serbian crime boss killed during arrest.*"

"What'd he do?"

"Very bad things," he says as he plods into the kitchen.

I get up and follow. "What kind of bad things?"

"The worst things," he says.

"That's not what I asked."

He twists the cap off a bottle of cheap red wine and sniffs at its mouth, then pours himself a glass. "Doesn't matter. Just be a teenager, Gwen."

I take the wine from his hand and sip it. Our deal is I can have a single glass of wine with dinner if the adults are drinking it, too.

"So, arresting Viktor Zoric," I say. "Were you involved?"

My dad takes down two plates and hands them to me. "I moved some papers around and wrote a little report. This time, someone actually read it."

I set the plates across from each other on the table. "So was he a murderer? Drug lord? What?"

"Enough, Gwen."

"I read the news. I'm vaguely aware that the world isn't all rainbows and butterflies."

"You want to know? Fine." He hands me another wine glass. "Murder, drugs, all that. But Viktor's main things were arms dealing and human trafficking. For prostitution. Women. Kids."

I wrinkle my nose. "Okay. I get it."

"Mainly they were sent to Europe, but also to Abu Dhabi, Shanghai. Los Angeles, too. Cargo containers on ships. That's how he sent them to LA."

"Thank you for that picture in my head." I scoop rice and vindaloo onto the plates.

"Put in a metal box with a little food and water and a bucket for a toilet," my dad says. "They were dead when Customs found them. Fourteen girls from Russia and Ukraine."

"Jesus. Stop already," I say. "Inappropriate dinner conversation."

"You asked, so I told you." He gestures to my chair. "Put it off as long as possible, Gwen. Finding out how shitty the world is."

As I sit, my dad pours wine into my glass with a flourish like a waiter in a fancy restaurant. *"Votre vin, mademoiselle,"* he says.

"Why, *merci*," I reply, and tuck into the vindaloo.

We eat without speaking for a few minutes, and the room is quiet except for the sounds of our chewing and the buzzing of the refrigerator and the thrum of the city outside our windows. The city's always there, reminding you with horns and sirens and shouts and screams that even when you're alone, you're alone in the middle of a hive filled with a billion other bees.

"So something happened today. A thing at school," I say. "I'll need you to sign something."

He raises his eyebrows as he wipes sauce from his chin with a paper towel. I reach over to my jacket hanging on a peg by the door and pull out the suspension form from Mrs. Wasserman.

My dad unfolds the paper and studies it for a second. "What the hell, Gwen?"

"It's just a one-day suspension."

"Just a one-day suspension? That's not a small thing."

I inhale deeply. "I know. I'm sorry."

"What happened?"

"Astrid Foogle, she said some things. So I swore at her in French and this teacher heard it and—now I'm suspended. Can you just sign it, please?"

"What did Astrid Foogle say, exactly?"

"Dad, they were nasty things, all right? Can we leave it at that? Please?"

"What concerns me, Gwen, is that you know better than to take the bait. Don't take it, and there won't be a problem."

A sort of electric fog comes over me. I look away, grip the edge of my chair. I'd love nothing more than to tell him about Astrid slapping me, but then he'd just be disappointed I didn't fight back, or at least rat her out.

"I mean, Gwen, this isn't the first time. There was that kid in Dubai, remember? What was his name? And that girl in Moscow, Sveta. Same thing there, really."

"Goddammit, just sign it!" The words explode out of me before I can stop them. I stand, the air catching in my throat when I try to breathe. I turn and head off in the direction of my room. My dad follows, calling my name, but I slam the door shut just before he reaches it.

He knocks politely, then asks if I'm all right. Sure, I answer. Perfect. What's wrong? he asks. This time I don't answer. I see the shadow of his feet in the small space beneath the door as he waits for a second, debating with himself whether or not to give me my space or keep pressing. In the end, he walks away.

What's wrong? he wonders. What's wrong is that I hate this place. I hate Danton and everyone in it. I hate his job and everything to do with it. There are people my age who've spent their entire lives in the same house. There are people my age who've had the same friends since kindergarten. They have a dog and a yard and a tennis ball on the roof that bounced there when they were ten.

I fumble through my nightstand drawer for my bottle of Lorazepam, work the spit up in my mouth, and swallow one of the tiny pills. It's a sedative for anxiety I've taken for a few years. *As needed,* it says on the label. But I'm running out because *as needed* has been way more often since coming to New York. It'll kick in about twenty minutes from now, putting a warm blanket over my shoulders and telling me Astrid Foogle and the slap and the humiliation don't matter as much as I think they do. It's like having a best friend in pill form.

Next to the pill bottle is my other sedative, a deck of playing cards. I slide the deck out of the tattered box and begin shuffling them, over and over. The tangible, mathematical rhythm of the plastic-coated paper against the skin of my fingers and palms is calming in a weird OCDish sort of way. I picked it up after watching street hustlers in Venezuela fleecing tourists with air-quote "games" that are really just cons. I got good at all sorts of tricks over the years, and now cards serve as a little therapy session while I'm waiting for the Lorazepam to start smoldering.

Through my window I hear sirens, big deep voices like those of fire trucks. Somewhere, something is burning. Collecting the cards and shuffling them again, I hear the shushing of a bus's air brakes and the honking of a taxi's horn. I hear a drunk on the street howling about how someone took his money, about how Jesus is coming back. Jesus, I want to get out of here. I push the thought out of my mind and work the cards, my fingers creating and re-creating and re-creating again an orderly, plastic world of chance and probability, a new universe of winners and losers every time.

It's 11:36 p.m. when I wake up—fucking Lorazepam—and now his birthday's almost over. I climb out of bed and open the door.

He's sitting on the couch with his glasses on, laptop open. I slip into the kitchen and get the box from the bakery out of the refrigerator.

Inside, the cupcake with the red frosting has fallen over onto its side and is sort of a mess. I take that one for myself. I dig through the drawers, find matches and a birthday candle—it's in the shape of a 5, brought back with us for some reason from Moscow, where I'd had my fifteenth birthday. Strange, my dad's sentimentality for little things.

I stand in the kitchen doorway, holding the plate with the two cupcakes until he looks up and notices me. He closes the laptop and puts his glasses in his pocket.

"Sorry for the crappy birthday," I say, sitting down on the edge of the couch next to him.

"Aren't you going to sing?"

"Absolutely not. Make a wish."

A second passes as he thinks, then he blows the candle out. With careful fingers he lifts the cake off the plate and takes a bite. "Lemon," he says. "You remembered."

I notice a paperback book sitting on the couch, half covered by his laptop. "What were you reading?"

With his free hand, he pulls it out and shows me. *1984* by George Orwell, an old paperback, worn out and shabby. "I wasn't. I'm loaning it to a friend," he says. "You ever read it?"

"No."

"You should. Dystopian future. Or maybe dystopian present."

The present. I grab my backpack from the floor and fish through it until I find the little box. "I got you something this year."

He takes it from me, squints at it, and wrinkles his nose. "Is it—a fishing pole?"

"Stop."

"No. A new car."

"Stop!" I say. "Just open it!"

My dad lifts the cover a little bit and peeks inside as if whatever is in there might bite him. Then his face goes slack. "Gwendolyn

Bloom, what have you done?" he says, the same tone as when he's angry.

He drops the box to his lap and holds the pen as if it were as delicate as a baby chick. I pull a notebook out of my backpack. "Here," I say. "Write with it."

He puts the pen to the paper and scratches out something like a signature, but there's no ink at first, just a dry scribbled indentation. Then it starts to flow, elegant blue, royal blue. *Love it!* he writes.

"Really? Are you sure?"

"More than love it. I'm crazy about it. It makes me feel like—*a real aristocrat*," he says with a bad English accent.

I laugh, and he puts his arm around me. With my head on his shoulder, I can hear his heart beating slowly and evenly. Strip away the house in the suburbs, strip away the scads of friends who'd just turn on you anyway, and so what? A family of two is still a family. It's enough. I'm about to tell him this, and even though it's corny as hell, I'm about to say it out loud, but he stops me by speaking first.

"I'll bring it with me tomorrow on my trip," he says. "I'll be the fanciest guy in the meeting."

Tomorrow? I pull away and sit up. "Where are you going?"

He cringes like he does when he forgets something. "I was going to tell you, but you fell asleep. I have to go to Paris tomorrow."

My shoulders sink.

"Just two days," he says. "Fly out tomorrow morning, have a meeting tomorrow night, and by bedtime the day after, I'm home."

Three

It's the same note he always leaves—*Don't eat junk food. Here's forty dollars for emergencies. Go to Bela and Lili's if you need anything*—but this time, scrawled in that elegant royal-blue ink from the pen I gave him. I lean back against the seat of the 6 train headed downtown and turn the note over to where I'd written the address of the used record store on St. Mark's Place.

On almost everything having to do with music, my dad and I disagree. But jazz is the exception. He'd take me to the clubs sometimes overseas, and I'd pinch my nose against the cigarette smoke and listen intently for two shows in a row. We made a kind of sport in the foreign cities we'd visit by trying to find the smallest, weirdest venues and most obscure local recordings. Too bad about his turntable that arrived in New York smashed to pieces. I'll get him a good one someday, when I'm rich.

It's a little before noon, and I already wasted my morning eating cold leftover vindaloo in front of the TV. But I'm going to make the most of the rest of this rare weekday sans school. So I get off at Astor Place and head toward St. Mark's. Little hipster bars, tattoo parlors, a taqueria with a sombrero-wearing mannequin out front. Maybe I should get a tattoo.

My dad told me his family settled in the tenements here more than a century ago, a dozen people to a room or something absurd like that. That was the way most Jews fresh off the boat lived then, my dad explained. His family is Lithuanian, and Blumenthal became Blum at Ellis Island, then sometime later, Bloom. Technically, they're not my ancestors, not by blood, but I say they still count.

My dad's an only child, and both of his parents died before I was born. A car crash in San Diego, where he grew up. The only real, true, DNA relatives I have are my mom's sister and her daughter. My aunt is married to a rabbi in Texas. I met her and her husband only once, right after my mom was killed, and I don't even remember what they look like.

There's a little bell over the door that rings as I step inside the record shop. A guy with a shaved head and gauge earrings looks up from the counter. The place smells good, like dust and vinyl and ozone. Long rows of low counters loaded with bins run up and down the length of the store.

I take some vinyl out of a few bins: *Bitches Brew* by Miles Davis, *Ellington at Newport*. Then I see hands flipping through the bin next to me and follow them up to a body and a face.

It's the clothes that throw me off. I'm used to him in the Danton uniform of white shirt and striped tie. Today he's wearing a red turtleneck sweater and khakis with a sharp crease, like he just stepped out of a Ralph Lauren photo shoot. His skin is smooth and dark brown, with a warm glow from inside him, like there's a lantern in his chest. At Danton, he keeps to himself, eats alone, talks to almost no one. His real name is Terrance, but the other kids call him Scholarship because the story is he got a full ride for computer science.

"Hey," I say.

Terrance looks up. "Hey," he says back.

"Terrance, right?"

"Yeah."

"I'm Gwendolyn."

"I know."

For a moment, there's an awful silence. A silence that's so awful I remember this is the reason I never talk to guys. Then Terrance smiles. "Aren't you supposed to be in school?"

"Aren't you?"

"Three-day suspension for altering attendance records," he says. "No sense of irony, those people. How about you?"

"One-day suspension," I say. "For telling Astrid Foogle to go fuck herself."

He arches an eyebrow as if genuinely impressed. "Brave girl," he says. "What are you getting?"

I look down dumbly at the album I'm holding and notice my hands are shaking. "Sonny Rollins. But I'm just browsing," I say.

"Sonny's cool," he says. "Charlie Parker is better."

"Of course he is," I say. "That's cheating. Try again."

He shrugs. "I've always been a Coltrane man."

I smile involuntarily. "I'm a Coltrane man, too."

He laughs, and my face turns red as his sweater.

"Sorry. I didn't mean to . . ." His voice trails off. "So—you like jazz. We must be the only two."

I gesture around the shop.

"At Danton, I mean." Terrance looks down, adjusts his backpack.

"I'm—I'm just hanging out," he says. "So if you want to—I don't know what your schedule . . ."

"Love to," I say before I can think.

Outside the shop we discover the sun is gone, replaced with inky purple clouds that seem to be creeping across the city, over the tops of the buildings. Neither of us has anyplace to be, and that's good because both of us seem content to be here. We walk along St. Mark's for two more blocks. Is the city strangely empty today, or have I just not noticed anyone else?

We talk about music we like, books we like, Danton students we hate. He says he thought I was "Greek or something." No, I tell him. American by passport, but just another diplobrat, same as the others. Cool, he says.

At some point, we cross Avenue A and end up in Tompkins Square Park. We stroll along a paved path beneath a canopy of bare trees. To one side, a homeless guy is sleeping between sheets of cardboard, dirty hands and shoes and bundles of clothing sticking out from the sides like an overstuffed sandwich.

"So—you have a scholarship to Danton?" I ask.

His eyes narrow. "What?"

"Your nickname. The others, they call you Scholarship."

"They call me Scholarship because I'm black. Ergo . . ."

"Ergo what?"

"Ergo how else could I get into Danton?" He shakes his head. At them. Maybe at me, too. "Only time I even exist is when they need a weed hookup. But fuck them. I'm not playing that part. My life isn't their movie."

My hand accidentally brushes his. "So make your own. You can be whatever part you want."

A grin flickers as if he likes the idea. "Who do you play, in yours?"

"My movie?" I shrug. "I don't really have one, I guess. It's just—random scenes, edited together."

"Even so," he says. "You still get to be the hero."

"The hero?"

"You know. Kicking ass, saving the world, looking fine doing it." He shadowboxes the air in front of him playfully.

It's a compliment, kind of: Me, saving the world. Gwendolyn Bloom, looking fine. I give him a thin smile. "Sure," I say.

But Terrance has stopped and is looking at two boys next to the dog run. They've set up a cardboard box and are dealing three-card monte. It's a street game that's not really a game at all, but looks like it is and that's where the con comes in. One of the kids shuffles three playing cards and calls out, "Find the lady, find the lady," to the passing joggers and office workers on lunch break.

The game used to be all over New York in the old days, my dad told me, but I guess not anymore because Terrance says he's never seen it. I've seen it lots of places, though, all around the world, and used to love watching the dealers fleece the tourists. With the help of some YouTube videos, I even learned to do it myself, practicing on my dad for Monopoly money.

While one of the kids deals, the other makes a big show of winning. He has a fat wad of cash in his hand and seems to be cleaning up.

"You want to try?" Terrance asks.

"It's a scam," I say. "You can't win."

"The other guy is winning."

"Because that's his job," I say. "He's called the shill. They're working together."

But Terrance is undeterred and sidles up to them anyway. He pulls out a twenty and lays it on the cardboard box. The dealer takes it and shows him the cards, a queen and two jacks bent slightly on the long axis so they're easier to pick up. Then the dealer flips the cards over and juggles their position, shifting the queen to the left, to the right, to the middle.

It's easy at first, which is the idea. But the trick, the key, the very core of the con, is to pick up the queen and another card with one hand, then release the second card while making the mark, the person being conned, believe you've just released the queen. The dealer is so fast, I don't even see him do it. Now Terrance is following the wrong card.

When the dealer stops, Terrance taps the card on the left. With a little smile, the dealer turns it over. Jack of clubs.

Another twenty comes out of Terrance's pocket, but this time the dealer tells him double or nothing. So out comes forty, and a round later, eighty.

"How'd you know?" he asks when we finally walk away.

"YouTube, a deck of cards, and lots of time. Ten thousand rounds later, I was as good as those guys."

"Then we should set up a game ourselves," he says. "You and me."

We wander deeper into Tompkins, past the crowded basketball court and a homemade sign taped to a post about a missing guinea pig named Otto. We find a bench that's clean, or cleanish, beneath some skeletal trees, and sit.

"So is it your dad who's at the State Department, or your mom?" Terrance asks.

"Dad," I say.

"What does your mom do?" he asks.

I consider lying. Usually it only gets awkward after I tell the truth. But this time, for some reason, I don't. "She's dead," I say. "Ten years."

"Mine, too," Terrance says. "Eight years. Sailing accident."

I open my mouth to fill in the how part, but he stops me with a hand on top of mine.

"It's okay. If you don't want to," he says.

"Thanks," I say.

Then the fact of both our moms being dead just sits there for a second, okay with itself. No fuss. No drama.

"So where do you want to go?" he asks.

"I'm fine just hanging out here," I say.

"No. For college."

"I haven't really thought about it," I say. "University of Someplace Warm. How about you?"

"Harvard. My dad, he endowed a chair there, so . . ."

"A chair?"

"Not a literal chair. It's, like, a faculty position. The Mutai Chair for the Study of Economic Something Something. I can't remember the whole name."

From somewhere deep in my pocket, my phone rings. I steal a look and see it's my dad. But instead of answering it, I turn off the ringer. I'll call him back later; no need to interrupt the moment and break the spell. The clock on the phone reads 2:42 p.m. Where did the time go? The wind whips through the slats on the wooden bench. I turn the collar of my army jacket up and cross my arms tightly.

"What's wrong?" Terrance says.

"Cold," I say.

"Want to get going?"

"No."

Then his arm is around me and he pulls himself close. My muscles go stiff. I feel the warmth from his body traveling all the way through his jacket and mine. Is there something I'm supposed to say? No, I tell myself, just shut up and let things be. I tilt my head to the side so it's resting on the shoulder of his suede jacket. He smells like fancy soap, the kind they have in expensive hotels.

34

"And after college?" I ask. "What then?"

"My dad says anything I want as long as I don't go into hedge funds like he did," Terrance says, running his hand along my arm. "But I'll probably, I don't know. I love writing code, the mental precision. There's beauty there. Math as art. Is that weird—math as art?"

I let out a little laugh. "Math music."

"What?"

"Math music. It's stupid, but that's what I call, like, Dizzy and Charlie Parker together, or Coltrane and anyone. It sounds like chaos, but it isn't. It's calculus."

"Math music," he repeats. "I like that."

Then his arm tightens around me, and I slide an inch closer, then another inch.

A fat drop of rain lands on my knee; a second lands on my hand. They start to explode and pop all around me, darkening the sidewalk like drops of brown paint. We both know we should get up and head for shelter—it's going to start coming down hard in a minute—but neither of us moves. A low rumble of thunder turns into a sharp crack. A purple cloud over the buildings in the distance flashes brightly, as if lit from within.

"The gods are conspiring against us," I say.

"Better go," Terrance says.

We dash through the park, the sky opening up above us, letting down sheets of rain in contoured waves that look like furious ghosts. If I believed in God, it would almost seem like a punishment for stealing a few hours of fun with a strange, interesting boy. We make it across Avenue A to the shelter of a tenement entrance. There's only a few square feet of space here, and we lean against the black steel door to get away from the ricocheting raindrops.

"You're shivering," he says. "Come here."

I hadn't noticed and I don't feel cold anymore, but I do it anyway. He presses his chest to me and wraps his arms around my back.

"So let me get this straight," I say. "It's the Mutai Chair for Something Something Economic . . ."

He laughs, and I feel his chest move against the side of my face. "Technically, it's the Terrance Mutai the Third Chair."

"The third chair?"

"No, my dad's name is Terrance Mutai the Third. That makes me Terrance the Fourth."

Now it's my turn to laugh. I hope he doesn't think I'm an asshole. "There's a number in your name? Are you royalty or something?"

"No," he says. "Just a pretentious snob."

"That's okay," I say. "Me too."

Then, tragically, and against all the statistical odds that apply to New York in a rainstorm, a taxi pulls to the curb and a woman climbs out. I could have stayed where we were, as we were, all day, maybe all week, but before I can protest, Terrance is pulling me by the hand into the back of the cab.

He directs the driver north along First Avenue toward my address. "Then a second stop," Terrance says. "Seventy-Second and Fifth, the Madisonian." I haven't been in the city that long, but I know enough to recognize one of the most prestigious blocks on the whole island of Manhattan. Here, even the very rich live on blocks like mine, in apartments that are too small, looking down on streets that are too busy. Terrance's neighborhood is reserved for the astronomically wealthy. Even most of the snobs at Danton would look at his address with envy.

The cab scurries along and the streets gleam black in the rain. Terrance and I are crouched down low in the backseat, the heat vents blasting. I notice my fingers are red and numb. He takes my hands in his and rubs them.

We turn down my street, and I tell the driver where to pull over. As we roll to a stop, I reach into my pocket for money, but Terrance says to forget it, the cab ride's on him. I turn to say thank you but find him right there, mere inches from my face. It's over before I know it, a quick, chaste kiss on the lips. I wonder what my expression must look like because he laughs. "Later," he says.

My mind races to break down and analyze every second of the past few hours as I enter the front door of my building and start climbing the stairs, second floor, third floor, fourth floor, Terrance the Fourth.

I lock the door behind me, two dead bolts and the chain. Had Terrance really just leaned over and kissed me? My God, what does that mean?

For a few hours, I wrestle with my homework. There's the regular Friday calculus quiz tomorrow, and even though I've only been out a day, I'm still behind. It's hard work, made harder by my mind constantly flying like a ghost back to the feel of his hands as they rubbed mine in the back of the cab, hands with long, thin fingers, hands befitting an aristocrat with a number in his name. That was the important part, wasn't it? Not the kiss. The way he rubbed my hands. God, he's literally the only thing I've found in this city that doesn't hurt.

Somehow I manage to get through the homework, and at eleven o'clock, I make a sandwich and pour what's left of last night's wine into a plastic cup and turn on the Mexican soap opera I watch to keep my Spanish tight.

Two secret lovers at a grand party—she in an evening gown, he in a tux—agreeing to meet in the *cobertizo*. Cabin? Shack? No, not in this rarefied world. It's an elegant boathouse, richly appointed in brass clocks and chubby leather chairs and a stuffed falcon on a shelf.

Dangerous, meeting like this, they both agree, what with the party so close, still audible, even. Do you love me, he asks. *Sí, Emilio,* she says, *siempre, siempre.*

The wine is warm in my stomach, and my brain is feeling furry. I slide down on the couch, my head sinking into a throw pillow, and think about Tompkins Square for the eight thousandth time tonight, how the rain looked like blobs of paint on the sidewalk. He's rich, I think—he must be, to live where he does. But so what? How much was holding me like that in the doorway as we hid from the rain worth? I don't know, but you don't measure it in money.

And that's what I'm thinking about as my eyes close and I feel myself falling backward, just falling backward through the warm wine buzz and into sleep. The soap opera is still on, a heated argument now. Emilio and someone—her father? And on the show, someone else is knocking at the door, but Emilio and the other guy just keep talking over it. Jesus, answer it already.

Then I snap awake. The knocking isn't on the TV; it's at the door to my apartment, firm and urgent. *Come now,* it says. I approach the door groggy but wary, and look through the peephole. It's Bela, dressed in a bathrobe. Behind him stand two figures in cheap-looking suits. One's a woman, and her dishwater-blond hair is tied back in a ponytail. She's pretty, I think, athletic, maybe forty. The other one is a guy, maybe late twenties. He has a heavy red face and his black hair is cut short like a military recruit's.

I unlock the two dead bolts and open the door as far as the chain will let me.

Bela wrings his hands. It's not nervousness, but something else. "These people—they need to speak with you."

"Can you open up, please, Gwendolyn?" says the woman.

I close the door, unlock the chain, and open it again. The woman steps forward and unfolds a wallet showing a badge and an ID card with her photo on it.

"Gwendolyn, hi. My name is Special Agent Kavanaugh and this is Special Agent Mazlow. We're from the Bureau of Diplomatic Security."

Now it's the man's turn to show his badge and ID, but I don't need to look at it. I know them already—not these two specifically, but I know their kind, what they do, what it means when they show up. I know the next words out of their mouth before they even say them.

"My dad," I say, my voice low, almost a whisper. "What happened to my dad?"

Agent Kavanaugh places a hand gently on my shoulder. "We'd like you to come with us, okay? Can you do that, Gwendolyn?"

I knock her hand off my shoulder. "What happened to my dad?" I repeat, louder now, almost a shout. "Is he all right?"

"Gwendolyn," Agent Kavanaugh says. "Your dad is missing."

Four

Kavanaugh and Mazlow stand on either side of me in an elevator that smells like disinfectant. The button for the sixth floor is lit up. BUREAU OF DIPLOMATIC SECURITY it says next to it.

When I visited my dad here in the drab concrete building downtown where the State Department has its field office, there were metal detectors at the front entrance, and I had to wear a red badge marked VISITOR. But there's none of that now. As we climbed out of the big SUV with sirens and lights that Kavanaugh and Mazlow used to get us here, the security guards just waved us through.

I'm deposited in a small conference room where mismatched tables have been pushed together and a collection of ratty chairs lines the walls. "Stay put," Kavanaugh says. "Mazlow will be right outside the door if you need anything."

She disappears, and I'm alone in the room, wishing they'd let Bela come with me. The fluorescent lights above me buzz and flicker, casting a sickly light over everything. The only window in the room is covered with closed blinds. I lift one of the metal strips and find that the window faces a hallway, and from here I can see into the room across from me. Kavanaugh is there, along with six or seven others. They're gathered around a whiteboard where they've written some sort of timeline:

20:37 SMS from Bloom at Café Durbin to Paris Station all clear

20:42 Phn from Bloom to daughter no answer/no vm

20:55 Call from Bloom to Feras/confirm

21:22 Leave Feras Meeting at Café Durbin/SMS to Paris Station all clear

21:32 Phn offline/dead

Kavanaugh is speaking to two men I recognize. One is Joey Diaz, a political officer like my dad. He's a handsomely stocky black guy who's been a friend of my dad's for years. They were stationed in Dubai together, and Joey, along with his wife and two kids, spent Thanksgiving and Christmas at our apartment there two years in a row. The other guy I've seen, too. Chase Carlisle is his name, and he's my dad's boss. I know little about him other than that my dad says he's from an old Southern family and knows everyone in Washington.

Carlisle's about fifty or fifty-five, I think, pink-skinned and wearing the standard-issue tired suit, buttoned uneasily over his middle-aged bulk. His hair, though, is the same as I remembered, sharp part on the side, dyed perfectly brown. As Kavanaugh speaks to them, Carlisle looks over in my direction, and I pull back instinctively, letting the blind fall back into place.

A moment later, Diaz and Carlisle come through the door to the conference room. Joey gathers me into a hug. "It's going to be all right, Gwendolyn," he says. "It's going to be all right."

"Why don't you sit, Gwendolyn," Carlisle says, his Virginia accent pleasant and soft.

"I'll stand, thank you," I say, trying to make my voice as calm as I can.

"Gwendolyn," Joey says, hands on my shoulders, eyes directly into mine. "Your father disappeared shortly after meeting a colleague of ours in Paris, someone we—"

"*Very* misleading, Joey," Carlisle says, cutting him off. "You're implying it's a kidnapping, and we have no evidence of that."

I lower myself into a chair and grip the armrests.

Carlisle stares right at me as if he's trying to remember my reaction. "All we know so far is that he's missing. That's it. That's all we have. Could he have been kidnapped? It's a small possibility. But there are other reasons he may have gone off the grid."

I feel my face clench like a fist, eyes pinched shut, mouth open, teeth bared. I hide behind my hands. Over the course of my life, I've prepared myself for the eventuality that he would end up in the hospital or even die on the job, but this—my mind stretches, picturing a thousand scenarios and tortures. Two tears break free from the inside corners of my eyes, run down along the crevices next to my nose. I force myself to look up. "Tell me exactly what you're doing to find him."

Carlisle's face is blankly professional. "You have my assurance that State is doing all it can. The FBI field office in Paris is already scouring the area. So are the French police, local and federal—"

I cut him off. "You have to assume he was kidnapped, though, right? I mean, that's how you're treating it, right? As if he were?"

"Of course," Carlisle says. "Yes. Absolutely. Right now, SIGINT is looking for what we call 'chatter'—intercepted conversations—about a missing American diplomat. But so far there's nothing. Which is a good sign."

"What is SIGINT?" I ask, blotting my eyes with a tissue.

"Signals Intelligence. They deal with cell phone interceptions, any sort of electronic communication." Carlisle takes a seat and consults his notepad. "Gwendolyn, did your father talk to you about work at all? What he does? Maybe he mentioned certain troubles he was having at the office?"

"No," I say. "I mean, the usual stress. And he was sad the last few days. The anniversary of my mom's death. But he never mentioned much about work. Just that he looked at papers a lot, wrote some reports."

Carlisle nods and makes a note. "Has your father spoken at all about a desire to, I don't know, retire? Leave the State Department and move abroad?"

Joey's hand slaps the table. "That's enough, Chase."

Carlisle fires a look at Joey, then turns back to me. "Gwendolyn, we know your father phoned you yesterday afternoon but didn't leave a message. Have you had any contact with him since then? E-mail, maybe. Social media."

"No," I say. "Nothing at all."

"Thank you. That's helpful." Chase sets down his pen and folds his hands in front of him. "I know this must be so hard for you. Do you have any relatives you can stay with for the time being?"

"I have an aunt and uncle in Texas. Georgina and Robert Kaplan. He's a rabbi in, I don't know where. A suburb of Dallas, I think."

"No one local?"

"I'm sure I can stay with Bela and Lili. The Atzmons. They're friends of ours who live in our building. Fifth floor."

"The Atzmons will do for the near term," Carlisle says as he stands.

"Probably best if you stay with them tonight. We'll be sure to come get you if there are any developments."

I open my mouth to speak, but Carlisle's already disappearing through the door.

The wipers tango quickly across the windshield, sweeping away the rain, pulling back, sweeping again, pulling back. I try to hypnotize myself with the motion, try to lose myself in it. The SUV Joey borrowed from the motor pool is creeping up Third Avenue through the 3:00 a.m. traffic. He doesn't bother with the lights or siren now, as if he senses I'm grateful to be here with maybe the one friend my dad has in the world who can actually do something to help.

"How're your kids?" I ask. "Christina is the oldest, right?"

"Yeah," Joey says. "She's twelve next month. And Oscar just turned nine."

"Oscar. I always liked that name."

It sounds like small talk, but it's a test. I'm closely watching Joey's face for his reaction when I say, "We'll all have to get together, you know, when my dad is back."

His head retreats a little, and I see him breathe in slowly. "Sure," he says with a smile that isn't real.

"My dad's not coming back, is he, Joey?"

"Of course he is," Joey says, but the words are hopeful and empty, the way you tell a cancer patient to get well soon.

I feel my face starting to clench up again. I turn away and lean into the cold glass of the window, where the rainwater is flowing down in little rivers. "What happened to him, Joey? Please tell me. No bullshit. I think I have a right."

Joey drums his fingers on the wheel. "Your dad was at a meeting with a contact of ours, someone we work with. The meeting was at a café. After the two of them left, he texted our office in Paris to say he was all right. But a little while later, his phone was either turned off or just stopped working. There were no police reports from the area, no signs of violence. That's all we know for sure."

I think of the timeline I saw on the wall of the room across the hallway. "Was the meeting with someone named Feras? I saw his name on the whiteboard."

"Yes," Joey says. "We have someone en route to speak with him now. But we don't know what role he played, if any."

"There was a guy, a Russian or Serb, I can't remember. I saw a picture of him the other night on my dad's computer. Viktor Zoric. Is he connected to Feras?"

"Not likely. But you can be sure it's being looked into anyway."

I press the palms of my hands into my eyes, and Joey reaches over to squeeze my shoulder.

"I don't get it, Joey," I say, my voice broken, barely there. "My dad shuffles papers around. What would anyone want with someone like him?"

A long moment of silence. "I think I need a cup of coffee," Joey says finally. "Come on, I'll buy you a Coke or whatever."

Suddenly the SUV veers to the right, cutting across two lanes of traffic. Car horns sound furiously behind us. He pulls to the curb in front of a little bodega, shuts the ignition off, and motions for me to follow as he exits.

The rain batters against my head in fat, frigid drops and runs down my face and neck and into my shirt collar. I raise my hood as Joey pulls me along by the upper arm like he's leading a prisoner. "It's not safe to talk in there," he says. "The radio. It's never really off. You understand?"

We stop beneath the awning of a twenty-four-hour corner store and stand before wooden shelves lined with bananas and oranges and apples and buckets of cheap flowers in plastic wrapping. There's no one around, not at this hour, and Joey grips me by the shoulders.

"Your dad," Joey says. "What is his occupation?"

"He's a political officer with the Department of State, a diplomat."

"Come on, Gwendolyn," Joey says. "What is your father's job? What does he do for a living?"

"Christ, Joey, what are you getting at?"

He breathes slowly for a moment. "Your dad doesn't work for the State Department, Gwendolyn. He has never worked for the State Department. It's called 'official cover.'"

He pauses a moment, eyes locked onto mine until the words sink in. If my dad doesn't work for the State Department, then there's really only one possibility left. I open my mouth to speak but have trouble forming the words. "He's a spy," I say finally. "He's CIA."

Joey gives me a sad smile. "Remember, you came to that conclusion on your own, got it? I never told you."

The only thing that shocks me is that I'm not shocked at all. It hits me like an answer to a riddle I've heard before but forgotten, the punch line of a joke I saw coming a mile away. Part of me always knew this, at least as long ago as our time in Egypt, maybe earlier, maybe Venezuela. I didn't know what the letters CIA stood for when I was ten or eleven, but I knew what my father did was different. None of the other parents took an hour to drive their kids to school, a different route every day. None of the parents had meetings at 3:00 a.m.

"And you?" I ask. "Are you a spy? How about Chase Carlisle?"

"What we are doesn't matter."

"So the answer is yes."

"You're free to believe whatever you want," he says. "Just keep your conclusions to yourself."

I turn away, unable to look at him. There's an old couple shuffling toward us, huddled together under an umbrella. I wait until they pass. "So all those postings overseas, my dad was spying?"

"He was a political officer for the Department of State, just a diplomat filling a desk job. Officially, that's all he ever was."

"But unofficially?" I ask.

"Unofficially he was a patriot, the best man I've ever worked with," Joey says.

Bela and Lili Atzmon have done this before. Or at least, that's how it looks to me as Joey tells them the official version—disappearance in Paris, circumstances unknown. Standing beside each other, they nod along coldly at the news, like doctors brought in for a consultation, their bathrobes like lab coats.

There is, I learn when Joey leaves, a ritual to be performed when a father goes missing. Lili builds what can only be described as a nest—a ring of quilts and pillows on the couch in her living room with me at its center, like a choked-up baby bird. Tea is prepared, the gentle herbal kind.

After the first hour, I'm cried out, my wells of everything run dry. Eyes hurting, nose raw and red, I stare down blankly, weaving my fingers through little holes in a crocheted blanket, trapping them like a net. Bela sits in his armchair, a glass of palinka in hand, while Lili is perched next to me on the edge of the couch.

"You're good at this whole comforting thing," I say.

Lili smiles, fusses with the blanket over my shoulder. "Where we're from, fathers sometimes disappear," she says.

My dad lied to me. In fact my dad has done nothing but lie for as long as I can remember. I think of all the times he would come home from Khartoum or Islamabad—or is that even where he really went?—and I'd ask him how his meeting had been, or how the official dinner had gone down, or how they'd liked the presentation he'd given. "Death by boredom," he'd say, and roll his eyes clownishly. Well, screw him, I think. Screw him and the years of lies. The years where the one person in the world he shouldn't lie to, he lied to.

My mind goes to the timeline written on the whiteboard at my dad's office, then to the conversation with Joey out on the street. I know I'm not supposed to say anything about that. I know it's supposed to be a secret. But Bela and Lili know the world, and they're all I have now. My mouth flutters open, as if I can't stop myself from speaking. "He's not a diplomat," I say.

Bela holds up his hand. "Of course, child. You don't need to say it."

I peer at him closely. "He told you?"

Bela shrugs. "He didn't need to tell me, just as I didn't need to tell him. Spies can smell one another across a room. Like dogs."

There's something strange in his eyes as he looks at me, apology and mischief.

"You—you worked for the CIA?" I ask.

From Bela, a genuine laugh. "Thank God, no. Someone else."

And it's all he needs to say. He'd spent thirty years in Israel. "Mossad," I say quietly.

No response from Bela.

So the kindly old shopkeeper had once belonged to one of the best and fiercest intelligence organizations in the world. Sure. Why not? Let's just pull back the curtain on the entire world today.

Bela clears his throat. "Your father made an arrangement with Lili and me. We are to provide help to you."

"I know. Keep an eye on me while he's away."

"No. Another sort of arrangement." He leans forward, hands gripping his knees. "The clandestine services, his and mine, can be cruel to the families of those who serve them. So in the event of—of something like this—he wanted us to make sure your interests were looked after."

"Like what?"

"Like that you're not fed bullshit."

My eyes clench again, but I force it away. There's really only one question worth asking. "I want you to—be honest, Bela. The truth."

"You want to know if he's dead."

I nod.

"If their intention—their immediate intention—was to kill him, you'd know. His body would have been found there on the street already. I'm sorry to be blunt."

"Do you think they'll let him go, whoever has him?"

"If whoever took him is given the money or favors or whatever they're looking for, then maybe," Bela says.

I look at him. "And if not?"

He shakes his head.

In the photo, Bela is a young man, thin as a rail, but good-looking despite the boxy suit. He had just gotten out of prison, Lili says, and was lucky not to have been shot. Shot, I ask? She tells me about the revolution of 1956, of Soviet troops and massacres in the streets of Budapest. Lili was a student of biology at the time, and Bela was a young professor of chemistry, barely out of school himself. He was sent to prison for two years after that, she tells me, and nearly died of tuberculosis.

I'm truly grateful to them for the distraction. And they're so clever about it, Bela and Lili. Distraction is an art, and they know a card game or silly movie would never keep my mind off the swirling tragedy in my head. So here is someone else's tragedy, someone else's tough times, close enough to my own, yet far enough from my own, so that I can absorb myself in it without guilt.

Lili refills my tea, while Bela yawns and opens another album. People around a swimming pool. Shirtless men with hairy chests and wives in dowdy swimsuits toast the camera with bottles of beer. "Tel

Aviv," Bela says. "1973." He taps a man and woman. "This is us, of course." Then he taps a squat, balding man with a wicked smile and a cigarette between thumb and forefinger. "This one was like a brother to me. He went on to become head of my service."

"These are your spy friends?" I ask.

"Every one of them," Bela says.

Lili closes the album. "Enough," she says. "No war stories tonight, Belachik. The girl must rest."

"I don't think I'll be able to sleep," I say.

"Of course you won't," Lili says, spreading the pillows and blankets on the couch into something resembling a bed. "But you must try."

They go to bed, and the tears come again a few minutes later, a slow, feeble stream that I hardly notice at first. I know if I just sit here the crying will get worse, so I reach for my backpack and pull out the book I'd been reading.

I open it to where I left off, but I see right away it's hopeless. There will be no fiction now. The letters on the page scatter like roaches and rearrange themselves into truth, covering the whole page with the only thing that needs saying tonight: he is already dead and you are alone he is already dead and you are alone he is already dead and you are alone

I slam the book shut, slam my eyes shut, and, goddammit, if I had a gun I'd put the muzzle in my mouth right now and blow the top of my head off. It is unbearable. Literally unable to be borne. The roof above me is collapsing. For the first time since I was seven, I fold my hands together and pray to a god that I know isn't there.

Five

For the second time in twelve hours, it's an urgent *come now!* knock on the door that wakes me. I spring up from the couch, nearly falling face-first onto the coffee table as I catch my foot in one of Lili's blankets. Whatever news the urgent knocking means, it can be only one of two things. He's dead or he's alive.

Bela shuffles in, angrily tying his bathrobe belt, and opens the door. The man on the other side is very young with red hair and pale skin dotted with freckles. He introduces himself as Special Agent Fowler and shows his badge and ID. Good news or bad news, it's Joey or Carlisle who would've come by. So why this Agent Fowler?

He unfolds a thick, densely worded document in front of me. "This is a search warrant for the home of William and Gwendolyn Bloom," he says.

I push past him and hear Bela and Fowler arguing behind me as I head down the stairs. On the landing below, another agent grabs my arms from behind as I try to get into my apartment.

Through the door, I see four guys in windbreakers with *Bureau of Diplomatic Security* written on the back pulling drawers out of cabinets, piling papers into cardboard boxes.

I hear a voice call from inside, a voice with an elegant Southern lilt. "Take the photos, too. Everything means everything." Carlisle, hands deep in the pockets of his pants, appears at the entrance of the hallway along with Joey Diaz. Carlisle nods when he sees me. "It's all right, Mike," he says to the agent at the door. "Let her in."

As the agent releases my arms, I rush inside but freeze at the sight of a cardboard box sitting on the kitchen table. It's filled with my school notebooks and my diary. "You have no right!" I shout at Carlisle, and snatch the diary out of the box.

Carlisle appears next to me and takes the diary back. "I am very sorry, Gwendolyn. I know how traumatic this must be, but I'm afraid it's necessary."

"What are you even looking for? My dad's the victim here!"

"Well, that's what we'd like to determine," Carlisle says. "I want you to know, your father is a friend of mine, a dear friend. That's why it pains me to do this."

"So why are you doing it?"

He leads me into the apartment by the arm and nods to the couch. We both sit. "Gwendolyn, I have to ask you something now. Can you foresee any circumstances under which your father would choose to leave us?"

"Leave us?"

"Has he ever talked to you about defection. To another country."

My mouth hangs open like a fool's. "Fuck you, Chase."

"There are people who have concerns about your father. Not me, not Joey. People in Washington." He looks at me sternly. "So answer the question, please. Has your father ever spoken to you about defection?"

I stand and walk out onto the landing, into Bela's arms. He takes me back upstairs. *"Fascists,"* he whispers.

I'm standing alone in my apartment two hours later, seeing what's been taken and what hasn't. Missing are all his papers and many of mine, all photos, all computers, and even the TV and Wi-Fi router. My clothes all seem to be there, though I can tell the drawers were searched. My books are mostly there but taken off the shelves and piled in precarious stacks on the floor. The rage boils in my veins, and even though the searchers wore rubber gloves, everything is now soiled, as if they'd coughed their accusation—*defection, treason*—over everything they touched.

The rage boiling in my veins is useless, though. I know this. The Diplomatic Security thugs have search warrants and holstered guns and declare their authority over my life with the words on the back of their official windbreakers, while I'm just a quavery-voiced child, hissing her tantrum to ears that give not a shit. How dare they accuse my dad? How dare they run rubber-sheathed fingers over my things? But power doesn't dare; it simply does.

Still, I will remake what they've taken apart, put back some order to my world. I will start here, in the bedroom, in *my* bedroom, with *my* books. My hands shake so badly as I pick up the first handful of them, I can barely put them back on the shelf. On the covers are the heroes from paper worlds who've kept me company in Paris, Dubai, Moscow, New York. If they were real, these brave girls, they'd stare at me with pity and disgust in their eyes.

But there are no heroes. There is no courage. Just diplomats who write reports. Just fat Chase Carlisles who tell you your father's a defector. Just security agents who wave search warrants about and paw through your life. Just me, a little girl with rage in her veins who burns it off by cleaning her room, like a little girl should.

Once the apartment is back in order—cushions back on the couch, the ring of dust around where the TV had stood wiped away, shoe-prints on the IKEA rug scoured with baking soda and paper towels that shred in my hands—I go to the toilet, bend over it, and vomit. For a while, I sit on the bathroom floor, back to the wall, my skin buzz-ing, my mind repeating the only truth that matters: *He is already dead and you are alone.*

It feels like an electric shock every time the phone rings. So Lili answers for me, and I stare at her expression for clues. But it always ends with her hanging up and shaking her head as she says, "Nothing new." You'd think these non-updates would get easier after three days, but they don't.

What I need is sleep, Lili tells me. And she's right. I haven't slept for more than a few hours since the night before my dad was taken. The exhaustion is now hallucinogenic, with swirls of purple and pink filling the world like ghosts. Lili walks me to my apartment and actu-ally tucks me into my own bed. The grief, the shock, all of it fades behind Lili's stroking of my arm and the narcotic fog of a triple dose of my sedatives.

Sixteen hours after I'd fallen asleep, I wake, still exhausted. But it's nearly noon, so I get up anyway, shower, take another pill. I pull a chair to the window and stare out at the world, trying not to think or feel. Let today be a quiet day. Let today be silent. But no.

The apartment intercom startles me with its grating electric war-ble. Someone's on the street below, demanding I get off my ass to see what they want. I actually laugh out loud. Such a quaint idea, asking permission to burst into my life. Why not just force your way in like all the others?

I shuffle to the intercom and press the button. "Yes?"

"I'm—I'm looking for Gwendolyn Bloom. Is this she?" It's a woman's voice I don't recognize.

"I'm Gwendolyn," I say. "Who are you?"

A pause, only the sounds of the street coming through the static of the speaker. "It's Georgina Kaplan," says the voice. "Your aunt."

It takes me a few seconds to process the idea of it, as if I'm not quite sure what the words mean. My aunt. My mother's sister. I press the button to let her in, then wait in the open apartment door. I haven't seen my aunt since I was, what, seven, right after my mom was killed? And why has she come?

I hear her moving tentatively up the stairs, heels clicking on the gritty tile floor, then she appears on the landing in front of me. She's a fit, pretty woman of maybe fifty. Her hair is a salon-bought auburn helmet that matches the perfect French manicure. She smiles with very white teeth, "Wow, Gwenny. It's been so long."

When she hugs me, I feel the firmness of her five-workout-a-week muscles. Hanging on her clothes is yesterday's perfume, and the smell of an airplane cabin, plastic and coffee.

"Gwen, Gwenny, I'm so sorry about your dad," she says, the Texas accent round and sweet as an apricot. "So sorry."

She holds me for a long time, then takes me by the shoulders and studies my face while I study hers. Thin wrinkles form deltas at the corners of her eyes and mouth, the only flaw in skin that's otherwise a mask of tasteful earth tones painted with department-store makeup.

"You're very pretty, Gwenny, like your mother," she says. "I'm sorry, can I call you that, or do you prefer Gwendolyn now?"

"Gwendolyn."

"Then that's what I'll call you," she says. "The man on the phone, Mr. Carlisle, he said you're being looked after by neighbors."

"Yes. Bela and Lili."

"I'm sure they're doing a great job, a *great* job, but Mr. Carlisle said maybe it would be better if you were with family. You know, if the situation with your father lasts longer than a few days." Georgina twirls a lock of my hair with her finger. "Well, isn't this just the prettiest shade of red?"

"Look, I appreciate your coming all this way," I say as I pull away from her. "But I'm sure you have a life back in Texas. There's really no need—"

"Oh, I don't mind. Really," she says, pursing her lips into something between a pout and a smile. "Robert's taking the synagogue youth group on a horseback-riding trip and Amber's going with him. Myself, I can't stand horses."

"It's really not necessary," I say. "My dad could be back anytime."

She pulls me into a hug, a hug full of pity and sadness, the kind reserved for funerals. "Of course he will, dear."

We avoid each other for the rest of the day. Or rather, I avoid her by hiding in my room while she keeps a patient, respectful distance. There's nothing wrong with her. Nothing evil. But this is *my* apartment, where I deal with *my* shit, which, maybe you've heard, Georgina, is pretty fucking significant right now. I hate the idea of her being here. How embarrassing to have a stranger hear you cry. In the morning, I try avoiding her again, but then, a moment before I'm out the door, she stops me.

"Sit a minute," she says, patting the spot next to her on the couch.

I'm about to say no, but I have no legitimate reason to be rude to her. She's come all this way for me. That's worth at least a conversation. I take off my jacket and sit down in a chair across from her.

"School," she says.

"What about it?"

"It might be a good distraction. When do you think you'd like to go back?"

I hate to admit it, but she's right. "A few days," I say. "Later this week."

"I'm so glad you agree." Then Georgina inhales sharply like there's something else she wants to say. "Look, Gwendolyn," she manages finally. "If this sounds premature, I'm sorry. But if this situation—the situation with your father—should go on more than, I don't know, a few weeks—"

I cut her off. "You can go back to Texas whenever you want."

"That's just it," she says. "I was thinking you might come with me. Temporarily. Until he comes back."

I stare at her, tamping down my anger, resisting the deep desire to tell her to get the fuck out. "Look, I appreciate you coming here. I do. But why would you want a stranger in your house? I mean, honestly, what am I to you?"

"But you're not a stranger, Gwendolyn," she says. "You're family. I'm sorry, but no matter how you feel about us, that's God's own fact right there."

"I don't want to be a burden to anyone."

Georgina clears her throat, presses her hands down on her knees. "A burden? Honey, you could never be a burden. I know it won't be New York City or Paris, but if you give it a chance, I think you'll like it there. And anyway, it's just for a while."

She comes over to me and sits cross-legged on the floor at my feet. Then she pulls her Louis Vuitton tote bag—the real thing, not a Chinatown knockoff—onto her lap and removes her phone. She opens the photos and turns the phone so I can see. There on the screen is a large suburban house in the middle of an impossibly green lawn, a white Cadillac SUV the size of a tank parked in the driveway. "You'd have your own room, of course—there's plenty of space where we are. You'd share a bathroom with Amber, but she's tidy, don't worry."

She scrolls to the next photo. A pretty girl with curly black hair in a cheerleading outfit standing atop a pyramid of other girls. "And there she is," Georgina says. "Amber's captain of the cheerleading team, but she's also a very good student. She leads a Torah study group at the school. You could go with her, if you wanted."

"I'm not religious."

"Just to make friends, then. Look, we're Reform all the way, very casual about it. You wouldn't even have to come to temple with us unless it was your choice." She puts the phone away and digs through the bag, looking for something else. "You'd be free to be your own person there. Be whoever you wanted."

I'd be lying if I said the sales pitch didn't work, at least a little. Life sounds easy there. Warm weather and nice people and space.

She pulls something else from her bag and sets it on my knee. It's an ancient, fraying black-and-white photo of an old woman with her large family spread out on the porch of a run-down house. There must be a dozen kids and grandkids. Some are sitting, some are standing, no one smiles. The date on the bottom of the photograph says 1940.

Georgina taps the old woman with her perfect nail. "Alona Feingold—your great-great-grandmother—goodness, do I have that right? I did all the research about her online. Born 1882 in Odessa. That's in the Ukraine, or maybe Russia now, I can't keep it straight. Anyway, she came over to America in 1913 with her husband and five children. This is Alona as an old lady with her children and grandchildren at their home in Fenton, Missouri. Only Jews in town, I'd bet."

On a young man's lap sits a toddler who looks vaguely like a picture I remember of me at that age. She's about two or three and wearing a clean white dress. "That's your grandmother Sarah. You never met Sarah because she died when you were just little. Lovely woman. Strong-willed."

My breath trembles, and I stifle it to keep Georgina from hearing. I had been only academically aware that I had an aunt and a grandmother and a cousin and family. A few lines of a sketch. But now, here they were, real people in all their detail. I brush my hair back behind my ear. "I've never seen pictures of them before," I say.

"Your mother wasn't very sentimental about family," Georgina says. "It was probably our fault, mine and your grandmother's. We were too conventional for her. So off she goes at eighteen to join the army. What a scandal it was for your grandmother—a nice Jewish girl joining the army! But she was always the brave one, your mom. Always the intrepid explorer." Georgina reaches up, touches my cheek. "Bet you're the same way, aren't you? Fearless. Always looking for adventure."

She has no idea how wrong she is. "It must skip a generation," I say.

Mrs. Wasserman's saccharine pity is in fine form as she looks at Georgina and me across the desk. She is a stage actor, projecting her sorrowful eyes all the way to the balcony. The staff, she says, has been informed that my dad went missing while on a business trip in Europe. But hanging in her voice is the busybody's question mark, an implicit plea for details, mundane or salacious. Neither Georgina nor I give her any, though, and I can see Mrs. Wasserman is disappointed. Still, she purses her lips in kabuki warmth and presses her hands over mine as she tells me Danton will, as always, be a safe space for me in this period of emotional challenges.

As I leave Mrs. Wasserman's office and walk to my locker, it's clear to me that news of my dad's disappearance evidently spread further than the staff. Conversations slam shut as I pass, and all eyes turn to me. Only when my back is to them do the whispers start. Rumors of intrigue and murder? It may be the case that my stature has actually risen. That I am now at least interesting.

Terrance approaches me at my locker. There's concern and empathy on his face, as if someone he cared about had been hurt. I almost ask him what's wrong. Then I realize the look is for me.

"Hey," he says as I stand in front of my open locker. "I heard about your dad. That he was captured or something. I mean, holy shit, Gwen, are you all right?"

Something good and warm pulses inside me at the sound of his voice, but right away I feel guilty and push it away.

"He wasn't captured. He's just missing." My voice is flat and cold. I don't mean it to come out that way, but it does.

"Do you need anything? Can I help?"

"I'm fine," I say as I close my locker. "Sorry. Gotta go."

I head to class and wonder if things would have turned out differently had I answered my dad's call when I was with Terrance in the park. Probably not. But maybe. It's all your fault, Gwen.

But it's to avoid thoughts like these that I'm back in school in the first place, and it mostly works. It's been eight days without news, eight days of nothing except the torture of my thoughts at what it means to have no news. Luckily, calculus cares not a whit about my troubles, and neither does the civilization of ancient China. To dwell on hard facts and long-ago events is the closest I've come to actual pleasure.

After the last class ends, I take the train downtown to my dad's office, where it's nothing but the same shit as all the days before. The only difference now is that I can sit and do homework in a conference room between interrogations. *Why did you write in your diary about Syrian refugees on April 23? Why did your father charge $79 at a flower shop on June 12?*

But it's clearer to me with each day that passes, with each pointless question, that they have no idea what they're doing, or even what they're looking for. It's obvious that looking for clues in a schoolgirl's diary entries and old credit card statements is the best they can manage.

I see Joey Diaz rarely, and when I do, he only squeezes my shoulder and tells me, "It's a marathon, not a sprint." I see Carlisle even less often. It's always some variation of *nothing new today*, said with a brusque, dickish tone as he stirs his coffee with a pen.

It goes this way for yet another week. Monday through Friday, I go to school, then to the building downtown. There they don't even bother with the interrogations anymore. I study in a conference room, the red VISITOR badge dangling around my neck, and the only time I talk to anyone is when an agent peeks in and asks if I want coffee. Gradually, I realize the badge is right. I'm just a visitor who happens to be there, not the object of inquiry, not even an object of interest. The automatic looks of pity I used to get from everyone have turned to looks of polite tolerance. And one day, when I catch Carlisle in a hallway and ask if he's heard anything new, he says, "About what?"

Every night, I return home to Georgina, where there is dinner waiting for me, and a recap of her day's adventures in the city. Every night, I look for a reason to hate her, this interloper, this stranger. But I come up empty.

The truth is, she's been nothing but kind to me. Nothing but sweet. Nothing but generous. And here, this part, this is where it gets weird: It's her love that she's generous with most of all. We're nothing to each other besides a strand of shared DNA, but that's not how Georgina sees it. She helps me with my calculus, and turns out to have majored in mathematics in college. She shares the dirty joke she overheard in the salon, then giggles along with me. She holds me when I break down, whispering into my ear *it's okay it's okay it's okay* until I dry out. And it's as she holds me that I realize I have to amend that conclusion

I came to that first night on Bela and Lili's couch, that truth I replayed like a chanted mantra a million times a day: *He's already dead and you are alone.*

Because that last part isn't quite true.

As I play with my VISITOR badge and work through a chapter on the Zhou dynasty in my history textbook, Chase Carlisle enters the conference room. He is different today. No more implied *fuck off* when he sees me. No more brusque, dickish tone. Instead, he smiles warmly, like a real human, and inquires after my health and the health of Georgina. When I tell him we're both good, he smiles warmly again, as if he cares about the answer. Then he sits.

"Gwendolyn, I need to speak with you about your father now," he says.

I ball my hands into fists under the table. "You have news," I say, a statement, not a question.

Carlisle inhales through his nose, places his palms flat on the table. "We do not," he says.

"You do not what?"

"Have news."

I blink at him. "So then . . ."

"Gwendolyn, for twenty days the NSA has monitored all communications from all possible sources—terrorists, suspected terrorists, criminals, suspected criminals—everyone. There have been no mentions of your father, nothing related to your father."

My lip trembles. "Look harder."

"French intelligence, French police, our own FBI—they've scoured every inch of Paris. They've interrogated the man your father met there. They've interrogated everyone that man knows, from his brother to the person who delivers his mail."

"And?"

Carlisle turns his hands, palms up. "Nothing."

"Nothing," I repeat in a breathy whisper.

"There is no evidence, Gwendolyn—none—that your father was kidnapped. If there were, we would go to the ends of the earth to find him. But right now, nothing indicates anything other than that he—walked away."

The buzz of the fluorescent lights above us is deafening. I bite my lower lip and feel my face expand into the tortured version of itself that's become so familiar to me. I force myself to breathe slowly. I count to ten in my head and open my eyes. "But you have no evidence for that, either," I say. "That he just walked away. You don't *know* that. You have no *proof* of that."

"No," Carlisle says. His eyes are wide, sorrowful. "But such cases—such instances when people simply walk away—rarely provide anything like proof."

The words burst out of me in a furious shout. "So keep looking!"

He nods slowly. "And we will. I promise." He folds his hands together, as if in prayer. "But on a different scale."

"What does that mean, 'a different scale'?"

"Interpol—it's a police network, worldwide...."

"I know what fucking Interpol is."

"Interpol has issued alerts. His passports—diplomatic, civilian, both—have been flagged. And border agents have his photo and biometrics in case he's traveling as someone else."

I stare down at my hands, trembling with a sudden violent palsy. "So—a missing person flyer on a telephone pole. That's what you're doing. That's the best you got."

"A question of resources, really. Manpower. So many threats in the world today. We just can't afford to—"

"You can't afford to save your own agent," I gasp, pushing myself back from the table.

Carlisle grimaces as if the words hurt him. "Unfortunately, without a crime, our best hope is waiting for him to surface on his own. Which means this may take a while." He leans forward, waits for me to look at him again. "In the meantime—"

"Go to hell." I cross my arms over my chest, squeeze tight.

"In the meantime, your aunt Georgina. I called her today, explained the situation. We are both in agreement that you should go with her back to Texas. Is it ideal? No. But on a temporary basis—look, Gwendolyn, it's the best option." He pulls a thick packet of paper folded in thirds and opens it on the table in front of me.

"What's this?"

"A court order. Giving your aunt and her husband temporary custody. Until you turn eighteen or your father comes back." Carlisle coughs, frowns. "Or is declared dead. Legally, I mean."

I get up to leave. Fuck him. Fuck Georgina. Fuck legally dead. "I know my rights. You can't just do that. There's—court hearings. Lawyers. Speaking of which . . ."

He intercepts me at the door, grabbing hold of the handle before I can. "It's an emergency order. Government attorneys met with the judge in her office this morning." He looks at me sadly. "Your attendance wasn't required."

"Get out of my way."

"There is no more you can do for your father here in New York," Carlisle pleads. "You are still a child, Gwendolyn. An intelligent one, absolutely, but per the law, still a child."

I push past him and through the door, stab the elevator button, and stab it again when it doesn't come fast enough. I turn around, thinking Carlisle might be coming after me, but he's not. He's just standing there in the doorway of the conference room, hands in his pockets, looking at me with what may actually be real human pity.

. . .

In my apartment, I find Georgina sitting on the couch, an empty suitcase open beside her. "It's just temporary," she says like she believes it. "Until he comes home."

"How could you do that?" I seethe. "Your fucking signature. Right there on the court order. While I was at school."

"I'm sorry, Gwendolyn. I am." Her eyes squint like she's about to cry, like she's the fucking aggrieved one here. "This is—it's for your own welfare. The only choice. You know that. In your heart."

I break down again. And once more, there she is, holding me, as if holding me was her right. But she is right. She is. And I know it. Or think I do. Maybe.

"When?" I say into her shoulder.

"This weekend," she says softly. "Sunday morning."

When I'm finally dry and done honking snot into a paper towel, she places her hands on my shoulders. "I have an idea," she says. "Let's go to dinner, my treat, and—you know I've never been to a Broadway show?"

"Tickets are, like, two hundred dollars or something."

"Dinner and a movie, then. Girls' night out!"

Her smile is so damn bright.

At the fancy Thai place Georgina picks out a few blocks from the apartment, I order soup and a Sprite, while she orders crab cheese wontons and pad something and a cosmo.

"All the ladies in New York drink cosmos," she tells me.

Maybe in 1997, I want to say. But it's a catty thought. She's sweet and trying so hard. So I say, "Oh, all the time," instead, and touch her hand. "I want to—I want to tell you—that I appreciate it. What you're doing."

She sets down her drink and blinks at me. I can see her eyes are wet. She wants me to come with her, maybe for only a little while, but maybe forever. And she's cool with that. She and Amber and the good rabbi are cool with that. I marvel at how big their hearts must be.

We finish and go to a movie. A comedy. Part two to a part one neither of us saw, but it was just about to start and there were tickets available, and who are we kidding that it was really about the movie in the first place. The popcorn is warm and the crowd not too talky. We laugh a little, and I even manage to get lost in the story for a few seconds now and then. The ugly girl isn't ugly after all. See what a new wardrobe and a sassy gay friend can do? This time, she'll get the promotion *and* the man. I just know it.

By ten, we're back in the apartment, and Georgina drinks a glass of white wine and reads the *New York Post*, clucking her tongue and shaking her head at things she says never, ever happen in Texas.

I tell her I'm going to read in my room and kiss her on the cheek as I leave. She jumps a little at the kiss, and then smiles. I close the door to my bedroom behind me, bury my face in the pillow. Fuck you, Dad. Fuck you for doing this to me. Fuck you for taking a job that can get you kidnapped. Fuck you for keeping the only other family I have from me so that they're nothing but strangers and photographs. Fuck you for making me choose.

But he had his reasons. Must have. Right, Dad? I look for a photograph that I always kept on my dresser—of my dad, mom, and me sometime around when I was five. We were on vacation somewhere, Crete maybe, just before we left for the post in Algeria. My mom is in a bikini and wide-brimmed straw hat. My dad is in a pair of baggy swim trunks, and his skin is red from the sun. But this, too, is missing, another item seized in Carlisle's raid. Where are you, you asshole?

Six

Bela greets me at the door with a finger held to his lips. "Lili is asleep," he whispers as he shows me inside. The apartment is too warm, and I can still smell whatever spices they'd used in their dinner hanging in the air. "Does your aunt Georgina know you're here?" Bela asks.

"In bed," I say. "Maybe too much to drink."

Bela turns to a brass cart parked against the wall where he pours from a bottle into two glasses. "Your turn, then," he says. "And don't tell me you're too young. I started drinking palinka when I was nine."

I take a glass from him, and he clinks them together. "To your father," Bela says.

"To my father," I say, and take a little sip. Rancid fruit burns a trail down my throat to my stomach, and I nearly choke.

Bela sits in his armchair. "So?"

I look at him. "So?"

"You are disturbed tonight. More so. Tell."

I settle into the couch, fold my legs up against my chest. "They've stopped looking for him, Bela. Officially, at least. They say he just—walked away. Abandoned everything and walked away."

Bela takes a drink and contemplates this for a moment. "This is the bullshit I promised your father I'd protect you from."

"No clues. No chatter. That's what they say."

Bela leans forward, touches my knee. "And do you believe it?"

It is a harder question than I want to admit. "No," I say.

"And I agree," Bela says. "It is they who walked away from him, Red Shoes. The CIA is coldhearted, to its own most of all. I have worked with them and I have worked against them, so I've seen their cruelty. With my own eyes, I've seen it."

My throat is thick. "Why? Why would they do that?"

"No idea," he says. "But abandoning their own when an operation turns bad is what they're known for. I'm sorry, but that is the truth."

I stand and walk around the room, looking at all the little knick-knacks on shelves, lace doilies, the little treasures from the world Bela and Lili used to live in but left behind.

I take a second sip of palinka. It goes down easier. "Chase Carlisle, he got a court order. Georgina has custody until I'm eighteen."

"So? You will like Texas," Bela says. "You can listen to the rap music, go to school. Get a nice boyfriend from the football team."

I manage to give him a little laugh.

"Or whatever teenagers do," Bela says, smiling at me and refilling his glass. "I know nothing of such a life. When I was your age, there was a war on."

"I feel like I'm at war now."

Bela nods. "So you are. And I suppose you are full of fear and think you have no power to do anything."

"What can I do? I'm seventeen, Bela. A child. Technically."

He comes over to me, places a grandfatherly hand on my shoulder.

"I know this, how your heart hurts. How afraid you are. I felt it, too. My own war started when I was thirteen."

"Thirteen?"

"You want to know about it, my war, my tiny part of it?" His expression—raised eyebrows, slight smile—something here he wants to tell me, something he wants me to learn.

"I do," I say.

He walks back to his chair and motions toward the couch. I follow and sit across from him.

"My brother and I, we were in the forest, gathering firewood," he says. "From there we could see the little shack where our family was hiding. My parents, two sisters, they were outside, in the garden we'd made. Carrots. Potatoes. Fall, it must have been."

Bela swallows, lets out a long breath, the memory hard to look at. I give him his space by staring down into the palinka left in my glass. The smell of it rises to my nose, sweet and toxic.

"That's when the German truck arrived. Eight soldiers. No, six. And an officer in a fine leather coat, handsome like a movie star." He stops again, looks away for a moment before continuing. "My parents and sisters ran, but—this officer, he was a real marksman. Four bullets from his pistol. That's all it took."

I feel the tears coming, for him instead of me this time. I blink them away. "I'm sorry, Bela. I had no idea," I say. "What happened to you?"

He gives me a smile, thin as a wire, sadness and regret and pride all at once. "To me? What choice did I have, Red Shoes? My brother and I, we got guns and went to war."

"You were just a kid," I say.

"Not after that," he says, then points to his stomach. "That fear you have, just here, in your belly?"

"Yes?"

"It is just a feeling. Only that. Ignoring that feeling, that's all it means to have courage." He swallows the rest of his palinka and stands. "Come."

I follow him over to a cabinet with glass doors filled with dusty old books, most of them in Hebrew, some in what I suppose is Hungarian.

"Your father, he gave something to me," Bela says, opening the cabinet wide. "The morning he left for Paris. Told me to hang on to it until he comes back."

"Why?"

"In the event his apartment was searched, I suppose." He pulls a single book off the shelf and hands it to me.

It's the copy of *1984* my dad had shown me the night of his birthday. I turn it over in my hands. "Why didn't you tell me about this before?"

"Oh, it would certainly not be for you, Red Shoes."

"Who else?"

A shrug from Bela. "Whatever business your father was up to, it should be handled by an adult."

I thumb through it, but it's just an old paperback, the cover battered and cracked, pages yellowing. Inside the front cover is a name and a 718 phone number scrawled in blue ink. "Do you know who Peter Kagan is?"

"The owner of the book, maybe. Before your father." He wanders back to the cart, pours himself another drink.

I stare at the book. "Can I take this with me?"

"As I said, I do not think it was meant for you." He downs the contents of his glass in one swallow. "Well, wonderful talk tonight, but Bela must go to bed. Do me a favor, Red Shoes?"

I stare at him. "Yes?"

"When you leave, make sure the door locks behind you."

I pause on the landing in front of my apartment, but don't go in. Instead, I sit on the stairs leading down to the third floor and pull the copy of *1984* from the pocket of my army jacket. It's just a ragged paperback, dog-eared from a thousand readings, printing faded. I thumb through it again, more carefully this time, but there are no notes in the margins and nothing highlighted. Only on the last page, the blank one at the very end, do I find anything at all. There, someone wrote in pencil, *12/14/95*. A date, and not one I recognize.

The only things making this book unique are that date, the name, and the phone number. I turn to the inside cover and look at the name again. The handwriting itself is just block letters written in blue ink, unique to no one. Then I look more closely, and this time I see it. It's not the handwriting itself I notice, but how fresh and deep and so very elegant the blue ink is. Oh, Dad. You really did like the pen.

I can't help but smile sadly at the idea of it. For a few moments, I scour my brain for the name Peter Kagan, but he's no one I've ever heard my dad mention. I pull out my phone and dial the 718 number written beneath the name.

The line rings once, twice, then a male voice answers: "Eleventh Street Diner."

I hesitate and hear the sounds of mariachi music on a radio and busy kitchen in the background. "Hello," I say. "Is—is Peter Kagan there?"

"Peter who?" the guy says.

"Peter Kagan," I say slowly.

"Never heard of him. Wrong number."

"Wait," I say on impulse, "where are you located?"

He gives an intersection in Queens, and I hang up.

If the number belonged to someone named Peter Kagan, it doesn't anymore. I tap my phone to my lips. Unless it never belonged to Peter

Kagan. Unless the two pieces of information, the name and the phone number, are only meant to look like they belong together. I look at the clock on my phone. 11:20. Not late. Not *that* late. Then I stand, balancing on the edge of the landing.

Down the steps I run, three at a time.

The 6 train downtown to Grand Central, then change to the 7 headed to Queens. It takes me all of twenty minutes to get from my apartment to the Court Square stop, where the map says I should get off.

I climb down the elevated platform stairs to the street and make my way toward the address of the Eleventh Street Diner only a few blocks away.

Amid the mostly low-slung garages and industrial shops closed for the day, the diner is easy to spot. It has a bright awning and seems to be the only sign of life nearby. Inside it's warm and the air smells of frying grease.

"Coffee," I tell the guy working the counter. "To go. Light and sweet." He wipes his hands on his apron and pours a cup, loading it with cream and lots of sugar. I take a seat at one of the four booths and stare out the only window.

As far as I can tell, there's nothing around that would be of interest. But my dad had chosen this place for a reason. It occurs to me that maybe this clue wasn't meant to remind him of the location, but to make it discoverable for someone else, maybe even from this very vantage point.

I let my mind explore for a while, walk down the street in front of the diner, past a closed-up taxi garage, a closed import-export shop, a self-storage warehouse, a shop selling used industrial equipment.

My eyes drag back across the block to the self-storage warehouse. A place where one keeps things they don't have room for—or don't want—in their home. But you need a key to get in. A key to open the lock. I pull out the book and turn to the last page: *12/14/95.* It isn't a date, it's a combination.

The bell over the door tinkles softly as I walk out into the cold and toward the warehouse. Though the building is mostly dark, there's a light on in a little office at the front. I climb the steps and enter.

A rail-thin man in a tank top with tattoos from his fingers to his shoulders sets down a magazine and looks up from behind the desk. "Help you?"

"Do you—do you have a storage unit for William Bloom?" I ask.

The man's chair squeaks as he swivels to a computer and slowly types in the name. "Nothing for William Bloom," he says.

"All right," I say. "Thank you." I turn to leave and place my hand on the door handle. But of course my dad wouldn't have used his real name, not for something secret. And now, with what I know to be his occupation, a fake driver's license or even a passport, something just good enough so that he could sign a lease on a storage unit, wouldn't be too hard to come by.

"Try Peter Kagan," I say.

"What?"

"Peter Kagan."

More slow clicking of the keyboard. "Last name Kagan, first name Peter, unit 213," he says.

My stomach jumps. "Do you think I could—you know, take a look?" I say. "I'm his daughter. I have the key."

"Leaseholders only, and Peter Kagan's the only name I got."

I pull a twenty-dollar bill from my pocket but keep it below the counter and out of sight. I've never bribed anyone before, but I know there's a way you have to do it, a way of handing over the money so that you can pretend the bribe isn't a bribe.

"Maybe there's—maybe there's some sort of fee I could pay," I say quietly. It's the line I heard my dad use once with a traffic cop in Moscow. I fold the twenty in half and hold it up for him to see.

The man stands and braces his arms on the counter. "Out!"

I cross the street but make it only a few steps in the direction of the train before stopping. The answer, or at least my best shot at an answer, sits in unit 213 in the building at my back. So why am I walking toward the train? If this is a kind of war—and it is—can a night clerk be all it takes to defeat me?

That fear you have, here, in your belly. It's just a feeling. Only that.

So instead of walking back to the train, I cock my head and listen. The only sounds I hear are faraway sirens responding to faraway emergencies. And when I look around, I see that in the shadows of the New York night, it's easy for a girl to hide. Doorways, parked cars, stacks of boxes. There's nothing but hiding places. It's one of the things this city does well. It may be the thing it does best. So I turn back and take a look. That's all, just a look.

The warehouse is on a corner of a wide, busy boulevard and a side street that's apparently so quiet there's not even a traffic light, just a stop sign. A dumpster sits askew against the warehouse wall, battered and listing to one side like a damaged ship about to sink. Above it is a drainpipe fastened to the wall with brackets, and above that, a window. From across the street it looks easy enough, but when I cross and look closely, I see climbing it will be next to impossible. The brackets are rusty, and the wall itself is crumbling where the screws hold the brackets in place. Then there's the window, with no discernible way of opening it.

It would be easy to get caught, easier still to fall and break my neck. But I ignore the fear, the *feeling* that is fear, and in my mind flashes thirteen-year-old Bela with a gun and the brave girls who live on my bookshelf.

I climb up on top of the dumpster, give the drainpipe a little tug, then hang my full weight from it. It stays firmly against the wall. I pray to the gods of gravity, the same ones who control my fate in gymnastics, to be merciful.

The pipe itself is about the same width as the balance beam, and although it's vertical, it all feels familiar. I hoist myself up and brace my feet against the bricks, but by the time I'm ten feet over the dumpster, I feel a little play in the brackets, as if they might give way. I get a good grip and shift my feet to the pipe itself, pinching it between my boots. Shimmying is harder than climbing the other way, but in less than thirty seconds, I'm at the window.

Holding on tightly to the pipe, I swing my feet up to the windowsill and give the pane a kick, but nothing happens. I kick again, harder this time, and my boot disappears through the glass. For a moment, I hang there as still as can be, waiting for the burglar alarm to sound, waiting for the night clerk to come running, but all I hear is the traffic on the nearby boulevard.

My breath catches in my throat. It takes more effort than I expect to kick the rest of the glass away and swing my legs inside. Shards still clinging to their positions in the frame pierce through my jeans and bite into my flesh. I cover my face with my arms when I pass the rest of my body through, protected by the thick sleeves of the army jacket. As my feet land with a crunch on the floor, I feel a trickle of something wet run from my forehead down the bridge of my nose. It's almost perfectly dark inside, but I rub the drop between my fingers and can tell from its viscosity that it's blood.

My hands are shaking. Come to that, so are my arms. Even my knees seem like they're about to buckle, so I lean against the wall for a minute. Calm down, I tell myself. Toughen up. It's just a little blood. It's just a little fear.

But it isn't fear; in fact, it's the opposite of fear. It's the nausea I felt after smoking a cigarette once in Moscow and liking it. It's the high I felt after Terrance kissed me. It's the buzz of stolen champagne from embassy cocktail parties. It's all that combined, together and at once. And so much more. It's as if something new has crawled inside me, burrowed into me, where it's making a little nest for itself in my belly, trying on my limbs to see if they're a good fit.

This new thing, whatever it is, must have decided it likes the fit of me just fine, because in a moment, the shakes and nausea are gone. In a moment, it has taken possession of me and is steering me down the hallway. It's very dark, almost no light at all, but some instinct—some instinct not mine, but belonging to this new something inhabiting my body—knows better than to use the small flashlight I keep on my keychain. The dark is where you work best, it says. It's where you belong. In no time, I'm seeing with my fingers, seeing the way the blind see. The cinder-block walls are lined with smooth metal doors, and each door is marked with a plastic strip bearing a raised number.

I decipher the number 217, then 215, then 213. I feel for the lock and find it. It's thick steel and very cold to the touch. Cautiously, I turn my flashlight on, narrowing the light to a small point with my hand. With the thumb of my other hand, I rotate the six wheels on the lock so that they read *121495*. With a small tug, the lock slides apart.

I pause, listen, and am careful not to make a sound as I work the latch free and open the door. The smell inside rushes to greet me. It's familiar, like the smell of every apartment we've ever had, the peculiar combination of smells a family gives and imparts like a stain on the things they own.

I close the door behind me and, confident that I'm now invisible to whoever else is in the building, drag the beam of my flashlight over the things that once made up my life: an old dresser I had when I was a kid, the matching bed frame and armoire from my parents' bedroom set. Strange to break into a building and find your own memories living inside.

But what had he wanted me to find here? The light probes around a box with the word *TOYS* in faded Sharpie across the side. I open it and peer inside. There's a collector's edition Barbie whose hair I cut off at age five. There's a blond-haired, blue-eyed doll who, when you pull the string, says in Arabic, "Hello, friend!" There are loose Legos and toy cars and a sparkly Hanukkah card I'd made for my parents that leaves silver glitter on my fingers.

I close the box of toys and move on to another, but all I can see in this one is old tax returns and VHS tapes and aquarium supplies for the guppies that lasted a week. Then, in the next box, among my old ballet slippers and school papers is a photo album.

Don't, I tell myself. *Don't.* But I do. I sit on another box and open it. A Polaroid of my mom, in army fatigues and the very jacket I'm wearing now, grins at me from a time before I was born. On the bottom of the Polaroid is printed *Bosnia.* In the next little plastic sleeve is a photo of me, as an infant, wrapped like a burrito in my mother's arms. She's wearing a hospital gown this time but giving the camera the same grin. Who took this picture? My dad wasn't in her life yet. So my bio dad, whose name wasn't even on my birth certificate? Not likely. I place my thumb by my mom's face, stroke her cheek, touch her hair. My throat tightens, and the photo album slips off my knees to the floor.

The white corner of one of the photos sticks out from the album, jostled out of place by the fall. I pull at it and find it's not a photo at all. It's an envelope, sealed, white and crisp and new. I sit up straight, then work a finger under the flap and pull it open.

Inside is a single piece of paper, and I study it by the light of my flashlight. There are no words, no *Dear Gwen, if you're reading this, I've been kidnapped and this is what you should do next.* There are only sets of numbers separated by spaces, *0130513 1192381 3271822,* that go on and on and on, densely packed, single-spaced, covering the front and back. God forbid my dad do anything simply. God forbid he be straightforward. For the trouble he's putting me through, is it too much to expect a little clarity? And how do I know this is even what I'm looking for? Because it's hidden among the things that are most valuable to him? Why not, it's as good a reason as any.

This—all this, everything—is beginning to feel like a game, like one of those murder-mystery parties where people dress up like gangsters and flappers and dole out clues to figure out who some pretend killer is. I flatten the paper on my lap and look closely, studying the numbers. They all seem so random, like a sort of code. Like a code. Because it's a code.

I close my eyes. Bela was right; this was surely not meant for me. But who else? I don't know what it says or what it's for, but it is this that my dad was hiding here. It has to be. Please let it be. I fold the paper and push it deep into the inside pocket of my jacket.

From outside the storage locker, I hear the whir of an elevator motor and the chime of it opening its doors on another floor. I scramble out of the room, lock it up again, and feel my way toward the emergency exit sign. It's just as I make it to the door leading to the staircase that the elevator opens and the guy with tattoos from the office steps out. In his hand is a baseball bat.

I slip through the door, run down the stairs, and exit on the first floor. For a moment, I can't figure my surroundings; then I see I'm near the front office. I approach cautiously in case there's someone else there now—but I can't hear any movement. So I step into the room, push through the front door, and dash through the night toward the train.

Seven

It's like a Fabergé egg inside the elevator that goes to Terrance's apartment, with brass and mirrors and even a little velvet-upholstered bench along the back. When it reaches penthouse B, the elevator doors don't open into a hallway but into a foyer paneled with wood and blue marble tile on the floor. There are only two doors, one that is very fancy, the other plain and marked SERVICE.

The fancy one opens, and a sleepy Terrance stands there in boxer shorts and undershirt. "Hey," he says.

"Hey," I say. "Your doorman's a dick."

Terrance blinks at me. "Two in the morning. So—yeah."

He gestures for me to come inside, and I follow him down a dark hallway. The first thing I notice about the apartment is the almost total silence. There's a clock ticking somewhere, but that's it. I can't remember a single moment since we moved to New York that I haven't heard sirens and car horns and shouts.

"Your dad home?" I say quietly.

"No. Dubai maybe." He rubs his eye with the heel of his hand. "Or Shanghai. Anyway, you don't have to whisper."

I approach the windows that stretch nearly from the floor to the ceiling. Through them I can see the nighttime void of Central Park, ringed by the city beyond, distant windows filled with gold light hanging there like a tidy arrangement of stars.

Then it disappears as Terrance flips on a light. "Sit down," he says, motioning me toward a cream-colored leather couch. "Can I get you something—soda, coffee?"

"No," I say. "Thanks, but no."

"Did they find your dad?" he says. "Is he all right?"

I settle into the couch, pull the sheet with the number sets from my pocket, and hand it to him. "I broke into a storage locker, and this sheet was stuck in the back of a photo album. It's a code, Terrance."

He squints at me with tired eyes. "Wait. Go back. You broke into a storage locker?"

"It's my dad's storage locker, so basically mine, too. Not important." I stab at the sheet. "This, it's a code, right? A secret code?"

Terrance looks at the sheet closely, bites his lower lip. Then a little laugh escapes him. "It's—I don't know. Maybe," he says after a moment. "Come with me."

I follow him to a room at the far end of a long hallway. It's his bedroom and larger than my entire apartment. There's an ancient armoire that looks as if it was stolen directly from Versailles, and a king-sized bed with a robin's egg–blue upholstered headboard that sits beneath a couple of Japanese anime posters stuck to the wall with pins. But the centerpiece of the room is a gorgeous glass desk where a pair of enormous monitors seems to float above the surface.

I sit on the edge of his bed as Terrance paces the length of the room, studying the sheet in his hands. "All the sets are seven digits long."

"I saw that, too," I say. "And I was studying it on the train over here. The first number of each set is only ever zero through three. Never higher."

Suddenly he stops pacing. "A book cipher," he says. "Could be. It's possible."

"A what?"

"A book cipher." He grabs a sci-fi novel from his desk and sits down next to me. "So, codes like this have existed since—pretty much since books were invented. Thing is, for all the NSA-level technology, if you do it right, a book cipher is still pretty secure."

He opens the book and flips through it to a random page.

"Let's say you want to write a message to someone, and the first letter of the first word is *M*. You find an *M* on the page, then—so, write this down."

I take a pencil and legal pad from his desk.

He runs a finger down the page, then across it, counting quietly to himself. "Page two-one-one, fourteenth line from the top, twenty-seventh character from the left side of the page." He looks at me. "You get that?"

"Yes," I say, staring at what I've written. It takes me only a few seconds to figure it out. "So—the number set would be *211,14,27*."

"Exactly." Terrance closes the book and stands. There's an excited smile on his face. The geek's smile. The smile of the thinker engaged in the joys of thinking. "You have to do that for every single letter. It takes a long-ass time."

"But it's secure," I say.

"Yeah. If it's truly random," he says. "The thing is, though, the person receiving the message has to not only have the same book, but the same edition, the same print run, everything. Otherwise the numbers don't point to the same letters."

It's all so clear to me as soon as Terrance's words are out of his mouth. I pull the copy of *1984* out of my jacket pocket, and he takes it from my hand as if it were some sort of relic, delicately balancing it on his palms.

We work through each number set, with me reading them aloud and Terrance jotting the results on the legal pad. It's the middle of the night and tedious work, but we're both electric with excitement.

When we finish two hours later, we stare at the neatly printed columns of letters, but there's still no obvious pattern. They appear random, containing no more logic than they had in number form. For a few minutes, we're both dead silent, aware only of each other's breathing.

"It's almost five a.m.," Terrance says.

I look at the clock on my phone. "Jesus," I say.

He looks at me as he sits down in front of his computer. "You should go," he says. "I'm going to keep working on this."

"Terrance—I can't even say how much this means."

"You'll be in school tomorrow?"

School. My last day at Danton. Tell him now? "I guess."

"Meet me for lunch. The diner with the orange awning." He looks at me as I slip into my jacket. "Whatever this is, I'll have it figured out."

I hover over him at the desk, kiss his scalp just above his ear. "Thank you."

Georgina is waiting for me, livid. Not that I can blame her. She lets out something between a gasp and a shriek as I come through the door. "Do you have any idea, Gwendolyn, *any idea* what I went through, what thoughts went through my head?" she shouts, eyes red from exhaustion and tears. "I wanted to call the police, but I woke up Bela and he said not to. Said you were a big girl who knew what she was doing. What in living hell *were* you doing, by the way?"

"I'm sorry," I say. "I went to a friend's house."

"Oh, a friend's house, a *friend's* house," she says. "Is this friend a *boy*?"

"He is."

She throws up her arms. "This, this shit you just pulled, will not happen again. Do you hear me?"

"We're leaving Sunday. So obviously it won't happen again. I just— needed to see him."

She seethes for a moment, then goes quiet and wipes her eyes. "Come here," she says softly.

She holds me, and I hold her. It feels good, mom-like, mom-ish. It feels right. But my mind is lost. What do I do now? My schoolgirl sleuthing has turned up the key. The very thing to cancel out this entire mind-fuck hell.

"Why don't you go to sleep," Georgina says. "I'll call the school, tell them you're sick."

"No," I say. "I'll be fine."

Somehow I make it through the classes before lunch. Then I dash out the door and around the corner to the diner with the orange awning. It's crowded with Danton kids who turn and watch me as I make my way to the booth where Terrance is sitting in the back. When I slide into the seat across from him, I expect a collective gasp and the pulling out of phones and snapping of a hundred pictures. *#pretentioussnobhookup*

He slides a file folder across the table, and I open it discreetly, just peeking beneath the cover. Three sheets of paper: the original number sets, the page from the legal pad, and a new sheet with seven rows, each 21 characters long.

"At first, the letters seemed random," Terrance says quietly.

"But—here, look." He points to the second paper. "The first two characters were *CH*. Skip ahead twenty-two characters, and you see *CH* again. Then twenty-two characters later, we have *LI*."

I look at him. "I don't get it. So what?"

"So if you break down the sets into strings twenty-one characters long, every string begins with either a CH or LI. What do those letters mean?"

I think for a moment, considering the letters in isolation. Something there just beneath the surface of my memory rises up: The way European countries are sometimes abbreviated. *FR* for France. *SK* for Slovakia. "Switzerland and Liechtenstein," I say.

"And what happens in both those countries?"

"Banking," I say. "Money laundering."

He gives me a proud smirk, then taps the file folder. "They're bank accounts, Gwen," he whispers. "Translate the letters besides *CH* and *LI* back into numbers, *1* for *A*, *2* for *B*, et cetera—fucking bank accounts."

My skin goes cold. "You're sure."

"Yes. No question." He looks around, making sure no one's too close. "So, the five Swiss accounts are held by a very private bank in Zurich. We're talking founded three hundred years ago. Still run by the same family. The two in Liechtenstein, same thing."

"So whose are they?"

"I can't tell." He shrugs. "That's all the info I've got."

"You're a genius, Terrance," I say. "My God, this—I can't thank you enough."

His face turns serious. "I have to know, Gwen. What are you going to do with this?"

The waiter appears, greasy apron, little notepad and a stubby pencil.

"Nothing for me, thanks." I look at Terrance, my mouth open, not knowing what to say. "Look, I—Terrance, I'm sorry" is all I can manage.

I leave the diner and gasp out loud. No more school, not for me, not today; I've learned enough. So instead I head in the direction of the apartment and every once in a while touch the pocket where I tucked the papers Terrance gave me to make sure they're still there. This, it seems to me, is not just another piece of the puzzle, but maybe the whole puzzle. This is the reason he disappeared. And this is what Carlisle was looking for in our apartment.

Terrance and I are the only two people with this information. We are the only two people who can do anything about it. The obvious course, maybe even the right course, is to turn it over to Carlisle, despite what I have to assume were my dad's wishes. Turn it over to Carlisle, and be done with it. Head to Texas and hope for the best and pretend this information doesn't exist. But that will not happen. Cannot. He is my father. He is my only father. You do not throw that away.

I reach our building and pull out my keys to head upstairs. But I know Georgina's waiting for me there, full of bright teeth and earnest hugs and a Crock-Pot full of sympathy, warm and bottomless.

So instead, I press the doorbell of the stationery shop.

Bela leans back in the office chair behind his desk stacked with papers and an old-fashioned accounts ledger, green pages, handwritten entries, columns of numbers. But he's studying the numbers Terrance has given me, eyes moving back and forth from one page to the other and back again. "I should never have let you have the book."

"But you did," I say. "So what do you think?"

"Very clever," Bela says. "Your friend Terrance, he should do this for a living."

"No. About the account numbers. They're why my dad went missing, right? He didn't just walk away? Someone kidnapped him because they wanted these."

"All things are possible, of course," he says.

"So you think he's been kidnapped?"

"I said it's possible."

I rise from my chair, walk through the cluttered storeroom of the shop. "I can find him, Bela. I know where he disappeared from. Who he was meeting with. I can track him down. Go to war, like you did."

"Mm," he says, dropping the sheets onto the desk. "That easy."

"No. But I have to try. I have to."

He gives a little cough. "Do you know violence, Red Shoes?"

I stare at him. "It took my mother. I was there."

"But can you make violence yourself?" As he asks this, he studies me. It's not kindly old shopkeeper Bela doing the studying; it's Bela the spy, Bela the soldier, Bela the survivor. "After my family was killed, I got hold of a gun," he says. "An old, dirty Russian revolver. A few days later, I came across a German officer in an alleyway in the village. This officer, fine leather coat, handsome like a movie star."

It's exactly the way he'd described the officer who'd killed his parents and sisters. I stop pacing and listen.

"This German, he was with the town prostitute, shtupping her against a wall. It was dark enough that I could get up close." He raises a liver-spotted arm, pointing his index finger to the side of his skull, just behind the ear. "I shot him. Right here. No more than ten centimeters away. They both, the officer and the prostitute, fell. The bullet had passed through him and killed her, too."

"It was—it was the same officer who'd killed your family?"

Bela waves a hand over his face and grimaces. "Oh, who knows. It took off half his head. But it's the prostitute I think about. Still. To this day."

He's silent after that, but continues to study me, evaluating my reaction. On its surface, it's a horror story—a story meant to shock and frighten. But peel it back and the meaning is different: such are the cruel things we must sometimes do.

"And it will come to that, you know. Should you go after your father," Bela says. He leans forward, places a hand on my shoulder. "That's what war means. Bullets and mistakes you have to live with forever."

I nod. "Thank you," I say.

"For what?" Bela says.

"For telling me. For the advice."

"Advice?" Bela gives a little laugh, rests his head against the back of the chair. "And here I thought I was telling you why Texas is better."

It's a terrifying world, the one he described. But if no one else is going to act for me, then I have a choice: remain a child and do nothing, or become an adult and do it myself. That, it seems to me, is the difference between the child and the adult, the difference between the girl hunted by wolves and the woman who hunts them.

We hold each other's eyes for a time. "Of course, times are different now," he says. "You have an alternative. But theoretically . . ."

"Yes?" I say, my voice a whisper.

"Theoretically, going it alone would be suicide. Such would be the act of a lunatic. You'd need help."

I wait expectantly, then prompt him. "Yes?"

"If one had a friend—say someone with connections to that world. The world of intelligence services. Someone to make a few phone calls. Arrange for such help . . ." He sighs and bats the thought away with his hand as if it were a fly. "Even so, better to go to Texas and forget all this business here. Bela's just an old, crazy fool, anyway."

I look down, press my hands against my legs. "I'm going, Bela. I have to. I have to try."

Bela inhales deeply, closes his eyes. "That is your decision?"

"Yes." I tuck the papers and copy of *1984* into my jacket. "These phone calls. You'll make them?"

"I will," he says. "Bela is owed many favors. And in Israel, such debts are taken seriously." He rises from his seat and seems suddenly younger than his years, suddenly taller than his old man's frame. He gestures for me to stand, and I do.

We embrace. It's not sentimental, not loving. It's the embrace of comrades.

For twenty terrifying minutes, I wait in the computer lab at the public library for a greasy keyboard and an Internet connection. I spend the twenty minutes justifying this, the most insane idea I've ever had. The math never comes out right. Courage I don't have plus an old man's promise of help doesn't equal success. It equals zero.

But here I am now at the computer anyway, logging onto the Air France site with fingers that seem like they're controlled by someone else. Then there it is: JFK–CDG 8:37 p.m. With all my traveling over so many years, I have more than 120,000 miles I can burn through, way more than I need for one-way coach to Paris. The cursor over the PURCHASE NOW button vibrates in perfect rhythm to the shaking of my hand. I give the mouse one final click. Three seconds later, from somewhere in my jacket, my phone gives a soft chime as the boarding pass arrives.

I scurry out of the library and time it just right, arriving at my apartment just when I would normally be coming home from school. Georgina gives me a hug, asks how my last day at Danton went. Fine, I tell her. Sad to be leaving.

"You're going to make new friends in no time," Georgina says, holding me tight.

I twist out of her hug and sit at the tiny kitchen table, then draw a circle on the scuffed wood with my finger. "About that," I say. "Some of my friends, they want to have a going-away party tonight. A sleepover."

She sits down across from me. "But you were gone last night."

"It's my last chance to see them," I say.

She blinks, sets her jaw. "And where is it?"

"Margaret Saperstein's townhouse."

"Will Margaret's parents be there?"

I roll my eyes. "Unfortunately. Her mom is, like, super strict."

Georgina goes through a few more questions, but I assure her there will be no drinking, no drugs, no boys. I can tell she still doesn't like it, but in the end, she gives in. How can she keep me from my own going-away party?

I retreat to my room and put what I'll need into my backpack. Not the things I'll want, just what I'll need. I'm as spare as a soldier, taking only a single change of clothes, along with the list of account numbers, my civilian passport, and a deck of playing cards. Add the clothes on my back and the boots on my feet, and I'm ready to go.

Georgina is waiting for me in the living room. Hands clasped, eyes suspicious. "Be back by noon tomorrow, Gwendolyn."

"Okay," I say. "And thanks."

"For?"

"Everything. Thanks."

She closes her eyes. "You're welcome, Gwendolyn. Have fun."

The thing inside me—the thing that first made itself known in the hallway of the self-storage warehouse in Queens—is growing with each step as I march north along the avenue and turn left on Seventy-Second Street. It stretches into me, pulling my skin and body taut like a wet suit. It forces me forward. You are the hero of this story, it says.

My first stop is a little branch bank, and I withdraw the entire contents of my savings account, a little more than $500. I tuck this into my pocket and continue along Seventy-Second to the grand door of the Madisonian. The doorman calls Terrance for me, and a moment later, I'm at the door of his penthouse. He's waiting for me when the elevator opens.

"Want to come in?" he says.

"No," I say. "I just need—look, can you promise me something?"

He tilts his head and looks at me. "You all right?"

"Just promise me."

"Fine. I promise. What the hell, Gwendolyn, what's wrong?"

What there is to my plan, I tell him, adding that someone may or may not be arranging for some kind of help for me on the other side, in Paris. As I finish, I see Terrance's eyebrows rise in an expression of such silly surprise that I'd laugh out loud if today were any other day. I hand him the copy of *1984*, along with the original coded sheet. "Keep this for me. Hide it."

"Gwendolyn—don't" is all he can think to say as he takes the book and folded paper in his hands. Then he finds words and tries to talk me out of it. For a long time, we go back and forth. He uses as his tools reason and facts, a whole orchestra of them. But in the end, they bounce off the armor of my stubbornness.

"Nothing I can say will stop you, will it?" he says.

"No," I say. "And there's something else. I need money, Terrance. Cash."

He's quiet for a second, then pulls out a silver money clip stuffed with what he has. It's a small wad, maybe a hundred dollars total, and he tucks it in the pocket of my jacket.

"No. I need more." I hate myself for saying it, and I see his face pucker a little as if he's just bit into something sour. An embarrassed laugh from me as I turn to leave. "Look, I'm sorry, I shouldn't have..."

Terrance's hand darts to my arm. "No. Wait." He retreats into the apartment and is gone for more than a minute. He returns with a coffee can in his hand. "It's around two grand, I think. It's all I have. My dad has more, but it's in a safe."

I peek under the plastic lid. It's filled with loose bills: twenties, fifties, hundreds.

"My secret stash."

I close my eyes, and my breath trembles with gratitude. "You're saving my life. You know that?"

"Or helping you lose it," he says, taking my shoulders in his hands. He's looking at me deeply, his face tight, eyes begging, the most serious boy I've ever seen. "I can go with you," he says.

For a moment, I believe he actually means it, but it's a ridiculous idea. He's a soft American rich kid who'd last about five seconds on the run. Which, come to think of it, is what I am, minus the rich part. "You're sweet."

"I mean it. I can help."

I place my hands lightly on his chest. A shrink would say I was subconsciously pushing him away, but the truth is I just wanted to touch him. "No, I need you here," I say. "If I need a computer nerd, or, you know, something normal and good to think about."

I laugh a little. I have to or I'll cry. Why can't the world just go on its merry, foul way and leave me here alone with him? I lower my head to his chest and hold it there. It's the closest we've been since hiding in that tenement entryway to escape the rain.

"I have to go now, Terrance."

"I know," he says.

But neither of us moves. When I do finally peel myself away, his shirt is wet where my face was. He leans down and kisses me on the cheek, but I turn my head and meet his lips. It's a dry kiss, silent and soft, mouths closed. But it counts, I suppose.

. . .

When I hit the street again, the wind has picked up, pushing me down Fifth Avenue. I stuff the pockets of my jacket with the contents of Terrance's coffee can and drop the can itself in the trash. Two thousand six hundred and fifty-seven dollars is what it comes to.

I hail a cab and tell the driver to take me to JFK Airport. As I sink low in the seat, I pull out my civilian passport. The diplomatic one I'd been issued as the child of a political officer is still back in the apartment—too dangerous to use now and probably flagged, just like my dad's. But what are the chances they would do the same to my civilian passport? Carlisle thinks I'm headed to Texas. Wouldn't want to stop me from going to Cabo with my new family, would he?

When I arrive at JFK, the flight is still an hour and a half away. I buy a cap from a store, the kind old-fashioned cabbies and newspaper boys used to wear, and push my red hair up inside it.

At the gate, a strange quiet seems to have fallen over everything. I barely hear the chatter of the passengers, the din of the announcements over the PA as they call business class, group one, group two, group three.

The crowd surges around me like floodwaters, heading toward the plane. But I hang back. This journey has close to zero chance of success, and the only hope I have is the unknown, unlikely assistance Bela may or may not be able to arrange. But he's just a crazy old man. Said so himself. And I'm just a crazy little girl. This, the insane shit I'm doing now, proves it.

The gate agent calls all classes, all rows, and ten minutes later, the boarding area is empty except for me and her.

She looks at me expectantly, eyebrow raised, *on or off?*

PARIS

Eight

The airport is sterile and too cold and smells of air cleaned with chemicals. The other coach passengers and I march like a column of refugees through the corridor toward the immigration booths. I'm shivering because the air feels almost arctic, or maybe it's because I'm exhausted, or maybe I'm just terrified. The line creeps slowly forward, and I try to guess which immigration agent I'll get. The young thorough one, the old friendly one, the one who hates her job and the rest of the world because of it? It all depends on this. Who will smile at the American girl with red hair and wave her through and who will decide she hates American girls and hates red hair and so let's dig a little deeper into her story, shall we?

I'm directed toward a sour and drawn agent who stares at me with the boredom of someone who's done this for fifty years. I push my blue civilian passport across the counter and greet him in French. He replies in English, telling me to take off my cap so he can see me better.

"Why are you visiting France, miss?" the agent asks with tortured French vowels unsuccessfully transplanted onto English soil.

"Tourism."

"For how long?"

"One week."

"And where will you be staying?"

"A hostel called Hotel Colette." I remember seeing the name when my dad and I lived here. It looked like a dump.

"What are you planning to see?"

"The Louvre, the Eiffel Tower, the Centre Pompidou."

But there's something here he doesn't like, something suspiciously tidy about my answer that makes him stare at me for a few seconds. I try not to swallow too hard or smile too nervously.

He flips through the pages of my passport, examining each stamp. "I see you have been to France already three times," he says.

"Yes," I say.

"And you have not seen the Louvre or Eiffel Tower yet?"

I smile but feel the corners of my mouth twitch uncomfortably. "They're worth visiting again, no?"

His hand lashes out, and the stamp falls on my passport like a hammer.

"Of course," he says. *"Bienvenue en France."*

An electric door slides open, dumping passengers out of the customs area and into the reception room of the terminal. Eager families and bored limo drivers holding up signs scan the emerging travelers for recognition. A French soldier in uniform, young and trim and gorgeous, bolts past me and into the arms of his mother, whose makeup is running down her cheeks in tears. A dad in a slept-in suit picks up a toddler and kisses him, then glares at his wife, who glares back. But mostly the passengers push past the crowd on their way to the

Metro or taxi line. I throw myself into the middle of them, hoping to disappear.

In my peripheral vision, I see a woman in a leather jacket with an orange silk scarf tied loosely around her neck. She's somewhere in her late thirties, I guess, very pretty, with a riot of black hair pinned up on top of her head. She's scanning the crowd, walking quickly along its edge, smiling expectantly as if the person she's looking for is somewhere among us. I look up toward the signs, trying to find my way to the subway, but when I look back again, her eyes are locked onto me.

So it's a case of mistaken identity, I tell myself. So I look like someone she knows. No big deal. Keep walking. Then her hand is on my shoulder, turning me forcefully to face her. Instead of shock and an apology that I'm not who she thought I was, she beams and gives me two quick kisses on the cheeks before pulling me into a close hug.

Underneath her elegant leather jacket and trim body, I feel plenty of muscle. She holds me tightly, and I smell a hint of very expensive, very French perfume. Her mouth two inches from my ear, she whispers in English, "I'm a friend of Bela Atzmon, understand?"

She pushes me away as if to look me over but still holds me firmly by the shoulders. "*Comme tu as grandi! Je n'en reviens pas! Tu es presque une adulte!*" she says, loudly enough for those around us to hear. She pulls me close again and resumes whispering in English. "There are two men by the newspaper stand; they're police detectives. Don't look. Just smile like I do, like we're relatives who haven't seen each other in ages."

"Are they here for me?" I whisper back.

"Let's not find out," she says.

We begin walking, and she holds my arm tightly just as if she really were a long-lost aunt. "No bags?" she says quietly.

"No, I just ran with whatever I had."

"Then let's go."

She guides me along, steering me with her grip, out the door and across the passenger pickup area to a parking garage. The morning sun is giving way to thick, rolling rain clouds. But to my sleep-deprived eyes, it's still way too bright, and I have to squint as I study her. What is this, and why am I getting into a car with her?

The garage is packed, rows and rows of small Citroëns and Fiats, but there are few people around. "How did you know who I was?" I ask.

"The red hair is a little obvious." She stops to unlock the passenger door of a battered old Volkswagen hatchback. "Get in," she says. "Quickly now."

"Wait," I say. "I don't—I don't even know your name."

"I'm called Yael," she says, and climbs into the driver's seat.

The wording is careful: *called Yael*. Not *I am Yael*. Not *My name is Yael*. I climb into the passenger seat anyway, despite my better judgment. She reaches for the ignition with a key, but I interrupt her. "Just a second. Can we, you know, talk a minute?"

She retracts her arm and eyes me coldly. "What do you want to know?"

"To start with—who you are?" I say.

"Yael. I told you."

"Then *what* are you? A private investigator? A spy?"

Her eyes dance over my face, deciding what to say. "I am someone who is asked to do favors from time to time."

"That's a very vague way of putting it."

"Yes," she says. "It is."

"Yael is—an Israeli name?"

"Will that be a problem?"

"No," I say. "Of course not."

The woman called Yael starts the car, and we wind through the parking garage to the roadway. She drives quickly but precisely, speeding up to the tail of a big eighteen-wheeler loaded down with fat metal pipes, then downshifting as she circles around it, quick as a rabbit.

I notice her eyes flicking back and forth from the road ahead to the rearview mirror. It's not a nervous gesture, but something she's been trained to do, something I remember my dad doing. Beneath the chic Paris clothes and the flawless Parisian French lurks something hard, something that comes from years spent in the streets of cities crueler than this. There's too much cold control, too much skill, for someone who is sometimes, as she put it, "asked to do favors." The woman who calls herself Yael is no errand runner. Somewhere in her jacket, I feel reasonably sure, is a pistol.

"So—why are you doing this?" I say. "I mean, why does Israel give a damn what happens to an American?"

Yael's quiet for so long I wonder if she's ignoring the question. Just as I'm about to repeat it, she answers. "This man, your father—his agency and mine worked together now and then. He has knowledge that we'd rather he not share. He is, for my government, more of a priority than he apparently is for yours."

It's very clear now, and very unsentimental. This has nothing to do with paying back Bela the debts he's owed. "Just business, then," I say.

"Always is."

She makes another turn, and I see we've entered the suburbs of Paris that don't appear in any tourist guide. It's all concrete apartment blocks here, public housing. The buildings loom up on either side of us like canyon walls.

"You'll need to tell me everything," Yael says. "Then my service will go to work. Data mining, mostly—matching a puzzle piece here to a puzzle piece there. In the meantime, I teach you how not to get killed."

"The data mining, how long will it take?"

"Could be a month, or tomorrow."

"A month—Yael, that's too long," I say. "We can't just wait around."

"Waiting is ninety percent of what we do in my profession."

"So what's the other ten?" I ask.

Yael eyes me and smirks. "Pure terror."

The car slows to a crawl in dense late-morning traffic, inching along a side street, barely moving at all. Yael slams the heel of her hand into the horn and curses. This commercial side street isn't the Paris people dream about, the Paris of accordion players and copper roofs turned green with age. This is the Paris of grocery stores and cheap sushi joints and dry cleaners. Daytime Paris. Sensible-shoes Paris. The sidewalks are crowded with businessmen and mothers pushing strollers. Yael finally finds a parking spot, and I follow her on foot for another block before she stops beneath a green awning marked STUDIO MARIE, ACADEMIE DE DANSE.

"Who's Marie?"

"I suppose I am," Yael says.

"You're a dance teacher?"

She swings the door open. "Sometimes."

Inside, the place smells pleasantly of sweat and effort, like a gym. Floor-to-ceiling mirrors and ballet barres line the walls. I wander through the room, tap middle C on a beat-up piano in the corner.

"Leave the piano alone," she says.

Yael moves to the back of the room, where she opens another door. There's a sort of graceful power in her walk, like a cat's. "Follow me."

We head up a narrow staircase to the floor above. It's a large room the same size and shape as the studio below us, but with a higher ceiling and windows covered by blinds. Yael pushes back a folding curtain that cuts the room in two, revealing an area where thick mats

100

cover the floor and a fearsome rubber training dummy—crudely made face locked in a teeth-baring growl—stands in the corner.

"What is this?" I ask.

"My home," she says. "And for now, yours."

"No, that part. It's like a martial arts studio."

Yael takes a bottle of water from one of the metal cabinets lining the wall and opens it. "The other thing I teach. Krav Maga. Heard of it?"

I shake my head.

"In Hebrew, it means 'hand combat.' You'll be learning from the best teacher in Paris."

"You—you're going to teach me to fight?"

"I'm going to try." Yael sips the water slowly, her eyes scouring me as if evaluating what I'm capable of. "Bela told his contact you're a gymnast."

"Well—it's just a hobby."

"Even so. It means you have balance, strength. You know your body and what it can do."

"Look, I'm sorry. I don't know what anyone told you. But I'm not a fighter. When Bela said someone would help me . . ."

"You thought he meant someone would do everything for you?" Yael says angrily. "I'm the only ground support you get, and this isn't a solo operation. We do this together."

"But finding my father is a priority. That's what you said."

"Yes. And such an important one that they assigned a dance teacher to the case." She shakes her head. "Someone in my government said to someone else, 'Why are we paying this Yael up in Paris?' So here we are."

On a cot in the corner of a tiny and otherwise bare room, I try to sleep. And maybe I do, but the waking kind, the in-and-out kind, where you're never quite sure what's real and what isn't. I hear New York outside the window, no, I hear Paris—little engines, high-low sirens. Beyond the door of my room, I hear Georgina on the phone, speaking French.

My eyes snap open. Gwendolyn Bloom, you heartless, selfish girl, what have you done?

I'd turned my phone off when I got on the plane, buried it under wet paper towels in the bathroom trash just after takeoff. How many voice mails from Georgina are waiting for me, each one progressively more panicked? She's talking to the police now. Blaming herself. If only she'd let me stay a few days longer. If only she'd shared just a little more of herself. Poor Georgina. I rewarded her love by killing her. My little war has claimed its first victim.

I shove the thoughts of her aside and banish the self-doubt and self-loathing to some dusty corner of my mind. I will be hard, I decide. I will be fearless. I force myself to stand. Force myself to walk out into the studio.

Yael has, inexplicably, laid out a large plastic sheet on the floor and placed a chair in the middle of it.

"How long was I out?" I ask.

"Ninety minutes," she says.

"What's this?"

She nods toward the chair. "Sit."

It reminds me of an interrogation scene from a movie. "What's with the plastic? So you don't get blood on the floor?"

"Your hair. You can't go out looking like that."

"I'll go out looking however I please."

"How many people will remember the girl with bright red hair they saw on the train, or sitting in the café, or asking strange questions about her father?" She slides her hands into a pair of rubber gloves. "The answer is all of them. Now sit."

I obey, and Yael goes to work. She dips a brush into a plastic bowl at her side and slowly attacks my hair, section by section. Her fingers push and pull and twist my head into whatever position she needs. I hear her whisper something in Hebrew that sounds like a long complicated curse.

"Have you done this before?" I ask.

"For three months, I was undercover in a Beirut salon."

I try to picture Yael chatting amiably with the wife of some Hezbollah cell leader while she snips away at her hair, fishing for gossip about her husband's friends visiting from Damascus. *Remind me where you live again?*

"Still, maybe we should see a professional," I say. "You know, someone who's done this longer."

"And when the cops come around? 'Done any work on a girl with bright red hair lately?' We'd have to shoot her," Yael says, slamming my head forward to reach the hair at the base of my skull.

"Shoot who?"

"The stylist."

"You're joking."

The silence lasts just a second too long. "Of course," Yael says.

An old-fashioned kitchen timer ticks away the minutes. I can smell the dye and feel it burning my scalp. I ask Yael if she's sure she did it right. She tells me she has no idea and to shut up and wait. When the timer finally rings, she rinses my head in the kitchen sink. It turns out, though, that Yael's not done yet. She steers me back to the chair and starts in with the scissors. I see lengths of my hair dropping to the floor. It's deep brown now, with a touch of auburn, too.

Yael rinses me again, and I'm finally allowed into the bathroom to inspect her work in the mirror. At first, the sight of it shocks me. My hair is shorter, stylish, more grown-up, *Parisienne*. Damn, Yael's not bad.

It's the sight of my face, though, that shocks me most. With this haircut, I see it in a new frame, as a stranger would. My God, what have the last weeks done to me? Is it possible for a seventeen-year-old to look old? My face is thinner than I remember, sallow and drawn. Worn out. Substituting terror for food does strange things to the human body.

Outside, Yael directs me to stand against an unadorned white wall. She holds up a digital camera and aims it at me.

"You'll be getting a new identity," she says. "Don't smile, just look at the lens."

The flash goes off once, twice, and then a third time for good measure. She sets down the camera and starts fiddling with a computer on a desk. I see the images of me flash across the screen like mug shots.

"I'm told you know several languages. Which one is your strongest?"

"English," I say.

"Obviously."

"Then Spanish and Russian," I say.

"Are you fluent? Can you pass as native?"

"So I'm told."

"Be sure. Your life may depend on it."

"I'm sure," I say, though I'm not sure at all.

That afternoon, in the kitchen, I take a seat at the table while Yael prepares the teakettle. When it's done, she sets a cup down in front of me and takes the chair next to mine. She's so close I can feel the warmth coming off her body.

The tea is the minty stuff you find everywhere in the Middle East, and it reminds me of my dad and our time in Cairo. Maybe that's what Yael means for it to do, make me comfortable and relaxed, a psychological trick to get me to open up. Or maybe she just likes mint tea.

"Start at the beginning, the day your father disappeared," she says with the gentle voice of a therapist, the voice I remember all the doctors and shrinks using with me after my mom was killed. "Leave nothing out. No matter how unimportant it seems to you."

Because she's so close, I don't have to speak above a whisper. I begin with my dad's birthday, with him telling me he had to go to Paris. I tell her about the agents, Kavanaugh and Mazlow, and about the timeline I saw on the whiteboard through the window. Feras. Café Durbin. Chase Carlisle and Joey Diaz.

Yael is mostly expressionless as she listens, and only occasionally stops me to ask a question or repeat something. Which floor I was taken to. Carlisle's job title. What else I saw lying around the room. As I answer, I see Yael close her eyes, not just listening to my story but learning it.

I continue, the story pouring out of me like dirty water draining from a bathtub. It's a relief to unload the weight. It's only after it's done, only after I tell her about breaking the code and the bank accounts, only after Yael gets up to make more tea, that I realize the mistake I've made.

My father had meant the code to be a secret. Now I had spoken of its existence to both Terrance and this woman named Yael, *called* Yael, whom I had met only a few hours ago. Her expression hadn't changed at all as I told her about the accounts, as if these new facts were of no more importance than anything else I told her. But, then, of course it wouldn't. She's a professional.

She pushes a fresh mug of tea in front of me and lifts her own, blowing across the surface and sending up little curls of steam. "The book you used to crack the code," she says. "Was it a common edition, one currently available? Something someone could find easily?"

"It was old. A cheap paperback. From the seventies, I think. I left it with a friend for safekeeping, along with the coded sheet I found."

"Give me your friend's name."

"It's not important," I say. "I don't want to get him involved."

"He's already involved. *His name*, Gwendolyn."

I look down, ashamed of myself as I give it to her.

"And the bank account numbers," she says. "Who has those?"

"Just me."

"You're sure."

"I'm sure. I have them in my backpack."

She nods at this and sips the tea thoughtfully. "Bring them to me."

Her tone is that of a commander, calmly certain of her own power over my actions, as if the idea of my refusing isn't even conceivable. Inside, I feel like I'm about to catch fire with panic. Of what relevance could the account numbers possibly be? But it's an idiotic question and the answer is obvious: The account numbers are what she's after.

I open my mouth to speak, but the voice that comes out isn't mine. It's a little girl's voice, high-pitched, weak, feeble. "Why do you—why do you need to see them?"

"Gwendolyn," she says, leaning forward, eyes locked onto mine, "this isn't a request."

What if I refuse? What if I make a run for it? She'd kill me before I made it to the street, that's what. Like a slavish little robot with no will of her own, I walk to the little room where my cot is and retrieve the folded paper from the notebook where I'd tucked it. Money. It's always about money. Always and everywhere about money. Well, she can have it, then. I'll search for my dad on my own.

Yael appears in the doorway, strong, looming, and holds out her hand. "And this Terrance you mentioned—you trust him absolutely?" she says.

"Yes."

"Certain?"

"Goddammit, yes."

She takes the sheet from me, unfolds it, and looks it over, just for a few seconds. Then she removes a cigarette lighter from her pocket and holds a flame to the edge. The fire hangs there weakly for a moment, and Yael turns the page upright, allowing the flame to climb.

"What the hell are you doing?" I cry out.

"Your father didn't go through the trouble of hiding this only to have you hand-deliver it to his captors." The flames are leaping into the air now, and Yael drops the paper into a wastebasket, where it flares for a moment before pulling back. "What you have here, it can only hurt you, Gwendolyn."

My words come staggering out of my mouth like an accusation. "So that's not what you're after?"

"What, the accounts?"

"Yes. I thought you . . ."

"No, Gwendolyn," she says. "I don't give a shit about the money."

A chill of relief washes over me. The world, for the past month, has kicked to death any hope I had for it, but here was proof that my trust in at least one of its inhabitants wasn't misplaced.

"So," she says. "Whose accounts are they?"

"I don't know."

Yael gives the wastebasket a shake to make sure the flames are out, then looks up at me. "Too bad. It would be useful information, especially since they're going to come after you."

"My dad—he didn't steal these," I say. "He would never steal."

"All right," she says, as if whether he did or would is irrelevant. Then she comes closer, places one hand on my wrist, the other on my shoulder. "Gwendolyn, listen to me. Remember this always: Anyone who asks for these account numbers is your enemy."

Nine

On Yael's orders, I change into a pair of borrowed yoga pants and an undershirt. I walk barefoot to the center of the mat where she's waiting for me. She's changed, too, into track pants and a tank top. There seems to be no fat on her body at all, just taut, ropy muscles.

She begins with a few basic stretches, bending at the waist and placing her palms flat on the floor. I follow along.

"Unlike karate or kung fu, there's no honor in Krav Maga, not in the version I teach," Yael says. "This is street fighting. We use our teeth, our nails—whatever it takes. No limits. No rules."

She drops to the mat, her legs in a wide V, and lowers her forehead to the floor in front of her. I do likewise and feel the tension of the long flight slowly ebbing away.

"Most of your enemies will be experienced fighters but untrained. That's why you are here with me." Yael jumps to her feet and goes to one of the metal cabinets. "While we wait for an assignment from the desk monkeys, we'll do what we can to make you ready. The basics. We won't have time to make you an expert."

I nod that I understand. "I just have to be better than my opponent."

"Not opponent. Enemy." She turns, a yellow rubber training knife in her hand. "This isn't sport. You won't be breaking boards with your forehead. What you learn here is exactly what we use in Israel to turn the soft dentist's daughter into an operative who can kill a man with her thumbs."

She hands me the knife, handle first. My hand grips it tentatively. I know it's just rubber, non-lethal, but it feels strange. I've never used any sort of weapon, never even held one. Yael steps back and says, "Now stab me."

I blink at her. "Stab you?"

"That's what knives are for," she barks. "Stab me!"

I push the blade at her halfheartedly.

Yael flicks it away with her forearm. "Again."

Another thrust, more forceful this time, but she flicks it away with her other wrist. "Again!"

A third thrust, deeper than the others, my muscles into it this time. But instead of deflecting it, Yael seizes my wrist and wrenches my arm into a coil so the tip of the blade points to my own chest. I gasp at the pain in my shoulder and wrist but keep struggling against her. Then Yael's foot lashes out and sweeps my legs out from under me. Within a fraction of a second, I'm on the floor, staring up at her, while she looks down at me. The knife I'd held just a moment before is now in her hand.

I grip my right shoulder and try to massage away the radiating pain. "That really hurt," I say.

"I meant it to."

I expect Yael to help me up or say something positive. *Good try* or *You'll do better next time.* But instead, she's circling me, her dancer's feet silent on the floor. "Are you going to lie there like a child, or stand up and learn?"

I struggle to my feet. "I'm ready. Teach me."

"Sure? Because to my eyes you are a lazy American kid," she says as she moves left, then right, a graceful buildup to the next violent something she has in mind. "I give you a knife, and in five seconds, you're on the floor, whining."

"I'm ready," I say.

"What?" she barks.

"Teach me!" I shout.

I see her fist fly at me, high and to my left. But my gymnast's reflexes have awakened, and I lift my arm to block it. It's at that moment that her other fist crashes into my right side, and the world becomes a bright, quiet place. All that exists is the blunt pain in my kidney just below my rib cage.

When I open my eyes, Yael is standing at the edge of the mat, her face reflecting the blue light from her phone's screen as she checks her e-mail. "Fucking pathetic," she says as she turns her back to me, her attention on whatever she's reading. "But then, from you—pathetic was what I expected."

The pain in my kidney is being pressed aside by a flare of anger so gleaming it nearly blinds me. *Regardez la* alpha bitch—back toward me like I'm too small a threat to even look at. I gauge the distance between us, gauge the height of the ceiling, then spring forward, two strides, three. A clean hurdle, nice long lunge. My palms hit the mat exactly where I want them to, and my shoulders shrug with all the power I have left, launching me into the air. Legs snap together, and this may really, truly be the tightest handspring I've ever done.

I feel one of Yael's legs slice through the air where my body will be in another tenth of a second. But she's too early. I twist to the side like a spinning javelin, and my feet find Yael's chest. We both crumple to the ground with me on top of her.

It's an obnoxious, show-offy attack, but goddamn if it doesn't work. I knocked the breath out of her and just maybe her arrogance, too.

It takes Yael a few seconds to get her wind back and pull herself out from beneath me. She stands and cradles the side of her head with her hand. I pick myself up and face her. She's steaming with anger, cheeks the color of fruit punch.

Everything on me hurts from my little stunt, but I'm not going to show it. "Still pathetic?" I say.

"You're subtle as a truck," she seethes as she glares at me.

It's the first thing I've heard from her that sounds like a compliment, and now, in her glare, I see that she's assessing me a second time. Reevaluating the girl she thought she'd been saddled with, substituting a new one.

"You're welcome," she says.

I look at her with an angry little smile. "For what?"

"For teaching you the first lesson of Krav Maga," she says. "How to get hit and get up again. It wasn't as bad as you thought, was it?"

She's right, in a way. The pain from Yael's blows hurt, but that's all it did. In a few minutes, I've recovered and the sting has faded. It hurt a hell of a lot less than the shame I would have felt from giving up. I think about Astrid Foogle in the hallway of Danton and her slap to my cheek. It hadn't been nearly as hard nor as skillfully delivered as Yael's blows, and yet it seemed to hurt a lot more. The pain of Astrid's slap, I realize, wasn't in the slap itself, but in what it meant—that she was powerful and I was not. Whatever pain remains from Yael's strikes feels somehow different, somehow less significant, because my getting up again and fighting back has removed the toxin of humiliation.

"Proud of yourself?" Yael says, tossing me a water bottle.

I take a swallow between exhausted breaths and nod.

There's a flare of something nasty in her eyes. "I'll lend you some shoes, and we can go for a run. Ten kilometers to start."

We dash through the wet streets, weaving between crawling traffic, pushing past pedestrians who stop and stare at the two crazy bitches running in the rain, soaked to the skin. She's always ahead of me. Always. I can never quite catch her. There's no kindly coaching with Yael, no words of encouragement, just shouted orders to keep up and foul-sounding, slangy curses I don't understand.

Her strides are long and even, and though she's twice my age, I'm now at least a good ten paces behind her. Two businessmen in suits walk side by side down the sidewalk. Yael never pauses, never breaks her stride as she shoulders her way between them.

"Putain!" one of the men shouts as the other spits a huge yellow-and-white phlegmy gob that narrowly misses her.

"J't'emmerde!" Yael calls back.

I take the path of least resistance and bound past the two men along the edge of the curb, snagging my hip on the side mirror of a parked Toyota.

Yael turns so that she's jogging backward and searches for me behind her. *"C'est inacceptable!"* she barks. *"Allez bouge-toi!"*

I grunt and dig deeply into whatever store of energy I have left. The real thing ran out long ago, and I'm now operating on pure, acidic determination.

She veers left into a park, using a bench to launch over the waist-high iron fence. I follow, but my sneaker slips as it hits the wet wooden slats of the seat, and my leap over the fence isn't clean. My foot strikes the ground on the other side at an angle, and I land hard on the pavement. I start to push myself up but there's a stabbing pain from my ankle and it won't take my weight. Somehow I hoist myself to one foot, hop to a spindly sapling, and grab hold of its trunk for support.

Yael appears next to me. "Ankle?" she says.

I nod, and she kneels on the ground to examine it. Her fingers are like ice as they push down my sock and gingerly probe the skin.

"I think I sprained it," I say.

"Just twisted," she says, no sympathy at all in her. "Come on, walk it off."

She weaves her arm beneath mine and across my back, my bad ankle between us. I take a delicate step, but it feels like a knitting needle is being driven right through the bone.

"You're all right," she says. "Push yourself."

But I push her away instead. "Would it kill you to be a little nice?" I seethe.

"Nice?" Yael's eyes are pitiless. "Do you think your attackers will be 'a little nice'? Do you think they'll say, 'Poor baby, let's give her a rest'?"

I hop to a rusty jungle gym at the edge of the park and grip the metal bars. Through bared teeth, I seethe and struggle to hold back a wave of tears from exhaustion and terror at the hole I've dug for myself by coming here.

Yael hovers behind me. I feel her there, standing silently as if she's about to kick my good leg out from under me and tell me to toughen up. Instead, she places a gentle hand on my shoulder, and it surprises me that she's even capable of a touch that doesn't cause pain.

"Come on," she says.

She laces an arm under mine, and I have to lean into her so I don't fall. On the street, Yael hails a cab, and we climb into the backseat. In the confined space, all I can smell is the stink of our sweat.

· · ·

I fell asleep around six last night to the sounds of Yael shouting *un, deux, trois, un, deux, trois* to the clomping dance class below. Now, eleven hours later, my body's sleep rhythm somewhere between New York and Paris, I sit on the edge of the cot and probe the floor with my toes, testing my ankle for a sprain. But the sharp knitting-needle pain from yesterday is gone, replaced by a dull, warm throb that ticks like a metronome beneath the gel packs Yael bound to my ankle with a bandage. I peel the bandage back and find the swelling is down, way down—Yael was right. Not sprained. Twisted. She'll gloat, then punish me.

I limp through the dark toward the kitchen, the Paris sky between the blinds inky blue with the first morning light. As I approach, the smell of frying bacon grows stronger, and I wonder if it's an illusion. But as I step through the door into the kitchen, I see Yael standing over the stove, spatula in hand.

"How's the ankle?" she says loudly over the hissing and popping of bacon in a frying pan.

"Better. Thanks." I stare at her for a moment, as if the idea of her doing something so domestic and kind, and for me no less, were a sort of contradiction.

"Sit before you fall," she says. "You keep kosher?"

As my groggy head struggles to make sense of the question, I limp to the table and fall into one of the chairs. "Kosher?" I repeat. "No. I guess I'm missing the faith gene."

"Me too. And even if we're wrong, God's got enough to condemn me without bringing up what I had for breakfast." She scrapes at the pan with the spatula. "Bacon and eggs it is, then. A real American breakfast for my real American teenager."

For a moment, I wonder if this is a trick and watch her suspiciously. Maybe the second lesson of Krav Maga is how to have sizzling bacon grease poured in your lap and take it like a champ.

114

There's a long baguette sitting on the table, and I break off a piece. Yesterday's. It would have to be. But not too stale.

"So, your ankle—just a little twist. You were trying to get out of finishing our run."

But I don't take the bait. She's not going to get to me, I decide, not today. "So—what's your story? Ever married?"

"Why do you want to know?"

"On the planet I'm from, it's what people talk about. It's called getting to know each other."

Yael probes at the bacon with a fork. "You don't live on that planet anymore. Anything you tell someone, they use. Anything you love, they go after. If you must talk, say only lies."

I rub my forehead and close my eyes, willing the kind Yael of a few minutes ago to come back, because it's far too early for this spy-philosopher shit.

"I *was* married," she volunteers suddenly. "Once. For a year."

"And?"

"A woman in this profession—I have a saying, a woman needs a man like—how did I put it?"

"Like a fish needs a bicycle," I say.

She shovels some bacon onto the plate and stares at me. "What? That's idiotic. I was going to say, a woman needs a man like she needs an Hermès scarf. Nice to have, but if you lose it, who cares, it's a scarf."

"So, disposable men," I say. "Lose one, get another."

"Not just men. Everyone." She sets a plate down in front of me. Eggs, burnt black and dry as leather. Bacon, floppy and barely cooked. "It's the nature of this profession. Trust is impossible."

"That's—very paranoid," I say. "I don't want to believe that."

"Really? It's the reason you're here, after all." She sits down with her own plate and begins eating. "At some point, you will be betrayed, and at some point, you will betray. That's a promise."

"No, this is a promise: I won't ever betray you." I set down my fork and look at her, and she looks back. "What you're doing for me—it means everything."

"Words like that always sound nice coming out of the mouth," she says, wiping bacon grease from her chin with her wrist. "I guarantee someone said the same to your father."

"So if I might betray you, why bother helping me?"

"Because our interests are aligned for the moment. Tomorrow—who knows?" She breaks off a piece of the baguette and stares at me. "Better eat. We have a long day."

Once more, I'm directed to the center of a training mat. You remember ideas best when you're near your breaking point, she tells me, therefore to my breaking point we go. Yael paces a circle around me. She holds in her hand a yellow training pistol made of solid rubber, the cousin of the knife we used yesterday.

"If you're already fighting hand to hand, and your attacker pulls a knife, run if you are able," she says. "But if he has a gun, continue the attack and disarm him. Do you know why?"

"Because the knife is only useful for the length of his arm, but bullets travel."

"Just so," Yael says. "Please take this."

She hands me the gun, then lies down on the mat, faceup.

"Come," she says. "Kneel over me."

I do as she instructs, straddling her hips. It feels awkward and too intimate.

"Now point the pistol at my face."

For a moment, I hesitate. Then Yael moves my hands for me, putting the muzzle of the gun mere inches from her nose.

"It would seem there's nothing to be done," Yael says. "I'm on the ground, and my enemy is on top with a pistol aimed at my head. A position of absolute disadvantage, no?"

I smile weakly. "I'm guessing you'll show me it's not."

Her hand slams across the side of the gun, pushing the muzzle away from her face and twisting it from my hand. At the same instant, her hips flick upward and send me sprawling to the side. Within half a second from the time it began, it's over. Just like yesterday with the knife, I'm on my back and she has the weapon.

We reverse positions with me on the floor, and Yael explains how it's done, breaking down the move part by part, and putting it back together. Once I get the hang of it, it's surprisingly straightforward. Slam, twist, flick. Slam, twist, flick. Do it again and again and again and again and your muscles remember it without bothering to ask your brain. It becomes a reflex. It becomes automatic. And that's the point, I realize. That's what Yael wants to build in me. She wants to replace my instincts to scream, or to shit myself with terror, or to lash out stupidly, with something better and more useful.

Slam, twist, flick.

By the time we've gone through every permutation of the drill again and again and again, I'm covered in sweat, mine and Yael's. I'm used to my own smell after a workout, but now I wear hers, too.

With the pistol in my hand, I stand over Yael, triumphant, swollen with adrenaline and pride.

But she senses my self-satisfaction. "You think you've won?" she asks.

I shrug, and she replies by sweeping out her leg and catching my bad ankle. My body twists to the ground, and suddenly the gun's in her hand again and the muzzle pressed to my temple.

"You're dead," she says without emotion. "Dead because you didn't finish what you started. You want your enemy to win?"

"No. Of course not."

"So don't just take the pistol. Use it. If you don't need to kill your enemy, you can wound him," she says. "Shoot him in the leg, or if you take his knife, cut his Achilles tendon."

She turns the pistol around and hands it back to me. Then we practice another thousand times.

We train from the time I wake up to the time I collapse on the cot, already asleep before my head hits the pillow. For three weeks, I learn how to punch, *the force comes from the body, not the arm*. Where to punch, *balls, throat, stomach, kidney*. Pressure points, *between upper lip and nose, between thumb and forefinger*. All of this—along with knee strikes, kicks, locks, holds—Yael squeezes into me with the force of countless repetitions so that it's in my muscle memory, deep as my own DNA.

The decade of gymnastics has kept me limber and on balance, and I have little trouble with the endurance Yael requires of me. By the time we near the end of the third week, I can tap into the radio frequency of Yael's mind, predict what she'll do next. She says it's all physical, that a trained fighter can see her enemy's pupils dilate one-fiftieth of a second before they strike, but to me it feels more mystical than that, like an ability to see a moment into the future.

My muscles ring with exhaustion, and one night I count fourteen bruises on my body. Eight on my shins, two on each arm, one on my jaw, and one, mysteriously—I have no idea how it got there—on the top of my left foot. The skin on my knuckles bleeds every day and heals up every night, leaving brown scabs to be torn open again in the morning. In the mirror, after I shower, I hardly recognize my own body. It's becoming taut, angry, bulging at the shoulders, along my arms, across my back. Like a boxer.

Yael ends every day's training by defeating me. Brutally. Mercilessly.

She begins the next day's training by teaching me to counter the previous night's beatdown. Curiously, I don't dread the defeats. The fear has been bled out of me. Yael's words from day one—that learning how to get hit and get up again is the first lesson of Krav Maga—stay with me always.

But as the fear bleeds away, it's replaced by something else. A head-spinning narcotic rush that awakens the thing I'd discovered inside me back in Queens. It seems to feed on what Yael is teaching me. It seems, in fact, to be starved for it. I believe, or would like to believe, that sometimes this thing truly scares Yael. Sometimes she beats me down so hard that I wonder whether she's teaching me to fight, or teaching that thing who, exactly, is still boss.

And so it goes until an afternoon at the end of the third week when, covered in sweat and with every muscle on fire, I turn to Yael just in time to catch a shopping bag she throws my way.

Inside is a chic leather motorcycle jacket along with a pair of dark jeans. "What's this?" I ask.

"We're going out," she says.

"To do what?" I ask.

She downs a bottle of water, wipes her mouth on her forearm. "The boys in Tel Aviv called," she says calmly. "They found Feras."

Ten

We ride the packed Metro for a long time, heading north toward the Gare du Nord train station and the areas beyond. African men in puffy down jackets and baggy pants, speaking a patois of French and their own native languages. Arab women in full burkas, pushing baby carriages weighed down by grocery bags hanging from the handles.

When I moved to Paris with my father, I'd been eleven, too young to do much exploring on my own. I stayed mainly in the western suburbs, venturing away from our neighborhood in Boulogne-Billancourt mainly to head to my school, which was farther west still. The Paris my dad and I would explore together on the weekends was mostly confined to the tonier parts, the 7th and 8th arrondissements, and only sometimes beyond.

Yael and I get off at the Pigalle station. A hundred years ago, artists slummed here, drank absinthe. But today it's a touristy neighborhood of sex shops and rip-off cafés. Six or seven girls about my age stand out front of a neon-lit strip club in fishnets and spangled lingerie, shoving coupons into the hands of every man who passes by, cooing at them to come in for a drink, only ten euros. They're speaking French and English, but their accents come from far to the east of here. Tall and fine-boned, bare skin pink from the cold. I see hate in their eyes. This, I'm pretty sure, is not the Paris they thought they'd end up in. Certainly it's different from any Paris I knew. As Yael and I pass, a man with a buzz cut and wearing an alligator-skin jacket eyes us, sucks on a cigarette, and barks to the girls in Russian to show more enthusiasm.

Yael presses forward, while I follow a pace or two behind. After twenty minutes or so, we cross a border into yet another Paris I never knew. Here there are no cheap sex shops, no visitors from America giggling at the freezing strippers from their café chairs, sipping espresso and smacking their lips at just how naughty and so very non-American it all is. This is the Paris of the Tunisians who wash the visitors' coffee cups, the Paris of the Senegalese who sell them little *Mona Lisa* magnets from blankets spread out on the curb by the Seine. The awnings over the shops are faded and torn, the buildings they're attached to chipping and tired, long ago having passed from quaint decay into the real thing. Halal butchers and travel agencies offering the very best prices on flights to Algeria. Kiosks that sell SIM cards and newspapers in languages with unfamiliar alphabets. The place is called Goutte d'Or, Yael tells me. Drop of gold.

The sun is almost gone by the time we find a small trapezoidal park. There's a fine mist in the air, barely rain at all. Yael fishes a newspaper from a trash can and wipes the seat of a bench dry.

"We'll wait here a minute," she says.

I sit beside her. "Where are we?"

"Hush," she says. "Let them get used to us before we talk. We're no one, just a couple of women in a park. Use the time to observe."

We're quiet for a while; then I see what Yael wanted me to observe.

Directly across the street from the park, right on the corner, is a small restaurant. CAFÉ DURBIN, the sign says.

I stop breathing. The air is suddenly frigid and I wrap my arms tightly around my chest. "That's the place?" I say in quiet French.

Yael places a gentle hand on my leg. "It is."

From here I can see inside. It's dingy and small, but lively, each tiny table packed with two or three men, drinking coffee or tea or red wine. I try to imagine my father there, entering the café, looking around for Feras. I try to ignore the shudder in my belly. Stay focused, and in the now, I tell myself; it's the only thing that will get him back.

"What does 'Feras' mean in Arabic?" Yael says quietly.

"It's a first name," I answer. "But I think in some places it can also mean 'lion.'"

"Exactly." Yael takes another look around, then leans in close. "In this case, Feras isn't a first name as I assumed, but a code name the Americans use for him."

"How do you know what the Americans call him?"

"Even allies spy on each other. For a time when they're not." Yael pauses as an old woman in a headscarf passes. "The boys in Tel Aviv searched their databases and found a hundred-something informants worldwide with the first name Feras, none of them in Paris. However, as a code name, Feras has a single hit: Hamid Tannous. He lives not far from here, somewhere over in the 19th arrondissement."

"He's an American spy?" I ask.

"Informant. But he's ours, too. He'll talk to anyone who pays him. The consensus in Tel Aviv is that he's the guy we want."

"How do we get in touch with him?"

"There's a protocol we use. He's something of a regular customer with us."

"So let's do it."

Yael turns to me, gives me the same smile she uses before kicking my legs out from under me. "Practice is over, Gwendolyn," she says. "Time for the real thing."

We cross a trestle bridge leading over into the 19th. Below us, trains creep slowly along the tracks like snakes in a moat. The neighborhood itself is old and crumbling, a forgotten or ignored corner of Paris. A man in a white thawb and sandals, down ski parka thrown over his shoulders, stands outside a computer repair shop, smoking a cigarette. He wishes us good evening in Arabic as we pass.

We take a left on Rue Marx Dormoy, then a right, then another left. Yael seems to know this neighborhood like she's lived here her whole life. The cars on the street form a narrow canyon with the building walls, echoing Arab pop music from inside the shops. Smells of grilling meat and peppers and sweet shisha smoke dance through the air in little swirls and eddies.

Yael pauses before the door to a little tabac kiosk where they sell newspapers and cigarettes and passes for the Metro. She looks at me. "Say nothing, understand?"

I nod and follow Yael into the shop. A bulky man with a mustache stands behind the counter, while a young man looks through the soda case and a pair of women in headscarves pore over a rack of magazines.

"A pack of Sobranies," Yael says in French, nodding to the rack of cigarettes behind the counter.

"Sobranie black or blue?" the man behind the counter says.

"The gold ones," she says.

He squints at her for a few awkward seconds. "We're out," he answers. "And I don't think we'll be getting any more."

"That's too bad. I'm buying them for a friend who's absolutely desperate for them."

The man straightens some papers on the counter, his eyes never leaving Yael. "Then your friend should come back tomorrow, in the afternoon. We might have some then."

"Any particular time tomorrow afternoon?"

The man shrugs. "The afternoon."

"You sure?" Yael says.

The man shrugs. "Hard to tell these days. I think they were discontinued."

Yael thanks him and leaves, with me right behind. Outside, I come up alongside her.

"Translate," Yael says when we're on the sidewalk.

"The cigarettes, the gold Sobranies. You were talking about Feras. He said Feras might be gone, but that he might be able to reach him. You should come back tomorrow afternoon."

"Very close," she says. "That was our *need to see you now* procedure."

"So now what? We just wait?"

"We'll be back soon enough." Then she smiles. "In the meantime—how about I buy you dinner?"

We take a different Metro line back, and I'm not sure where we are. The doors of the subway open at a stop called Place Monge, and Yael grabs my elbow. "Come on," she says, and tugs me through the doors just as they're about to close. "Time to celebrate your first night in the field."

Is this a new Yael? Some kinder version of the merciless asskicker I've known these last few weeks? I'm wary of her motives, but the idea of a celebration appeals to me. Trying to make contact with Feras is the first real progress I've made. And there's something buoyant, almost giddy, in my chest. I had felt only powerlessness, frustration, fear since my dad disappeared, and now I'm feeling something else.

Excitement? Yes, it's exactly that. This clandestine life—maybe it suits me.

We climb out of the Metro station into a neighborhood I don't know. It's shabby in a Brooklynish sort of way with people everywhere, streets lined with bars and boutique stores and restaurants advertising Indian and Thai food on hand-painted signs.

Yael guides me into a little bistro. It's packed with people and throbbing with laughter, clinking glasses, and the sizzle of a grill. There's a crowd of customers waiting in the tiny foyer for a table, but a waiter recognizes Yael and waves her in. We're seated at a tiny table covered with brown butcher paper.

"My niece is down from Belgium," Yael says to the waiter.

"Well then, welcome," the waiter says to me. He's a good-looking guy, maybe Moroccan or Algerian, and he winks as he hands me a menu. "Keep your auntie out of trouble tonight."

Yael orders a *côte de boeuf* with *frites* for us both, a glass of house red for herself, and a bottle of mineral water for me. When the waiter leaves, Yael leans across the table. "No wine for you. The first rule of fieldwork is you need to stay conscious of your surroundings. Tactical awareness, it's called." She scans the room for a moment. "The table at your six o'clock, directly behind you," she says. "What color shirt is the man wearing?"

I rub my temples. I had hoped there wouldn't be any more training today, but Yael clearly has other plans. "Blue?"

"Trick question. It's two women."

"Look, can we not do this now?" I say. "It's been a long day."

The drinks arrive, and Yael makes a toast. "To you and your father," she says.

"And to you," I say.

We clink our glasses together, and she takes a sip of her wine. "So, you have a boyfriend back in New York?" she asks.

"I thought you don't discuss personal stuff."

"I don't discuss *my* personal stuff," she says. "So out with it—boyfriend?"

I look away. God, everyone in this room seems happy tonight. "A friend is all he is, I think."

"But you want something more?"

"To be honest, I didn't have time to think about it," I say. "All this happened just after I met him."

"Things will be normal again," she says. "Then, maybe."

It's a stupid thought, the idea of anything being normal again, but I smile back at her as if it weren't. "And you?" I ask to change the subject. "It's a two-way street."

"Not a chance," she says.

"So tell me, I don't know—the last time you were in love. Something that's completely over. No harm in that."

Yael laughs to herself in a sad sort of way. "I'm learning nothing is ever completely over." Then she takes a sip of wine and sighs. "Fine. But I'm warning you, it's sappy and pathetic."

"I'm all about sappy and pathetic."

She looks away thoughtfully. "Ten years ago—no, longer. One of my first jobs right out of training. I was working surveillance with another agent. We were in Budapest. Have you been?"

"To Budapest? No."

"One of the world's perfect cities. Hard not to fall in love there," she says, eyes focused on the butcher-paper tablecloth, wine glass hanging languidly between her fingers. "He and I spent a lot of time in parked cars together, looking out of windows in dark apartments together. And there it was, despite all the rules against it. I fell in love with the guy I was working with."

"And did anything happen?"

Yael shakes her head. "No. Not so much as a kiss."

126

"Why not?"

"First of all, he was married. Also, from another country's service. Very bad combination." Her mouth is smiling, but her eyes are sad, like the memory of him can't decide which way it wants to go.

"Maybe someday you'll meet again," I say hopefully. "Who knows."

"Who knows," she repeats in a way that means there's not a chance in hell.

The waiter appears carrying a platter holding our *côte de boeuf*—a single enormous slab of dead cow flesh, its surface black and still sizzling. He slices the meat into ribbons, and blood wells from within it, forming red lagoons on the plate. I consider turning vegetarian on the spot. But Yael digs in, and so I take a small, tentative bite. It's delicious.

When Yael is finished eating, she leans back and rubs her stomach. "I have to use the ladies' room," she says, and excuses herself from the table.

The waiter reappears and tops off her glass of wine. I sneak the glass closer and take a sip. It's cheap stuff, and it tastes like overripe cherries and dirt and goes perfectly with the meat. I down the rest of it and signal the waiter for another. He smiles at me as he refills the glass. *"Soyez prudente,"* he says. Be careful. I drink it down to the level it was when Yael left the table and slide the glass back into place just as she reappears.

Yael pays the check, and we head out. The wine has left me feeling warm, and I know in a while I'll be sleepy and a little buzzed. The neighborhood is still crowded with what looks like all of evening Paris—couples with arms thrown over each other, friends in tight, inseparable knots. They weave in and out of doorways, the restaurants and bars packed. What would it be like, I wonder, to come here when the world wasn't crushing me with its weight? Like one of the darker, more interesting corners of heaven, I suppose.

"You all right after the wine?" Yael asks me. "Not feeling too sloppy, I hope. Have to keep your tactical awareness up."

"No," I lie. "I'm fine. How did you . . . ?"

"Waiter told me," she says. "Even allies spy on each other."

I repeat the rest of it in my head: *For a time when they're not.*

Yael places her hand on my arm and stops me. "I have a bladder like a mouse," she says. "Let's stop here so I can use the bathroom again."

We've drifted out of the neighborhood we'd been in, the charming Paris-Brooklyn hybrid, and the bars and restaurants here are louder, seedier. The one we're standing in front of has a neon sign that says LA CHÈVRE MAIGRE. The skinny goat. There's loud and very bad French speed metal pouring from the door.

"Let's find a little café somewhere," I say.

But she pulls me in anyway. A tough crowd has gathered for the performance. Bikers in leather vests, guys with shaved heads and tattoos on their faces. Bodies shake violently, drunk and furious at the world. They're squeezed together around a small stage where a band is hammering away at their instruments. It's hard to make out faces and details through the thick cloud of cigarette and pot smoke, but I can see there are very few women.

"You can hold it," I say to Yael, just loudly enough to be heard over the music.

"Don't be such a child," she says. "Wait at the bar."

She disappears down a dim hallway, while I cross my arms and try to hide in the shadows. It's only seconds before a few men start circling. A guy with blond hair clipped short and a grimy denim jacket shoulders through them.

"Out slumming it with Mom tonight?" he says in French. His breath smells of beer and cigarettes.

I ignore him, or try to, but he's a wall of meat looming over me and it's hard to pretend he doesn't exist. There's easily an eighty-pound difference between us, and where the hell did Yael go?

The guy braces his arms to the wall on either side of my head. He's tall and heavy with a round pink face that reminds me of a horrible pig. I duck under his arm and steer down the dark hallway to find Yael. He calls out after me, "Where you going, little princess? Back outside to hang with the fags?"

I push through the door of the women's room. It's a filthy closet with the walls painted black and a single lightbulb hanging naked over a dirty sink. My boots slide through a wet pool of something on the floor as I head for the only stall, calling Yael's name. But it's empty.

Outside the bathroom, the pig is waiting for me at the end of the hall. My options are to go through him or through the steel emergency exit that likely leads into an alley or courtyard. I take the second option and slide out the door into the cold night air. In a loud stage whisper, I call out Yael's name, but there's no reply. All I've managed to do is go from a dark crowded place to a dark deserted place.

The courtyard is littered with trash and broken glass and stacks of wooden crates. It's open to the sky above, and I can hear the sounds of Paris traffic not too far away. I circle the space looking for an exit, but all I find are the locked steel doors I suppose lead into other bars or restaurants and a pair of tall wooden doors secured with a chain. Through them I can hear people laughing and shouting out on the sidewalk.

"Looks like Mommy left you behind."

I whirl around to see the pig standing before the closed door of the bar. An icy panic seems to lift me from the ground, and for a moment, I feel like I'm floating, in contact with nothing except my fear. I want to shout back at him, tell him to stay away, but as I open my mouth, I know that all I can do is scream.

He moves toward me slowly, no more than a silhouette in the dark courtyard, but a confident silhouette. There's a little swagger in his walk, a certainty in his own strength. Only when he's about four feet away do I finally get my shit together enough to take a step backward. I hear the crackle of broken glass beneath my boots.

The shadow of his face widens into a smile as he advances toward me. I step back again, but my back hits a tower of crates stacked against a wall.

His arm lashes forward and cups my mouth as his other reaches around my waist. A scream makes its way out of my throat, but his hand mutes it and it comes out as a weak little bleat. He pulls me forward into him so we're pressed together.

I squeeze my eyes shut, and all I can hear is a sound like a waterfall, the full-blast roar of my blood in my veins. His hand leaves my waist and scrapes upward along my back while the fingers of his other hand snake into my mouth and try to pry it open. They taste of salt and dirt.

Then the thing inside me opens its eyes once again. It stretches its legs into my legs, stretches its arms into my arms. I am no more than the clothes it wears.

My jaw bites down hard, teeth cutting through the flesh of his fingers until they hit bone. A baritone scream fills the air, and his fingers snap out of my mouth, nearly pulling my front teeth out along with them.

A taste like metal rolls over the surface of my tongue, and I spit the pig's own blood back at him. Stumbling a step backward, he eyes his fingers to see if they're all there. I throw my entire weight behind my fist as it rockets forward, aimed at his throat. But he moves, and I collide with his shoulder instead.

The blow doesn't seem to faze him, and he fires a careening missile of a punch that arcs out to the side before coming in toward my head. It's sloppy and slow, and I catch his wrist in the air. The elbow of my other arm swings into his cheek and snaps his head to the side.

But before I can follow up, he charges forward, his shoulder landing in my stomach and smashing me backward into the stack of crates. With sheer weight, he pushes me down onto the ground.

My elbow strike had landed hard, and now a dark stream of blood trickles from the corner of his mouth, but he's smiling, pinning my arms while he straddles me. He reaches around to the back waistband of his jeans and produces a small knife, the blade a slim triangle of steel that gleams even in the dark. He lets it linger in front of my face for a moment, showing it to me, letting me appreciate it. This is what she saw, my mom. A blade catching the light, in the moment before it cut her open.

But my body knows what to do and does it without asking. My leg hooks around his, then my hand slams the knife away just as my hips flick upward and to the side, throwing him off me. I hear the knife skitter across the ground.

I leap to my feet just as he starts to rise. My hand arcs through the air, forming a blunt ax that lands hard on his throat. The blow is so powerful I feel the soft cartilage of his windpipe bend and crackle beneath the edge of my hand. He collapses to his knees, pressing his forehead to the ground as he chokes loudly for air.

But the thing inside me isn't done just yet. My eye catches the knife lying there amid the broken glass, so I snatch it up and hold it loosely in my hand. The backs of his legs are dangling there, so very open, so very vulnerable. I remember Yael's words about always finishing what I start.

I move in closer and seize the heel of his work boot. The leather parts neatly as I pull the blade across it, but then I stop just short of the skin over his tendon, unable to go farther.

131

"Do it."

The voice comes from the other end of the courtyard. It isn't a whisper, but a hard and certain command. I look up as Yael steps out from behind a stack of crates and into the dim light beneath a doorway.

I let out a furious gasp. She has obviously been there the whole time. Seen the whole thing happen. Fury wells up inside me.

But the man's leg jerks in my grip. He's recovered some of his air and is staring at me, teeth bared, eyes narrowed into slits. What is it I see on his face, aggression or fear?

Yael's voice calls out once more. "Do it."

And so I do.

Eleven

There's a cut on my elbow, a gash about two inches long. Maybe it's from the broken glass when the pig pushed me to the ground, or maybe from something else. Yael presses a cotton pad drenched with alcohol to it. It feels like cold fire.

"I'll hate you forever for this," I say, and mean it.

"That's unfortunate," she says.

The kitchen feels too warm and the sweat covers me like shellac. I haven't been able to stop shaking. "You set me up," I say.

"Yes," she says. "I needed to be sure."

"Sure of what?"

"That you could. If you had to." She peels the cotton pad away. "If you're going to be in the field with me, I can't have you crumble when it matters. You need stitches."

"He was going to rape me, Yael."

"Oh, to start with, I think." Yael browses through the first-aid kit spread out on the table—bandages, scissors, tweezers, tape—until she finds a needle and thread. "Anyway, I would have stepped in if you couldn't handle it."

The fury is so loud inside my head that I can barely sort through it enough to pick out individual thoughts.

"And the point is, you did handle it," she says, trying to steady my arm with one hand, the needle poised in the other. "Hold still."

"I can't."

She presses my arm to the table and begins. The first pass of the needle and drag of the thread through the edges of the wound hurt worse than I expect, but not as bad as everything else. My voice is quavering. "The point is, Yael. The point is this was real, okay? That man, he had a fucking knife."

"Real? Of course it was real," she says, her face turning red with effort to keep my arm still as she makes another pass with the needle. "I told you, this isn't a sport. He wasn't trying to level-up to green belt."

I watch the needle as it moves in and out, in and out. "I'll never be able to forget him, Yael. The face. The way the knife—*Jesus!*"

"Sorry." She wipes away the blood with a tissue. "Be sure not to forget the part where you won."

"Yes, by crippling him."

"By doing what you had to." She puts down the needle and ties the stitches off. "Finished. It will hurt like hell; then it will itch like hell. Resist the urge to scratch."

"So don't you feel guilty, even a little?"

She places a wide adhesive bandage over the wound. Her fingers are very gentle. "Justice isn't some abstract thing, Gwendolyn. What you did tonight, that's what it looks like. Ugly and mean."

Against every probability, I sleep well. But the whole night long, strange dreams come and go, vivid nightmares in which somehow I'm just passing through, not afraid at all. In the morning, I open my eyes and stare at the ceiling over my cot, trying to remember them.

In the kitchen, I find Yael is already up, reading a French-edition *Vogue* at the table and drinking coffee. When she sees me, she rises and pours me a cup.

"Sleep well?" she asks.

"Strange dreams," I say.

"To be expected. Your mind is trying to grapple with it, the new you." She opens a drawer beneath the counter, removes a small booklet, the cover crimson red, and tosses it onto the table in front of me. "Speaking of."

"What's this?"

"Call it a graduation present. It came a few days ago, but I was saving it."

I turn the booklet over and see *Rossiskaya Federatsiya* in embossed gold Cyrillic letters at the top, followed by *Russian Federation* in roman letters. It's a Russian passport that looks and feels very real. I open it and recoil when I see a photo of me staring back.

Though the face is mine, the name isn't. Sofia Timurovna Kozlovskaya, it says. The birthdate, printed in official type, makes me twenty-two years old.

"Who—who is this?"

"It's you," Yael says. "Turn to the next page."

I do, and see an official-looking visa with the logo of the European Union, complete with silver-colored, holographic seal.

"A work visa," she says. "You can take up residence anywhere from Ireland to Greece and be legal."

"But who is"—I turn to the previous page—"Sofia Timurovna Kozlovskaya?"

"Sofia, the real Sofia, was a stripper who died of a heroin overdose in Munich two years ago. What you're holding in your hands is not a fake. It's her passport, only with your picture."

"How did you get this?"

"Maybe the cop who finds her gets paid, maybe a friend of ours makes it disappear from her belongings," she says. "I don't work that side of it, so I don't know. Point is, what you have there, it's gold. Anyone in my profession would kill for a passport that bulletproof."

I drop the dead woman's passport to the tabletop. It feels so ghoulish, so wrong.

Yael opens the drawer again and pulls out a thick packet of papers folded down the middle. She sets it on the table next to the passport. "Sofia's information," she says. "Birth certificate, school transcripts, a biography of her parents, information on the city where she grew up. As for the rest of her life, that's up to you to invent."

"What do you mean?"

"First rule of a cover identity: Go native when you can. Second rule: The believability of your story is in the details. Study these documents and fill in the holes. What's her favorite color? Who were her childhood friends? How old was she when her dog got hit by a car?"

I open the packet and scan over the documents. I turn to her father's death certificate: cirrhosis of the liver, when Sofia was only fourteen. Father's employment record: a rubber factory outside the city of Armavir in southern Russia. Her school records: high marks in German, low marks in math. The information is all very real, very tragically specific.

"Take the morning," Yael says. "Write down your biography. Then memorize it."

"But doesn't Sofia have a death certificate?"

"Conveniently misplaced. It's Russia. Things like that happen."

"What if someone starts digging deeper?"

"No backstory is perfect." She settles into the chair at my side. "So you make it up. Improvise."

I close my eyes—the new me.

"Now get to work," Yael says as she takes my hand and squeezes it hard. "Start making a life for yourself, Sofia."

My breath pulses against the window in a circle of fog that expands and retreats, expands and retreats. With my finger, I draw a little face in it, but then Yael makes a sound that means stop it and so I do. Just as she has instructed me, I keep one eye on what's in front, and one eye on the side mirror of the little Volkswagen to see what's behind. I'm ordered not to say anything unless I notice something out of the ordinary. But everything feels out of the ordinary now, and I wonder if I'll recognize it when it comes. An Arab man peeks his head out of a video store and looks around, then pulls back inside. A woman in a full burka walks past pushing an empty laundry cart, then comes back the other way a minute later, the cart still empty. What's ordinary here?

Yael's breathing is calm, flat, like she's sleeping, but she's trained herself to do that. There's tension on her face as she keeps an eye on her own mirror where she can see the door of the tabac a half block behind us.

We've been here for about an hour now. The sun is nowhere, invisible above featureless gray clouds. I have to squint at my watch to see it's only five in the afternoon.

My mouth feels dry and pasty, and I ask her if we should get some coffee or something. No, she says, it would look suspicious, two women drinking coffee in a car. More suspicious than two women sitting in a car doing nothing? I ask.

"Let's have a little quiz," Yael says. "Where were you born?"

"Novokubansk."

"What was your father's name and profession?"

"Timur Naumovitch Kozlovsky. Supervisor at a rubber factory."

"Before that?"

"Lieutenant in Spetsnaz."

"And what is Spetsnaz?"

"Russian special forces."

We continue the quiz to the slow rhythm of the windshield wipers cutting across the glass every few seconds. I close my eyes, trying to see all the facts and names and places in my memory. Then I hear Yael hiss, *"Là-bas!"*

My eyes snap open, and I turn. Over where? I follow the direction of Yael's squinted eyes to a pale, skinny man in jeans and an Adidas track jacket standing under an awning across the street from the tabac. He has a mane of thick black hair that needs cutting and a scraggly attempt at a beard.

She starts the engine, pulls out of the parking spot, and swings an expert U-turn in the narrow street. The man's eyes follow our movements, though he's trying to pretend he doesn't notice. His body tenses up as if he's waiting for someone to hit him. I stare back. He doesn't look like the monster I'd pictured, the man who kidnapped my dad, Feras the lion. But so much the better, so much the easier to get my hands around his throat when it comes time for that.

Yael slows down, lowers her window, and speaks to him in Arabic. It takes me a few seconds to work the translation in my head because it sounds so strange: "There used to be a store here that sold art supplies. Do you know where it has moved?"

The man looks at us warily, as if we've gotten the wrong guy; then he takes an uncertain step forward. I can see him more closely now. He looks barely twenty-five and has a spray of red pimples across his forehead. "The shop you're looking for went out of business in March of last year," he says.

"March?" Yael says. "Are you sure it wasn't April?"

"No," he says. "March."

Yael scans up and down the street. "Get in the car, Hamid," she says.

From the backseat, I can see he's shaking—from the cold but also from something else. The pimples are more like red welts, like the product of some disease. "Where's the usual guy?" he says. "I only ever speak to him. Jean-Marc, he called himself."

"Relax, friend. Jean-Marc is on vacation, and I'm filling in," Yael answers, placing a calming hand on his forearm.

He jerks his arm away. "Do you have someplace we can go? They're looking for me," he says, switching from Arabic to French.

"We can drive for a bit. You'll be safe with us."

"Safe? I've been hiding in basements for, like—two months, maybe. And why are there two of you? Jean-Marc always came alone."

A gentle smile from Yael as she pulls into the evening traffic of a busy boulevard. It's the warmest look I've ever seen on her. "She's just a trainee, that's all, Hamid. Nothing to worry about, okay?" Her voice is motherly. "Tell me why you've been hiding in basements."

"Do you have any food? I don't know when I ate last."

"I can stop and buy you something," Yael says. "Or give you some money."

Hamid shakes his head. "Too dangerous. Look, forget food. You have to get me out. Tonight. Right now."

"Why is it dangerous, Hamid?"

He looks at her, eyes narrowed. "Because they're hunting me. Same ones. Same people who did . . . that other thing. Every time I try to step outside, there they are. I almost didn't come tonight. One more minute, and you would've found a corpse waiting for you. I'm sure of that."

"Someone's after you because of what you did to the American?" she says. "Is that why, Hamid?"

"I didn't do shit to anyone. Look, you've got to get me out of France. I want to go home."

"Maybe it's possible," Yael says as if considering it. "But first I need to know what happened to the American."

"I don't know. We had coffee, went for a walk, then the van—"

"The van?" she asks.

"Yes, along the street. It was stopped, and there were two men, I don't know the word, the kind who fix toilets."

"Plumbers," I say.

Yael gives me a look to stay silent.

"Yes, two plumbers. They carry a long pipe, block our way. But then two more come out of the van. One puts a needle in the American's neck, and other one comes for me. They were good. Professionals."

"It's interesting you got away but the American didn't," Yael says.

"Get away? I run, and he shoots at me. Bullet cuts my shoulder," he says, pulling his jacket and shirt aside. There's a nasty-looking stitched-up wound, pink and purple giving way to green.

We pull up to a red light, and a motorbike pulls up noisily beside us on the passenger side, its engine chortling. There are two riders in tight black leather jackets and full helmets. The one on the back looks over at us and flips up his face shield. He's good-looking, from what I can see of him, and he gives me a flirty wink before looking away.

Yael leans over to Hamid, taking a closer look at the wound. "You went to a doctor for stitches."

"For a gunshot, a doctor will call the police. I saw a veterinarian I know who takes cash. He stitches me up like a torn shirt and gives me some pills for dogs. Does it look infected?"

"No," she lies.

The light turns green, and we start moving. We're somewhere in the industrial streets behind the Gare du Nord train station. The air smells of oil and fish.

"These plumbers," Yael says. "Tell me about them."

"They were Germans," Hamid says. "That's all I could tell."

"Germans? How do you know?"

"Because they were speaking German—how else?"

The motorbike is back, gunning its engine as it follows us, coming up close to the rear bumper. Another light, and Yael slows to a stop. The motorbike pulls up again on the passenger side.

Odd how empty the streets are here in the evening, I think. I look over at the motorbike. The passenger looks over at us, his eyes invisible now behind the reflective glass of his face shield. He pulls his messenger bag around to the front and opens it. Then his gloved hands emerge gripping a strange, stubby object with a small opening at one end, which he points at Hamid's window. It takes my mind a full second to realize it's a gun, and just as I do, the world erupts in an orange ball of flame and exploding glass.

I'm pressed to the floor of the little Volkswagen. I can hear nothing and it's mostly dark, but I feel the clacking vibration of cobblestones as we fly along the Paris streets. The wind is whipping around me in a silent tornado, and glass pebbles are everywhere, piled up in the contours of the seats, catching the light of streetlamps and looking like a king's fortune in diamonds.

I see a hand covered in black ink reach between the front seats and grab my jacket. It pulls me up, and I'm staring at Yael, whose face is also spattered with black ink and whose mouth is shouting words I can't hear. She takes my hand and guides it to Hamid, to his chest that is the source of the black ink. Three—no, five—holes, each the diameter of a dime, spit the stuff out, pour it, billow it. I nearly faint at the realization of what it is, but pull myself together and press down hard on however many holes I can cover with my hands, but this only causes the others to spurt even more blood. So I shift my hands to other holes, but it's no use. Hamid's eyes are still open and very alive, but every time he closes them to blink, I feel certain they won't open again.

We're racing down the winding, narrow streets of the empty industrial neighborhood, the cars parked on either side so close I could touch them. The motorbike is keeping pace, no more than ten or fifteen meters behind us, its headlight bobbing in the rear window like a pursuing ghost.

Yael makes a hard left, and I topple over, losing my grip on Hamid and crashing into the side of the car. The motorbike doesn't so much as slow down as it takes the corner. My hearing must be returning because I hear the two engines like a shrieking opera duet between the Volkswagen's tenor and the motorbike's squealing soprano.

I scramble back into position, bracing myself this time so that on the next turn I won't let go of Hamid. I can feel him breathing, shallow, barely there, his eyes only half open now.

Hard left. The tires squeal. Hard right, then right again. But the motorbike won't give up. In fact, it's gaining. They're going for Yael now, pulling up on her side, the passenger leveling the submachine gun. I try to shout a warning, but just as my mouth opens, there's another burst of orange flame from the barrel, a long succession of shots, the sound impossibly loud, like the universe itself being ripped open. The dashboard in front of Yael comes alive, pieces of it popping up and dancing on end as bits of plastic fill the air like confetti. Yael flicks the wheel to the left, and the motorbike leaps out of the way and onto the sidewalk, too quick and agile for her. Then it disappears from view.

There is no explosion as I would have expected. Only the crumple of metal and flesh against metal and concrete, sudden and fatal. A few pieces of the motorbike skitter down the road after us, as if not ready to give up the chase. We come to a stop half a block later.

The quiet and stillness of the world surprises me. But there's no stillness for Yael. She's out the door the second the car stops, hobbling back toward the wreckage behind us, clearly wounded but clearly not badly enough to stop her. I keep my hands pressed to Hamid's wounds but am able to turn my head far enough to see her limp up to the concrete base of a streetlamp. The motorbike and driver are piled against it like heaps of unrecognizable trash. The figure of the passenger lies in the roadway.

There's a pistol in Yael's hand now. Has she taken it from one of the pursuers? Did she have it in her jacket? I squeeze my eyes shut, unable to watch, but Yael never fires. It's obvious even from here that she doesn't need to.

I hear her limping back to the car, her shoe dragging across the cobblestones. "You can stop doing that," she says, leaning into the car, the pistol held loosely in her hand.

I look to Hamid. He's perfectly still now, mouth wide, eyes closed, and I peel my hands away from his dead body. Air catches in my throat.

Yael's voice is stern, businesslike. "Don't you dare cry. We don't have time." She's gripping the car door for support and presses a hand to her side. Blood creeps from between her fingers.

I scramble out of the backseat and try to scoop an arm under hers to keep her from falling over. She pushes me away and drops the gun to the ground.

"You're hurt. I'll call an ambulance."

"An ambulance? And how to explain the presence of three dead men and a wounded Israeli?"

"I'll drive you to a hospital, then."

"The car is too shot up. Steering's gone." She pinches her eyes shut in pain. "I have a number I'm to call if this happens. The embassy sends someone. We'll see whether they get here before the cops do."

"I'm staying with you."

"You'll end up in a French jail. You won't get your father back."

For a moment, I stare at her. "Get my father back?" I shout. "Hamid's dead, Yael. The only lead I had is dead."

She grabs my arm and squeezes hard, half in pain, half to make her point. "And I'm sure Hamid's mother will be very upset, but as for you, you have something better now. Do you not see this?"

The truth is I don't see it. But then I turn to the bodies behind me on the road and realize she's right. The men who wanted Hamid dead are more valuable than Hamid himself. Or would be if they weren't twisted corpses lying amid the parts of their motorbike.

She answers my question before I can ask it.

"They have papers, Gwendolyn. Passports, ID cards. They have mobile phones with names and numbers and pictures of everyone they know. Start there."

I feel her body shudder against mine, and I help her down onto the car seat. She curses in Hebrew, and a small cry sneaks out.

"I'm staying right here until you get help."

Her hand reaches out and grips my jaw, then twists my face toward hers. I feel her breath, hot and wet, coming through bared teeth. "You little sentimental shit. Either all this—Hamid, the blood, the fucking bullet in my side—means something, or it was pointless. You will be hard, Gwendolyn, and continue on alone, or you will be nothing. Which will it be?"

Her grip releases, and I stagger backward. For a long moment, there's only the sound of the Paris night and Yael's labored breathing.

Then I decide.

The left leg of the driver is still pressed into the concrete base of the streetlamp, fused with the engine block and rear wheel of the bike. I probe the pockets of his jeans until I find a thick wallet, then move to his jacket. There's no structure to his torso anymore, no rib cage, just what feels like raw, warm meat. I find his phone and passport and put them in my jacket pocket. The body of the passenger, the man with the gun, lies in the roadway about ten feet away. It's more intact but folded in half the wrong way. The crash knocked his shoes off, but the messenger bag is still looped around his chest. It's there in his bag that I find his passport, along with extra magazines for the gun, a bottle of Pepsi, and an apple. I never do find the second one's wallet or phone.

In the distance, the high-low wail of French police sirens. I look back at Yael, who is standing again, watching me, both hands now holding her side. She's leaning against the car door, maybe waiting until I'm gone to fall over.

Two blocks from the scene, the police sirens are louder, but the streets are still empty. The only vehicle I see is a windowless white van that speeds past me in the direction from which I've come.

BERLIN

Twelve

Connecting to Tor Servers:

Svaneke.gcqtor01.BigBertha (Slovenia)

Anonymousprox.altnet01.Rhymer (Japan)

SoixanteDix26.fortef07.Carre (Canada)

Unnamed.Unnamed01.Alterform (Thailand)

<<Congratulations! You are now connected to Tor Anonymous
Chat!>>

<<Entering Private Mode / Secure>>

<AnonUser Red is now connected>

AnonUser Scholar: jesus h where the hell u been?

AnonUser Red: just needed a friendly voice.

AnonUser Scholar: im here for u.

AnonUser Red: r u on safe computer?

AnonUser Scholar: yes u?

AnonUser Red: yes

AnonUser Scholar: where are u?

AnonUser Red: europe

AnonUser Scholar: can u b more specific?

AnonUser Red: no

AnonUser Red: sorry

AnonUser Scholar: r u safe?

AnonUser Red: dont know

AnonUser Scholar: cops were here

AnonUser Red: ?????

AnonUser Scholar: day after you left

AnonUser Red: regular nypd cops?

AnonUser Scholar: other kind. feds

AnonUser Red: u talk to them?

AnonUser Scholar: fuck no !!!

AnonUser Scholar: dad calld lawyer

AnonUser Scholar: lawyer told feds to fuck off

AnonUser Scholar: my dad says he wil sue

AnonUser Red: lol

AnonUser Scholar: right? fuckers

AnonUser Red: I'm feling down

AnonUser Red: sorry feeling down

AnonUser Scholar: hows it going? u close to finding him?

AnonUser Red: i don't know

AnonUser Scholar: i want to help u

AnonUser Red: just b there

AnonUser Scholar: i am. always

AnonUser Red: u r saving my life

AnonUser Scholar: how?

AnonUser Red: by just being there

AnonUser Scholar: i want to help more

AnonUser Red: i wish you could

AnonUser Red: but its not safe

AnonUser Red: got to go

AnonUser Scholar: g wait

AnonUser Red: sorry gtg

<<AnonUser Red has signed off>>

AnonUser Scholar: i miss u

Thirteen

It's all men here, Skyping with family back home, looking at porn, gaming. I'm the only woman in the Internet café, and they remind me of it with their eyes every second I stay.

"*Funf Euro, zwanzig,*" the bored kid behind the counter tells me. I pay and head out onto the street. It's afternoon in New York but night here. Very night. The rain doesn't seem to stop, ever. It followed me from Paris, and here in Berlin, fills the black air with icy crystals that sting the skin of my cheeks. I make my way down the street, keeping close to the buildings and out of the buzzy yellow cast of the streetlamps. I pass the creepy bars, the creepy porn shops, the creepy cop hanging out on the corner looking for someone to hit, sticking to myself, eyes down, nothing to see here.

This will be my second night on the Berlin streets. I have money, but three hostels in a row asked for my passport, and I don't know how good the Sofia papers really are. At the Internet café, I searched the Paris news sites. All I found was a single article about two unidentified bodies found on the street, apparent victims of a motor-cycle accident. No word of Yael. No word of Hamid. No word even of the shot-up Volkswagen. It could mean she got away clean, or it could mean the opposite, that she was captured and maybe French intelligence got involved. How long before they link Yael to me, then me to this Sofia? How long before they tell the Americans?

There's a knot of junkies in front of the entrance to the Zoologischer Garten Bahnhof—the Bahnhof Zoo, they call it here, both because it's the train station next to the zoo and because it is a zoo in itself. One of the junkies has found half a discarded pizza, so they ignore me as I slide past them and through the doors. It smells like piss in the train station, fresh and still hot, but it's out of the rain and well lit and relatively safe. I spent last night here—my first in Berlin—and the cops left me alone because I don't look like the other *Penner*, bums, spread out across the floors and benches. I'm reasonably clean and my clothes reasonably neat, but by now, the cops will have seen me hanging around and the one thing I can't risk is them taking me to jail for vagrancy and finding out who I really am. Which, come to think of it, is a good question.

Still, Berlin is a good city for a girl on the run, no matter who she is. Cheap, dark, and a whole stew of nations and languages to get lost in. Of the languages I speak, German—which I picked up when my dad was stationed in Vienna—is my worst and I can't even come close to passing for native. But it turns out a lot of the younger people speak English, and you never have to dig too deep to find a Russian speaker anywhere. So I try to speak my rusty, elementary-school German with a Russian accent, squishing the vowels, frowning more. It's easy so long as I remember to do it. Nobody cares too much for pronunciation and grammar in the Berlin of refugees and runaways.

My best bet in the Bahnhof Zoo is the cheap little döner kebab joint on the street level. It's open until three a.m., and the Turkish guy working the counter didn't kick me out last night for falling asleep in one of the booths even though all I bought from him was a single kebab and a bottle of Coke. Lucky for me, he's working again tonight and actually smiles hello as I enter, the first smile of any kind I've seen in Berlin. A slab of döner meat the size and shape of a piano leg spins on a vertical skewer, and he expertly shaves off an extra thick pile of it for me and mounds it onto the pita. He throws on shredded onions and cucumber, then drenches the whole mess in spicy white yogurt sauce. It's basically the same as the gyros I loved in New York, and to my mind, no food ever served to an emperor or pope is better.

I give him five euros, the inflated train-station price, and park myself in an out-of-the-way booth near the back. The food is warm and delicious and an effective stand-in for a bed and blanket and kiss good night. The grease runs down my chin and onto my neck, but I'm so hungry I don't bother wiping it off until I'm finished. A group of drunk soccer fans rolls in wearing their blue-and-white jerseys, chanting and singing, but I'm so tired I fall asleep anyway, slumping low in the booth, my head on the table.

I ran from Paris—Jesus, how I ran. To the Metro, back to the dance studio, then away again, every man on the street a cop, every car or motorbike another killer. I grabbed what I could from Yael's place. My backpack, my clothes, my new ID, some food for the journey. Left behind were the remains of my old self—my army jacket and old passport.

I vomited twice, first outside the Metro, then in the bathroom of a dirty little café near the Gare du Nord. It was there I washed the blood from the passports and wallet and mobile phone I'd taken. Hamid's killers were German. Berliners, specifically—Gunther Fess and Lukas Kappel. Thus my destination. I used the cash from the wallet to get a ticket on the overnight Paris-Berlin express.

154

The killers were just a little less than handsome, if you judge from their passport pictures and not from their corpses. Athletic young guys in their twenties, they looked a little like the douchey junior stockbroker types who hang around in the fake Irish pubs on Third Avenue. The phone I took from Gunther, the driver of the motorbike, is a newer iPhone. There was no e-mail account set up on it, no social media, and all the texts had been deleted. A work phone, apparently, scrubbed clean of everything incriminating. Almost everything. Everything except the photos: The two killers at play. Their friends. Parties at clubs. Lots of women. Lots of bottles. Lots of coke on the tables.

The guy working the counter wakes me up reluctantly and points to the door. *"Tut mir Leid, Kumpel,"* he says. Sorry, buddy.

I say no problem and head out into the train station. The cops seem busy expelling everyone who's still inside, so I keep my eyes down, shoulder my backpack, and head for the exit. Of course, it's still raining. The nasty, sentient kind of rain that seems to intentionally alter its trajectory to find its way inside my collar. Instinctively, I hunch my shoulders up and wish to the gods a hat or newspaper would come blowing by on the wind. I round the corner from the train station and walk along the perimeter of the zoo. There's a fence around it, but a small margin of shrubs and trees sits between the fence and the sidewalk and I look around for someplace dry enough to bed down. Most of the choice spots are already taken, but then I see a fat maple tree with a low, heavy limb that looks just right. I pick my way toward it through the bushes, but as I sit down, I hear a woman's voice hiss at me, *"Raus hier!"* Get out of here!

I look over and see two white eyes peering at me from under a tarp worn like a hood. A thin hand reaches out and motions for me to go away, then returns to its place cradling a bundle held against the

155

woman's chest. I look closely and see the bundle is a child of maybe three or four, black hair peeking out from under the edge of a dirty towel used as a blanket. The kid's mom looks up at me, and in the scattered light, I recognize frightened eyes.

"I'm just looking for someplace to sleep," I say.

"Not here, addict. I don't want trouble."

Quietly, I start to move away, but against all logic and reason, I stick my hand in my pocket and come out with a thick wad of the money I'd gathered, a mix of euros and dollars. I hold it out to her, but the white eyes stare back suspiciously. "Please," I say. "Take it." But she must sense a trick is coming and just glares at me. I set the money down on the ground before her and leave.

There are simply no good options, and I know I'll have to give the Sofia passport a try at a hostel eventually. I wander for a while, considering where and how and what I'll do if the desk clerk calls the cops. I head back toward the train station and notice an underpass. I sneak underneath, relieved to be out of the rain, and lean against a wall to think.

A woman in a short blue skirt and bare legs enters from the far end, blond hair pulled back in a greasy ponytail. She puts a cigarette in her mouth as she stops in front of me, then pats the pockets of her leather jacket.

"*Hast du Feuer?*" she says. Then, as if on a hunch, she says, "*Spichki?*" The Russian word for matches.

I answer back in the same. "I don't smoke."

"Then what use are you to Marina?" she says, and walks away.

But before she makes it to the end of the underpass, a car enters and slows to a stop in front of her. The woman bends over, leaning into the open window.

I push off from the wall and head in the other direction. Then a shout echoes off the tiles of the underpass. It's high-pitched but more angry than frightened. I turn and see the woman pulling hard to get her arm out of the open window, bracing her other hand on the door for leverage.

Without thinking, I bolt back toward her. When I reach the car, I seize the driver's hand, pulling back his thumb where it's digging into her jacket sleeve. I shove the woman back and find enough room to drive the heel of my left hand forward, slamming it into the man's chin. He lets out a yelp, and suddenly the woman and I fly backward. We land together on the sidewalk.

The tires of his car chirp just as I'm about to jump back to my feet, but the car is already speeding down the tunnel, the roaring of its engine vibrating off the walls.

"You okay?" I ask the woman in Russian as I climb to my feet.

"Fine." She searches the ground for something, then picks up a tiny plastic bag between thumb and forefinger and holds it up in front of her, inspecting it for damage. "Answer me this—how desperate does he think I am? A blow job for *ein wenig Gras*? Fucking loser."

I take her hand and help her to her feet.

She shoves the little bag of weed into the pocket of her jacket and looks me over. "So, *novichka*" —newcomer—"what are you called?"

"I'm called Sofia," I say.

The deal Marina and I strike in the underpass outside the Bahnhof Zoo is a straightforward one: twenty euros a night for a place on her couch until I run out of euros or she runs out of patience. We ride together on the subway to her place, far to the east of Berlin center.

It's dangerous, this arrangement. But it's also anonymous with no passport required. And I'd be lying if I said there wasn't some comfort in Marina's presence. Her age is hard to guess, but she's definitely older than me by, what, five years? Even though I've lived lots of places, I was the coddled child of a diplomat, and the streets of Berlin may as well be another universe. This is Marina's territory, and she knows the strange physics here, which direction gravity goes, and whether two plus two equals something other than four.

"*Novichka*," she says from across the aisle of the empty car as she scrapes at something under her fingernail with a key. "Where you from?"

"Russia," I say.

She rolls her eyes. "No shit."

So she thinks I'm for real. *Cover identity rule one: Go native when you can.* "The south," I say. "Armavir, it's called. By the Black Sea."

"Near Sochi?"

"Six, maybe seven hours by bus," I say. *Cover identity rule two: The believability of your story is in the details.*

"Practically in Turkey," she says. "That explains it, then."

"What does it explain?"

"When I first saw you, I thought, this Sofia, she's a Jew. And that's fine. Jews I don't mind so much." Marina leans forward in her seat. "But now I'm thinking, this one's a Muslim. So don't bring any of that jihad shit into my house, got it?"

"I'm not Muslim."

"I'm talking generally. Whatever jihad shit you're carrying—religion, politics, someone after you—everyone seems to be on some holy war. Just don't bring it near me." She stands, grasping the handrail, and comes across the aisle, the better to glare down at me. "Too many refugees lately, which means too many cops. Too many cops means trouble for Marina."

"Got it," I say. "No drama, no cops."

"Just so, *novichka*," she says. "A few more months, I'm going to be a bartender. You know what kind of money bartenders make?"

"And—what do you do now?"

"Fuck for money," she says.

The words shock me, and Marina grins when she sees me flinch.

"You got a problem?" she says.

"No," I say. "Absolutely not."

But she hears judgment in my voice. "Marina does with her body what Marina pleases, got it?" she says. "Your Allah or Jesus or whoever the fuck doesn't get a vote." She's quiet for a moment, deciding whether I'm worth the trouble. Then she looks out the window. "Here we are," she says.

We transfer to a trolley that runs down the center of a wide boulevard. The streetlamps catch the buildings in gray light, showing off their crumbling, communist-era glory. "They don't look much better even in the daylight," Marina says, reading my mind. *"Gnily zubie."* Rotting teeth.

A few blocks of the same rumble past the window before Marina tugs my sleeve to get off. I follow her through the massive concrete buildings and realize the only way to tell them apart is by the unique face of each one's decay. Sagging ears here, a listing awning-nose there. Hers is the one with the spray-painted RAUS AUSLÄNDER— Get out, foreigners—next to the entrance.

There's no lock on the building's door. You just have to know the trick to turning the lever: push and lift, then turn. The elevator's broken, Marina says, and has been forever. I follow her up the stairs to where she lives on the sixth floor. There's a TV on loud in one of her neighbors' apartments, and the toxic reek of crack or meth or death hangs in the hallway.

She locks the door behind us, then gives me the grand tour. The tiny kitchen, the tiny bathroom, then the living room where there's a plaid couch, sagging low in the middle, and an old swiveling recliner. Beyond this is a small bedroom with two single beds, one on either side of a window. The one on the right is sloppily made and has a Hello Kitty throw pillow on it. "That's Marina's," she says. The one on the left is drawn tight and has an Orthodox crucifix hanging over its head. "Lyuba's," she says. "My roommate—she's a cam girl."

"A cam girl?"

Marina nods. "Also a piano teacher."

I crash down hard on the couch, exhausted beyond exhaustion, and although I need a shower, and although I need to brush my teeth— Jesus, has it really been since Paris?—I simply can't move, not even enough to take off my jacket. I close my eyes, but all I see is a kaleidoscope of colors and shapes and faces and things. I try to shut off my ears, too, try to ignore the noise from the city outside, but Berlin refuses to shut up. It's just like New York in this way, always there, starved for attention even when you're trying to sleep, making itself known with distant sirens and rumbling trucks and buzzing sodium lamps.

And just when it's disappearing. Just when the world's going silent. The click of a lighter and the rolling fug of marijuana smoke. I open my eyes and see Marina, dressed now in a tattered T-shirt. She's curled up in a chair, bare legs folded up against her chest, brown ceramic weed pipe held lazily in one hand. She's looking at me, watching me, like I'm an animal in a zoo.

Probably a minute passes, the two of us just looking at each other. Finally, she lights the pipe again and inhales. "As a rule, I don't ask," she says with clenched throat, then exhales. "But you're not the usual kind of runaway."

I'm too tired to understand, and as Marina laughs at the confusion on my face, she gestures to the room, but really, to all Berlin.

"How is it you end up on Marina's couch?" she says. "Daddy hit you? Boyfriend get you pregnant and want to marry? I can help you with that."

"No," I say. "I'm just—looking for someone."

She shrugs. "Lots of someones here."

"And you?" I say. "How did you end up here?"

Marina taps the pipe over a plastic ashtray. "Marina doesn't 'end up' anywhere, *novichka*. Marina chooses. Father runs away, mother marries a bus driver who likes little girls, so, *pffft*." She flicks her fingers, sending her old life skittering across the floor. "Off I go, *nach Berlin*. Four years, this July."

"Congratulations," I say, the word coming out as a question.

She refills the pipe, carefully pressing the fresh weed into the bowl with the butt of her lighter. "Anyway, Marina needs only Marina. Just as Sofia needs only Sofia." She thrusts the pipe at me. "Want?"

"No thanks," I say.

"Suit yourself," she says, putting the pipe to her mouth. "How old are you anyway?"

I try to remember the age on the Sofia passport. "Twenty-two."

She laughs, coughing a geyser of smoke at the ceiling. "Twenty-two my ass."

"How old are you?" I ask.

She wipes spittle from her mouth on her T-shirt. "Seventeen," she says.

I close my eyes until Marina thinks I'm asleep and wanders off to bed. For a while, I try to imagine Marina's life, what it's like to *fuck for money* as if that were no big thing, to have no family and not give a shit, as if that were no big thing, either. Life as an endless war of all against all, and *ein wenig Gras* is what you get if you win.

But as I wonder what it's like to be Marina, I wonder if maybe she isn't right. If it's true that Sofia needs only Sofia, then why am I here at all? Silly to continue an epic, pointless quest to find a father who's not even my biological father. A father who lies to his not-even-biological daughter for her entire life. A father who killed my mother with a wrong turn because he refused to be an accountant or mail-man like all the others.

This connection to him is just imagined. A child's fantasy. And, like Marina and Sofia, Gwendolyn is too old for fantasy. Grow up, Gwendolyn. Let him go. Children bury their parents. It's the way things work. You already did it once.

Morning is starting in Berlin. The light—soft blue and yellow fighting it out—finds its way to my eyelids. I turn over, bury my face in the couch cushion, but trucks snort angrily past on the boulevard. Morning deliveries of strudel or whatever Berlin trucks deliver. And somewhere, in some other room, a clock is ticking.

When I wake, Marina is gone, replaced by someone I assume to be Lyuba. She's a wispy blond, curled up in the same chair Marina had sat in, smoking a cigarette and reading a Bible. She is doing so lan-guidly, beautifully, leg draped just so over an arm of the chair, hand with cigarette just so, draped over the other arm.

I check my phone: three in the afternoon.

"Where's Marina?" I say.

"Don't know," she says.

"I'm Sofia," I say.

"Did I ask?" she says.

"Mind if I take a shower?" I say.

"Do. I can smell you from here," she says.

In the bathroom, I have to duck under improvised clotheslines crisscrossing the room, heavy with drying panties and bras hanging by paper clips. But the sink and shower are surprisingly and spectac-ularly clean. I steal a little toothpaste and brush with my finger. Then I take a shower, letting the water scour the terror and exhaustion and fear down the drain in tan swirls.

When I'm finished, I dress and tell Lyuba I'm going out. If she hears me, she doesn't acknowledge it.

Outside, the rain is gone, and there's even a weak little sun in the sky. Somehow, the neighborhood in daytime is less ominous than the neighborhood in nighttime, and the concrete apartment blocks have an orderly symmetry about them even in their decaying state. An old woman in a striped smock hoses the sidewalk in front of a pharmacy and glowers at me as I pass, as if irritated by having to share her world with the young. I find a café tucked into a corner and spend a euro on coffee and a day-old sausage roll. The roll is tepid and greasy and terrible, but it's cheap calories and that's all that matters.

For a long while, I nurse the coffee and think, staring down at the Formica tabletop as if the facts and inferences and suppositions were spread out across it. But there's no librarian to ask for help, no textbook telling me how to do this. So how do I even start?

Start with the reason you're in Berlin, a voice tells me, start with the two men who killed Hamid. It seems logical you don't send a novice to Paris for a job like that. You use someone who has done this before.

I open the iPhone and thumb through the pictures once more. There they are: Gunther punching Lukas in the groin. Lukas bent over a line of coke as Gunther downs a stein of beer. Lukas punching Gunther in the groin. The world of men having fun: coke and beer and ball punching. They are not totally alike, though. Gunther is leaner than Lukas, and fairer. And their wardrobes are different, too. Lukas preferred, at least on this night, a form-fitted undershirt, while Gunther preferred a baggy striped oxford rolled up at the sleeves, thug-prep.

Then I see it, the thing they have in common. The tattoo. On the inside forearm of each. It's a crude outline of the European continent, the Spanish snout nuzzling an unseen Mediterranean, balancing on Italy's stiletto-heeled leg and the Balkan-Greek haunch. And around Europe, a coiled, equally-crude cobra, it's head about where Norway and Sweden and Finland should be.

Two teenage girls enter the café noisily, distracting me from my thoughts. One is a prissy-looking redhead with good shoes—Germany's answer to Astrid Foogle. The other is a blond with short hair who wears pink sneakers. They order coffee and chocolate croissants, then take a table in the middle of the room. The redhead discloses some heretofore-secret news that causes the blond to gasp, *"Doch!"*

Astrid Foogle. Wonder if she's found a new enemy yet? And Mr. Lawrence. Ask me about the benign indifference of the world now, fucker. I have a better answer.

I rise to leave just as the woman working the counter clears out the display case, removing a tray of cakes and rolls to make room for fresh inventory.

"How much?" I ask, nodding to the old ones.

"I was going to throw them out," she says.

"I'll give you three euros for them all."

She puts her hands on her hips and sucks at something in her teeth. "Five," she says.

I clear away an ashtray and a spread of magazines and a skyline of liquor bottles from the kitchen table in the apartment and set the bakery box down in the center. Lyuba approaches like a suspicious cat and carefully picks out a pastry, eyeing me the whole time. I ask if Marina is back, and she gives me a silent nod. I lift a fragile, crumbling fruit tart with what looks like raspberry filling from the box and wrap it in a napkin.

Marina is on her bed, legs crossed beneath her, a stack of note-cards on her lap. "Don't bother me. I'm studying."

I set the tart on the bed before her like an offering. "What are you studying?"

"Cocktail recipes." She picks up the pastry and scrunches her nose. "What's this?"

"I thought you might be hungry," I say.

"You brought some for Lyuba?"

"Of course."

"You shouldn't do that. Now she'll expect it every day, and when you don't, she'll hate you for it." She peels back the napkin and starts eating.

"She hates me already."

"Lyuba's from Moscow. They breed them to be bitches there."

I notice a homemade bandage of cotton and masking tape over Marina's right earlobe. Blood has soaked through and stained the cotton brown.

"What happened to your ear?" I say.

"Leo," she says, and wipes her mouth on her sleeve.

"Leo?"

"Leo is our *sutenyer*. He tore out my earring."

I struggle with the word. "*Sutenyer*?"

She squints at me. "Marina fucks for money, Lyuba does cams, the *sutenyer* takes a cut. What kind of Russian are you not to know this?"

Pimp, she means. I smile defensively. "They call it something else in Armavir."

"Anyway, mostly Leo's a teddy bear. Handles the bad clients."

"If he's such a teddy bear, why do you let him do that?"

"It's not about 'let,' *novichka*. If not him, someone worse." She shrugs in resignation. "The world belongs to men. It is theirs. *We* are theirs. Trees, rocks, sky—theirs."

"So what you told me, about how all Marina needs is Marina. That was just an act?"

"A wish. For someday." She sets the stack of notecards on the bed.

I climb onto the bed next to her and pull out the iPhone, scrolling through the photos until I come to one where the tattooed arms of both Gunther and Lukas are visible. "I need a favor, Marina. I want you to look at something."

She takes the phone and studies the picture. "VIP room at Rau Klub. You can tell from the orange couch they're on."

"The tattoo both of them have. What does it mean?"

She shrugs casually. "Criminals. Mafia."

"You're sure it was taken at Rau Klub?"

"Of course. I work it sometimes. Marina's dream, Marina's absolute dream, is to be a bartender there. A thousand euros on a good night."

"Can you work it tonight?" I ask. "I want a look."

"Take you, you mean. Who doesn't even know what a pimp is." She studies me carefully with squinted eyes. "You run from mafia like these guys, country mouse. Not toward them."

"Just for a look. Please."

A shake of her head, a sigh, then a long pause. "You can look, but anything more and Marina is gone, understand?"

Fourteen

You hear Rau Klub before you see it, the thump of house music drumming the air like distant cannon fire. To get there you get off the U-Bahn at the last stop in a nasty-looking wasteland and walk maybe a kilometer down a road lined with closed-up factories.

It's a dark path but well traveled, filled with club kids all heading the same direction like we're all on some sort of pilgrimage. It's mostly German being spoken, of course, and a little Russian and Turkish, but no English. Either the tourists haven't heard of Rau Klub or it's too rough for them to dare. Once in a while, a Benz or BMW or rented limo crawls past, the driver tapping the horn for the road to clear, the kids squinting at the windows to see who's inside.

Marina walks barefoot, holding her shoes in one hand. "Stay sober," she says. "This place—dogs and devils. You will see." She steps delicately around a puddle of some evil-looking brown liquid.

Rau Klub's zombie carcass of a building is a massive old factory made of brick, the holes where its windows used to be pulsing pink and blue, pink and blue. We pick our way across a weedy yard toward the entrance, stepping over bottles and crumbling chunks of masonry. "Careful of needles," Marina calls out.

I'm freezing in the short dress she loaned me, which comes complete with a cutout for almost my entire back, and it's hard to walk in the cheap shoes she made me buy, tacky heels made of plastic. But Marina says I look hot, and so she's not surprised at all when the bouncer spots us in a line of maybe two hundred freezing club kids and motions for us to come to the front.

Lights strafe the bodies of the crowd on the main floor, piercing through the haze of smoke and steam. The machine-gun rhythm from the amps pushes at my chest. I'd been to clubs before, in Moscow, sneaking out with the other diplomats' kids, but that was for fun. Now I'm here to work, and Rau Klub feels like a dystopian-futuristic version of the party on the *Titanic* after all the lifeboats have left.

Following Marina up a wide metal staircase, I see just how vast the place is. I'm not sure what used to be manufactured here, but it was something big. Rusty metal tanks rise up along one wall, and a web of pipes snakes across the ceiling. Bodies are everywhere, squeezed together in a single, squirming mass. The music reaches a crescendo, and on cue, a thousand police whistles blow at once and glow sticks appear in the air, waving frantically as if to signal a rescue plane passing overhead.

There's another bouncer at the top of the stairs, an obese guy in a beret who greets Marina in Russian. He steps aside and nods for us to enter.

A slightly quieter, slightly less crowded version of the world downstairs spreads out before us. Toothy smiles glow like cartoon Cheshire cats in the blue and pink light, and shining eyes follow us newcomers into the room. Men recline in banquettes, attended to by women in short skirts and pretend smiles. *My, aren't you just the cleverest and handsomest and richest man in the world!*

A gunshot pops, and I nearly jump out of my skin, but instead of screams, I hear peals of laughter from a table in the back where a man in a cuff-linked shirt and loosened tie is spraying his harem of six teen-age girls with champagne bought with bonus money.

Marina orders two ginger ales at the bar. Never drink alcohol on the job, she tells me, just pretend to. I remember Yael's speech about tactical awareness. Not so different, the prostitute's dangers and the spy's. Thirty euros is what the two drinks come to. Thirty euros for two sodas. But at least the prices have thinned the herd, and Marina is able to find two empty bar stools.

"Read the crowd. Best not to make your move right away." She looks up and smiles at some of the men as they pass. "Then pick out your mark. I'll take the wallet; you get the watch." This said so drily I wonder if she's joking.

A kid in a leather jacket who looks vaguely like a famous actor is drinking vodka with his bros and singing songs in drunken German. Marina nods in his direction. "A soccer player from Munich. He tips well, but his mates are assholes. You'll be lucky if they pay you."

"You know them?"

"Them specifically? No. But you learn the species quick."

"How about that one?" I point out a guy of about sixty with gray hair down to his shoulders. He's dolled up in torn jeans and a bright paisley shirt, and lecturing a slender, model-gorgeous black woman of about twenty-five, who's picking at an olive in a martini glass as if there's a hair on it.

Marina squints and nods. "Profitable. Likes giving jewelry. That sparkling shit around the African's neck ain't glass." She leans in con-fidentially. "All you need to do is listen to him cry like a baby about how he's getting old and his kids are all drug addicts and nothing matters anyway."

It's a fascinating world, this club, and Marina is an expert guide. We go through a few more—the visiting businessman chatting up a pretty young guy, the peacocks in suits and sunglasses, manes carefully slicked.

At the top of the stairs, four men appear, and the Russian bouncer scrambles to get the rope out of their way. Their laughter is loud and comes out in sharp, high-pitched brays. Bullies' laughter. Shoving and punching each other with every step, they stumble across the floor to a table with a sign on it that says RESERVIERT. Everyone in the room looks at them before quickly looking away. Track pants. Untucked silk shirts. Puma sneakers.

Marina nudges me. "See the tattoos?"

I study their arms where their sleeves are pushed up. Same as in the photos of Gunther and Lukas.

"So what species are these?" I ask.

"*Schlägertypen*," Marina grunts. Typical thugs. "That means money and pain. First you get one, then the other."

A swelling of fear in my stomach, but it's time to go to work. I push back the stool and stand.

Marina's hand clasps my wrist. "You said just a look. Don't be an idiot."

I smile at her. "Just going to the bathroom."

As I cross the room, I feel Marina's eyes on me, protective but wondering how much protecting I'm really worth. For the benefit of the boys, I put a little swish in my walk, but feel like a five-year-old in mommy's heels and so give it up after a few steps. It's enough, though; they notice. As I pass their booth and head to the bathroom at the far end, I hear one of them gush, *"Feine Schlampe."*

Fine slut/bitch/whore, it means, but I would know the meaning even if I didn't understand German. The tone of it is clear enough. I keep walking, ignoring them—making a show of ignoring them—and disappear into the restroom.

At the row of sinks, two blonds are snorting coke off the porcelain edge. Two more club girls linger in front of the mirrors, arguing while they adjust their skirts and hoist up their boobs and glance hatefully at each other. On a stool against the wall sits an elderly woman, round and swollen, handing out towels. She stares ahead blindly, seeing nothing.

The fear and adrenaline rise inside me, and sweat begins to blister from my forehead. The old woman hands me a towel, and I drop a one-euro coin into the basket next to her. I mop my forehead and stare into the mirror, trying on a few smiles for the boys.

It's showtime. I steady myself and march out, back toward Marina. One of the *Schlägertypen* gets up to follow me over. Marina rolls her eyes when she sees him and pulls her clutch into her lap.

I sit down again, and the boy puts one arm around me, the other around Marina. *"Was geht ab?"* he says. What's up?

"Verpiss dich," I sneer, my Russian accent as thick as I can make it. Piss off.

He's good-looking, about twenty, with shaggy dark hair and a little stubble. The charmer of the group, I'm guessing, sent out as a scout. He turns to Marina. "Your friend tells me to piss off. Don't you think that's a little rude?"

Marina slips out from under his arm. "I'm out of here," she says in Russian, eyebrow cocked, meaning, *If you're smart, you'll follow me.*

I'm terrified of being left alone, but all I can do is smile at her and watch as she leaves. The guy plops down on her stool, his hand sliding down my arm to my hand. "So, what's up? What's your name, girl?"

"I'm called Sofia," I say.

"And I'm called Christian."

. . .

Christian's friends are more or less as I guessed they'd be, douches of a dangerous kind. Each successive round of beer and shots of vodka—there are three of each in the first hour—inspires them to ever higher levels of douchery, as if there were a competition going on between them. Idiotic banter about soccer and cars alternates with impromptu wrestling matches. But in between, I catch snatches of conversation. They are in mourning, of a sort, for someone they knew. A funeral today. No, two of them. My palms start to sweat.

Christian tries to make small talk—*What about you, girl?* He asks me about my favorite season, my favorite color, my favorite soda, my favorite childhood pet. I reply as best I can, filling in the blanks of Sofia's life just as Yael has taught me. Autumn, blue, Fanta, a rabbit named Alyosha. *So much in common,* he says.

But mostly they treat me like furniture. Something that's just there. I endure the occasional hand on my leg, the occasional lewd question—*Tell me, Sofia, are all the Russian girls in Germany whores?*—but otherwise I'm just another club girl, and a Russian one at that, who won't understand most of what they're saying.

Then a new song comes on, nothing I've heard before, but there's a collective gasp. The boys stir, then rise. They clink their glasses together, order more shots. This was their song. Gunther's favorite. Lukas hated it.

A shiver rolls from my shoulders outward down to the tips of my fingers. My theory was right. Follow the path to the watering hole and there I'll find the rest of the herd. I calm myself, force myself to be casual. "Who are Gunther and Lukas?" I ask.

Christian breathes deeply and rests his hand on my thigh. "Our mates," he says.

"Oh?"

"They died last week. Motorcycle accident."

"I'm sorry," I say. "Here? In Berlin?"

"Paris."

I close my eyes, hear the rush of blood in my veins. I reach for my ginger ale, drink it all. Reach for someone's water, drink that, too. What do I do now, Yael?

"What's wrong?" Christian asks.

"Nothing," I say. "Let's dance."

We descend the staircase to the dance floor below, and I pray he can't see my knees and hands shaking as I grip the railing. Every fiber in my body wants me to run to the exit, the evolutionary-instinct lizard brain telling me there is danger here, fire and predators. But Christian is my in. My in to Hamid's killers. My in to my dad's captors. You will be hard, Gwendolyn.

On the floor below there are bodies, too many of them. Moving through the room is like passing through gelatin. Every step, every breath a battle to not suffocate. But I lead him by the hand to the dance floor. We will dance together, Christian and I. Just long enough to get him to go somewhere private with me. Then I will torture him to get the information out or fuck him to get the information out. Either way, same result.

"Look," Christian says. "Look, I'm sorry—I hate dancing. I suck. And really, I gotta get back to my friends. The funerals—you know."

Inside, I seethe. But Sofia smiles. "What's your number? I'll text you. We can hang out."

He gives me a kind of nervous schoolboy's laugh, then tells it to me. I send him a one-word message, *Sofia.*

He checks his phone. "Got it."

I head back to Marina's place on the U-Bahn, replaying the scene at the Rau Klub, planning what comes next. In the window of the train, I catch a glimpse of my face, the tunnel walls streaking behind the

173

reflection. The stuttering fluorescent lights in the car give my skin a terrible pallor, and there are deep shadows beneath my cheeks. My eyes have retreated into caves and the muscles of my jaw flare as my teeth bite down hard.

Something curious going on in my stomach and in my head: the terror I've lived with from the moment I found out my dad was taken is—what? Transforming? The word seems inadequate. The concept I'm looking for, it's what happens to the guy in the Kafka story when he becomes a cockroach. Metamorphosize? I look it up in my phone.

> (To) Metamorphose. Verb. 1. To change significantly in appearance or character, sometimes by supernatural means, esp. more beautiful or grotesque.

That's it. The terror is metamorphosing into the thing inside me I first discovered in New York, the thing that Yael trained and refined. The thing is the flip side, the counterpoint, the shouted answer to the terror's question. Asks the terror: What will become of me? Answers the thing: This.

My anger clouds my thinking, and since anger is the oxygen the thing inside me breathes, it's in an eager mood tonight. Get Christian somewhere private at all costs, it tells me, tie him to a bed, and go to work on him with pliers and a cigarette lighter until he gives you the answer. But this, I know rationally, is no way to get information. I learned that from my dad as we watched news reports together of the torture of terrorists. "A man will admit to anything when you torture him. That he's a terrorist. That he's the devil. That he knows tomorrow's winning lottery numbers," he told me.

So, that other thing, then. Why not? Fucking him instead of torturing him—violence would be better, and less stomach-turning, than fucking him. But we'll see. Anything it takes. Anything to win.

I miss the train stop and have to walk back from the next one. My mind remains on Christian and his friends. How could this collection of shitheads I met tonight have kidnapped my dad? What qualifies this band of petty fools who swill beer like water and try to punch one another in the balls to even look in my dad's direction? I had pictured the evil that stole my dad from me to be powerful because it was large and brilliant and monolithic, an aircraft carrier that played chess. But here it is, an evil powerful because it is small and unthinking and many.

And it is this that makes them even more frightening. How can I win? Beat them in a spelling bee? As I walk, I notice people on the streets, bums and drunks and guys whose eyes gleam in the streetlamps like blades. But they only watch me warily as I pass, as if I'm the danger, as if I'm the one who'll pull them into a doorway or alley and cut them open.

Marina and Lyuba are asleep in their beds when I get back. I close the bathroom door gently behind me, so as not to wake them, and hang my head over the toilet. I heave a few times until there are tears running down my cheeks. But my stomach is mostly empty and nothing comes out except a string of spit. With the loofah hanging from the spigot in the tub, I scrub at my hands and forearms, trying desperately to get clean of dirt I can neither see nor smell.

There's a note on the couch in scrawled Cyrillic handwriting. *Wake me when you get back*, it says. I slip into Marina's room, sit on the edge of her bed, and touch her arm. Her head turns and she blinks at me. "You scared me tonight," she says. "I was worried."

"Sorry," I say.

She's about to say something else but squeezes my hand instead.

Fifteen

I dig through the kitchen to make an improvised breakfast feast for my roommates and myself. There's black tea and honey and yogurt and a carton of eggs and half a loaf of dense, flavorless rye bread that the label says is essential for achieving *"überlegene Darmgesundheit."* Superior bowel health. I do what I can with the ingredients and serve it to Marina and Lyuba at the table.

Lyuba looks at me with narrowed eyes through the smoke of her cigarette and eats only the rye bread. "The tea is very weak," she says as she gets up to leave. She's out the door a few minutes later, claiming a piano lesson for some "rich little sissy" in a grand Charlottenburg flat.

Marina takes Lyuba's plate and finishes it. "I'm surprised you came home."

I start to clean up. "I wasn't looking for a hookup."

"Not a hookup, *novichka*. I'm surprised you're still breathing." Marina brings the plate to the sink and grabs a dishtowel. "You said you were looking for someone. Is it one of them, those gangsters? Is this about some kind of revenge?"

I scrub at a pan with a sponge, then scrape at the burnt egg with my fingernails. "Not revenge."

Marina lets a pair of dry plates drop to a shelf with a clatter. I jump at the sound. "I told you, don't bring your shit into Marina's house. Lyuba doesn't think you're even Russian. Did you know that? Says you're a fake."

"Armavir is a long way from Moscow."

"That's what I said to her. She's a paranoiac. Listening to too much Putin, thinks spies are everywhere. But, Sofia, after this mafia drama yesterday—if you want to stay here even one more night, you need to tell what game you're playing at."

I shut off the water and turn to her. "I'm looking for my father," I say. "He ran away, and I think he fell in with them. Those men from the club." It's the bare minimum I think she'll accept.

Marina rolls her eyes. "So there it is. The great mystery of Sofia reveals itself as sentimental bullshit." She hangs the towel over the sink. "Papa ran away for a reason. Better to leave him with his new friends. You'll both be happier that way."

I'm about to reply to her, tell her that's not how it is, but she's already left the kitchen. A moment later, I hear her bedroom door close.

My phone vibrates in my pocket. It's a text from Christian: *was geht ab baby.* I sit on the edge of the kitchen table, staring at the screen, thumbs hovering over the keyboard. What I want to write back is *What's up, baby, is that I want to make you bleed.* What I type instead is *Nicht viel. Du?* Not much. You?

He writes back immediately in slangy, abbreviated German that takes me forever to decipher. But after I do, I find out there's a party tonight in an area called Neukölln, and I'm going as his date.

. . .

I meet Christian outside the Hermannstrasse U-Bahn stop. It's already dark out but fluorescently bright beneath the awning of the food stand on the corner. He's leaning against the wall and eating sausages covered in what looks like ketchup, poking at them with a toothpick and slurping them into his mouth. His jacket is flashy red leather, and his sneakers are gleaming white and brand-new. "You like currywurst?" he says as he chews, holding out the little paper basket. "I can get you a new toothpick. Or you can use mine."

I shake my head and try to force a smile. I am Sofia tonight, I tell myself, cute and shy, quiet and mysterious.

He looks me up and down. "No dress?"

I'm wearing jeans and my Doc Martens and the leather jacket Yael bought me over a black T-shirt. "I thought maybe tonight was casual."

"No, of course! I mean, you look great! Really. You'd look great in anything." This said genuinely, a teenage bashfulness coloring his face. He is, despite the ketchup on his chin, handsome, like he belongs in some boy band I would have listened to when I was twelve. Not the lead, but the quiet one, the object of a million secret crushes.

He tosses the rest of his food in a trash can and wipes his mouth with a napkin. "You been to Neukölln before?" he asks. "Used to be rough. Now it's all faggy. Lots of artists and shit."

He walks next to me down a street lined with tired apartment buildings on one side, and tall weeds on the other that cover a chain-link fence and railroad tracks just beyond. I can't tell if it's a bad neighborhood or just run-down and badly lit.

"Whose party is it?" I say.

A nervous laugh. "It is at my boss's apartment, but don't worry. I told him you were cool. It's like—for my mates who died. A 'celebration of life' we say."

A funeral after-party. At the boss's apartment. Nervous terror stirs in my stomach. Where did all the confident bravado I felt last night on the train disappear to? "So—a memorial service."

"Yes. A little fancy. Which is why I thought—maybe a dress for you. But whatever."

"So tell about your boss," I say. "Cool guy?"

"Paulus? Supercool. And his apartment—you will see." He exhales sharply and shakes his head. "Two units, one on top of the other. And he put in a stairway so you can go between them. Mahogany bar. Jacuzzi on the roof. Sweet-ass TV, like, I don't know, two meters wide."

"Cool."

"I think in a few years, maybe I can get such a place." He claps his hands together in excitement. "Maybe they'll have a TV three meters wide by then."

"And what work do you do, Christian?" I say, casually as I can. "You didn't tell me last night."

His voice deepens by a half octave all of a sudden as he plays the grown-up. "I'm a wholesaler. We buy things, sell things. Computers. Whisky. Car parts. Whatever. West to east, north to south. All over Europe."

"And here I thought you did something, I don't know, dangerous." I give him a sideways look and a smile. "I like dangerous."

"Oh, it can be!" he says, eager not to disappoint. "Maybe all the tax papers aren't there sometimes. Maybe an import stamp is missing."

"Sounds scary. All those forms. You might get a paper cut."

His face changes to embarrassment. "There's more to it than that. These people. My crew. We're nobody to fuck around with."

"Mm," I say, making sure he hears the doubt in my voice. "Is that right?"

But he pulls back and his voice becomes defensive. "Five hundred euros this jacket cost me, you know. Fucking limited edition. Believe

179

me, Sofia, you don't get what you want in this world by being a meek little loser bitch."

"*Genau,*" I say. Precisely.

The Celebration of Life is in a graffiti-covered building at the very end of the street. House music and rattling windows, men laughing and shouting. Christian leads me by the hand up the building's stairs, past couples making out and smoking weed. The guys look like slightly older versions of him, and the girls in short dresses look like better-dressed versions of me. He enters the party with a triumphal shout that receives a few shouts back. There's a thick crowd around the enormous TV Christian told me about, playing some shooting game set in a destroyed world.

We squeeze our way to the kitchen at the back of the apartment, and Christian hands me a bottle of beer and a full shot glass. I don't see a way around it, so tactical awareness be damned. We clink the glasses together, and I swallow the shot in one go, a thick, sweet liquor that leaves my lips sticky as glue.

Christian takes my hand, twirls me around, and presses his body against my back. His lips, also sticky, start exploring my neck. I try to wriggle away, but he just holds me tighter. "Hey!" I say, swatting at his head. "*Nicht doch!*"

One of his bros from last night at Rau Klub approaches with a wide grin and gives Christian a hard punch in the shoulder. "Where's your fucking manners? She said knock it off!" But Christian brays with laughter at what is, evidently, a joke. The two start play wrestling, or maybe wrestling for real, but either way, I'm able to break free. I slip through the jostling crowd, their noise deafening, and look for some-place less crowded. I find a corner where two women in short dresses are smoking and speaking Russian to each other.

A pale woman about twenty with white-blond hair gestures to me with her cigarette. *"Russkiy?"*

I nod.

"God, not another one of us," she says. "Which one do you belong to?"

"Him," I say, pointing to Christian. "Red jacket."

"Oh, Christian's just a baby," says the other woman, this one maybe in her late twenties with elaborate pinned-up black hair. She's swaying back and forth a little, already drunk, and introduces herself as Veronika. "I'm with Paulus. You can have him if you want."

The women laugh, and I try to.

"Which one's Paulus?" I say.

Veronika points to a man standing nearby. Late thirties, with his head shaved completely bald, and a tailored black T-shirt over a body that's muscular and very lean. He's doing shots with Christian and two other young men. He pours another round. Then another.

"They get grabby because of the coke and liquor," Veronika says, the words slurring out of her mouth. "Trick is to hide downstairs until the coke runs out, and they pass out playing video games."

At an open window on the far side of the room, a group of men are gathering. A well-muscled guy wearing a tank top roars as he lifts a beer keg over his head. Shouts of encouragement. Chanting. Then the beer keg disappears through the window. There's a crash. The wail of a car alarm. Weeping shrieks of laughter.

The blond crushes out her cigarette on the floor and takes me by the arm. "Time to disappear."

We slink discreetly through the party toward a spiral staircase in the room's center. Veronika catches the eyes of a few other women and gestures with her head for them to disappear, too.

The blond leads the way, while I follow with Veronika, who's gripping the railing tightly, heels clicking uneasily down the stairs. "The boys know the rules," she says. "This area is just for the boss and me. Private. Access denied."

The lower level is much quieter. White leather couches, a glass coffee table, a shitty abstract painting in a curlicue gold frame on the wall. Three other women join Paulus's girlfriend, the blond, and me on the couches. Someone produces a bottle of vodka. Someone else a small mirror and clear plastic tube full of white powder.

Besides me and the two Russians, there are two German women and an Austrian. Conversations the women started upstairs continue and I catch a few pieces. Sex problems. Where to shop. Clinics that won't report black eyes.

Veronika sits next to me and drains a glass of vodka. As she refills it with the bottle, she speaks to me in quiet Russian. "Is Christian treating you well? I started drinking at noon, so I'm being a nosy hag."

"Oh, yes," I say. "He's a sweetheart."

"Well, he's young. Look around. You see what bastards they become," she says, taking another sip. "This business of theirs. It makes them mean. And after Paris, they're all acting like madmen."

Paris. How drunk is she, and how far do I dare push her? "Christian told me about that," I say. "Gunther and Lukas, so sad."

"*Sad?* Please. They were idiots and thugs, just like every one of those monsters upstairs." She puts a hand on my shoulder, another on my leg. Commiserating girlfriends. "Anyway, I'm sick of talking about it. At least Paulus can't blame me for that shit show. No, he cannot. I should dump his gangster ass."

I smile and pat her arm conspiratorially. "Just like my aunt used to tell me: A woman needs a man like she needs a silk scarf. Nice to have, but if you lose it, who cares, right?"

"*So true!* And they never listen, you know. It's like they're born without ears. I told Paulus he always regrets the jobs he takes from that ghoul Boris or Bandar or *Buh*-something. Always. Too much work, not enough money. Fucking Paris." Veronika slides the mirror and coke in front of her and makes two narrow lines with the edge of someone's health club card. "You want? Keeps a girl thin."

"No," I say. "Thank you."

"Won't have that figure forever, you know." Veronika bends at the waist, snorting first one line, then the other. When she comes up again, her nostrils are red and she wears an immense smile. She grabs my hand and places it on her chest. "Feel my heart. Feel it. Kicking like a racehorse."

And so it is. "You okay?" I ask. "Maybe, you should—slow down."

Veronika stares at me for a moment with what looks like anger. Then lets out a raucous laugh. "Oh, little girl. Do yourself a favor and get out of here. Get out of here before you become me."

Heavy footfalls on the staircase. I look up to see Paulus coming down. He stops halfway, stares directly at Veronika. "Why are all of you down here? Up! Now! Let's go!"

The women all rise, and Veronika curtsies to Paulus. "As you wish, *Liebling*."

I follow them halfway up the stairs, then stop. The party is louder than before, in full swing now. They won't even notice I'm not there.

I slip back down the stairs into Paulus's home and look around. It's just a gangster's gaudy apartment—*Schlägertypen*. Too much leather, too much glass, too much expensive, ugly shit. How long do I have before someone comes looking for me? Ten minutes? Two?

I pass the kitchen and head into the hallway. Here's the bedroom, an enormous bureau, an enormous armoire. Here's the bathroom, marble everywhere. And here's a locked door. I pause, listen to the party again. The clomping of a hundred feet, screeches of laughter, a shout, something landing hard on the floor.

Paulus, where would you keep the key? In your pocket, of course, but maybe—I head to the living room. Quietly as I can, I open the closet, rummage around through coats and jackets, but come up with nothing. Shit. So maybe Paulus changed before the party. Maybe the key is in his pants, lying on the floor in the bedroom.

But the bedroom floor is tidy, the top of the bureau, too. In the armoire and drawers of the bedside tables I find nothing other than a novel in Russian, loose change, a few receipts. The fear is coursing through me now like a narcotic, but I give myself one last moment. In desperation, I search the hamper: T-shirts, socks, underwear, Veronika's and his. Fucking gross. I search a department store shopping bag: silk nightgown, price tag still attached. I search under the bed: a single cardboard box from a courier.

I slide it out and see it's already been opened. There's no shipping label inside, no customs form. Only a beautiful wooden box packed in foam. It looks like a humidor, but when I lift the lid, I see it's something else entirely.

A pistol plated in gold nests in a bed of form-fitted velvet. I move a little notecard aside to see it better. It's gaudy as hell and exactly the sort of thing I'd expect someone like Paulus to collect. A brass plate in the lid says:

Česká Zbrojovka Uherský Brod
Made in Czech Republic
Limited Edition 64/100

The notecard on top of it, though, isn't gaudy. It's made of thick paper with rough edges and feels like linen. On the inside, written in blue ink, it says in English: *As ever, a pleasure doing business. Your admiring friend, BK.* For a moment I squint at the initials. What had Veronika said? *That ghoul Boris or Bandar or Buh-something.*

Time's up, I tell myself. Time to get out of here, back to the party. With the package put back exactly as it was, I slide it under the bed and head down the hallway toward the living room. Forget the key to the locked door; it's just too risky to be down in the area Veronika said was *private, access denied.*

As I'm turning into the living room, I freeze. Christian is standing at the bottom of the stairs. He stares at me, eyes narrowed with anger. "The fuck are you doing?"

Swallow the terror, I tell myself. Be Sofia. I approach him, put my hands on his chest, and give the sexiest smile I can manage. "Waiting for you," I say.

He yanks my hands away by the wrists, gripping them tightly. "You can't be down here. You know that."

Knee to the groin, thumbs to eyes. Blind him. Run. But I don't. "Christian, let go, you're hurting me," I say instead. "I wanted you to come find me, so we could be alone."

His face slackens, and I see uncertainty. Then he releases his grip.

More footsteps on the stairs, hurrying this time. I wrap my arms around Christian and pull him into me. His mouth meets mine, and I slide my tongue between his teeth. I feel his body tense with shock.

Then he's ripped from me with a violent shove. Paulus switches his eyes from me to Christian and back again. "You little bitch," he says. "Little street thief." Then he turns to Christian. "And you. Either you're stealing, too, or too stupid to realize she was."

Christian tries to stammer something but fails. Paulus grabs me by my jacket and pushes me hard against the wall. "What's your story? A thief, or were you planting bugs? You working for the cops?"

"Paulus!" cries Christian.

"Shut up."

"Paulus!" Christian shouts again, stepping forward, the awkward teenager, forcing himself to be brave. "It was me. My fault. I invited her down here. I wanted—I wanted someplace to be alone."

"Bullshit," Paulus says. "Veronika told me she didn't come up with the others."

Christian inhales sharply, rubs his mouth with his hand. "All due respect, Paulus. But Veronika is drunk and stoned. No offense. But you saw it yourself." He gestures toward me. "She said she would, you know, sleep with me tonight. But I couldn't wait. So I said we could sneak down here."

My eyes are trained on the side of Paulus's head as he stares at Christian. Then his hands relax and he lets go of my jacket. "Fucking children," Paulus seethes.

"I'm sorry," says Christian.

Paulus seizes me by the back of the neck and shoves me toward the stairs. I grab the railing and manage not to fall. "You," he says, pointing a trembling finger at my throat. "Get out of my house."

Then he turns to Christian. "And you. You stay right the fuck here."

Sixteen

With my phone plugged into the wall and the power cord stretched as far as it can, I lie on Marina's couch, staring at the screen and the three unanswered messages I've sent to Christian:

Bist du ok?

Bist du ok?

??????????

I typed the first on the U-Bahn back to Marina's, and the second an hour later, and the third an hour after that, the whole time wondering in what ways Paulus was torturing him. The fact is I need Christian. He was my way in. Then I screwed it up for both of us. Without him, there's no more access to the men who took my dad.

And while the thing inside me worries and clenches its teeth at the strategic loss, my heart, my human heart, aches for the boy, just a little. He's a thug, and a sloppy, grabby drunk, but he was brave in the end. He stood up for me. That's worth something, right?

After a long while, I'm able to sleep in fits and starts but wake up every so often to phantom vibrations of the phone resting on my chest. I get up just after dawn, pace the living room, and send Christian another sad, hopeless *Bist du ok?*

I brush my teeth and shower, phone turned all the way up and resting on the edge of the sink. But no reply comes in. As I brush my hair and get dressed, I hear Lyuba and Marina moving around in the kitchen. When I open the door, however, I see a third person standing between them. He has a scrubby red beard and a round, bean-shaped belly. Lyuba points to me, and he cocks the lapels of his denim jacket, taps the toe of his cowboy boot on the floor.

For a while, he and I look at each other silently. Then he turns to Marina and sends a hard slap across her cheek. She lets out the high-pitched but undramatic yelp of someone who's used to this. I watch as she shrinks back, slouching near the kitchen door, the confidence she always wears gone.

The man steps toward me, and I step back into the living room, keeping a few meters between us. Better to be here in an open space if I'm right about what's going to happen next.

"I'm Leo," he says in Russian. "And you call yourself Sofia, is that right?"

"That's right."

Leo nods, steps closer. I don't retreat this time. "The protection tax is three hundred a week. Which is pretty fair, right, Marina?"

She looks up, her cheek red from the slap. "Yes, Leo."

"What's that now?" he says.

"Yes, Leo," Marina repeats. "Very fair."

His eyes narrow. "But for you, with late fees, penalties, I figure a thousand. How about it?"

My muscles tense, poised and at the ready. Whatever fear is in me blurs into the background of my mind, behind the desire to punish this man, behind the knowledge that I'm capable of doing it.

I cant my head to the side. "I'm going to take my things now, Leo. Then I'll walk out the door." My voice sounds certain, even cocky, in a way I've never heard it before. And I like it. "As for my money, it's mine. It belongs to me. That means I'm not going to give it to you."

I step to the side, take up my backpack, and shove my phone and charger and the few things of mine that are lying around inside. Leo is staring at me with an expression of curiosity. I've presented something new to him.

As I move toward the door, I face Leo and turn as he turns, never letting him see my back. Then he makes his move, a sloppy grab for my left arm.

The muscle memory Yael beat into me kicks in. I catch his hand and twist it away from me. Leo's arm is now a lever steering his body to where I want it—groin pushed forward and to the side. I launch my knee into his balls with the force of a baseball bat. As he doubles over, I seize the sides of his head, digging my nails into his hair and scalp, holding him tight.

Two more knee strikes, to Leo's face this time, and on the second strike, I hear something crack. I let him go, and he takes a few steps back, falls to his knees. Then Leo raises his eyes to mine. They shine with humility now. This is what happens, Leo, when you try to take what isn't yours.

Marina's right about Leo being a teddy bear. It took me maybe four seconds to bring him down, and that just isn't acceptable. So I pivot on my right foot and arc my left leg through the air. My toes meet his head at the temple and snap his neck to the side. He does a half turn and collapses, landing hard on the floor.

Leo is unconscious, or near enough that he doesn't protest as

I fish a small pistol from the pocket of his jacket along with a roll of euros. The roll is made of smaller rolls, paper-clipped together, one from each girl on this morning's rounds, no doubt. Leo stares back at me dumbly. Maybe comprehending what's happening to him, maybe not. His nose has swollen to twice its natural size and is the color of eggplant.

Elation washes over me like bath water, and I feel my lips flutter into a profane smile. Behind me, I hear Lyuba shrieking and Marina calling Leo's name.

I stare down at the pistol in my hand. It's a little thing but heavy for its size. There's a sliding mechanism on the side that's meant to be moved with the thumb. An orange dot embedded into the metal reveals itself as I work it. The safety?

Leo stirs on the ground, pawing with his thick fingers through his pockets looking for the gun. I level it at him and pull back the hammer with my thumb until it clicks into place. It's what they do in the movies to get the other guy's attention, and it works. Leo holds out his hands in front of him in surrender, fingers spread, shaking. A voice inside me says to leave now, to leave it at this. But Yael told me a good warrior goddess always finishes what she starts.

Lyuba and Marina rush past me. I expect them to continue beating him, to take out of Leo what Leo took out of them. But Lyuba, tears flowing down her cheeks, takes his head into her lap and cradles him, wetting her fingers with spit to wipe away the blood on his face.

Marina turns to me, red with fury. "Oh, you stupid bitch! No jihad shit, I told you!" She comes in close, unafraid of me, unafraid of the gun. She snatches the roll of money out of my hand. "I worked four years to get it this good."

"He's not going to own me, Marina," I say. "And now he doesn't own you, either. This is your chance. No more Leo."

"There's always another Leo! Ten more by tomorrow! I go some-where else—Paris, Chicago, fucking wherever—look, there's Leo!" She raises her hands to the sides of her head, sinks her fingers into the mass of her hair, and lets out a gasp. "Are you this stupid about the world? You going to stick around and take the other Leos down for us too?"

I blink at her, my mouth wide with shock. "I'm sorry. I thought—I was helping you . . ."

"You get to walk away now. In fact, you'd better. But what hap-pens to Marina when you leave, Sofia? Ask yourself what happens." Marina shoves my shoulders hard, and I stagger back. "Want to be a hero, Sofia? Leave this world you don't understand just as it is. Save your own ass. Let me look after mine."

She bends down, picks up my backpack, and throws it at me. I catch it but remain standing where I am.

Marina points to the door. "Now go fight your war in someone else's house."

Triff mich, reads the text from Christian. Meet me. This is followed by the address of a Turkish restaurant in a neighborhood called Pankow. I agree, setting our date for three hours from now.

Sunlight glares off every surface in little bits of photonic shrapnel, stinging my eyes. It's the first warm day my body can remember. Inside the S-Bahn headed to central Berlin, I lean back in my seat and feel the sun filtered through the dirty window on my face, evaporating the tears. My plan now is to get new pants that don't have Leo's blood on the knee. Then find a cheap hostel where I can take Christian. Nothing fancy. Nothing where they check the passports of Russian girls too carefully.

I am so sorry, Marina. I am so very sorry. The sight of Leo, bloated and bloody, had left me gleeful and proud. It was the right thing to do. I was sure of that. And I'm the one who did it. Strong, powerful me—me the hero of this story. Now, Marina, you'll have to cut Leo's throat to finish the job I started—or not. But either way, it's you I left behind to clean up the blood. I couldn't even be bothered to grab a mop. Please forgive me. Please take Leo's money and run as far and as fast as you can.

But as for Leo's gun, that's in my pocket. Every time I touch it, my breath catches in my throat. Oh, the things we'll do together, you and I.

All is in order. My pants are new and clean, the room is rented, and Christian is at the Turkish café when I arrive. I weave through the room of Turks and Syrians and North Africans who are gathered around tiny copper tables sipping at cups of strong tea in glass mugs with filigreed silver handles. A few men in the back are lounging on low couches with red cushions and passing around a shisha pipe. The smoke smells of apples and reminds me of autumn.

Christian rises to his feet when I walk in and moves with effort as he pulls my chair out. He has a black eye, swollen but not too bad. Bruises elsewhere, though, I'm sure. "I'm sorry about last night," he says shyly.

"*You're* sorry? Christian, *I'm* sorry. It was my fault."

But he waves this away. "Nothing I couldn't take." This said with a kind of pride. He swallows, gives me an anxious smile. "I was worried you wouldn't want to see me again."

I place my hand on his. "You saved me last night. I don't know what he would have done if you didn't step in."

"Look, Paulus said if he sees me with you, I'm out. So this, us, has to be on the down low, okay?"

Hence the Turkish café. "Of course."

The waiter arrives, and Christian orders tea and baklava for us both. "Enough Paulus bullshit. Let's talk about you," he says when the waiter's gone. "Where are you from?"

I give him fleshed-out details from the dossier on Sofia's life I'd read in Paris. What it was like growing up in my part of Russia. Never enough food and too much violence. Papa drank vodka and couldn't find work for two years. Mama died of the flu. "I miss the birch forests and the cranes," I tell him, thinking it sounds like a particularly Russian sort of detail. He nods along, swallowing every bite.

"Not so different, Russia and my part of Germany," he says.

"Oh?" says eager Sofia just as the tea and baklava arrive.

He tells me about his hometown close to the Polish border, deep in what used to be East Germany. Dad left him when he was six, he says, and mom followed two years later. His grandmother, a sour old communist, raised him to believe in the strengthening power of poverty. Shoes always too small, nothing but potatoes for dinner all winter long.

I pick politely at the baklava on the little plate before us. For Christian, life as a petty gangster is an upgrade. Limited-edition leather jackets and dreams of a TV three meters wide will always beat potatoes for dinner.

When I look up, I see he's staring at me, eyes soft, his face very close to mine. Time for me to go to work. Time for me to be bold. "I liked that Veronika," I say. "We talked a lot. Told me all about Gunther and Lukas."

But Christian isn't in the mood for Gunther and Lukas. His chair squeaks on the floor as he moves it close to mine. "You know now, don't you? About the business. About my business. What goes on."

"But that's what I like about you. The world doesn't give you an opportunity, so you just take it anyway. I think you're brave." I lean in closer, put my lips very softly against his. It's a tender kiss, very sweet, and I make sure it lasts a good five seconds before I whisper, "I think it's exciting, the thing that happened."

"The thing?" he whispers.

Another kiss, another whisper. "Paris. Veronika said—Paulus took an American."

But I see right away that I've gone too far. Christian leans back suddenly, looks around, wipes his mouth.

"Yeah, that was—a gig, just a job." He swallows nervously. "Some shit for some Czech. I don't know—it's not something we can talk about, okay?"

I cut him off with my lips on his. Longer this time, I cradle his head. *Some shit for some Czech.* Around us, people turn their heads to gawk.

Christian gently pushes me away. "Jesus, we can't do that kind of thing here."

I push back my chair. "So let's go someplace we can."

Christian walks next to me down a wide boulevard, his hand in mine as I lead him to the hostel. We turn left onto an everyday commercial street of cell phone shops and döner restaurants that leads to the U-Bahn stop a few blocks away.

I catch sight of our reflections in the window of a flower shop and catch someone else's reflection, too. Five or so paces behind us is a very fit guy with Oakley sunglasses covering his eyes. His blond hair is cut short, and he wears jeans and a leather jacket. Nothing wrong with him. Normal. Generic. Just—there. Always five paces behind us.

"We have to be careful," Christian says.

"Yes, we do."

"Is your place far?" he says.

"Two stops," I say.

He's saying something else now, but I don't hear it. My attention is on every shopwindow we pass and the fit guy in the Oakleys. You don't see glasses like those often in Europe. And just then, I pick up another scent, too, this one from across the street. Another very fit guy with short hair, brown this time. No sunglasses on this one, but he's dressed the same way, leather jacket and jeans, like some sort of uniform. He crosses the street and falls into step beside his twin. No talking between them. Just two guys. Again, totally normal.

I give Christian's hand a squeeze. "We're being followed," I say, just loud enough for him to hear.

I feel his body stiffen next to mine, and he steals a casual look over his shoulder.

"Recognize them?" I ask.

"No," he says.

"Friends of Paulus?"

"No," Christian says again. "You better go," he says. "Straight, then right. You'll hit a boulevard in two blocks."

But I need Christian, need whatever information is left in his head. "No. I stay with you."

In any case, it's too late for him to protest. The two men are right there, closing the gap, just a pace behind now. The blond one, just behind Christian, flicks his wrist and a metal baton extends from its handle. I hear it whistle through the air toward the back of Christian's head, but I pull him away and it slams into the meaty part of his shoulder.

The second man circles an arm around my neck, and when I try to drive my elbow into his ribs, he catches it, then slides his hand forward to my wrist. He's pressing me to the ground and buries his knee in my back. Everything Yael taught me is simply of no use.

Christian is brawling with the blond man but not getting very far. His attacker is clearly well trained and is driving heavy boxer's blows to Christian's chest and jaw. Then Christian goes down. His attacker kneels on top of him and—two times, three—smashes Christian's head to the sidewalk.

A large Volvo SUV glides to the curb, and someone opens the back door. My attacker tries to hoist me up, but I wrench away from him. Just as I'm getting to my feet, he spins and lashes out his leg. The sole of his sneaker lands in the center of my stomach, and my breath explodes from my mouth as I fold in two. My vision narrows to a dark tunnel as I stumble backward. I try to catch my breath, but there's only a crushing pain as my lungs gasp for air.

Both men now are coming for me, and I stagger away from them. With what strength I can manage, I feel around in my pockets until I find Leo's gun. The two approach, hands out, ready to grab me. I flip the pistol's safety and level it at a blank spot between them. The pistol leaps in my hand as it fires with a loud crack.

The blank spot between them turns out to be a panel on the Volvo, and a small hole appears on its surface. I fire again, letting off four more shots, one right after the other. There's screaming in the streets now, shouting. People run in every direction except toward us.

Then the attackers are diving into the backseat of the Volvo, and the SUV roars away from the curb with five bullet holes in its side and the back door still open. It disappears a few seconds later, and the sound of its engine is replaced by sirens.

I ran before the cops got there, ditching the gun in a garbage can half a block away. But there was no way in hell I was going to let the only lead I had disappear on me, assuming he was still alive. So I circled the block and stayed near the back of the crowd that had gathered for the show, hoping no one would recognize me, which no one did. An ambulance had arrived, the name of a hospital printed on its side, and I watched as they loaded Christian in. It took off with sirens blaring and lights flashing. Would they do that, I wondered, if he were already dead? Then the police started closing off the area and taking statements, so I slipped away.

I replay it again and again in my mind. Who had the attackers been? Was their target Christian or me? For five hours, I prowl the neighborhood around the hospital named on the side of the ambulance. My plan is fucked, and not only because Christian, if he's still breathing, is likely now in the relative safety of a hospital room. There's also a police car parked in the fire lane outside the hospital's front door. As well as a plain white Volkswagen sedan. Plain until I recognize that it has special license plates and an odd radio antenna. Just police detectives, or someone else?

As I reach hour five of my stakeout, however, I decide to make the only move I have left. I enter the hospital through the emergency room and find a door in the lobby that leads to the rest of the hospital. I inquire about Christian at an information booth. He's been admitted, the clerk tells me. Fourth floor, room twenty-two.

The machines attached to Christian whir and chirp with an even, mechanical rhythm. *He's alive*, every chirp says, *he's alive*. Both his eyes are black, one cheek is misshapen, and his jaw is off center. But there's no ventilator, and the graph of his heartbeat on the monitor has the reassuring certainty of a math problem coming up with the same answer every time.

There's a light tap on the door, and a nurse enters. She has stringy brown hair that doesn't quite touch the shoulders of her green scrubs. Her name tag says URSULA.

"He's going to be all right?" I ask.

She shrugs, then makes a note on a clipboard.

"What's wrong with him?"

"You family?"

I nod.

"Concussion, hairline fracture to his left cheekbone, four broken ribs," she says as if reading off a grocery list.

"Do the police know who did it?"

A sigh from Ursula. "Police are looking for two white men and a Volvo. But there was a woman with the victim, and they're looking for her, too."

"A woman?"

The nurse looks at me for just a moment too long. "American. Some runaway, they said."

I look away but feel her eyes on me. *How did they know?* "When is he expected to come around?" I ask, making my Russian accent as deep as I can.

"Anytime now. The next month will be one long headache, but he should be grateful he's alive." Ursula picks up a small remote control with a single button and passes it to me. "If you're here when he wakes, you can give him this. It's a morphine drip. Press the button; get a treat."

"And what stops him from overdosing?"

"He can only do so many doses per hour. It's enough to take away the pain and get him high as a kite, but no more."

Ursula makes a move toward the door, then stops. "Do me a favor, tell the nursing station when he wakes up."

"Okay."

"There are cops waiting in the cafeteria to talk to him."

My eyes follow her as she exits. She knows who I am. Maybe. Or will figure it out.

I draw the curtains over the windows facing the hallway, then turn to Christian, helpless in his bed. He looks younger like this, unconscious, like a child of ten instead of a thug of twenty. There's a bandage drawn in a tight loop around the crown of his head and his swollen left cheek puffs out like the top of a muffin.

"Christian, wake up," I whisper in German, not bothering with Sofia's accent anymore.

No movement. I rest a hand on his shoulder, one of the only parts of him not bandaged up, and shake him gently.

"You need to wake up, Christian."

His body twitches slightly, and he shakes his head, as if saying no in a dream. So I clasp his shoulder and squeeze, driving my nails into his skin with all the pressure I can manage. Christian's body wiggles, his eyelids flutter open, and the metronome beeping of his heart monitor speeds up. But his eyes settle on me, and even through the swelling, I can see him attempt a smile.

"Do you hurt, Christian?" I ask, gentle as a kindergarten teacher.

He manages a weak nod.

"Do you want me to help make the hurt go away, Christian?"

Another weak nod.

I take up the remote control for the morphine drip and press the plunger. It only takes a few seconds before his face slackens and his eyes turn milky and compliant.

"Tell me where the American is, Christian," I whisper.

His pupils shrink as they focus on me. There's confusion in his face. "What American?" he manages, so quietly I can barely make the words out.

"The American Paulus had kidnapped in Paris."

I hear the tempo of his breathing rise, and his eyes start their confused dash around the room again. "Bad things, Sofia."

My blood goes cold. "What bad things, Christian?"

His mouth opens and closes without sound, a fish on the cutting board. "We do bad things there," he whispers. "At the warehouse."

Gently, I tell myself. Gently. "Is the American there, Christian? At the warehouse? Is the American at the warehouse?"

"I saw him."

"Saw who, Christian?"

"The American."

"At the warehouse? You saw the American at the warehouse?"

He's staring straight up at the ceiling, floating on some narcotic cloud. "Is Sofia a spy?" he says slowly, his face sort of pinching up. A tear forms at the corner of his left eye and breaks loose, running down his temple to his ear. "Tell Paulus I'm sorry that Sofia's a spy. He knew she's a spy. He said she was a sneak. Sofia the sneak."

A delicate decision: press the button on his morphine drip again and risk losing him to unconsciousness, or don't press again and risk him shutting up. I press again. His face slackens, and the milky, compliant look returns to his eyes. He's about to drift off, so I slap his face, lightly at first, then more forcefully. His eyes can barely focus. "Not now, Christian," I say. "No sleep now. Where is the warehouse?"

"Tell Paulus I'm sorry."

"Paulus says he'll forgive you if you tell me."

His eyes look away. I can tell he's fighting the morphine, trying to find where his better judgment has gone. I place my hand on the bandages around his chest where the broken ribs are and press. His body jerks involuntarily, and his eyes focus again. He tries to bat my hand away, but he's far too high and weak.

"Where is the warehouse, Christian?"

His face pinches up with agony, and I press harder. "On Adlergestell," he grimaces.

"Where on Adlergestell? The cross street."

"Jesus, it hurts."

"Answer me or I swear on my mother's soul that I'll kill you in this bed, Christian."

"Dorpfeldstrasse."

I know he's too far gone and that's all the information I'm going to get. As I release my hand, his face relaxes. "Sofia the sneak should be careful," he says through the drugs and whatever's left of the pain. "We do bad things at the warehouse."

"Good night, Christian," I say, and give the button three more clicks.

Seventeen

The ride to Adlergestell and Dorpfeldstrasse lasts one thousand years. A train, a bus, another train, a trolley, and through it all, I run a little play in my head, rehearsing the dialogue of what I'll say when I find my dad, what my dad will say when he's found. Absent are any thoughts of what my dad will look like, or how I'll get him free, or how we'll get away. You can't have a plan until you have facts. Since I have no facts other than a vague location, I'm going to stick to the little play I'm rehearsing for when it all works out, because, let's be honest, a made-up play is probably all it'll ever be.

We do bad things at the warehouse.

I climb off at the Adlershof stop. The neighborhood is one of bad restaurants and suspicious blandness. A pale man in track pants and an undershirt with a cigarette hanging from the corner of his mouth pushes a baby carriage. An Asian guy in a bloodstained butcher's apron leans against a wall drinking beer from a bottle. Beyond a row of trees and a chain-link fence, I hear the huff and shuffle of a commuter train.

The interior is filled with yellow light, sleepy heads in the windows, bobbing as they head home to more prosperous towns beyond Berlin's edge.

A skinny old man with a gray beard, like an emaciated Santa Claus, rides past me on a bicycle, weaving back and forth across the sidewalk like a drunk. From the beat-up radio strapped to his rear fender with duct tape, I hear old German folk music: tubas and trombones, a bass drum, music for his parade of one.

It's mostly apartment buildings here. Nothing that could be described as a warehouse. But then I see it. A small one-story building that looks like an abandoned gas station is hidden deep in an empty parking lot, a place you'd never notice unless you're looking for it. A sign making some vague mention of auto body services and used car parts is nailed up over the door, but that's the only indication of its purpose. I walk past it at first, eyeing it in my peripheral vision to see if anybody's there. There isn't, at least not that I can tell.

There's a garage attached to the building, and a wooden fence higher than my head that seems to extend all the way around to the back of the property. The fence abuts the windowless wall of a small apartment building on one side and an alleyway lined with small, unkempt trees on the other. I walk down the alley, stepping over broken glass and discarded tires and trash, until I notice that the wooden fence extends past yet another building that sits behind the auto body shop. It's much larger and made of brick stained deep brown by at least a century of smog and smoke. Small arched windows peek out from the second story, some of them boarded over.

I test one of the limbs of a tree, then hoist myself up to peer over the fence. Below me, parts of dismembered cars are arranged in tidy stacks, windshields over here, doors over there. The older building faces the junkyard with three large arched doors locked from the outside with chains and padlocks. If there's anything in this neighborhood that can pass for a warehouse where Christian and his friends do bad things, this is it.

From the back, as from the front, the whole compound appears empty. The gathering evening dusk provides good cover, so I swing my legs over the fence and land beside a dozen or so car hoods stacked in a neat pile. Bits of glass pop beneath my boots. I freeze and wait tensely to see if the proverbial junkyard dog is more than proverbial, but there's nothing, only the sound of traffic and my own breathing.

The locks and chains securing the large arched doors of the warehouse are solid and new—gleaming and heavy things designed not to yield easily. But it's the doors and handles themselves that catch my eye. They're old wood and rusted iron, the kind of thing a banker back in New York might pay six thousand dollars to use as a dining room table.

A few seconds of scavenging around the yard is all it takes before I find what I'm looking for: a steel bar about a meter long. I slip it behind the chain of the third arched door and give it a twist so that it works like a tourniquet, tightening the chain against the old iron handles. The metal is stronger than I thought, and I have to put my entire body into it, but after a few moments of pressure, I see the handles start to bend inward toward each other. As I twist, shiny iron nails that have been buried in the wood for a century or more start to appear, millimeter by millimeter. I feel every muscle in my body, from my forearms to my butt to my calves, throwing itself behind the effort. The iron nails groan and screech each time the bar turns; then there's a final pop as the handle on the left surrenders to my strength and springs free of the door.

For just the briefest of seconds, I see a flash of Yael's smile in my head, feel her pride being transmitted like a radio signal from wherever she is now—Paris or Tel Aviv or hell.

· · ·

I swing the door open only a few inches and peek inside. There's an old brown-and-gold-plaid couch, a coffee table made of tires and boards and covered in beer bottles, and a Formica kitchen table near the back piled high with what look like still-sealed iPad boxes. The smell of marijuana and cigarettes and beer follows on the stale air. I slip inside and close the door behind me.

There's only a little light filtering through the small, dirty windows set high in the back wall, so I take out the flashlight on my keychain and bounce the beam around the room. Take-out food containers are littered everywhere, complete with skittering colonies of roaches. There are boxes lining the walls and stacked to the roof marked Johnnie Walker, Marlboro, Apple, Gucci. I shoot the beam through an open doorway into the next room and see even more boxes, scores of them. Whatever it's all worth—authentic merchandise or bootleg— you don't measure it in thousands, but in millions.

I step carefully through the trash on the floor, trying to be as quiet as I can, until I find a staircase connecting the ground level to both the upper floor and basement. It's a question of odds, really: Where would you keep a prisoner, upstairs or down? I head down the staircase, my flashlight beam slicking over crushed-out cigarette butts and food wrappers and a mouse trap snapped shut around a mouse skeleton. There's an open wooden door at the bottom of the staircase, and beyond it, more stacks of boxes.

I enter slowly, ears awake for any sound. The ceiling here is low, with wooden beams running overhead. In the spaces between the beams, fraying electrical wires and a few pipes snake their way around the room.

What I'm looking for I find in the farthest corner of the farthest room. At first, I assume it's a large industrial freezer, the walk-in kind they have in restaurants, except the skin of this one is just squares and rectangles of scrap metal, rusty and welded into place. A door, also skinned with metal, hangs ajar from a single sturdy hinge that runs down its entire side, while a pair of sliding bolts and a massive clasp where a padlock would go are attached to the opposite side of the door. Judging by the construction and the size of the bolts, whatever was put in the room was meant to stay in the room. I pause with my hand on the door and correct my thought: It doesn't look like a freezer; it looks like a gas chamber.

I pull the door open tenderly, somehow clinging to the idea that my dad will be inside, waiting. But of course he isn't.

The walls and ceiling of the cell are lined entirely with old sofa cushions fastened with bolts. Suffocation is the aesthetic theme. Suffocation of screams, suffocation of hope. I find a light switch just outside the room and flip it on. A bulb in a cage is mounted at the center of the ceiling. The place sickens me, but I force my eyes to stay open, to stay cold and impartial. Observe and infer, I tell myself. Learn what you can.

Fact: Two metal rings—dull steel on top, shiny metal on the bottom—are screwed into the concrete floor approximately one meter apart. Inference: The shininess on the undersides of the rings suggests someone had been chained to them, pulling on them repeatedly and for a long time.

Fact: The only space on the walls not covered in cushions is the opening of a small vent near the ceiling where a PVC pipe a few centimeters in diameter runs through the wall. Inference: But for the vent, the place is airtight.

Fact: There is a metal drain in the center of the concrete floor with what initially appears to be substantial amounts of rust around the edge. Upon investigation—scraping at the rust with a fingernail—I determine it's not rust, but blood. Inference: Prisoner was tortured and/or murdered in this room.

I am sure my father has been here. I can still smell him, or think

I can, or imagine I can. The scent is mixed with fear and suffering, and I swear on my dad's life and my mom's memory that I will turn whoever did this into a corpse.

But I'm too close, getting too emotional to be objective anymore. So I wipe away the tears, exit the little cell, and begin scrutinizing the room outside. I pick up stacks of paper resting on top of a row of crates and scan, discard, scan, discard. There's shipping manifests for truckloads of handbags, receipts for pizzas and beer, a magazine of Japanese porn, an instruction manual for a microwave.

But as I get to the bottom of stacks of papers, I notice the crates beneath them. They're made of rough pine and so new I can still smell the sap. Stenciled on the top of each one:

Česká Zbrojovka Uherský Brod
CZ 805 Bren 5.56x45
Made in Czech Republic

I rack my memory, trying to find why there's something familiar about these words. Then it comes to me: the name of the manufacturer of the gold pistol I found in Paulus's bedroom—made in the Czech Republic, limited edition, the sixty-fourth of one hundred. I remember the note, too: an expression of gratitude after the conclusion of a business deal, signed BK. *Boris, or Bandar, or Buh-something.*

There are nine more labeled exactly the same way—*Bren*, it's a kind of gun, isn't it? And two labeled Semtex—also apparently a product of the Czech Republic. After hanging around government types my whole life, I damn well better know what Semtex is. It's a plastic explosive, and the go-to choice for demolition crews and armies and terrorists all around the world. In addition to iPads and Gucci bags and cartons of Marlboros, Paulus has hidden away an arsenal.

Above me, the floorboards creak, and I barely notice it until they creak again. I freeze in place, my ears cocked like a dog's. A footstep. Then another. Someone's here.

I kill the flashlight and look around for an exit, but there's only the staircase. On the floor above, I hear the footsteps of someone trying to move silently. They're slow and carefully placed, made by someone trying to remember where the floorboards squeak and where they don't.

From the top of the stairs, a man's voice calling in German-accented English: "Gwendolyn Bloom. Show yourself, please."

Paulus needs no help navigating the basement in the dark. He knows the place intimately and steps through the maze of trash and crates with ease. He's moving toward the only visible light, the feeble bulb burning in the cell. The door to the cell is wide open and inviting. Come closer, it says. Even closer.

He seems cool and unconcerned, carrying an excellent leather jacket over his right arm, his pistol still holstered under his left.

He stops a meter or so from the cell's entrance and sets his coat carefully on the crates of assault rifles. With hands on hips, he says my name again. You have to dig deep into his tone to find the threat.

A pause as he listens for me, then two steps forward, just a few centimeters from the entrance to the cell. I wonder if he's thinking that I've already left or questioning whether I was ever here at all. Paulus leans forward, sticking his head into the cell. The light from the bulb gleams off his precisely shaved scalp as he turns his gaze from one side of the cell to the other.

It's at this moment both my feet land with perfect accuracy into the small of his back, launching him forward into the cell. He crashes across the floor, the pistol tumbling from his holster and bouncing across the concrete to the far corner.

I release my grip on the copper pipe from which I've swung and seize the door. He scrambles toward me, but I slam the door closed and throw the bolt into place just as his weight hits it. I hear a sound, like a car horn far away, and realize it's his scream of rage, barely audible through the cell's insulation and finding an outlet only through the narrow PVC vent.

The cobwebs are still laced thickly across my clothes and face and hands from where I'd hidden myself between the joists in the ceiling, suspended there horizontally, my ankles over a copper pipe while my hands gripped another pipe, my whole body high above the floor. As Paulus had descended the staircase, I'd climbed atop an old filing cabinet and wedged myself in the tight space, worried the pipes would give out, or that my legs would, or that he'd hear my breathing. But as he entered the room and approached the cell, I was silent and still as the dead.

I pull a battered wooden chair to the side of the cell and stand on it so that I'm close to the PVC vent.

There's silence at first, then a little chuckle. "Do you know what a Yellow Notice is?" he says in English. "It's what Interpol issues when someone goes missing. Like the missing American teenager Gwendolyn Bloom."

I ignore him. It's just his theory. He can't be certain. "Who is that?" I say in Sofia's accented German.

"Not you, then? Well, if you see her, tell Gwendolyn they have turned it into a Red Notice. 'Wanted for questioning in relation to a murder,' it says."

"What murder?" Sofia says.

"The murder of Christian Leitzke." His voice trails off. I hear the clicking of a cigarette lighter, and a moment later, the smell of smoke drifting through the vent. "I'm sorry, hadn't you heard? Found suffocated by a pillow in his hospital bed an hour or so ago. A friend of mine found him and phoned me straightaway."

I close my eyes. Poor Christian. Poor hapless, smitten Christian. Sorry it had to be you. There's no use anymore in pretending. "You do it yourself, Paulus?" I say in English. It's the first time I've heard my natural voice since arriving in Berlin.

"So it is Gwendolyn Bloom I'm talking to!"

"Why'd you kill Christian, Paulus?"

"Had I killed him, it would be for telling you where this building was. But the police have a different idea. A nurse was shown your picture. She said you were a few kilos lighter and your hair was different, but she had no doubt it was you. Congratulations, by the way."

"For what?"

"Losing the weight."

He's trying to egg me on, make me stupid with anger. But I won't let him. I've got him now, and every move I make has to be calculated. I can almost hear the clock ticking on what will be my last chance to bring this whole thing to its conclusion, yes or no, alive or dead. "What did you do with him?"

"Christian?"

"The American."

Silence as Paulus thinks. "He's your family, yes? Same last name."

"Yes," I say.

"Uncle? Father? He's your father, I think. Who seeks revenge for an uncle?"

"I'm not after revenge. I want to find him."

"Find him?" A little laugh from Paulus. "Then I'm afraid today there is more bad news."

I pinch my eyes shut and bite hard into the palm of my hand to stop from screaming.

"The end for him was bad," Paulus continues. "*Schmuddelig.* How to say in English?"

Grimy. Filthy. Nasty. Messy. Horrible. "How did it happen?" I say, my face wet.

"I did it myself. With a knife. Here. In this room. About the body, we drove it east. To a swamp by the border with Poland."

I have to lean into the wall, grab the edge of the cell to keep from falling.

"He spoke of you, you know. Right before I did it," Paulus calls out, clearly enjoying this. "He was begging. 'Please don't,' he said to me. 'I have a wife and children,' is what he said. Screamed it. Crying like a girl."

My eyes flicker open, and I repeat Paulus's words in my head. "What did he say exactly?" I ask Paulus. "The exact words."

"The usual, 'Please don't,' things of this nature. Begging," he says.

"And after that." I say.

"'I have a wife and children.'"

Wife. Children. *Dead. Plural.* "You're certain?"

"*Genau,*" Paulus says. "Precisely this. How could I forget? He was just so goddamn sincere."

I force myself to focus on the texture of the steel wall of the cell, force my breathing to slow down. Paulus lied. Or maybe not. I have to muster the rationality to pull on this thread and find where it leads. But he's also playing a game—keep me listening, keep me talking, keep me here until his friends show up.

I lean in to the vent and speak. "Now I have to kill you, right? Isn't that the way this is supposed to work?"

Another of his confident laughs. "With what? I'm the one with the gun, and even if you had one, there's two centimeters of steel between me and you. Besides, you're not a killer, *Mädchen.* You've got tits but no balls."

I think of the crates of Brens. Can I even get the crates open? Do they come with bullets, or are they sold separately, like batteries? Not that it matters because I have something else in mind anyway.

"Very solidly built, this cell of yours," I say. "So if I plug up this pipe, how long do you think your oxygen will last?"

He's quiet for a moment, absorbing the prospect of suffocating, calculating the cell's volume, his rate of breathing, dividing it all by the number of hours. "At least a day or two," he says finally.

"See, I was thinking a few hours, but then again I'm just a *Mädchen* with tits and math is so very hard for us," I say. "Which is why I thought—let's add fire to the mix. Old building, oily old timbers, lots of shit that can burn. Mind passing me your cigarette lighter through the vent?"

"My friends will be here any minute."

"Your friends love you enough to save you from a burning building, Paulus?" I pick up his jacket and start rifling through it, removing a wallet and a nasty-looking folding knife, both of which go in my pocket. Then I find a pack of gum, car keys, and finally exactly what I was looking for. "Never mind about the lighter. I found matches."

I grab a piece of paper from the floor, a shipping manifest, and twist it into a torch. *"Auf wiedersehen*, Paulus," I say, then light the end and stuff the torch into the pipe.

A muffled scream, terrible and high-pitched, comes out through the pipe. I remove the torch and stamp it out on the floor. "What did you say?"

"It wasn't true," Paulus shouts. "The story about killing him. He's alive. Or he might be."

I freeze in place. A stretched and contorted fool's grin breaks across my face, and I rest my forehead against the wall of the cell. But then, of course that's what he would say. What choice does he have now? I make my voice calm. "What did you do with him?"

"We traded him," he says instantly. "For some guns, other things."

I look at the crates. "What kind of guns? What kind of other things?"

Silence for a moment, then, "Why do you ask this?"

"Paulus, answer me or I'll burn you alive."

"Brens. And an explosive called Semtex."

And there it is. The note. The pistol. Christian's words—some shit for some Czech. All of it makes sense now. "Thank you, Paulus."

"Excuse me?" he says. "I cannot hear you."

I stand on my tiptoes and repeat what I just said closer to the vent.

"Again, please? I'm having trouble hearing you. Speak directly into the pipe if you would."

As I move in front of the vent, an explosion of heat and the roar of ripping air rushes past my left cheek. I topple backward off the chair and land hard on my back. The reek of cordite and sulfur from the gunpowder singes my nostrils.

I raise a trembling hand to my face and find that the bullet didn't touch me. He missed blowing my brains out by millimeters. I pull myself to my feet and take up Paulus's jacket again.

A trickle of smoke like from the burning tip of a cigarette is still curling from the end of the pipe as I climb back onto the chair. He's swearing at me in German, screaming *Fotze* this, *Schlampe* that. He's probably deaf now from firing the gun in such a confined space, so I don't bother saying good-bye as I stuff the jacket into the vent as tightly as I can.

The glass boxes of the Hauptbahnhof glow from within, suggesting less a train station than the X-ray of one. It's transparent except for a steel grid skeleton. All the rest is clear, and I can see the people circulating through it like blood cells.

I am calm as I enter, walking only as fast as the other Berliners—observe, Polizei, how very ordinary and un-murderer-like I am. Inside, it's the sort of calm anarchy that must be unique to Germany, everyone in a polite, sober rush. I mimic the others as closely as I can: moving quickly but not in haste, not smiling but not glowering, either.

An orderly queue for the ticket counter: a Muslim woman with a little boy ahead of me, a college kid with bad acne behind me. Two cops with submachine guns under their arms walk by slowly, eyes on faces. I try not to look away, thinking it will look suspicious if I do, but in the end, I can't help it.

Eighty euros gets me a one-way ticket on the next train to Prague, leaving in twenty minutes from track 14. Once the train leaves, all I have to do is keep to myself for about four hours until we cross the Czech border and I'll be safe, or at least safer than I am here.

But that's still twenty minutes away. And tonight the Hauptbahnhof is Cop Land. They're everywhere. Mean-looking guys in dark blue jumpsuits with machine guns and dogs, as well as smart-looking guys in suits with badges around their necks. I doubt the American teenager wanted for questioning in a murder is putting the city on lockdown, but I have to assume they've heard my name, and it's a good bet they've seen my picture.

The bathroom stall reeks, but at least it's out of anyone's sight. I lean against the door and go through Paulus's wallet. There's a condom, an ID card, and a sheaf of almost a thousand euros.

I know I'm going to regret leaving Paulus alive. Yael would have had me kill him, no question. She would have had me burn the warehouse down around him and not give it a second thought. And I wanted to. As badly as I've ever wanted anything. I was even going to do it. But Paulus was right about me at least in that sense: I'm no killer. Not because I can't, not because the thing inside me won't let me, but because it's the one barrier I haven't yet vaulted over on my way to the abyss. I will preserve that little corner of my seventeen-year-old self, that narrow slice of Gwendolyn Bloom, for as long as I'm able.

After fifteen minutes, I leave the stall and head toward track 14. Everything I took from Paulus's jacket except the cash and the folding knife lands in a trash can on the way.

The cops are out in force in the bowels of the station, too, measuring up everyone on the platform, letting their dogs sniff around the luggage. Is it possible they have my scent?

The whoosh of the train approaches like a descending angel, and I hang back a little until the angel issues an electronic chime and the doors slide open. I step through the doors two seconds before they close. There's a hiss of brakes, another chime, and a muffled announcement. Then we start moving.

I find an empty second-class compartment and drop into one of the window seats. Outside the platform is streaking by, cops heading for the stairs, a few latecomers throwing up their arms in fury for being latecomers.

There's no one else in the compartment, but I raise my hand to hide my smile as I lean back and put my boots up on the seat across from me. The platform becomes a dark tunnel, which becomes a weedy urban neighborhood, which becomes the suburbs, which becomes the countryside.

I've escaped.

PRAGUE

Eighteen

I sleep a little, the dense, frosting-covered sleep of the victorious. There was a ticket check a few minutes after we left the station in Berlin, but no one's bothered me since. And so, after victory comes the reward. In this case, a dream. It's one of those dreams you know is a dream from the very first, and so you shush the voice that says none of it is real in the hope that the dream will go on and on and on.

I am on a train just like this train, riding through countryside just like this countryside. The announcements come over a staticky loud-speaker: *Queensboro Plaza, Thirty-Ninth Avenue, Thirty-Sixth Avenue.* The N train as it jostles and wobbles and rockets through a version of Queens replaced by rural Germany. At the Broadway and Thirty-First Street stop I am joined in my little compartment by Terrance.

"Is this seat taken?" he says, indicating the one next to me. He's wearing the pressed khakis and turtleneck sweater from the day I saw him in the record shop. I open my mouth to speak, to tell him it's me, Gwendolyn, but no words come out.

He doesn't seem to recognize me and at first I'm alarmed, but then I understand. How could he? I'm no longer the same girl he knew in New York. Just as my voice is about to come back, he puts on a pair of headphones. But because it's a dream, I hear the music, too. It's a slow, sad, lovely piece by Miles Davis. Just trumpet and a scratchy drum at first, then a polite, unobtrusive piano, then a saxophone starts in.

Then we're not on the train anymore, but behind the steamy windows of that bar at the Waldorf Astoria, the one I've only ever seen from the sidewalk. The saxophone hands off the melody to the trumpet and picks up the harmony, like a conversation between the two: warm, civilized, the saxophone nodding to the trumpet, *I understand, I understand.*

We are sitting in a tufted banquette, alone amid a crowd of rich people. It's late. I'm tired. I lean into him. He smells of cologne and normalcy.

A waiter approaches—bow tie, white shirt, vest. "Dresden," the waiter says, and I wake up.

We're pulling into the Dresden station, and a few people shuffle off and on. Newcomers scan across each compartment, looking for someone quiet or chatty or nice or worth hitting on. I scowl and spread out, trying to look as hostile and unappealing as possible, and mostly it works. A thin guy with brown hair pulled into a greasy ponytail pauses in the doorway, studying my face before moving on. He seems to be looking for someone specific, and I'm not her.

The train chuffs and begins moving again, the homes and graffiti-covered buildings of Dresden's bad part of town slipping by. I heard it had been a gorgeous place before World War II—like Florence, Italy, except in Germany. Beautiful, medieval, irreplaceable. But a few months before the war ended, the Yanks and Brits firebombed the whole thing, burned it to the ground, boiling tens of thousands of soldiers and workers and mothers and children alive in their own skins. I read about it once in a book by Kurt Vonnegut.

I pull out my phone and send a text to Terrance: On a train and fell asleep. Had a dream about you.

A reply comes back exactly twenty-seven seconds later. O rly? What about?

Miles Davis was playing, I write back. We were at Waldorf. The bar.

A longer wait for a reply this time. It's afternoon in New York. I picture him sitting in class, thumbing his response under the desk. I think abt u a lot.

I smile, blink a few times. I think abt u too.

Anything u need. Im here.

Strangely, I believe it. It's an absolute in my mind, an axiom, that though I hardly know the guy, he means what he says. Then, as if reading my thoughts, a follow-up:

I can come and b with u. Help u. I'll get on a plane. B there tomorrow.

Even though I'm alone in the compartment, I spread my hand across my face so no one can see the expression on it, which is mine and mine alone, torture and gratitude all at once.

Thank u. Maybe soon. Not now.

The truth is, I want him here desperately, but I know better. I know that what's coming next will be infinitely harder than what's come before and a soft Upper East Side kid won't last a second. The help he could provide—his skills, his resources, his kindness—would all be squandered here.

I start to type something back, but it's too long and too sincere. It's the kind of thing that should only be said face-to-face. So I delete it. Damn my luck, having to go off to war when all I want to do is run away with that beautiful boy and live off wild berries and love.

. . .

The train moves past the outskirts of Dresden, picking up speed, the buildings becoming a blur. Close to the border now. We'll be in Prague in an hour. The conductor comes through again, and I can hear the clicking of his ticket puncher as he works his way through the new passengers who just got on.

I grab my backpack and head to the restroom, where I wash my face, cleaning off the dried Berlin sweat.

A knock on the bathroom door: polite, inquiring.

"Einen Moment," I say.

Another knock, more insistent.

"Einen Moment!"

And one more knock, just to piss me off.

I yank the door open to find the guy with the ponytail who got on at Dresden. There's maybe three or four days' worth of stubble on his face and a small pistol in his hand.

"Step back," he says in English.

I try to slam the door shut, but he shoulders it open again.

"Get the fuck against the wall," he seethes, one hand gripping me by my jacket lapel, the other leveling the pistol at my face. He squeezes himself into the tiny bathroom and kicks the door closed behind him.

The man's English isn't native, and his accent isn't German. Still, I have to assume this is a gift from Paulus, which means Paulus has somehow gotten free. It wasn't all that hard to figure out where I'd be headed, so one phone call later a friend meets the train in Dresden. I should have burned the fucker alive.

"Here's what will happen," the guy says. "We will soon cross the border into Czech. At the first stop, you and I will get off the train. We will do this quietly, and without making trouble. Clear?" His left hand paws over my body and through each pocket in a quick frisk for weapons. The knife I took from Paulus—where is it? The backpack. Sitting next to the sink.

The lights above the mirror flicker with the motion of the train, which is slowing down. I feel myself tilting toward the back of the car and suppose we're climbing a hill. My new friend with the gun shifts his weight to brace himself.

"How much is Paulus paying you?" I ask.

"What?"

"How much is Paulus paying you? Maybe I can top it."

"Who's Paulus?"

I make a calm assessment of the situation and try to think of what Yael would advise. As I was so many times in training, I seem to be in a position of absolute disadvantage. He has a gun; I have nothing.

I eye my backpack and nod in its direction. "Do you mind if I get something out of there?"

"No."

"No you don't mind, or no I can't get something out of there?"

His eyes narrow with confusion. "No—you cannot."

"I need a tampon," I say in English, then with the German pronunciation, *"Tahm-pohn."*

He gets the gist of it and grimaces. "You wait."

"Not the way it works. I need it quick. Right now. Otherwise it's going to be very gross for both of us."

He hoists the backpack and starts rifling through it.

"Make sure it's not one of the used ones."

He blinks at me in confusion, shuffling through whatever notecards he has in his mind on the topic of women and tampons. Then he shoves the backpack at me and brings the muzzle of the gun close to my face. "You get it," he says. "But do not try anything."

I take up the backpack—heavy with clothes, toiletries, everything

I own—and give him a submissive, reassuring smile. We never break eye contact, my new friend and I, as I dig through it and find what I'm looking for, Paulus's knife. "Thanks," I say.

As he starts reaching for the bag, I thrust it hard at his face. His gun hand swings toward me, but I grab the pistol and twist it away, snapping his trigger finger all the way back. The shout of pain is nearly deafening.

Somehow he finds space to swing his left fist, and it lands on the side of my head as I reach for the door. The pistol tumbles from my hand and into the space beside the toilet. I lash out with the knife, but he dodges it easily and sends his knee into my stomach.

I get the door open, snatch my backpack, and stumble into the train's corridor, but he's right there, attached like a shadow. I slash at him with the knife again, but he dodges it and grabs me from behind, circling an arm around my neck while his other hand, the one with the broken trigger finger, takes hold of my right wrist. He twists my hand so that the knife is pointing at my chest, and he begins the slow work of bringing the blade closer and closer. I resist him the whole way, but with his arm still tight around my neck, my oxygen is dwindling.

The train rattles and screeches around a curve. Outside, I see lights from a few houses blur past. We're picking up speed again as we head out onto what I presume is a straightaway.

The knife is just a few centimeters from my chest now. My oxygen is gone, and so is my strength. With everything I have left, I fire my left elbow back into his side where his kidney is and bring the heel of my boot onto his toes. He flinches, and for just a quarter of a second, releases the pressure on my hand and neck long enough for me to break free. I pivot around and slam the sole of my boot into his stomach. The air rushes from his lungs as his body closes up around itself.

I dash along the train's corridor toward the front of the car and pull desperately on the lever of the door, but it's stuck or I'm too panicked to figure out how to open it. I glance behind me and see my friend moving toward me. He's retrieved the pistol and is aiming it at me in his outstretched left hand.

"Drop the knife," he says.

I look down at the useless knife in my hand, and hear Yael's words from my training: run from the knife, rush toward a gun.

On the wall next to me is a metal hatch with EMERGENCY BRAKE written on it in Czech, German, and English. I open the hatch, grip the red handle, and pull as hard as I can.

The power and speed of it shocks me. The air is filled with a terrible squeal of steel biting into steel as the wheels lock up on the tracks, and everything seems to bend forward. I'm pressed into the car's door and see the gunman careening toward me at the same speed the train was going a moment before.

He slams into me with the force of a truck, and my knife plunges deep into his chest. Then the gunman's body slips to the floor, his last emotion, utter surprise, painted on his face. Through the windows in the doorway between cars, I see a pair of what I assume are Czech border cops rushing toward me.

I close the slippery folding blade, slide it into my pocket, and pull the train doors open. The cool air of the Czech night hits my face and invites me into the darkness.

It's a good meter or so to the ground, and my feet land hard in the brush. Then I'm half running, half tumbling down a hill, toward the town below me. I crash over a rotting log, and find myself on my back, facing the train. A cop stands silhouetted in the doorway, the beam from his flashlight bouncing around the weedy hillside. Then he jumps down to the ground, braces his flashlight over a drawn gun, and sweeps back and forth through the brush. I hold my breath and stay perfectly still as the beam passes just in front of me. Suddenly the light clicks off and the cop climbs back inside. Why aren't they coming after me? Not their jurisdiction? Waiting for backup? Afraid of the dark? I have no idea, but I'll take any opportunity I can find because it sure as hell won't be long before the entire police force comes rushing in like floodwaters.

I crouch beside a garage, certain someone will hear me panting. My hands, my arms, my whole body is shaking violently, convulsing, struck by a seizure made up of at least two species of fear: fear of the cops, and fear that the murder I've just committed will never stop replaying itself in my mind. The blood covering my hands and clothes appears black like the ink from Hamid's chest. When I try to wipe it off, it just spreads around like grease. How easy it had been, how casually I had reached out and pulled the emergency brake. Newton's first law of motion had done the rest: an object in motion tends to stay in motion. My physics lesson for the day.

Then the convulsing of my limbs stops, and the steam that clouds my mind clears as cold rationality steps in once more. Evaluate the situation, form a plan, take action.

I walk as quietly as I can along the edge of a hillside where it butts up against a row of small garages and yards. I can smell a river not too far away, the polite stink of fish and rotting plant life. From here it looks like a small, drama-free town, and I can see through the back windows of tidy houses where tidy families are already in for the evening. A mother, a father, and a daughter of maybe six eat dinner at a table. A woman watches TV on a couch while the man next to her reads a book through glasses perched on the end of his nose. A trio of teenagers plays video games while the mother of one of them fusses through a stack of bills in the next room. What would they think, these tidy families, knowing a murderer still covered in her victim's blood was passing by, watching them through their windows?

The curve of the hillside moves farther from the train tracks, and

I follow it, keeping out of the street and to the little dirt alleyway behind the garages. This would be the route taken by teenagers and secret lovers, and it is thankfully dark and mostly invisible.

It doesn't take me long to find what I'm looking for: a string of four dark houses in a row at the end of a block, the occupants either not yet home for the night or out of town. I pick the third one in the row and peer through a rear window, scanning it for signs of life. A black cat lounging on a couch, aristocratic as a queen, stares back at me with bored eyes. She yawns, rises, and walks gracefully to a row of four bowls of food set out for her on the floor.

Four bowls. It might mean her owners are away. I knock gently on the back door just in case, watching through the window to see if anyone stirs, but all remains motionless except the cat.

The blade of my knife slots into the little gap between the door and the jamb right where the lock is. I tug back on the knife's handle and hear the wood groan. On the third pull the doorframe gives with a muffled crack.

I push the door shut behind me, and the cat, curious now, approaches and does a figure eight between my ankles. I scratch her head and have a look around. In addition to the four bowls of food, I find a pie tin of water and a pile of mail beneath the slot in the front door.

It appears two teenage boys share a room on the second floor and sleep in bunk beds. There are magazine pictures of cars and girls in bikinis and a poster of Jay Z tacked to the walls. Their closet is fruitful hunting ground. I grab a T-shirt and jeans from the younger one's stuff and a green coat that looks like my mom's army jacket that I left in Paris as I made my hasty escape.

In a small, windowless bathroom, I turn on the light. The blood on my hands and forearms and chest and belly and face is drying into a nice shit-brown paste. I strip and ball all my clothes except my boots into a trash bag. Then I scrub at the blood on my body with a stack of hand towels. The only ones within reach are the embroidered kind with little reindeer and snowmen on them, the ones reserved for company at Christmas. I feel bad about that, ruining the family's good guest towels.

In the cabinet under the sink, I find some barber's clippers and go to work on my hair, shearing it off to about a centimeter in length, so short I can see my scalp through it. It's a good, if primitive, disguise; once I put on the stolen clothes, I look like a teenage boy, at least from a few meters away. I'm hoping it'll be enough to pass through the streets without cops taking a second look.

I collect the hair and wash the blood from the sink with toilet paper and cleanser from the cabinet. Then I retrace my steps, wiping everything I've touched. I tell myself it's to erase the evidence, but it's more than that. I don't want this family dirtied by my visit. They're part of a cleaner world than I am, and the sickness in me might be contagious.

I walk north of the little town, figuring the cops will focus on points south, closer to Prague. At a truck stop a few kilometers away, a Polish truck driver named Witold agrees to drive me to Prague for ten euros. We haggle for it in our elementary German, the only linguistic overlap we can find. He is unfailingly polite on the hour-long ride to the city, guilty of nothing more than singing along to Led Zeppelin and Aerosmith on the radio. But even for this he apologizes and offers me half a liverwurst sandwich in compensation.

Witold drops me off just west of the Vltava River within sight of a bridge he says will lead me to the Old Town. *"Das Prag, das du dir vorgestellt hast,"* he says. The Prague you see in your imagination. He smiles at me as I climb down, wishes me good luck and to be careful. He's the first normal person I've known in months, and I wish I could continue on with him to wherever he said he's headed.

A trolley wrapped in ads for Samsung shuffles along the bridge, its interior lights pulsing. From somewhere comes the baritone clang of a church bell, eleven times, twelve. Midnight in Prague, and the bridge is still full of teenage couples, somehow still in love after a whole month. A guy offers to sell me weed or coke or heroin, whatever I'm looking for. Another guy lies facedown on the ground, a hat with a few coins in it cupped in his outstretched hands.

There's a café on the other side, and through the windows, I see warm yellow light and old-fashioned waiters in bow ties and aprons serving plates of steaming food and tall glasses of beer to a well-dressed crowd. Where have they all come from—the opera? A play? The idea of food is, by necessity of my circumstances, an afterthought. But somehow I'm hungry, less for a dinner of duck and dumplings than for the steaming, delicious company of decent people. Briefly, but only very briefly, I consider going in, but I can't risk being seen. For all I know, I'm famous by now, my face slathered all over television, wanted for murders in two countries.

Flashing lights from a cop car partially blocking the street in front of me. It's probably something dull and routine, but this new me has to avoid all cops, and so I do, turning down a narrow side street where I disappear into invisibility and stumble back in time a few hundred years. The street here is cobblestone, with narrow ruts worn in parallel lines where centuries of horse-drawn carts and, later, automobiles have passed, each one taking a little of the street away with them. My footsteps echo against the walls of medieval buildings on either side, drowned out only by the grinding motor of a scooter as it flies past.

The street divides, and I take the route on the left, only to circle back to where I started. So I take a right instead, and that street, too, ends up dividing and dividing again. There's no logic to it, only a complex anarchy, as if the city grew from the ground like a forest, all chaos and organic beauty.

And then I stumble out into a square and very nearly gasp at the sight. Witold was dead right. Here it is, the Prague you see in your imagination. It's a fairy tale of amber light and stone worn smooth by time and the hands of countless millions of visitors seeking to touch beauty. Damn my luck for seeing it in the context of my circumstances. I'm jealous of the knots of tourists dumbly making their way from out-door café to outdoor café, of the families posing for pictures, even of the boys drinking beer and leering at the girls.

Somehow I break myself free of the sight and focus on practical priorities, the first of which is where I'll bed down for the night. A hotel or hostel is out of the question if the police have my identity, and I have to assume they do. I'll keep an eye out for another version of Marina, but I can't count on being that lucky two cities in a row.

I wander a bit away from the crowds and discover a tiny, curving side street with a building on one side and a wall about three meters tall on the other. I have no idea what's behind the wall. Maybe a park or a courtyard, someplace private without junkies or crazies. I look around and see I'm alone on the street, then grab hold of a carriage lamp jutting from the wall and lift myself up. From the top of the wall it looks like a private park, like a smaller version of Gramercy in New York, but it's hard to tell in the darkness. Not knowing what's below me, I lower myself slowly, trying to be as quiet and careful as I can.

My feet touch something hard, but as I put my weight on it, it shifts. I feel around with the toes of my boots until the strength in my fingers gives way, and I fall to the ground. Probing around in the dark, I feel narrow slabs of stone jutting up at odd angles from the earth and packed together as closely as crooked teeth.

It's a cemetery.

I close my eyes, force the little girl fear away, and open them again. It's just another place, I tell myself, and a private one at that. The yard is dense with gravestones, as if they were a crop in some morbid, overgrown garden. I pick my way over them to an open pathway just touched by moonlight. The stones, I see now, are mostly in Hebrew, and the dates on them are hundreds of years old. The ground is hilly and packed to the point of bursting with the bodies underneath, no doubt stacked five, eight, a dozen high.

For only a moment, I consider climbing back over the wall. But the fact is, I'm not going to find anywhere else more welcoming than this tonight, and I have more real things than ghosts to worry about. I find a place between two rows so close to each other I have to lie on my side. The stones are still warm from the heat of the day and feel almost soft against my body. You're welcome here tonight, traveler, they seem to say.

I pull my jacket tightly around me and go to sleep among the dead.

A quiet, dreamless night passes, as if I were just one more of the lifeless bodies here. The ground is soft and the tombstones' embrace tight, allowing me a cleaner, deeper sleep than I've had since Paris.

I wake up to sunshine and the prodding end of a shovel tapping the bottom of my boot. As my vision clears, I see that the shovel is held by an old man with white hair wearing blue workman's overalls. He addresses me in what I take to be Czech, then in slow English. "No drunks here, okay? Go back to where you come out."

"I just needed a place to sleep," I say slowly, showing him my hands so he sees I'm not a danger. "My money and passport were stolen. Understand? Stolen?"

"You are English? American?"

"Yes," I say. "I mean no. I speak English. A little." I'm not sure who I should pretend to be.

He squints at me as if peering past the short haircut and teenage boy's clothing. "You are a girl," he says, more to himself than to me.

"I meant no harm, sir," I say.

"If your money and passport are stoled, maybe I call police for you."

"No," I say too quickly, then force a smile. "No thank you. I will call them myself. Later."

The deep wrinkles around his mouth purse up, a decision being made inside his head. "Maybe you need food?"

"I'll be okay," I say. "Thank you anyway."

"A little breakfast," he says. "Then you go."

He's the caretaker of the place with a little apartment above the museum attached to the cemetery. It's Saturday, he tells me, the Sabbath, so there will be no visitors today.

I sit at a little table while he fusses with some bread and cheese at a wooden counter. There's a boxy old TV on the table next to me; it's playing the morning news. I can't understand the reporter, but they cut to a shot of my train the evening before and a police crew with dogs working down the hillside where I'd fled. Don't turn around now, I will the old caretaker. Wait for the weather report. The shot cuts to two men carrying a stretcher bearing a body beneath a black plastic sheet.

The caretaker sets a platter of thick orange cheese and rough rye bread on the table. He sits, then tucks a napkin into the collar of his coveralls and makes a sandwich. "You hear about this, maybe?" he says, tilting his head to the TV. "A killing, some man on the Berlin train."

"Do they—know who did it?"

"Who make the killing?" The caretaker shrugs. "If they know, they do not say."

My shoulders relax a little with relief. Maybe they really don't know who did it. Or maybe they just aren't letting on. Either way, I'm in the clear for the moment.

"About your passport," the caretaker says. "More easy if I call police for you. You have not Czech."

I smile politely. "You are kind, but no thank you."

The furrows around his eyes deepen as he chews. Is it suspicion or something else? Then he smiles a little. Crooked yellow teeth, two of them capped with gold. "Are you Jewish?" he says.

"My parents were."

"Jews understand sometimes no police is better," he says. "It is, for us, bad history."

"I'll be fine on my own," I say.

"In Praha, many criminals," the caretaker says, using what I assume is the Czech name for Prague. "Criminals hitting, taking, you know?" He gestures broadly, as if to encompass the whole world. "But bad for alone womans most."

"Thank you for the warning."

"I know someone. Hedvika. She is in Praha 10, Vrsovice—not far. She has place. You take, maybe. Small money only. You have small money?"

"I do."

The caretaker rummages through a pile of papers until he finds a torn envelope and a pencil. "Maybe Hedvika is good for you. Not too much questions. For her, no passport, no problem."

The caretaker, I think, is no stranger to this world where *sometimes no police is better.* He hands me the paper with the address scrawled across it. From his description, it seems like precisely what I need: a room in an old woman's house, cheap and on the down low.

When breakfast is finished, I clean the dishes, the only thing I can offer him in return for breakfast and his kindness. As the caretaker sends me off, I shake his hand stiffly.

"Thank you," I say.

He nods gravely. "Careful in Praha."

Nineteen

From a cigarette kiosk I buy a transit pass, along with three new SIM cards. The directions the caretaker gave me are easy enough to follow, and soon I find myself in a little neighborhood of little apartment buildings in Prague 10, old but well kept.

The woman, Hedvika, is ancient and has the globular body of a snowman. In her colorless smock that is either a dress or a nightgown, she shows me around the small three-story building she runs as a rooming house. It's an old place but scrubbed to within an inch of its life. Here, she explains in German—a good lingua franca in this part of Europe—is the kitchen. All may use the icebox, but stealing is grounds for eviction. Here is the sitting room, no smoking, no loud television. Here is your room, no overnight guests, payment in advance every Monday by noon. We work out an agreement: twenty-five hundred crowns or a hundred euros a week, either currency is fine. I pay her for the first week, and she leaves me alone. She never even asks for a name.

There's not much space in the room and not much furniture. It's little more than a cell, really. A bed built for one, a wooden chair, a wooden table, and a small, three-drawer bureau for clothing. The bathroom is down the hall, and I'll have to share it with the men, Hedvika says, so always lock the door and don't leave my underwear lying about.

Guys who look like they might be Vietnamese and Syrian and Latino mumble hello as they pass me in the hallway. Workers with no papers, maybe. But hard to tell. Just people who need a room, *no passport, no problem.*

I'm exhausted and want to sleep, but I won't let myself. There's too much to do. I've jumped to the conclusion that my dad is in Prague, but the evidence is only circumstantial. A few bits of conversation with Veronika and Christian. A note to Paulus signed *BK*. Some crates of guns. The claims of a man who believed I was going to kill him if he didn't tell me what I wanted to hear. After only a few unproductive minutes of sorting it out, the tiny room starts to feel claustrophobic, and I head out to wander and think.

A sky the color of a battleship weighs down over Prague, putting a steel shield between the city and the sun. It might rain, or the sky might just collapse down on us, hard to tell which. I have a soul-deep desire for something, but I don't know quite what: a ray of sunlight or a glass of orange juice or just a goddamn flower.

I stumble upon a small park with a playground in the corner. There's a little girl in a pink dress hanging upside down on a jungle gym while an older woman, her grandmother maybe, reads a book on a bench. It's about as cheery a sight as I can hope for right now, so I sit down on the ledge of a low wall not too far away and watch.

The little girl says something in Czech, then repeats it, louder this time. *Look at me,* I assume. The grandmother looks up and smiles and nods, then throws a look in my direction. She pretends to turn her gaze back to her book, but I can tell I'm on her radar of dangers. After another minute, she gets up, gathers the girl, and leads her away, casting a glance over her shoulder at me as they move down the sidewalk.

A solo raindrop, a scout for the rest of the storm, lands on the knee of my dirty jeans, spreading out into a little circle of darkness. Another one catches my scalp, and tickles through what's left of my hair and down my neck. I close my eyes and picture Tompkins Square Park and Terrance on that afternoon just before everything turned to shit.

I pull out my phone, install a new SIM card, and dial his number. There's a hiss in the sound of his phone ringing that only emphasizes the hours and ocean between us.

His voice is quiet, like at the far end of a tunnel. "Hello?"

"It's me," I whisper.

The static of distance, of signals moving through storm clouds, through space, through satellites, and down again.

"It's—me, too," he says.

"We know who we are," I say.

"Still. Dangerous to talk."

"I'll get a new SIM when we're done."

"Did you find—accomplish it?"

"Not yet. But I'm close. Well, closer than I was."

"Can I help?" he asks.

"Yes," I say. "Can you chat online soon?"

"Twenty minutes?"

"Fine. The usual way, Tor proxy."

"Is that why you called?"

"Partly."

"And the other part?"

I close my eyes, feel my eyelids becoming hot, feel my breath catch in my throat. It means everything to me that for this moment another human being is with me, listening to me, even if he's as far away as the moon. "Just, you know, to hear someone normal."

"Are you all right?" he asks.

"Yes," I lie.

Connecting to Tor Servers

Anonymousprox.altnet01.Rhymer (Japan)

CaravanServ.hamd08.SamizdatGambol (Serbia)

MacherKurland.glick04.Storytime (Canada)

BigMacMcGarey.Alerform03.Gambol (Jordan)

<<Congratulations! You are now connected to Tor Anonymous Chat!>>

<<Entering Private Mode / Secure>>

<<AnonUser Red is now connected>>

AnonUser Red: thanx for helping

AnonUser Scholar: no prob so great to hear ur voice

AnonUser Red: need your mad hacker skills

AnonUser Scholar: skills not mad but I can try

AnonUser Red: not much to go on

AnonUser Red: czech guy with initials bk

AnonUser Red: sends gun and bombs to Germany

AnonUser Scholar: terrorists???

AnonUser Red: no

AnonUser Red: maybe. Idk.

AnonUser Red: arms traffickers I think

AnonUser Scholar: what else?

AnonUser Red: that's it

AnonUser Red: all I got

AnonUser Scholar: serious?

AnonUser Red: YES!!

AnonUser Red: sorry frustrating fr me to

AnonUser Scholar: give me five

AnonUser Red: ???

AnonUser Scholar: minutes

AnonUser Red: u there?

AnonUser Red: u there?

AnonUser Red: U THERE?

AnonUser Scholar: one min

AnonUser Red: k sorry

AnonUser Red: ??????????????

AnonUser Scholar: shit takes time!

AnonUser Scholar: this is what I got

AnonUser Scholar: lots of ppl with initials bk

AnonUser Scholar: but one guy is big czech criminal

AnonUser Scholar: name is Bohdan Kladive

AnonUser Scholar: sorry Bohdan Kladivo not e at end

AnonUser Red: holyu shit

AnonUser Red: are u sure?

AnonUser Scholar: criminal records to 1992

AnonUser Scholar: arms trafficking

AnonUser Scholar: and human trafficking are the big ones

AnonUser Scholar: big kingpin now

AnonUser Scholar: pablo escobar level shit

AnonUser Red: for real? how do you know?

AnonUser Scholar: yea all of it in interpol database

AnonUser Red: mind=blown

AnonUser Red: how did u get into Interpol database?

AnonUser Scholar: ;)

AnonUser Scholar: kidding its public

AnonUser Scholar: kinda

AnonUser Scholar: just need to knw how to search it

AnonUser Red: still youre a genis!!!!

AnonUser Red: genius

AnonUser Scholar: gracias but it was no prob

AnonUser Red: where does kladivo live?

AnonUser Red: ??

AnonUser Scholar: he's super dangerous

AnonUser Scholar: no fkng way

AnonUser Red: need to know

AnonUser Red: pls

AnonUser Red: fucking PLEASE

AnonUser Scholar: no address for him

AnonUser Scholar: probably moves a lot

AnonUser Red: what city

AnonUser Red: just the city

AnonUser Scholar: Praha 1

I switch over to a normal unsecured browser and Google Bohdan Kladivo. Links to article after article appear on the screen. *In Praha, many criminals.*

The stories in the Czech press focus on Kladivo's local dealings. His stake in Prague's casinos. His connections with judges and police officials and powerful figures in the Czech government. There's a sensational headline from a Prague tabloid, and the translation comes back: JUDGE FOUND BEHEADED IN KARLOVY VARY. It's a gruesome piece, complete with pictures. Another article speculates on the group's deep reach into Prague's petty street crime and features a profile of one pickpocket who refused to pay tribute to Kladivo and had his right hand cut off with a circular saw.

My eyes close. The idea of my dad being held by men like these—but I break the thought off. Don't think that. Stay productive.

Then I dig further, beyond the articles in the Czech press. I find a piece in the *New York Times* linking Kladivo to arms smuggling in

Sudan and Iraq and Syria. In the *Guardian* I find a diagram showing the routes of Kladivo's mysterious cargo flights—Russia to Syria, then Syria to Moldova, then Moldova to China—contents of the planes unknown.

I scroll to the next article, this one in *Der Spiegel*. It claims Kladivo's organization handpicks women and children from Eastern Europe and Russia for lavish auctions, in which the victims are sold off to wealthy clients around the world. *Fleischkurator*, the article labeled him. Curator of flesh is one way to translate it. Curator of meat is the other.

But my own flesh goes cold when I arrive at an article in the *Economist* only a few days old about how Kladivo was already transforming the nature of organized crime in Europe—creating new supply channels, innovating decades-old systems—mere weeks after the death of his former boss, the Serbian crime lord Viktor Zoric.

The man I'd seen a picture of on my dad's laptop. The man with a bullet hole the size of a dime in his forehead. "Very bad things," my dad had said when I'd asked him what Zoric had done. "The worst things."

I start back to Hedvika's place. Now that I know I'm in the right city, and after the right man, I have to figure out how and where to find him. Flashes of faces and bits of conversation play back through my mind. Hedvika telling me rent is due Monday, in crowns or euros, either currency is fine. The caretaker as he eats his breakfast and warns me about Praha's criminals, *bad for alone womans most*.

As I pass a shop, an old man staggers out from beneath the entryway, a liver-spotted hand outstretched, and asks me something in a weak voice. I'm about to veer around him, but then I don't. Karma being what it is, I dig through my pockets for a little change, but all I find is a few bits of paper, a book of matches, and the deck of playing cards I took with me from New York. I reach into the pocket of my jeans, find a few coins, and give them to the old man.

The deck of playing cards.

I pull it from my pocket and turn it over in my hands.

It is the beauty of Prague 1 that draws the tourists, and it is the tourists who draw the criminals. You see it all around the world, everywhere fat tourists gather. They're like a natural resource, wild berries just waiting to be picked.

From my seat along the stone rim of a fountain, I can see almost all of the Old Town Square with its beer tents and overpriced souvenir stalls and pods of tourists shuffling back and forth, oohing and aahing and grinning for pictures. I see also the pickpockets and swindlers working them. All the usual suspects are here, all the swindles that seem to translate well across culture and language—the short change, the currency swap, the broken camera—the things I've seen time and time again all over the world. What I don't see, though, is three-card monte.

As for the cops, they're everywhere but seem to ignore the cons. In the three hours I spend observing Old Town Square, no one is ever arrested. I see an upset tourist talking to a cop, and he hands her a leaflet, which she drops to the ground in frustration before storming away. I pick it up and see instructions in several languages on how to fill out a police report online.

I set up my box between two beer tents and begin the shuffle. Three cards bent along the long axis so they're easier to pick up—the queen of hearts, jack of spades, and jack of clubs. I juggle their positions, shifting the queen to the left, to the right, to the middle.

What I need and don't have, though, is a shill, a partner who pretends to be playing the game and winning. So if my mark picks the right card, I'll have to resort to the time-honored method used by solo cons everywhere: shouting that the police are coming, then folding up the game and running away.

My first marks appear quickly, a trio of drunk German boys wearing jerseys from the Munich soccer team. They sway and stumble, beers in hand, as they watch the game.

"Follow the lady," I bark. *"Folgen Sie der Dame."*

They move closer, and one of them ventures a finger forward, tapping on the leftmost position. I flip the card and whaddayaknow, the queen! I shuffle again, back and forth, juggling and swapping the three cards. He taps center. Winner again.

"Zeigen Sie mir Ihr Geld," I say, still shuffling. Show me your money. He pulls out a twenty-euro note, and wins a third time. I slide a twenty to him over the box.

Come on, his friends urge, let's go. But the greed bug has bitten, and the boy pulls out more money. Double or nothing, I tell him, and he agrees. I pick up the queen, flick down the jack of spades, then shuffle one more time. He taps the right side, and I flip it over. Jack of spades.

He tosses forty across the table, resenting my victory but hooked and eager to prove to himself and his bros that he's not a loser. He produces two more twenties as I continue the shuffle. He slaps his hand down on the left side. Jack of clubs. Too bad.

An American couple—white sneakers, baseball caps, the husband in a NASCAR T-shirt—sidles up for a look. On their practice round, the woman picks correctly. I tell them in fake broken English to place a bet.

"Oh, I just don't know," the woman hedges, the rounded, chubby Midwestern vowels floating through the air, delicate as balloons.

"Too bad," I say. "I can tell you'd be good at this."

The man pulls a ten-euro note from his pocket. Which turns into a twenty after his first loss, and a fifty after his second. His face turns pink, and he exhales sharply as if I'd just kicked him in the stomach. The two storm off, shaking their heads.

After an hour, I'm ahead over a hundred euros. After two hours, I'm ahead three hundred forty. I feel sick fleecing tourists like this, but the money goes a long way toward making me feel better again.

As I head back toward the edge of the square, two guys in matching Puma tracksuits fall into step beside me. They're young, and pretty good-looking, especially the tall one, with a weightlifter's neck that's as wide as his head. He says something in Czech, grabbing my arm just above the elbow and squeezing hard. I look at him blankly, and he tries again in nearly unaccented English. "From the river to Narodni is ours, you understand?" He has the air of the unchallenged schoolyard bully about him, and he shoves me against the wall of a beautiful old church at the edge of the Square. "How much you make today, boy?"

"I'm not a boy," I answer in English thick with Sofia's Russian accent. "And it's none of your fucking business."

He lifts my chin with his finger and studies my face. "No shit," he says. "Libor, check this out. A girl."

The other one—Libor, evidently—grins and makes a comment in Czech.

"I'm called Emil," the tall one says. "Heard of me?"

"No."

"This, this whole area, belongs to me. It belongs to Emil. So I tell you what. You give me the money and stay the fuck away, got it?"

"Don't you mean it belongs to Bohdan Kladivo?" I ask.

The two look at each other. "You deal with us, you deal with him," says Libor as Emil reaches for my jacket and starts pawing through the pockets.

With one hand I seize Emil's wrist, while I strike the inside of his shoulder with the other. He lands hard on his side, and I twist his arm behind his back, pinning it. Libor starts shouting as I dig my fingers into the gelled hair on Emil's scalp and slam his forehead into the cobblestones—only once, and not too hard. I'm just trying to make a point.

Then Libor grabs me and pulls me away. Emil springs to his feet, a small trickle of blood running from the edge of his scalp down his forehead to his nose. He begins reaching into the jacket of his tracksuit, but Libor holds out his hand and says something about the police. Emil punches me in the stomach instead.

Twenty

We leave Prague 1 and head south along the river in Emil's BMW station wagon. Libor sits beside me in the backseat, pressing a small pistol into my side with one hand, while the other touches my back, my shoulder, my ass, my leg. I make a note to cut grabby Libor's hand off at some point in the future if I live through this.

If the articles about Kladivo's reach into the very bottom levels of street crime are correct, I have no doubt that a thousand links up the food chain from Emil and Libor, I'll find him. My little stunt was just my way of knocking on Kladivo's door.

Outside, it's still Prague, but more suburban here. After just ten minutes, we pull off the street and into the back service entrance of a structure that stands out among the low apartment buildings and shops in the neighborhood. It's a grand mansion abutting the river, three stories of gray stone that looks well over a hundred years old. There's a distinctly Austro-Hungarian-Empire vibe to the place, and we stop in front of a plain door that might once have been used by the servants. Emil and Libor hustle me up the stairs into a gleaming commercial kitchen.

The waitstaff, in bow ties and vests, very pointedly refuse to acknowledge our presence, as if there were nothing remarkable about two men in Puma track suits and a woman with a nearly bald head passing through their kitchen. Emil throws open the door and leads me into the next room.

I've never been in a casino and have only ever seen them in movies. But my impression that they were noisy places filled with flashing lights and old people wearing fanny packs is evidently wrong. This is a James Bond–style casino with crystal chandeliers, men in jackets and ties, women in dresses. I've seen no sign advertising this place out in the front of the mansion, so apparently people—the right people— just know of its existence. I hear laughing, the clacking of chips, the shuffling of cards, the *clickety-click-click* of the roulette wheel.

We linger outside the door for a moment like awkward party crashers, enduring pinched-nose looks from patrons who glance over at us from their seats. A barrel-chested man with thinning dark hair heads toward us quickly. The combination of his tuxedo and comical run-walk makes him look like a penguin in a hurry. With a hiss, he sends us all back into the kitchen.

He and Emil exchange sharp words in Czech as he corrals us down a hallway and through the door of a decidedly less fancy room. There are others here, five or six guys, variations on the tracksuited-thug theme, who mill around as if this room were their clubhouse. They hang out on beat-up leather couches and barstools too ratty to keep out on the casino floor.

The man in the tuxedo circles around an old wooden desk stacked with folders and ashtrays and coffee cups and drops into a chair that groans beneath his weight.

He and Emil argue heatedly in very fast Czech. The drift of it seems to be that the man in the tuxedo is furious with Emil for bringing me here, while Emil is trying to explain. The other guys in the room look on, curious but staying out of it.

The boss snaps his fingers twice and points to me. "Your name," he says in English.

"Sofia," I say.

"I am Miroslav Beran, but everyone calls me 'the Boss.' Do you know why they call me the Boss, Sofia?"

"Because you're the boss?"

"Just so!" he says with the false enthusiasm of the chronically put-upon. "Tell me, please. Where are you from? Armenia? You a Gypsy?"

"Russian."

"My young colleague here, Emil, says you were conducting a gambling operation in Praha 1," he says wearily. "*Sofistikovaný* is the word he used to call your game. Sophisticated. All gambling in Praha 1 is Emil's business. It is his *thing*. Do you understand?"

"Yes," I say.

"For this crime, and also for smashing his head to the street, Emil believes you should be shot," Beran the Boss says. "Emil must come to me before shooting anyone, you see. It's a new rule we have because of what happened last time. Isn't that right, Emil?"

Emil says something in protest, but the Boss raises a finger and Emil goes quiet.

The chair squeaks as the Boss rises and circles back to me, arms folded over his chest. "We are not unreasonable men, Sofia. Thieves and Gypsy pickpockets we tolerate—everyone must make a living. But gambling operations in Praha are in direct competition to our interests. Do you know what is the punishment for running something in direct competition?"

"No."

The Boss leans in, touches my face gently, and turns my head as if appraising a show dog. "First time, off comes a finger. That's for the men. For the women, something else. Do you want details?"

I twist my head away. "It wasn't gambling," I say. "It was a con. A trick."

"Emil says it was a game of cards."

"It's called three-card monte. It looks like a card game, but it's not," I say. "You can't win. Not the way I play it."

The Boss says something in Czech, and one of the tracksuits scrambles to retrieve a deck of cards from a desk drawer.

"Show," the Boss says.

The attention of the room is piqued again, and the crew leans forward with curiosity as I remove the jack of clubs, the jack of spades, and the queen of hearts and bend them lengthwise. I instruct the Boss to follow the queen and start the shuffle along the edge of the desk, slowly at first, letting him easily follow the cards' movements from position to position. Then I stop and give the Boss a nod.

"She is exactly here, of course," the Boss says. As I turn the queen over, he gives a satisfied smile to the room, drinking in the laughter. He slaps me on the shoulder. "Maybe this can fool Emil, but not me."

"Then bet something," I say.

"Pardon, please?"

"If you're so confident, bet something."

A hand slaps a fat roll of euros fastened with a rubber band onto the desk. I follow the hand up the arm to see Emil at the end of it.

"I bet the girl," Emil says to the Boss. "She wins, she walks away with my money—three thousand euros. I win, she belongs to me."

The Boss smiles. "What does 'belongs to you' mean, Emil? You keep her as pet?"

Low whistles from Emil's friends. I can hear them whispering excitedly behind me. The Boss seems amused with the prospect and scans the room to read the general consensus.

The fear mounts in me, every rational cell of my body up on end, straining toward the room's exit, screaming get out, get out.

A nod from the Boss. "Agreed," he says to applause and low whistles.

But silence falls over the men as I pick up the cards and begin juggling them, sending the queen left, then right, slipping her under the jack of spades, throwing the jack down in her place.

Emil's watching with laser focus, so I pick up the speed. This isn't a game, I repeat to myself, it's a con. So as I shuffle, I let the queen fall faceup, making as though it were an accident. Then I pick her up again but very quickly replace her with a jack. I finish with a flourish, tossing the cards onto the table. The concentration in Emil's face is evident, and he studies me for clues. But I'm made of stone and show not a thing.

Too easy, he's thinking, she's tricked me. Then he thinks again, maybe not and it's exactly as easy as it appears. He glances up at the Boss, but Beran is a casino pro and as unreadable as I am.

Emil extends his index finger toward the card on my left, then switches suddenly to the card in the center.

"Is that your answer?" I say.

A pause as he exhales slowly, facial muscles twitching. "Yes," he says.

The room gasps—actually gasps out loud—when I turn over the jack of clubs. I jump as Emil's hands shoot into the air, thinking he's about to hit me, but he spins around as he throws out a long string of curses that are met with laughter from the rest of the room.

He's pointing at me and screaming angrily to the Boss in Czech, appealing his case, I suppose, arguing I cheated or that it wasn't fair. He's right, of course, but it's not like I didn't tell them I would cheat. Only this time, the Boss had been my shill, showing the crowd how easy the game was until the real mark stepped forward.

The Boss stares him down. "Are we not *cestný lidé*? Men of honor and sport?" he shouts, not just to Emil but to everyone in the room.

Sheepish nods all around. The Boss pulls a cigarette from a pack on his desk and lights it. He exhales thoughtfully. "Take your money, Sofia. You have won and are free to leave."

Emil paces back and forth, eyes drilling into me with hate. God knows what he would have done to me had he won. God knows what he still might to do to me.

I step forward and pick up the roll of money. It feels hefty and wonderful in my hands. I don't think I've ever seen so much cash together in one place. "What's your usual cut?" I say to the Boss.

"My cut?"

"The money you get from each game that goes on in Praha 1?"

"Thirty percent."

I peel off nine hundred euros and set it on the desk. "I want to work for you," I say.

The Boss arches his eyebrows, and I hear a few snickers from the crew. "As you see, we are men only here," he says.

"I just made you nine hundred euros in less than a minute."

The Boss inhales deeply, and his nostrils flare. There's a long pause as he considers and looks around the room, taking its temperature. Then he smiles the contrarian's smile and shrugs. "Why the fuck not?"

At nine o'clock the next morning, the casino is closed to customers and is strictly employees-only. It'll open again in the afternoon, but for now the tracksuited crew is gathered in the bar, sneakers propped up on stools upholstered in expensive green leather, crumbs from their breakfast of bread and cheese and salami dropping to the plush carpet. Their conversations shut down as I walk in, and heads turn to follow my progress across the room. A thin boy, cleaning a disassembled pistol with a wire brush, arches his eyebrows when he sees me and shakes his head. *This place is going to shit.*

Beran the Boss—in daytime dress of jeans and a white dress shirt open to the middle of his chest—stands behind the bar drinking mineral water from a bottle in between bites of sausage and sauerkraut. He smiles when he sees me, as if he's surprised I showed up.

"Come with me," Beran says, and I follow him down the corridor to his office. He shows me to a chair, and I sit primly, back straight, hands folded in my lap.

Beran opens a metal cabinet in the back of the room and takes out a long dry-cleaning bag on a hanger. "I will need your passport," he says.

I produce it for him and set it on the desk.

"Take any drugs?" he says. "Heroin, methamphetamine?"

"None."

"Truly? Not even a little marijuana now and then?"

"Marijuana when I was young. No longer."

He drapes the dry-cleaning bag over the desk. "Undress."

"Excuse me?"

"Undress. Take your clothing off."

I knew in my heart it would come to this. I was willing to fuck Christian, so why not Beran the Boss? You don't battle and weasel and scrape your way across Europe's sewers and come out a virgin on the other end.

My jacket and shirt fall to the floor, and I try not to tremble. My pants join them a moment later. Beran looks up and eyes me with detachment.

Don't be weak, I say to myself. The end justifies the means. I reach around my back to the bra clasp and am about to open it.

"Enough," Beran says. "Hold out your arms."

Like a doctor, he takes my hands and twists them, scanning me from wrist to shoulder. "You're clean," he says, a hint of surprise in his voice. "You will pardon my rudeness, but I needed to check you for needle marks or wires. I do not permit addicts to work for me. Or informants."

He holds up the dry-cleaning bag by its hanger and strips away the plastic. It's some sort of uniform: white shirt, embroidered maroon vest, short maroon skirt, a little maroon bow tie. "Please," he says. "Put it on."

My hands shake with relief as I climb into the clothes, but I have no idea what this uniform is all about. There's no mirror, but I'm certain I look ridiculous. "Is this a waitress uniform, sir?" I say.

"You are to be a dealer, Sofia. Here in the casino. Blackjack. Poker. Baccarat."

"But I don't know any of these games," I say.

"You can count, and I've seen you handle a deck of cards. That puts you above most of the others already."

"I thought I could work—"

"With the boys? Emil and Libor?" He shakes his head. "Out of the question. I would have a rebellion on my hands. The only women here work in the casino."

A word of gratitude seems required, so I thank him for the job, even though this isn't at all what I had in mind.

"It is nothing," he says warmly. "I hire only talented people from the streets. Smart people who are, what's the English word, like children without parents?"

I search my memory. "Orphans?"

"Orphans. Just so," the Boss says, opening the office door for me. "People who won't be missed."

My name tag says Sofia, and the uniform is too tight—made that way on purpose, the other girls tell me, to cup the buttocks and breasts just the right way and to prevent us from hiding casino chips inside baggy clothes.

My teacher, a fellow dealer named Rozsa, throws down three cards: queen of diamonds, eight of spades, seven of clubs.

"Twenty-five," I say instantly, then repeat the number in Russian, German, and Czech, the rudiments of which Rozsa is teaching me as we go. The Czech language, it turns out, is similar enough to Russian that I have no trouble getting a handle on the basics like numbers.

Rozsa is tiny, with pale skin and black hair cut into a bell-shaped bob. She reminds me of a darker, rougher version of Tinker Bell. She throws down three more cards: jack of hearts, ace of spades, and two of diamonds.

"Twenty-three or thirteen," I say. The ace can mean either a one or an eleven, whichever is more advantageous.

We run the counting drill again and again until Rozsa is satisfied. "You're a natural, Sofia," she says in crisp English, sweeping the cards together with an elegant flick of her wrist. "Now, what do we do about your face?"

"My face?" I say.

"Yes. With that hair and no makeup, you look like a boy with tits. Come."

She leads me to the bathroom and spreads the contents of her purse on the counter. "This," she says, holding up a tube of lipstick. "Do you know what it is?"

"Of course," I say.

"Then show."

I pull the cap off and smear it around my lips. The truth is, I've worn makeup only six or seven times in my entire life. I hate the stuff, lipstick especially—something about the taste and smell.

Rozsa clucks her tongue and shakes her head as she snatches the lipstick from my hand. *"Ach,"* she says. "Let me do it. Make a face like so."

I copy her expression and stretch my lips as Rozsa spreads the stuff around. The lipstick is followed by eye shadow and eyeliner and blush. "Have you met the other dealers?" Rozsa asks as she works.

I tell her I haven't, and she fills me in, confirming that it's just as Beran had said, that we are all orphans of one sort or another here, drifters from Europe's damp, shadowy corners. Rozsa lists off the ones she likes: Marie and Vika, the Romanian Gypsies, are her favorites. Followed by Aida the Croatian Muslim and Gert the daughter of German radicals. As for Ivan the Ukrainian anarchist, he's quiet at first, but cool once you get to know him. Finally, Rozsa tells me about herself—Hungarian, speaks nine languages, and is a practicing witch. I raise my eyebrow at this latter point, and she tells me she dreamt of my arrival at the casino, saying that in her dream a woman with short hair whose name started with the letter *S* would show up one day soon, bringing with her a gift for them all.

"What kind of gift?" I ask.

"The dream did not say," she says.

"And how did your dream end?"

At this, she smiles, and I can tell she's about to lie. "I don't remember," she says.

I'm about to press her for more information on the dream, but suddenly Rozsa turns me by the shoulders so that I face the mirror. Staring back at me is a face I haven't seen before: cheekbones pink from the blush; eyes wide and alive thanks to the ten different things

Rozsa did with them; mouth full and plump from the lipstick. I look like a premonition of my adult self, a woman a good five years older than I really am. My new face is pretty only in a matter of speaking. I look like what I'm quickly becoming: a hard woman, crueler than the girl she left behind, cynically hiding behind a mask of skillfully applied makeup.

"You like?" Rozsa asks.

"I—I don't know," I say.

"It is a woman's, ah . . ." She waves her hand in the air, impatiently searching for the English word. *"Verkleidung,"* she says finally, finding the German word instead.

"Disguise," I say.

"Yes, that. If men want to see their women pretty and happy, then we will wear the disguise and pretend." She begins gathering her makeup back into her clutch. "The men in charge here, they demand pretty and happy, always. You must be careful."

"I know. Emil and the others are dangerous."

"Pfft, they are nothing," she says as she turns to me. "It is Beran and the ones above him who you should fear."

The skin on my neck tingles. There's information to be had here. Rozsa is friendly, but she's also wise, and this is her world far more than it's mine.

"Isn't Beran the boss?" I say naively.

"Of the casino and street boys only." She puts her hands on my shoulders, tilts her head. "You know who is the owner of this casino, yes?"

My body tenses—please, Rozsa, let me hear you say it aloud. I shake my head.

"His name is the devil," she says flatly. "But he calls himself Kladivo."

· · ·

Even as Rozsa says the words, what wells inside me isn't fear, but pride. I've found the devil, and now I've come for him. So with confidence and calm hands, I work my first table of customers in the devil's casino.

I call out the total of the cards in four languages, and a heavy, unshaven Russian smoking cigarette after cigarette gets his third blackjack in a row. I summon the waiters, and they appear a moment later with a silver ice bucket from which is sticking the neck of a champagne bottle. It looks like the mast of a sinking ship.

Eventually, the Russian loses, though. As does everyone. Some of the dealers show no emotion as they sweep the bets from the table, but Rozsa says it helps your tips if you give a little sympathetic smile. I do, and it does.

I go back to my room at Hedvika's place that first night, and for the next twenty nights afterward, with more money than I know what to do with. I'm earning more than my dad earned working for the government. I start eating at cafés instead of bringing street food back to my room. I buy some new clothes, some makeup of my own, and a pair of stylish flats for work. I have to remind myself every night to fight off the prosperous novelty of it all and remember why I'm here.

I've taken the job in the casino to get close to the thugs holding my dad. Monitoring them isn't difficult, as they're coming and going from the casino all the time. In only a matter of days, there's a rumor going around that I'm a lesbian. Rozsa informs me of this—it's the short hair, she says, and the fact that I kicked Emil's ass. In any case, the boys seem to believe that lesbianism should be taken as a challenge to try harder, and the race is on to see who'll sleep with me first. It is Emil who tries hardest of all, perhaps seeing it in his inscrutable scrotal logic as a way to resurrect his dignity and standing among his fellow bro-thugs.

Maybe you come with me sometime, baby, see my sweet-ass

apartment. You ever drive a Porsche before? They're full of poor dead Christian's cheap seduction and English they learned from American TV bad guys. It takes all my strength not to rebuff them. Instead, I swallow hard and smile back, ask them about their apartments, tell them no, I've never driven a Porsche before. I have to watch the glasses I drink from, never letting them out of my sight.

In between fatuous questions about their Porsches, I make inconspicuous inquiries about Kladivo. But all I ever hear is that he's largely a mystery and occupied elsewhere, appearing at the casino only for a few brief moments now and then before disappearing just as quickly.

It is difficult to be patient. Every time I look at Beran the Boss or Emil or Libor or the twenty other thugs making their way through the casino, I wonder whether they laid hands on my dad, whether they punched him, or slit his throat, or threw a shovelful of dirt on his body. Because I will do the same to them when the time comes.

The devil called Bohdan Kladivo arrives a few minutes before the doors open on my twenty-second day at the casino. He is referred to by the others as Pan Kladivo—the polite title, Pan, somewhere between "mister" and "sir" in formality.

He is short and slightly built, his thinness accentuated by a very expensive, very trim pin-striped suit. Black hair sweeps back from his forehead and frames a thin face with delicate birdlike features while his quick-moving eyes study the world over the top of silver-framed glasses. The other thugs I have met exude strength; I fear them for their muscle and temper. But Bohdan Kladivo exudes intellect, and instantly I fear him for his mind and what looks like surgical rationality. To him, I feel certain, every problem is a tumor, and the one true solution is always the knife.

The Boss makes a fuss over Pan Kladivo's arrival, pointing out a new chandelier, new felt on the tables, and the new girl they've found—me. I smile coyly and incline my head in a little bow of respect. But there are things more important than chandeliers and felt and me on Bohdan Kladivo's mind because he does nothing more than pass over us with his eyes as he leads the Boss off the casino floor into the kitchen.

"He is, in German, *gestört*," Rozsa says as the kitchen door swings shut. "How please in English?"

"Troubled," I say.

"Exactly this," she says. "Troubled."

"About what?" I say.

"Everyone has worries." Rozsa shrugs as she leaves my side. "Monsters, too."

I stand at my empty blackjack table for an hour. Weekday afternoons are like that, and I'm grateful for the small mercy. It would be hard to count the cards when my mind is on fire with the possibilities of what is being discussed between Kladivo and Beran the Boss in the casino office. I want proof that they still have my dad, that he's still alive, but I'd settle for even the barest hint of evidence.

"You are available?" asks a voice to my side in English.

I turn and see Bohdan Kladivo standing there, hands held primly in front of him.

"Your table, I mean." He smiles. "Is your table available?"

My mouth flutters for a moment, but I finally manage to say, "Of course, Pan Kladivo."

He sits at the middle stool, pulls a five-thousand-euro chip from his pocket, and places it in front of him.

The cards aren't in his favor, a ten and a six against my eleven. He taps his middle finger on the table, and I toss out another card, a five, giving him twenty-one. I turn my second card over and reveal a seven, giving me eighteen.

"Congratulations," I say, sweeping up the cards and giving him another five-thousand-euro chip.

"You're Sofia Timurovna, yes? Do I have the patronymic right?"

My middle name he means, which in Russian is always a modification of the father's first name. Timur in my case. "Yes, that's right," I say.

"Pan Beran says you are a shining star here. Intelligent, excellent with the cards." He doubles his bet to ten thousand. "Where are you from in Russia?"

"The town of Armavir, in the south," I say as we play through the hand. "Nineteen. You win again."

He stacks up all his chips, twenty thousand euros in total. I throw down a jack and a four for him, a pair of eights for me.

"An admirable people, the Russians," he says. "Disciplined. Loyal. Another card, please."

"Then maybe we know different Russians," I say as I deal him a three, which gives him a total of seventeen.

He declines another card, and I deal myself a four, giving me twenty. "Dealer wins," I say. Just as I would with any other customer, I sweep his stack of twenty thousand euros away.

Bohdan Kladivo eyes me for a moment. Then he fishes a thousand-euro chip from his pocket and pushes it to me across the felt. "For you," he says. "You are the only dealer here who would dare do that."

"Do what, Pan Kladivo?" I say.

"Allow me to lose."

I drop it into my little slot for tips as I would any other and give him a simple thank-you. This too he seems to appreciate and lets his eyes linger on mine until I look away.

"You're new to Praha," he says. "Do you have a boyfriend yet?"

My stomach turns. "I don't date," I say.

"Yes, this is what Pan Beran says. Speculation is you are a lesbian, but I think you are just being wise not to date the men here. They can be—rough."

"I'm just a woman who doesn't date."

"I am not asking for myself, you understand," he says. "I'm asking for my son, Roman. I believe your character would be a good, we may say, *influence* on him."

I incline my head and smile politely as I can. "I'm sorry, Pan Kladivo. As I said, I do not date."

"A decision I must respect." He sighs and removes a small notepad from his suit jacket. "However, in case you change your mind, let me give you my mobile number."

He jots his information down on a piece of paper with a fountain pen. The silver nib catches the light like the blade of a scalpel, and along the side of the pen's piano-black body, I see the inscription *To Dad, Love G.*

Twenty-One

Rozsa makes tea that smells of black licorice and wet summer soil. I sip it and am grateful for the warmth, even if the flavor is terrible. It's medicine, she tells me, and therefore supposed to be terrible.

Somehow I made it through the rest of my shift, a blur of playing cards and stacks of chips and stacks of money seen through veils of cigarette smoke. Rozsa found me sitting on the ground at the tram stop outside the casino afterward, my face, she says, pale as a dead man's.

So tea and something to eat at Rozsa's apartment. She would have none of my protests that I was fine and would really just like to go home. She even sprang for cab fare to her place, a dingy closet of an apartment above a café a long distance west of the river.

It's all I can do to stay in Russian Sofia's skin tonight, to remember to pronounce words as she would, and sip my tea as she would. I want desperately to let Rozsa know everything, to tell the truth, to unburden myself of my own story. What I tell her instead is that my current sorry state was simply a migraine brought on by all the cigarette smoke. In reality, my head aches with the deepest sense of shock and panic I've felt since the day my dad was taken.

There it was, the pen. The proof I'd been looking for. But what now? What do I do? What I need is Yael the ass-kicking ninja warrior goddess Israeli spy to tell me, but what I get is Rozsa the Hungarian pixie who fancies herself a witch.

"What you taste is anise and something—in Hungarian it is *edes gomba*," Rozsa says of the tea. "Medicine for, not the body, but the unseen part."

"The soul," I say.

"Soul. Precisely that."

I pick a little at the roast duck she brought up from the café, but I have no appetite for dead things just now.

Rozsa fusses just like Lili did back in New York, plumping the pillows in a little nest around me, tightening the blankets around my shoulders. Good at this, these Hungarians.

"You're a strange kind of cat," Rozsa says, settling into the couch beside me with her own cup of tea. "One minute, peaceful and quiet. The other minute, like your tail's on fire."

"It is on fire," I say under my breath as I take a sip.

"You know, the other night I was thinking about you and couldn't sleep. So I got up and read your tarot."

"Tarot cards?"

"Yes. Do you believe, Sofia?"

I haven't believed in God since I was a kid, and so consequently I don't believe in tarot cards or Ouija boards or tooth fairies, either. "That's not really my thing," I say.

"You don't need to believe in gravity to fall on your face." She smiles. "Would you like to know what they said?"

"Sure," I say to indulge her. "Go ahead."

She leans forward on the couch, pressing the tips of her tiny fingers together. "The first card I drew, which speaks of your past, was six of cups. It means childhood, innocence. But these things are gone, in the past. The second card, which speaks of your present, is the fool."

I manage a small laugh and take another sip of the awful tea.

"Do not mistake—the fool is not stupid," Rozsa says. "The fool is clever, wise."

"And the third card?" I ask.

Rozsa retreats a little in her seat. "The death card," she says. "But when I pulled it, it was upside down."

Of course it would be that. "Which means?"

Rozsa shrugs. "About that, I am not certain. I'm new to this. But the old women from my village say an upside-down death card does not always mean death."

"What then?"

"It is unclear." She reaches forward, presses a hand on each of my knees. "The death of someone else, perhaps. But maybe, also, a change. The end of something."

I pinch my eyes shut and press my palm to my forehead. I'm getting sleepy, and that warm-blanket sensation I got from my sedatives is spreading from my stomach to the rest of me. The tea—anise and *edes gomba*—whatever the hell that is.

"Like I said, I'm not a believer," I say.

"I know," Rozsa says. "But I am."

I lean over onto the couch, into the nest of pillows and blankets. The room spins a bit, then stops, then spins the other way. Rozsa slips beside me, pressing her body to mine, circling an arm around me to keep me from being thrown off the earth as it whirls and whirls.

Suddenly, I'm at a ball in an elegant home, wearing a green gown and white mask. It's a dream, obviously, but clear as a film. There's a fire burning in a fireplace, reflecting orange on the faces of the men—they are all men—gathered in the room. I'm carrying a tray loaded with six gold cups that look like old-fashioned church chalices. One by one I hand them out, to Kladivo, to Emil, to Beran, and three other faces I can't see. When they're all gone, I set the tray on a table, over which is a mirror framed in gold. I take off the mask and see not my face but a skull.

I allow a week to pass before making the call so as not to appear too quick and eager. Bohdan proposes dinner: himself, his son, Roman, and Sofia.

We meet at a restaurant by Hradcany Castle, the seat of the Czech government. The tablecloths are white, and the walls are purple velvet and the candlelight burns gold. Rozsa loans me a sleeveless black dress for the night. It's short on her and even shorter on me, which makes it so much the better for my purposes. Bohdan smiles and looks me over when he and Roman see me in the restaurant's lobby.

It's clear the son has inherited his father's fussy aesthetic but not his looks. Roman is tall, and even beneath the excellent suit, I can tell he's muscular. His dark-blond hair is parted just so, and he has the confident air of the well-off Wall Streeter. But as I rise from the velvet couch and greet them—a kiss on the cheek for each—the son gives the father a look, and I can tell my presence was a blind date ambush.

This is, Bohdan Kladivo tells me when we're seated, the finest restaurant in all of Prague, perhaps in the whole of the Republic. Whether this is true or not I can't say, since I taste exactly none of the flavors in the foie gras or roast quail or asparagus with delicate cream sauce the waiter says has a hint of juniper in it. The men drink wine—the '82 Chateau de Something—and offer me a glass. No thank you, Sofia says, preferring the mineral water.

It's clear from the first that these are gangsters of a different sort than Emil and even Miroslav Beran. These are gangsters who under-stand the wine list, who know which fork is meant for salad and which for meat. Still, I can't help but study their hands as they work through the business of dinner, stabbing with their forks, squeezing the necks of their wine glasses. Bohdan Kladivo's are fine and delicate with long fingers. A pianist's hands. His son's are large and paw-like, with strong fingers built for strangling.

"And are your parents still in Russia, Sofia?" Bohdan asks.

I smile sadly. "Mother died when I was seven. Father when I was fourteen."

"A tragedy," he pronounces. "Family is important. It is, one may say, *indispensable*. Perhaps someday God will grant you a family of your own."

"Perhaps," I reply with a smile.

I push the limits of the Sofia identity, flirting lightly with both men, but especially Roman. Bohdan seems pleased with me, but as for his son, he'll require work. I make up stories about Sofia's small city of Armavir. I tell of her love for books and learning. I tell about over-coming hardship and seeking fortune in Europe, which culminates here, tonight. *Such an honor to dine with you both.* Then I shyly pro-pose another toast, this one to their health.

"Did you attend university, Sofia?" Bohdan asks.

"Unfortunately, no."

Bohdan waves a dismissive hand. "Like me, then. You and I, our university was the real world." He gestures to Roman. "Roman, however—Yale. 'Ivy League,' they call it in the United States. He was even on the rowing team."

"You are very lucky to have gone there," I say to Roman.

"He is lucky to have a father who paid for it." Bohdan grins. "Isn't that so, Roman?"

Roman refills his wine glass. "Very lucky."

"Now the king pays for the prince's foreign automobiles and all his parties with his, one may say, *close friends.*"

A harsh look passes between the two men, lighting a fuse that it's up to me to pinch out.

"And do you enjoy music, Roman?" I offer.

A relieved little smile. The first of any kind I've gotten from him. "I do," he says.

"Jazz," Bohdan says. "The one music the king and prince agree on. What is your opinion of jazz music, Sofia?"

"Oh, I like it very much." I inhale, hold the breath for a moment. "My father—my father did as well."

Bohdan's eyes brighten. "Did you know Praha was the capital of jazz in Eastern Europe? It's true. All of it was underground, of course. The communists didn't like it. It was considered dangerous, one may even say, *decadent* music."

Busboys appear and gather the dinner plates while a waiter brings dessert menus. But Bohdan waves him away and lights a cigar. Smoke billows around him like a blue cloud.

He looks at me through the smoke, as if wondering whether certain questions should now be asked, and deciding they can wait. Then he looks at his watch and arches an eyebrow. "Roman, there is a set starting soon at the Stará Paní. You should take Sofia."

I see the muscles in Roman's neck tense up. "Perhaps Sofia has someplace to be. Perhaps she must work tomorrow."

"Nonsense. She's with the boss's son," Bohdan says. "Besides, a date with a Russian woman is never to be missed. Is this not correct, Sofia Timurovna?"

"It is correct, Pan Kladivo."

We leave soon afterward, Bohdan disappearing into the backseat of a Mercedes, the door held open for him by a bodyguard. Then the valet brings around Roman's car, a sleek Audi, jet black and elegant. I climb into the passenger seat, and Roman slips behind the wheel.

"Look, if you don't want to go out, I understand," I say.

"It's fine," he says, putting the car in gear. "I just wasn't expecting this tonight. My father—he wants to reform me, he says."

"Reform what?"

"Who knows."

We cross the river and crawl through the ancient streets of Prague 1, barely fitting through the narrow lanes, and park near the Old Town Square, where just weeks ago I was hustling tourists. Stará Paní is audible from the street, a racing saxophone and drum riff.

The club sits at the bottom of a steel staircase. It's an elegant place, like an old-fashioned speakeasy, with a stage at one end and little lamps on every table that reflect up on the faces of the smartly dressed patrons. The band is strong, too, a sax, piano, bass, and drum quartet.

We settle into a couch in a small VIP area off to the side. A waitress appears, says hello to Roman by name, and looks me over. Roman orders a beer for himself and a mineral water for me.

The set continues, but Roman isn't listening. He's focused on his phone, thumbing text messages and looking around impatiently. It's clear we're here for no other reason than to satisfy his father. I move closer to him on the couch, let my hand brush against his leg. But Roman only adjusts himself so we're no longer touching.

Another text, another thumbed response. He leans in close to me. "I'm sorry, Sofia. I have to go."

"Is everything okay?" I ask.

"It's—look, I have to meet someone. For business," he says.

"I see."

"I'm just, you know . . . not looking for anything right now." He removes a thick roll of cash from his pocket, peels off a few bills, and hands them to me. "Cab fare home," he says.

He throws down another few bills for the drinks and disappears up the staircase. Who's he meeting? I wonder. About what? I wait a moment, then follow him out.

The street outside is mobbed with T-shirt–wearing tourists, but in his excellent suit, Roman is easy to spot. I follow at a distance, always at least a dozen people between us. It's hard going on the cobblestone streets in my heels, so I take them off and carry them. Someone whistles, someone else propositions me, but I ignore them and stay in pursuit.

Roman turns down a narrow lane, then onto another wide street, then into the doorway of a bar. I take up a position across the street in a dark space against the wall where the streetlight doesn't reach. There's nothing really special about the bar. It's in a narrow white building about a hundred years old—practically new for Prague— and a bouncer in a denim vest sits on a stool just outside the entrance.

As I wait, I wonder what's happening inside. Meeting his real girlfriend, or is it a business colleague, as he said? An hour passes, or maybe just less than that. Then the door to the bar opens, and Roman stumbles out, followed by another man. They're both drunk, weaving a little as they walk. They're laughing, touching each other on the shoulders, sharing a joke.

The crowds on the street are thinner now, and so I have to hang back even farther as I follow them. They walk for ten minutes or so, then stop in front of a modern, very stylish apartment building. I can't hear their conversation, but it's easy to understand even without words. Roman looks at his watch, the other guy motions to the building, Roman shakes his head. There's an awkward pause, the other guy looking at his shoes. Then Roman reaches out, lifts the man's chin, and kisses him. It's a deep kiss that looks like it means something to them both.

. . .

268

In another context, in another life, I would think it was sweet and touching. But where does this leave my plan?

The kiss continues and catches the attention of three passersby. They're fiercely drunk and start whistling and calling out, "Faggot! Faggot!" in English. Roman and his boyfriend break the kiss off and try to ignore them. The boyfriend squeezes Roman's hand and disappears into the building while Roman starts down the street, his steps weaving and uncertain.

The drunks stumble after him, and I can hear them speaking to one another. Midtwenties or so, dressed in Burberry knockoff polo shirts. From their loud conversation, I gather they're British men here for a stag party, and disappointed the "Prague birds" weren't as easy as they'd been told.

Every once in a while, one of the men continues his taunt, coming up with something obscene to shout Roman's way. But if Roman hears them, he's either too smart to show it or too drunk to reply. He stops briefly along the side of a building and rests his head against it.

The men sense some weakness in him now and use the opportunity to close a little distance. Roman turns down a narrow, vacant street that empties out into the Old Town Square.

One of the Brits heaves a beer bottle that strikes Roman sharply in the back of the head. Roman turns, and even in the dim light, I see fearsome anger on his face. Still, the men aren't intimidated. One of them grabs Roman by the shoulders and head-butts him in the nose, snapping Roman's head back. Then all three start in with round after round of sloppy punches that last until Roman crumples against the wall and slides to the ground.

His body is limp, and the three men stand there for a moment, deciding whether the fun ended too soon. Leave him alone, I think to myself. You've done enough. Then one of them starts kicking him, driving his sneaker into Roman's stomach and side and head. The rest join in.

I rocket forward, drop my shoes to the ground, and grab the largest of the three attackers by the wrist. I wrench his arm into a lock that spins him around and sweep my forearm against his throat, sending the back of his head into the cobblestone wall. He lurches at me, but I catch him in the jaw with a fist that twists his body away.

The second attacker seizes my shoulder from behind. My elbow flies back into his stomach; then I turn and drive the heel of my hand up under his chin, sending him toppling backward. He's incapacitated but likely only for a few seconds. I sense movement at my side and turn. A big, drunken swing from the third attacker misses my head by a good six inches. I answer with a fast kick to his groin. He doubles over and staggers a few steps. But as I move toward him, I notice the other two attackers backing away, hands raised.

I look to Roman. He's still on the ground, still only semiconscious, but has a pistol in his hand and is trying to level it at them. Two of the attackers turn and stumble off down the alley, while the third runs off in the other direction.

Roman swings the pistol around, looking for a target. Gently, I wrap my hand around it and force the muzzle down. "Put it away," I whisper.

Blood burbles from Roman's nose. "The fuckers," he gasps.

But he's drifting off again, back into unconsciousness. I check his pulse and see that it's strong, but he needs a hospital and there's no way I can carry him by myself to the car. For only a second, I consider shouting for help, but a man with the last name Kladivo probably doesn't want the police coming around asking questions about what happened and why.

I pull his phone from his pocket and figure out how to access the contacts. I thumb through them until I see the word *otec*—father, same as in Russian. I press the name, and the phone dials.

"Pan Kladivo," I say when he answers. "It's Sofia. Roman's been hurt—attacked. He's breathing but unconscious. Do you want me to call an ambulance?"

A pause, then a calm voice. "No. No ambulance. Where are you?"

"Praha 1, near the Old Town Square. A little alley . . ."

"Are there shops nearby? Give me the names."

I tell him the names of a pizza restaurant and a wine store, both closed for the night.

"I'll have someone come to you. Don't move."

"Thank you."

"Sofia?"

"Yes, Pan Kladivo?"

"Were you—were you with him?"

"No, Pan Kladivo. I came only later."

A pause. In the background, I hear soft music and the tinkling of glasses as if he's at a party. "Someone will be there soon," he says, and then the line clicks off.

For five minutes, I wait by Roman's side. He's breathing deeply and steadily, which I take to be a good sign. Then two figures appear at the end of the alley, coming from the direction of the square. As they step into the light of the streetlamp, I recognize Emil and Libor.

"The fuck happened?" Emil says.

"Three men attacked him," I say.

They stand dumbly over Roman for a few moments, debating in Czech what to do. Then they hoist him up, one under each arm, and drag him toward the square.

I start off in the other direction, but Emil grabs my arm. "No chance," he says. "Boss says you come with us."

I follow them to Emil's BMW and help them fold Roman into the backseat with Libor. I climb into the passenger side, and we take off through the dense late-night Prague traffic.

"Who did it?" Emil asks as we leave the city and start into the suburbs.

"Three British guys," I say. "I don't know why they picked Roman."

Emil laughs under his breath. "I bet I do."

We say nothing more the rest of the ride. The apartment buildings give way to small houses, then to large houses the farther we get from the city. The car turns onto a private gravel road with signs giving what look like ominous warnings in Czech about what will happen to those who dare trespass here.

We approach an iron gate set into a stately stone wall. Beyond it is a large stucco mansion, an enormous place with a well-manicured yard. A man in a gangster-issue tracksuit approaches, shielding his eyes from the headlights with one hand, and carrying a submachine gun with the other.

Twenty-Two

Roman is laid out on a long wooden table in the kitchen like a dish being prepared. An improvised mattress of quilts is wedged between him and the planks, and above him hangs a rack of copper pots and pans. A few of Bohdan's personal security crew hang around waiting for orders.

Bohdan, shirtsleeves rolled up and tie loosened, stands with hands on hips, supervising the work of a private physician summoned to the house. The doctor is deferent and frightened, keeping his eyes low.

I sit where Bohdan tells me to sit, in a wooden chair pulled away from the wall. From here, I can see Roman clearly. He has only just now regained consciousness, and the doctor is sewing stitches into a cut on his cheek. Roman's eyes are on me, deep with panic. The physician dabs away some blood and announces that he's finished.

Bohdan snaps his fingers as he gives an order in Czech. He's commanding everyone to leave, apparently, because everyone does, even the doctor. I begin to stand, but Bohdan seizes my shoulder and forces me back into the chair. "Not you," he says.

When the door to the kitchen is closed, Bohdan turns and looms over me. "Leave out nothing," Bohdan says. "Leave out nothing or I will know."

"Three men, three British men, drunk, came up to him. They were harassing him, saying—terrible things. They grabbed him, and Roman tried to fight them off. He fought like—like a lion."

Bohdan shakes his head as he turns to Roman. "You hear that, Roman? She calls you a lion. Such loyalty. Despite everything, you are still the king of the jungle in her eyes." He approaches his son, leans in close. "You were with—that fellow?"

Roman closes his eyes and says something in Czech.

"In English, so that Sofia may hear and understand," Bohdan says. "Do not be a coward."

"I was with—a friend."

Bohdan's shouting causes me to jump in my seat. "A *friend*? One of your *boyfriends*? One of your *lovers*?"

The humiliation in Roman's eyes seems even more painful than his physical wounds. *"Ano,"* he whispers. Yes.

Bohdan nods and leans against the edge of the table. "I have only ever asked for you to keep your sickness discreet. Yet even this you cannot do. Have you any idea what will happen if it is discovered my son is a sodomite?"

"I'm sorry, *táta*."

"And you?" Bohdan says, pointing to me. "How is it you happened to be there?"

"We had—gone separate ways," I say. "I went to another bar and happened to see Roman on the street."

"And what did you do, file your nails and watch like a useless bitch? Or did it occur to you to get help?"

Roman interrupts. "She fought them. The men knocked me to the ground, and she fought them."

Bohdan cocks his head and squints at me. "This is true?"

I nod. "Yes, Pan Kladivo."

Bohdan leans in close to me, so close I can smell his cologne. "How is it you learned to fight?"

"My father was a soldier. Spetsnaz," I say. "My father believed a woman should learn to defend herself just as she learns to sew and cook."

"Roman, is it true the woman fights like Spetsnaz?"

"It is," Roman says. "Better than your own men."

Bohdan sighs and rubs at his temples. "Sofia, I will arrange for someone to drive you home."

"I could stay and help him. . . ."

Bohdan opens the kitchen door. "You are no longer needed, Sofia."

One of the tracksuit crew, a thin guy with short bleached hair and a tattoo of a diamond on his neck, takes me by the upper arm and hustles me out the door to the back seat of a Volkswagen. He says nothing on the ride, not even asking for the address to Hedvika's place, which he apparently already knows.

Back in my room, I lie in bed for three hours, unable to sleep, unable to even think of anything beyond Roman's beating and how it affects my plan. By four in the morning, my eyes are just beginning to close. And that's when they come for me.

There's a sharp rap on the door, and I hear voices and the rattling of keys. Before I can ask who it is, the door opens, revealing Hedvika in a thick quilted nightgown, hair bundled up in a net. Two men stand behind her, one of them the driver with the diamond tattoo, the second, someone new. He's thick and pushing fifty, with flushed cheeks and a gray mustache turned orange under the nostrils from cigarette tar. Poor Hedvika looks both terrified and furious.

"You are to come with us," the second man says as he begins yanking open drawers and throwing everything I have onto the bed. The other guy pulls a folded trash bag from his pocket, snaps it open, and starts stuffing it with my possessions, everything except my cell phone, which he puts in his pocket. I pull on my jeans and a T-shirt, but my boots and shoes are already in the bag and they ignore me when I ask for them.

When they finish, there is nothing left of me in the room, no sign that I was ever there. I see the man with the mustache counting out bills and placing them in the palm of Hedvika's hand. Paying her for the trouble, and a little something extra to just shake her head if anyone comes around asking about me.

There is no question of my not going with them. "It is ordered by Pan Kladivo," one of them says. For only a brief second, I consider running, but I'm barefoot and wouldn't get more than a few meters before one of these two gunned me down.

I'm ushered into the side door of an unmarked van. The back is separated from the front passenger compartment by metal mesh running from floor to ceiling. They take hold of my arms and push me to the van's floor. Arms twisted behind my back, I feel steel on my wrists and hear them ratchet handcuffs into place. I lash out with my legs, but the guys catch them and cuff my ankles, too. Diamond tattoo kneels on my back while the second one slides a black fabric bag over my head.

The van door slides shut, and we're moving a few seconds later. The big guy is still here with me in the back. I can smell him—beer, cigarettes, and sweat. I can feel him, his mass looming there in the space. There are no seats back here, and very little to hold on to, so as the van turns a corner, I tumble against the back doors.

"The passport you showed Miroslav Beran at the casino is an obvious fake," the big guy shouts in Russian. "What's your real name?"

"Sofia Timurovna Kozlovskaya," I answer.

For this answer, a slap to the side of the head.

"What's your real name?" he shouts again.

"Sofia Timurovna Kozlovskaya," I say again.

A slap to the other side, this one harder.

"What's your real name?"

"Sofia Timurovna Kozlovskaya."

A boot lands in my side, and I topple over. The van is accelerating and the road beneath us is smooth, as if we've just entered onto a highway. What I'm counting on—what I have to count on—is that the passport Yael gave me is as good as she said it was. And even if it's not, I have to stick with the story to the end. If they still have my dad, telling them my real name is a sure way to get him killed.

Hands grip my shirt and yank me forward. "We checked the records, you little bitch!" my interrogator shouts. "Your passport says you're from the city of Armavir, but the hospital has no paperwork on you."

It's clear from his accent he's a Russian native, so I answer in Russian, working to get my own accent absolutely perfect. "Because I was born in Novokubansk. Armavir is where I grew up."

He slams me up against the wall of the van. "I know Armavir as well as I know my own prick. Tell me, what color is the roof of the opera house?"

"The roof of the opera house is blue."

"Bullshit! There is no opera house in Armavir!"

"The roof of the opera house is blue," I repeat.

"You told Pan Kladivo your father was Spetsnaz," my interrogator screams. "We know he was a factory worker."

"After the army, he was a factory worker," I shout back. "He died when I was a girl."

"Aw. Poor little slut," he growls, then boxes my ears. "What did he die of?"

"Vodka."

A punch in the left kidney. "What kind of factory did he work at?"

"Rubber," I yell. "His factory produced rubber."

A punch to the right kidney. "Rubber for what?"

"Your mother's dildos."

But he's tiring from the game, and after he shouts a few more questions and throws a few more punches, he stops. He's breathing hard, wheezing. Then there's the click of a lighter and the smell of cigarette smoke.

The waiting, the guessing at how it'll all turn out, is over I suppose. Something's gone wrong, some hole in my story found, some bit of intelligence gathered. The evening that began in a restaurant by a castle will end with my body in a barrel floating in a swamp. It occurs to me this might be too great a leap of logic, but truly I can see no other conclusion.

We're still on the highway. Even through the walls of the van I hear the thrumming of truck tires and the snort of air brakes as we pass big eighteen-wheelers. I lose track of the time. The interrogation and beating seemed like hours but was probably no more than a few minutes. My body hurts, and I feel myself bleeding from the wrists where I've pulled at the handcuffs in futile rage.

After a very long time marked only by the sound of traffic and the clicking of a lighter as my interrogator starts a new cigarette, the van slows, and we make a hard right. The road here is more pothole than pavement, and I bounce and roll around the back of the van like a toy ball. It's this way for ten minutes or so. Then we slow again and take another right.

We must be nearing the end now. My stomach turns to iron, and I wonder how they'll do it. Shoot me? Strangle me? And why here? Why not in Prague? The answers don't really matter, I guess. They're just something to keep the fear boiling. My body is numb with resignation. No atheists in foxholes, the saying goes, but there's clearly no God here, either, so I guess we're even. It's all inevitable and clear as day.

Even through the hood over my head, I can tell the driver has opened his window. The air pressure has changed, and I hear a dense symphony of crickets. I smell the delicious, damp air of a forest at night.

Beat me? Slit my throat? Rape me first?

My interrogator yanks off my hood without warning, and I sit up to get a better look. Bugs spin in the light of the headlamps as we approach a mud puddle almost as wide as the road itself. The driver curses, and the rear wheels spin as we crawl through it. Up ahead, a chain-link gate moves as the backlit silhouette of a guard pulls it open.

The van wallows into the middle of a courtyard illuminated by four sodium lamps that shine down onto the mud below in gray cones of light filled with moths. Buildings line the sides of the yard, painted green maybe forty years ago and not touched up since. We roll to a stop before a long two-story structure. The whole place has an institutional quality to it, like an army barracks.

We are not alone, however. There are a half-dozen cars also parked here: two Range Rovers, three BMW sedans, and a Mercedes that looks exactly like the one that took Bohdan Kladivo away from the restaurant.

The driver turns off the ignition and comes around to open the side door. It shocks me how meekly I let myself be taken from the van. I don't fight, don't even resist. Instead, I let them hoist me up by each arm. After a few steps, I realize their grip is surprisingly painful, not because they're squeezing, but because I can barely walk and they're dragging me. My body is accepting what my mind will not: that this is how it ends.

The mud beneath my bare feet is cold, and I can smell the forest, its wetness, its life. A moth touches my cheek, my forehead. My interrogator pushes open the door to the building. Fluorescent lights flicker and buzz, casting the dirty linoleum floor in a sickly blue. My feet drag and shuffle along, leaving behind the undignified footprints of one who is about to die badly. My escorts stop at an open office door, tap politely on the frame, and the figure of Bohdan Kladivo rises from a chair.

He is a different species from the man who sat across from me at dinner not eight hours ago. In the fluorescent light, his face is drawn and skeletal, the devil from a medieval woodcut, just as Rozsa had said. He is once more in his expertly tailored suit, with tie cinched up at his neck, the fat knot like a pedestal for his Adam's apple.

My interrogator says just a few words in Czech, and Bohdan replies with a single nod as if the interrogator has just confirmed what he'd suspected. Bohdan approaches me, places a hand on my shoulder, and guides me farther down the hallway. My two escorts follow.

"Do you know what this place is?" he says next to my ear, voice low and confidential.

"No," I say, the word barely coming out.

"We call it our *tábor*—our camp. But under communism, it was something else: a jail run by the secret police."

We're at the top of a metal staircase, and his footsteps ring as we descend. Mine are silent, and the staircase is cold as a sheet of ice on my bare soles.

"Torture. Executions. A bullet to the back of the head was the usual way," he continues. "They happened right here in the basement."

We walk along another corridor parallel to the one upstairs, only this one is lined with steel doors, each with the faded stencil of a number painted on a small metal hatch at eye level.

"After I sent you home, I said to myself, who is this woman who fights like a man but is loyal like a mother?" His eyes are narrow, filled with urgency. "Surely, a woman such as this is one of two things, a treasure rarer than diamonds, or a spy sent to trick me."

"I am not a spy, Pan Kladivo."

"But you can forgive this old man's paranoia, no?" Bohdan pauses in front of cell number seven, traces a finger along the barely visible stencil. "This cell, this one was mine. For five months. Spring and summer of '86. For *chuligánství*, it was called. Hooliganism. Selling blue jeans and cassette tapes of American rock music."

My knees are about to buckle. "I have done nothing to betray you, Pan Kladivo."

Bohdan places a hand on each of my shoulders, inhales deeply, then smiles. "I know that now, Sofia Timurovna. You are no spy."

My mind races to untangle his words. Have I heard him wrong? Has he misspoken? He believes me? My interrogator appears in front of me, unshackles my wrists, then kneels and unshackles my ankles. I gasp in relief, and Kladivo pulls me into an embrace, holding me tightly.

"And I apologize for the way my men treated you in the van," Kladivo continues. "One cannot be too careful. Do you understand that?"

"Yes, Pan Kladivo," I say.

He pulls back from the hug, places a hand on my cheek. "That is why, Sofia Timurovna, I must now ask for one more piece of evidence of your loyalty. One more, we may say, *proof* of your friendship."

Bohdan Kladivo twists the handle on the door to cell number seven and pulls it open. Inside I see the figure of Miroslav Beran, tuxedo shirt rolled up to the elbows. He's standing over another man who's kneeling at the center of the cell, arms tied behind his back, face terrified and pleading. After the shock passes, I recognize him as one of Roman's attackers, the largest of the three, the first one I grabbed.

There's a wooden table in the corner of the cell. On it are a pair of pliers and a power drill and a blow torch—the tools for whatever they have planned for him next. The prisoner's chest is heaving, each breath a labor, moments away from a heart attack. He's staring back at me, and I see the recognition in his eyes.

Bohdan stands beside me in the doorway. "I am lucky to call the Praha police commissioner a dear friend. He made inquiries at hospitals and found this one preparing to leave with a few stitches. A few stitches hardly seems enough for beating my son, does it, Sofia Timurovna?"

"No, Pan Kladivo," I say.

The man opens his mouth, chokes, then finally manages to speak. "Lady, I'm sorry—look, my mates, we had—you know, we were just funning, got a little outta hand is all—can I just—I can get money. . . ."

Miroslav Beran swings a fist into the side of the man's head, and he topples to the side. With a white handkerchief pulled from his pocket, the Boss mops sweat from his brow, then scowls at the blood on his knuckles. For the crime of bleeding, he launches a sharp kick with the toe of his patent leather loafer into the man's side. The prisoner manages no more than a hollow gasp for a response.

Bohdan steps forward and crouches before the prisoner. "You recognize this woman, do you not?"

The man nods.

"And is it true she attacked you after you beat up the fellow?"

Another nod. "She did, sir. She did. Fights real unfair-like. My mates and me were just having a bit of a row, you know, a bit of a dustup with the guy. Then she showed up and took it way out of proportion, sir. Way out of proportion."

Bohdan rises and turns to me. "Do you know how I survived as an inmate in this place, Sofia Timurovna?"

"No, Pan Kladivo."

"Discipline," Bohdan says. "It is the thing Roman lacks. It is why he cannot, we may say, *suppress* his weaknesses. But I see discipline in you, Sofia Timurovna."

"Yes, Pan Kladivo. I have discipline."

Bohdan says something to Beran in Czech, and Beran removes a pistol with a silencer from the waistband of his trousers. He extends it to me, butt first. My eyes move from the gun to Kladivo's face, but there's only a faint smile and eyebrows raised in expectation. I take the gun. It's a well-used, heavy thing. The sharp edges around the sight and hammer and trigger guard are burnished to a shiny brass from being pulled free from waistbands and holsters a million times.

"Show me, Sofia Timurovna. Show me how disciplined you are."

My mind refuses to acknowledge the meaning of this, refuses to issue the order to my hand. But the thing inside me, growing since New York, stronger since Paris, more violent since Berlin, fills me now. Has replaced me. And it seems to have no problem with what's being asked of it. The math is already done: Finding my father means getting close to Kladivo means demonstrating loyalty means killing the bigot means:

There is a sound like a hammer hitting metal. I see a fan of red appear on the wall and floor behind the prisoner's head. This is followed by a sound like a faint chime, and I feel something burning against the side of my bare foot. I look down to see the brass shell casing resting there against my skin, smoke still rolling upward from its mouth. The pistol is still in my hand, smoke coming from its mouth, too.

Twenty-Three

The sun is coming up, purple light turning orange turning yellow. We're slipping along the highway toward Prague, the ride so smooth and gentle in the back of Bohdan Kladivo's Mercedes we might as well be flying. The seats of the sedan are the color and texture of butter. I grip them to stop the shaking of my hands, certain my nails are going to leave permanent marks. Bohdan opens a panel between the seats, a small refrigerator, and offers me a bottle of water. But it's all I can do to stop from throwing up, and I shake my head.

"A man always wishes for a son, and a son is what God gave me," Bohdan says, his voice soft. "But perhaps I should have wished for a daughter."

I wonder how he can't see the hatred in my eyes.

"What you did back there, in the cell," Bohdan continues. "It showed—in Czech the word is *Síla*. Strength, it means. Also power. Authority."

Unable to look at him, I stare out the window.

"I understand how you must feel, Sofia Timurovna. But a woman who seeks to rise in this world must be crueler than even men."

I have to focus, show him it meant nothing to me, show him my will is capable of matching my actions. "You are right, Pan Kladivo," I say.

The city appears in the distance, the red-and-beige apartment buildings, the new glass-and-steel towers, the spires of Hradcany Castle. I wonder if Roman's two other attackers are running through its streets looking for their friend.

Bohdan pats my hand paternally. "Your current employment in the casino is, we may say, *suboptimal*."

"What?"

"Your skills. They are wasted there. So from now on you work for me. No more dealing cards. It is preferable for you?"

"Yes, Pan Kladivo. It is preferable for me," I say.

"You can be an example of discipline to my men. You will also make a good partner for Roman. Who knows, he may yet change his habits because of you."

"A good partner?"

"Companion, and maybe someday, lover. But matters of the heart are the Lord's business, not mine. I will pay you well, of course."

"You're paying me to be his girlfriend?"

Kladivo shrugs. "To the world's eye, yes. Myself, I am not so antique that I cannot accept my son is a faggot. From you, I ask only that you be an example to him, a companion at his side who will temper his ways and show him what discipline looks like."

"May I open the window? For some air?"

Kladivo nods his assent, and I press the button to lower it just a crack. The air is cool and smells of diesel.

"In this modern world, a woman mustn't be content to sit about if she aspires to do the work of a man," Kladivo continues. "Are you prepared for that, Sofia? To learn this business of mine?"

I would rather die. But of course I smile, as much as I'm able to, and say, "Yes, Pan Kladivo. I would like nothing more."

He sighs contentedly. "Then it is as I thought. But remember what I said about women who seek to rise in this world."

"That they must be crueler than men," I say, and force myself to turn to him. "Then that's what I'll be, Pan Kladivo. And thank you. For the opportunity."

We leave the highway and are winding through the cobblestone streets in a smart neighborhood just west of the river. Stately old mansions mix with expensive-looking new buildings, everything either pre- or post-communist, as if the second half of the twentieth century hadn't happened at all. The Mercedes comes to a stop before an apartment building with windows divided by brightly colored mullions into strange geometric shapes. It glistens like a faceted jewel in the morning light.

"What's this?" I ask.

"Roman's apartment," Kladivo says. "And now yours also."

Kladivo escorts me to the apartment door, hand on my elbow. Behind us, the doorman stands deferentially, eyes down, the trash bag containing my things in his hands. I fumble with the key in the lock, so Bohdan steps aside and the doorman unlocks it for me.

"Would you—like to come in?" I ask.

Kladivo gives a single shake of the head. "An eventful night, so use the time alone to rest. Roman will be back later."

The silence inside reminds me of the silence in Terrance's apartment, a luxurious hush over everything. In the living room of the apartment, there is a pair of low couches in cream-colored leather bracketing a plush Bokhara rug the color of blood. There's excellent art in the hallway and a well-stocked wine refrigerator in the kitchen.

I find the bathroom and begin filling the tub with steaming water. It takes me a full five minutes just to figure out how to turn it on. Everything is white marble and dark wood and gleaming surfaces. Gorgeous, really. Like from a magazine about bathrooms. Such a magazine exists, I seem to remember, in some faraway life. As for this world, the one I'm living in, there are freckles of dried blood on my feet from the British tourist whose head I blew open.

The tub is large and fills slowly. I think of my dad and the conditions Kladivo must be keeping him in. Surely there's no hot bath for him, wherever he is. But as I sit on the edge of the tub, it occurs to me I may know exactly where he is.

If he's still in Kladivo's possession, there's a chance he's being held at the secret police station I've just come from. And why not? It's a ready-made prison, private and secure. Had I been only a few meters away from him and not known it?

I turn the tub's faucets off, then strip and slide into the water. It's too hot and my skin turns red, but that's the point. It's about sanitizing. It's about cleansing by pain. I order myself to cry, or at least feel guilt, over the man I killed, to prove to myself there's some normal human emotion left in me. But it doesn't work. Besides, sucker punch a gangster on the street, call him faggot and try to kick him to death— how do you think that story ends? Stupid asshole walked into this voluntarily. He could have just walked away from two men kissing and had another beer with his mates. Could have, but didn't, and now some guy with bleached hair and a diamond tattoo on his neck is tossing his body into a hole in the ground. That's how I justify the murder, anyway. That's how I stop myself from taking Roman's razor and cutting my wrists.

But there is a lesson here I'm meant to learn. I passed the first test, a cursory examination of the Sofia identity and a basic interrogation. But there will certainly be other tests, and for those Sofia won't hold up. Not under the kind of scrutiny a man like Bohdan Kladivo can bring to bear on me. We're way beyond the Spycraft 101 Yael taught me, and I will not take well to questioning under the pliers or the power drill or the blowtorch. I need an option. I need an out.

I open the drain of the tub and towel myself off. There's much to do before Roman gets home.

Everything is untouched in my bag of possessions, even the money. I dress quickly and am about to head out when I stop at the front window. There's a small Škoda hatchback parked across the street, and two young guys in leather jackets are leaning against it, smoking and staring straight at the entrance to Roman's building. Not talking, not checking their phones, just standing there smoking and staring. That's right, I think. I'm Pan Kladivo's property now, bought and paid for and put away in the nicest closet in Prague. Are they protectors or captors? It doesn't really matter, I suppose.

I go from room to room, inspecting the windows for a possible alternate exit. But they open only a few inches, and even if I could squeeze through, it's a five-story drop to the roof of the neighboring building. So instead I slip out of the apartment and down the staircase from the twelfth story to the basement. I follow along a corridor to the garbage collection room where the chutes from every floor empty into a compactor. Just as I suspected, there's a door leading to the outside, and if I've kept my bearings, it will open into the alley running parallel to the street.

My hunch is correct, and the alley is empty. I find a piece of scrap paper on the ground and fold it into a little wedge that I insert into the latch to keep the door from locking behind me.

Then I put the hood of my jacket up and disappear around the corner.

. . .

Graffiti covers the walls of the subway staircase. Bored, drugged-out teenagers hang out on the station benches, their eyes large and drawn back inside skeletal faces, their bodies drowning in T-shirts three sizes too big.

I push past them to the street. Run-down shops with run-down cars parked outside them. A babushka, old as the earth, pauses to adjust the polka-dot kerchief on her head and scolds me for looking like a boy. Proud women wear their hair long, she says.

There's a butcher shop and a little bakery, an auto repair garage and a travel agent. But the shop I'm looking for sits a little farther down, between a shop selling used musical instruments and a tanning salon. The sign out front says in Russian RESTAURANT SUPPLIES.

The front of the shop is rolled up like a garage door, and I step inside and pretend to browse. Metal mixing bowls, strainers, and plastic ashtrays are stacked in crooked columns that rise to the ceiling. A fly buzzing around a bare lightbulb leaves its post to circle me for a second before disappearing out the shop's door. I take a few items and head to the counter where an obese guy with gray skin sits on a stool.

I drop the items on the counter, and he starts tallying them on a pocket calculator. Then I lean in close and speak in Russian. "My boss sent me to this shop because we're having a hell of a rat problem," I say.

The guy looks at me over the dirty lenses of his glasses. "Traps and poison, aisle seven."

"Yeah, I saw those. Thing is, it's a bad rat problem. My boss sent me here, to your shop specifically, because he said you have the good stuff."

"The good stuff?"

I nod in the direction of the door behind him, what I assume is the stockroom. "The *real* stuff," I say. "Like we had back home."

The clerk braces his hands on the counter and, with considerable effort, lifts himself to his feet. He disappears into the other room and emerges moments later with a small cardboard box.

"Manufactured in North Korea," he says.

"The best?" I say.

"Fucking Rolls-Royce."

I pick the box up and turn it over in my hands. The entire package is yellow and looks like one big warning label with skull and crossbones stamped next to boldface and underlined Korean text.

"Do not handle pellets with bare hands," he tells me. "Myself, I wouldn't even handle the box with bare hands."

I drop it to the counter. "Does it work fast?"

The clerk snorts a little laugh. "A minute. Maybe two."

"Does it—hurt?"

"They're rats; they don't understand pain," he says, eyeing me, "But if I'm wrong, so what."

It's a time-honored tradition among spies, the suicide pill. Nazis at the door? Bite down hard. You'll be dead before they ever touch you. Concentrated cyanide is the usual way, but a pellet of North Korean rat poison will do in a pinch. At least that's what I'm counting on.

The key is two ingredients banned almost everywhere but North Korea, cyanide and thallium. They are to rat poison what onion and garlic are to cooking. That's what the connoisseurs on the Internet say. It took me ten minutes of research to find that out. It took me ten more to find a place in Prague where I might get it. Walk into any Russian shop in the world and there's always a better selection of everything from caviar to vodka to rat poison waiting in the back. You just need to know how to ask.

I enter the apartment the same way I left, avoiding the street out front and Bohdan Kladivo's men. In the bathroom, I pull out a tube of lip balm, break off the end, and throw the rest away. Then I tuck two pellets of the rat poison into the tube and squish the end of the lip balm on top of them. Now I have my out. My alternative to the pliers and blowtorch. Should it come to that. When it comes to that.

Just as I slide the tube into the pocket of my jeans, I hear the apartment door open. I force a smile, step out of the bathroom, and find Roman.

His face is still swollen, his hand is bandaged, and he walks with a limp. I stand in the hallway, watching as he sets his phone and wallet on a table by the entrance and examines his face in a mirror. He ignores me when I say hello, and when I go to take the suit jacket draped over his shoulders, he flinches. He's just a means to an end, I have to remind myself. Do not pity him. Do not care what happens to him.

"How are you feeling?" I ask.

"I have a new, very important assignment from my father," he says.

"What is it?" I say cheerily.

"I am to take you shopping."

"What do you mean?"

"New dresses. New shoes. New everything. My father says you are to look the part of a proper Kladivo woman and I am to help you do it. 'Something faggots are known to be good at,' he said to me."

The pain in Roman's voice is plain. He's still wearing the shirt from last night, and fumbles with the buttons as he tries to undo them.

"I can do that," I say, unfastening one of the buttons for him.

"Don't touch me," Roman says, brushing my hands away. He slowly works through the rest and shrugs the shirt off. His torso is muscular and toned, but there's a wide bandage wrapped around most of his chest.

"What's that?" I say.

"Cracked ribs." Roman looks down at the floor, mouth pursed like he just bit into a lemon. "How much did you see last night?"

"Just the attack."

"Don't lie."

"I saw enough. But I want you to know that I don't care."

He nods at this, looks away. "Well, I'm through with that now."

"Roman, why don't you—why not leave?" I pick up his shirt for him, try to see his expression. "Prague, I mean. Europe. Go someplace where . . ."

His sharp eyes glint at me in the light. "I'm not a faggot," he seethes. "This, *this business*, is who I am. You're welcome, by the way."

"For what?"

"Saving your ass. If I hadn't told my father you'd tried to help, you'd be dead, too." He snatches the shirt away and takes a step closer, looming over me. "And now my father thinks you're something other than a little street slut. But we'll see, Sofia, We'll see what you are."

"Okay, Roman," I say, turning my eyes low. "Why don't you rest now. I'll bring you some tea."

Lest members of the public wander in and touch the items on display with unwashed hands, the shop on Pařížská Street—just a stone's throw from the cemetery where I spent my first night in Prague—must be entered by first pressing a buzzer. The saleswoman, Claudette, speaks English to me as she shows me gowns. She is unfailingly polite with her voice, but her eyes could not be more forthcoming in their contempt. She has transformed street urchins before, turning them into proper mistresses and sometimes even wives. But this only ends one way, sweetheart, Claudette's eyes say. And we don't take returns.

In the dressing room, I linger a few moments more than necessary, taking in the image in the mirror, not quite believing it. My naturally black hair—dyed so often, I haven't seen it in years—has grown back a little since I sheared it off. It lies sleekly flat from the sharp part on the left side. Beneath it is an angry face of sharp lines, and an angry body thicker and harder than it had been even when training with Yael. The translucent sheath of pale skin is taut over the brass layer beneath, and it makes me look like I'm made of stone. It's a new kind of beauty on this stranger: beauty through strength, beauty through fury. It's frightening and wonderful, and for the first time ever in my life, what I see in the mirror pleases me.

I come out of the dressing room and display myself in gown after gown for Roman, who lounges on a couch upholstered in silk. He pretends to enjoy it, howling with praise each time I step from behind the curtain, cracking lewd remarks. Finally, when he can take the boredom no more, he declares the event over.

"Which do you like the best?" I ask him.

"Whichever one you do, my lovely angel." His speech is slurred. Since the night of the beating, he's been popping Percocet and shooting up with the morphine prescribed for the pain. I wonder if he's still stoned? Stoned again? He re-ups the cocktail every few hours, so it's hard to tell where he is in the cycle.

"The green one, emerald. With sequins," I say.

A dismissive flick of his hand. "Perfect."

It costs as much as a car, the green one, emerald, with sequins. It's literally the most expensive thing I have ever owned twenty times over. Roman pays for it in cash, but he struggles to count the money correctly and I have to help him.

Out on Pařížská Street, our two bodyguards stamp out their cigarettes and fall into step ten paces behind us. They're the same two from outside Roman's apartment and have been with us all day. I glance in their direction over my shoulder. "Can't we get rid of them?" I ask.

Roman ignores the question. "We're going to Das Herz tonight. You'll need club clothes."

I translate from German. "The heart?"

"No. Das Herz is a person. A DJ. He's performing tonight, and we are to be there. People don't respect a king they can't see, my father says. It's part of the business, being the public face."

"And what about the rest? The part that's not public," I say. "Your father wants me to learn."

"So you will, soon enough." Roman's phone rings from inside his jacket, and he answers it. A brief conversation in Czech, and then he hangs up. "It's over. Like I told you it would be," he says to me. "Janos was his name. Liked to be called 'Jimmy.'"

"Who?"

"The faggot you saw. Who followed me out of the bar." There's an implied smirk in his voice.

"You—you broke up with him?"

"He's dead," Roman says. "Shot. In his apartment, eating breakfast."

My skin beads with sweat and I feel a rush of nausea. "Your father, he had him killed?"

"No," Roman says. "I did."

Everyone in Prague under the age of thirty has turned out for the Das Herz show at the club called Fume. It's south of Prague 1 in the semi-demolished ruins of a communist-era hospital.

Roman and I are seated in the VIP area on the third story, right at the edge where the floor falls away. We preside over the party happening below within the jagged, blown-apart foundation walls that look like the inside of some enormous creature's jaw. Beautiful people dance beneath the moonlight and strobes on what would be the creature's tongue, oblivious that they're about to be swallowed. Das Herz stands on a platform behind an impossibly complicated spread of turntables and Mac laptops, headphones pressed to one ear, arm pumping in the air.

We are here so that we may be seen to be here. Among the

glamorous. Among the people who mean something. Das Herz is only last week out of rehab in Helsinki, and this is his first gig in nine months. Reporters have come for the occasion and will remark on Twitter about how even Roman Kladivo, the gangster and heir apparent to the biggest crime family in Mitteleuropa, showed up with his new girlfriend.

There is Cristal champagne in the ice bucket at our feet, sent over by an American rapper everyone but me seems to know. There is cocaine on the table before us, being snorted by Roman's coterie of tracksuited friends. Someone shows off his new tattoo—a pink-orange devil riding a motorcycle. Someone else shows off his new Glock 9mm—a handsome pistol of plastic composite with a fifteen-round magazine.

"What happened to you?" someone important asks Roman, taking note of the swollen eye and the bandage on his hand.

"Car accident," Roman says. "Flipped my Lambo on the 18." Lambo is short for Lamborghini, saving time for those who have to use the word often.

He's still on Percocet and morphine. These and the champagne and the whiskey and the beer are making Roman especially friendly tonight, eager to show off his new girlfriend and position as the reigning and very hetero king of Prague's club scene.

I smile at all who come to pay tribute and laugh generously at their jokes. I accept the caviar sent over by the visiting pop star from Japan. I kiss the cheek of a sultan's son from Dubai.

But the celebration is thankfully short-lived. It's only half an hour into the show when an intruder arrives. It's Emil, sweating, angry. "You don't answer your fucking phone?" he shouts at Roman in English over the music.

"Relax. Have a sniff. Let me get you something. Where the fuck did the waitress go? *Servírka!*"

"Four, maybe five texts I sent you," Emil says. "Roman, there's trouble."

"There's always trouble," Roman says. *"Servírka!"*

"Libor got picked up by the police. Stolen merchandise, they said."

Roman pinches the bridge of his nose. "So bail him out in the morning."

Emil glances in my direction. "Libor and me, we have that thing tonight. You know, the cargo we were supposed to pick up, then drop off at the *tábor*."

Tábor—it's the word Kladivo had used for the secret police station.

"Let me help," I say.

Emil gives a shrug. "Look, no offense to the boss's girlfriend..."

"Take her," Roman says. "Take Sofia."

Emil laughs incredulously. "Seriously, Roman..."

"My father says she is to learn the business," Roman says, squeezing Emil's shoulder.

"So what?"

A kind of nasty smirk crosses Roman's face. "So teach it to her."

Twenty-Four

It's midnight, and a light rain has started falling along Sokolovská Street. This stretch of it is mostly asleep, metal shop shutters rolled down, curtains pulled over apartment windows. There's a wood fire burning somewhere. It smells cozy, and I wish I were there, reading Kafka all snuggled up in a blanket, or whatever normal people do in front of a fireplace in Prague. Instead, I'm drinking coffee from a paper cup, the strong Turkish stuff with the texture of river mud I bought at the last open kebab stand two blocks ago.

It's here Emil is supposed to pick me up after he went to get the truck and I went back to the apartment to change out of my club clothes. Down the street, I see a small, boxy truck turn the corner, yellow headlights strafing the pavement in front of it, heading straight toward me. Even from this distance, I hear the hip-hop blasting from inside.

It slows to a stop in front of me, and I climb into the passenger seat. Emil's face glares at me, his anger at working with a woman, me, especially, looking somehow more dangerous in the blue cast of dashboard lights. He accelerates down the street and makes a left. In a few moments, we're on a highway heading north.

"Why does Roman want you slamming it with the street side now?" Emil says. "Thought you were too fancy for us."

"The English phrase is 'slumming it,' not 'slamming it,'" I say over the awful Czech rap blasting from the speakers.

"Fuck do you know? You're Russian," he says.

"Can I turn down the music?"

"That's *me*. That's *my* album. MC Vrah is my name. It means, like, gangster, assassin. Did you know I was a rapper?"

I turn the music down anyway. "What are we picking up?"

"Cargo. That is all I am permitted to say." He cuts into the left lane, guns it past a row of trucks, the colorful tarps covering their trailers rippling like sails in the light of the sodium lamps.

There's a knapsack in the space between the seats, and I pull it onto my lap. "What's this?" I ask.

"What we're trading for the cargo," he says.

I unzip the knapsack and pull out three clear plastic bags stuffed with yellowish crystals that look like rock candy. Each one weighs a little over two pounds, I estimate, or a kilo each. "Drugs?" I say.

"You just come in from the farm? Crystal meth. The finest. Imported from Oklahoma," Emil says, then adds proudly: "That's a territory in the United States."

I have no idea how much the three kilos are worth, but it must be a lot. Considering we're taking the truck and not a car, we have to be trading it for something substantial.

"Almost forgot," he says, digging through his jacket. He pulls out a pistol and places it on my lap. "In case."

"In case what?"

"You'll know," he says.

We drive without talking for a long time, the only sounds coming from the highway and the speakers, a low, grating drum machine and the voice of MC Gangster-Assassin. Then Emil downshifts as he moves over to the right. The lane separates from the rest of the highway and we pass beneath a sign marked NĚMECKO. Germany.

We cross out of the Czech Republic sometime after 2:00 a.m. There are no real border crossings anymore, just the remnants of them: boarded-up guard posts and barrier arms permanently raised. What the European Union did to ease the burden on commerce and travel also eased the burden on criminals. People like Emil, and now, apparently, me.

We exit the highway a few kilometers past the border and pass through a little village where every building is dark for the night. He slows down and takes a left at the very last street before it turns to farm fields. It's an alley, and we follow it to a loading dock behind a little shop.

There's a guy in jeans and leather jacket waiting there, leg cocked on the wall. When he sees us, he flicks his cigarette into a puddle like some German James Dean and approaches.

"*Was geht ab*, bro," Emil says through the open window.

The two slap their way through a complicated handshake that ends in an embrace and backslap.

James Dean notices me and nods. "Who's the chick?" he says in English.

"Sofia. New girl. Boss thinks it's a good idea to have women around these days," Emil says.

He gives me the once-over and a nod. "I'm called Fischer," he says. Then he looks back to Emil. "These guys in there? Serious-as-hell gangsters. No fucking around, okay?"

The door of the loading dock slides up. The serious-as-hell

gangsters look the part, with leather jackets worn and patched over, work boots shifting uneasily on the ground. But Emil takes them in stride and climbs out of the van. "Come on," he says to me.

Fischer, Emil, and I climb up the loading dock and into the back of the shop. The garage door lowers behind us with the sounds of clanking chain and squeaking metal wheels. Fischer introduces them, Russian names all around.

Their lead guy, Max, stands behind a workbench and smiles at us with all the sincerity of a dogcatcher to a dog. He has a thin gauze of blond hair and wears patches on his jacket—a bat with its claws around a grenade, a skull with two hammers crossing beneath it. "You bring it?" he says in English, nodding to the knapsack in Emil's hand.

Emil pulls the three bags from the pack and lays them out on the workbench. One of their guys, the smallest of the group, opens a bag and removes a sample with a pair of tweezers. He places it into a test tube and retreats to a counter where he has a few portable lab machines set up. All eyes are on him and the testing, and I can smell the tension in the air. I finger the gun in my pocket.

Finally, the tester turns around and speaks loudly in Russian so the others can hear.

I lean close to Emil and interpret. "Very pure. About ninety percent."

Max extends his arms and grins. "Three kilos, top quality."

"Just as promised," Emil says. "So, you have the cargo?"

Max nods to his men, and two of them head off into the shop. "So, as agreed, ten units?"

"Correct," Emil says. "Ten units."

From somewhere deep in the shop I hear two men shouting followed by high-pitched yelps. Then, rounding the corner, emerges a group of young women—girls, actually. The youngest is maybe fourteen, the oldest maybe seventeen. Beads of sweat appear on my skin, and a sudden and powerful nausea takes hold of my stomach. This is the "cargo." These are the "units."

They're bound at the wrists with zip ties and being herded with sticks. The men lash out at them arbitrarily, with no purpose but to hurt.

"Hey! No fucking bruises!" Emil shouts, then turns to me. "Tell them!"

I shout the translation.

They're brought to the front of the room. Ten girls, hunched over, shaking, shivering, eyes wide with fear. They are, each one, extraordinarily beautiful, shockingly so. The kind of beauty every woman wants and every girl's parent fears. A few of them stare at me, finding room enough next to their terror for hatred. They've learned to expect this from the men here, but they'll reserve an even worse place in hell for me.

My jaw and fists tighten. Pull out the gun and set them free. In the name of whatever good is left in you, Gwendolyn, do the right thing. But I don't. There's nothing I can do, I tell myself. I have a pistol with, what, maybe eight bullets? Even if I were an expert shot, I'd be dead on the floor before I could drop just two of the Russians. That's what I tell myself to stop from doing it. Because I'm a coward and because I'm selfish.

Max walks around the workbench to stand next to Emil. "Nice, yes? The redhead, she is from Petersburg. I think, maybe I make extra cost for you, but no. I give her to you as . . ." He looks at me. *"Podarok?"*

"Present," I say. "Gift."

"Yes, gift. I make it to you and maybe we do more business together, okay?"

Emil reaches forward and takes the redhead by her bound wrists. "No track marks," he says.

Max shrugs. "As you ask, no junkies. Top quality all."

Emil moves on to another girl. She recoils as he touches her black hair. "Where are the rest from?" he asks.

"Poland, Romania, Russia, Albania. I don't know. As you ask, we find only best for you."

"And are they clean?" Emil asks.

Max squints.

"Disease? No. We have doctor look. Clean as soap." He pats Emil on the shoulder. "You find HIV, syphilis, whatever, you call me. Refund, no problem."

Emil holds out his hand, and Max shakes it. Very gentlemanly, the whole thing.

Someone rolls up the garage door, and Emil sends me down to unlock the back of the truck. I stand on the deck, helping each one in, grabbing them by their thin forearms and pulling them up. Two or three girls start crying. One of them even resists, but Emil yanks her head back by the hair and puts a pistol to her cheek and that's the end of that.

I reach for the redhead's arm, but she refuses and climbs in on her own. Then she spits in my face and calls me a devil-bitch in Russian.

The windows are down, and Emil is rapping along with Lil Wayne on the radio, slapping his hand to the rhythm against the outside of the truck's door.

"Stop it," I say.

"What?" he shouts over the music.

I press the power button on the radio with the palm of my hand and the music goes silent. "Stop it. Stop hitting the door, and for Christ's sake, stop singing."

Emil's smirk glows in the dashboard lights. "See, this is why Roman never should send a woman for this job. The girls back there, they're just whores, you know."

"And what's the difference between them and me?"

He shrugs. "You're the one sitting in front."

I close my eyes, unable to stand it any longer, the rage like a heat within me, threatening to melt my skin. *Hand in my pocket. Hand wrapping around the butt of the gun. Finger finding the trigger.* This, the mission to find my father, ends tonight. Ten lives for one, maybe two. It's an easy choice, isn't it? No made-up god's made-up morality would ask otherwise. Watch his brains explode and grab the wheel.

"We're bringing them to the—what is it, the *tábor*?" I ask.

"Yes," Emil says.

"And what happens to them there?"

Emil thinks a minute as he lights a cigarette. The smoke whips out the open window. "The *tábor* is for, like, to hold them. You know."

"Hold them," I repeat. "Rape them?"

Emil grimaces. "They are whores, Sofia. It is not rape if they are whores."

I flip the safety with my thumb, and slide the pistol from my pocket, keeping it hidden next to my thigh. But first, a confession from Emil. It's not enough for him to die; he needs to know the reason. "Are they raped at the *tábor*, Emil?"

"Are you kidding? Fucking Pan Kladivo would cut our dicks off. We just keep them there. Until the auction."

He's talking about the auction I read about on the German news site. *Fleischkurator.* Curator of flesh. Curator of meat. Only a foot or so between us. I'll have to be quick about it, fire as soon as I raise the gun.

"Every few months," Emil continues. "Big party at the casino. Special girls like these only." He studies my face and seems surprised by my expression. "This angers you? About the girls?"

"Doesn't it anger you, Emil?" I ask.

304

It's a tricky question for Emil's mind, and he considers it carefully. "Maybe," he says finally.

"Why maybe?" I ask.

"When I think about it, it's like—these girls are too young. I think, maybe that redhead wants to be a schoolteacher or something back in Petersburg, but now we make her a whore." Emil squints at the road ahead, the philosopher deep in thought. "But that's why I don't think about it."

Of course you don't. And thank you, Emil, for making this so easy for me. I steal a look down at the pistol, tighten my grip. *Now.*

"It's like that old fag who's there," Emil says suddenly. "Who is he? What the fuck did he ever do to Pan Kladivo? None of my business, so I don't think about that either."

My body freezes in place. "The old fag?"

"Yeah, the old guy. Not *old*-old, but gray, or he's gray now. At the *tábor*. In the last cell."

I slip the pistol back into my pocket. "Oh," I say. "Him."

We get off the highway at the first light of dawn, trundle over a bad two-lane road, then turn down a gravel path surrounded on both sides by forest. Ahead I see the gates of the *tábor*.

We park in the middle of the yard, and Emil turns off the engine. As he exits the truck, I slide my iPhone from my pocket, launch the GPS app, and wait for it to pinpoint my location. But there's nothing. No signal at all.

"You coming or what?" Emil shouts from outside. "These whores won't unload themselves."

I slip the phone back into my pocket. "Coming," I say.

The guard from the gate plus five more from the main building gather behind the truck as I raise the door. The girls are huddled at the far end of the hold. The oldest stands in front of the others, arms stretched out as if to protect them.

One of the guards, a pudgy little thing who looks like he's still a teenager, finds sudden bravado. "Come on, bitches! Out!" he screams, rapping the butt of a Kalashnikov rifle on the deck. *"Ubiraytes! Raus!"*

The women jump at the violence of the command but don't move. Emil orders everyone in to get them. I look away, I have to, as each guard grabs two women by the arm and drags them out. The pudgy one pokes at them with the muzzle of his gun, herding them toward the building.

In the kitchen of the *tábor*, Emil helps himself to coffee as the guards bring the women to the cells. When the guards return and sit down for their breakfast—someone's brought pastries—I stay off to the side, leaning against the counter. Emil and the others are engaged in an animated conversation, and the gist of it seems to be the quality of the women downstairs. Two Kalashnikovs on the table next to the food, and everyone with some kind of pistol. I haven't a chance, not now.

The room is kitted out like a frat house and smells of old towels and cooking grease. The cheap, communist-era office furniture is supplemented by someone's mother's old couch and an enormous LED television playing highlights from last night's soccer match.

Then, in the corner, I spot a desk and an old two-way radio. I walk over to it. It looks at least fifty years old. Switches, dials, a wire running up to the ceiling where it disappears.

"Don't touch," someone shouts.

I look back at the table. All eyes are on me. "Why not?"

"No mobile service here, no landline," says the pudgy kid. "Radio is the only way to call Prague. Coded only. Always."

One mode of communication. No calling for help if the radio goes down.

"The women downstairs," I say. "When do they eat?"

"When we say so," says one of the men.

"How about now?" I say. "They should eat something."

A murmur at the table, a little laughter, then the pudgy guard rises and unloads a large cardboard box of American protein bars from a cabinet. "Only one each. If more, they get fat."

My footsteps ring on the metal treads as I repeat the journey I took with Bohdan Kladivo. Each step doubles the dread building in my stomach, each step adds a turn to the metal coil in my chest. I don't know what will be worse—finding my dad here, or finding he's gone. The protein bars inside the box are rattling against one another, and I have to force my hands to be still.

The corridor at the bottom is empty and exactly as I remember it, with numbered cell doors lining the wall, each with a little hatch covering a window, and a long narrow slot at the bottom.

I slide open the hatch of the first window. The box wobbles and nearly falls to the floor as I move my hand instinctively to muffle my gasp. The women from the truck have been stripped naked and two sit curled up on the cot, while two more are on the floor in the same position—bare arms wrapped around bare legs folded up against bare chests. For the first time, I can see them clearly. They shiver and stare straight ahead. Only one turns her head to look at me through the window. Her expression is fear slowly giving way to panicked sorrow. She knows what'll happen next. She's heard the stories. I guess her age to be around fifteen.

I slide a dozen bars through the slot in the bottom of the door.

In the second cell are the remaining six girls in more or less an identical state. The oldest of the group, the one who tried to protect them in the truck, sits with her arms around them, hiding her own fear for their sake. She reminds me of Marina. Once more, I repeat the pathetic gesture and slide a dozen protein bars through the slot in the bottom of the door.

Are there others? I open the third cell and find it empty, but blankets are twisted into contorted shapes on the ground, fingerprints and the leftover residue of human breath smudge the window in the door where someone has tried to see through from the other side. This was the only testimony the women who'd occupied this cell had left behind, little smears of life and desperation. Who knows where they ended up or if they're still alive.

I check the fourth cell, and the fifth, and the sixth. These appear to be recently vacated, too, though I get no comfort from this. Eyes closed, forehead pressed to the cool stone of the wall, I picture what the fates of the previous occupants were. This place, this *tábor*, it's clear to me now, isn't a prison at all. It's the holding yard outside the slaughterhouse where the living are turned into meat.

Inside me, nausea turns to hate, and hate turns to rage, and I swear on my own life that I will make the men upstairs and both Kladivos, father and son, die for this.

I move on to the last cell and slide open the hatch over the window. Inside is a single figure, this one a male, stretched shirtless on a cot. His face is turned against the wall, but I can see a bushy beard on the side of his face, brown turning to gray. The man's hair is shaggy, as if uncut for months. He looks like a picture of a prisoner of war from a textbook, the victim of some atrocity. The man turns onto his back and stares up at the ceiling. His rib cage is in full view, like a skeleton's.

He notices the hatch covering his window is open and lifts his head to squint at it and see who's there. Despite the beard, despite the loss of thirty pounds, despite the change of skin color from peach to gray, I see it's my father.

Twenty-Five

I must be silhouetted in the window because he can't seem to make out my face or at least he doesn't recognize it. My hands go to my mouth, covering a soundless cry. He's alive. Alive, but only just.

Then, footsteps on the stairs. I close the hatch over the window and look away, pressing my palms into my eyes, trying to catch my breath.

"You done?" It's Emil from the end of the corridor.

"Yeah."

"Hurry up. I want to head back to the city."

"One second."

When I'm sure Emil's gone, I pull the gun from my pocket and weigh it. Could I hit them all before one of them gets a Kalashnikov? It's not even a maybe. Of course I can't.

I turn back to the hatch on my father's door. I'm about to slam it open and beat on the window until he recognizes me when logic seizes control. *Don't,* logic says. *Think.*

There's no way to determine how he'll react. There's no way to shout explanations to him through the cell door without the men upstairs hearing. There's no way to prevent it all from backfiring just as I'm within sight of the finish line.

I force myself to pull away, then climb the stairs back to the main floor.

"I'm ready," I tell Emil.

"Were you crying?"

"Fuck you," I say. "Let's go."

As I climb into the truck, I silently promise my dad and the women downstairs that I'll be back for them. Then I make the same promise to Emil, and the rest of the men, too.

I stand over Roman in his bed with his own pistol raised and pointed at his head. He's on his back, snoring like a fool, his chest rising and falling beneath the bandage around his ribs. Justice requires that I kill him. There's no doubt that upon his brains exploding against the headboard, the clouds will part, birds will sing, and a chorus of Kladivo's victims will deafen me with their collective sigh of gratitude and relief.

But I will not pull the trigger. Will not because it will neither free my dad nor free the women in the cells. He's not the only man in this army of the wicked. Roman's not even the only one named Kladivo. But I will pull the trigger someday soon, and that's enough to get me through the next moment. I place his pistol back in his ankle holster and set the thing among the perfectly arranged bottles of cologne on his dresser. Then I pick up his clothes from the night before. Put his suit on a cedar hanger and hang it from the doorknob. Bundle up his shirt that smells of spilled liquor and put it in the laundry hamper.

Behold, Roman, how your mistress cares for you.

I return to the living room and the bottle of wine I opened when I got back to the apartment at seven-thirty this morning. It's the good stuff, brownish red and tasting of rancid grape juice and dirt. But right now this isn't about the taste. It's about medicating. It's about trying to unsee what I've seen, and escape the shivering shapes of those girls, those poor girls, those poor terrified girls.

"I thought you didn't drink."

I turn to see Roman standing at the end of the hallway, dressed in a bathrobe.

"Today seemed like a good day to start," I say, aware of the slur in my words.

He nods. "How did it go last night? The pickup with Emil?"

"I didn't know the cargo we were picking up was women."

He nods indifferently. "I'd like a coffee."

"What?"

He gestures toward the kitchen with his head. "I'd like a coffee. Make it for me."

I look at him as I make my way into the kitchen. A Yale-educated monster in an expensive robe.

Roman follows, instructing me in the proper use of his espresso machine. That lever, not this one. Fill to this line, not that one. "It's from goddamn Italy, so you've got to be gentle with her," he says. Roman's enjoying this, directing me in some petty domestic chore. He leans against the wall, watching his good little housekeeper-concubine.

I finish making it and push an espresso cup toward him across the counter. "They're going to be auctioned, yes? The girls at the *tábor*?"

"I always use a saucer," he says, gesturing with his cup. "For my coffee."

I find the saucers in a cabinet and take one down for him.

He studies me for a while, sips his espresso, then studies me some more. "Who told you about the auction? Emil?"

"Yes."

"Well, you wanted to learn the business," he says. "So there it is—the business."

"They were—children," I stammer. "Kids, Roman."

"Just the way life is. Some people are worth more than others." He sets his cup and saucer on the counter and puts his hands deep in the pockets of his robe. "Good coffee, by the way. Machine can be a little tricky, but you did it right."

"I'm glad."

A moment passes, then Roman grabs the front of my shirt, shoves me against the wall. He pulls a long knife from the butcher block on the counter and holds the point in front of my nose. The blade doesn't tremble or shake. He holds it dead steady. "You know what they had back in their villages, those girls? Fucking nothing. We put them in Versace, cut their hair."

Kill him now. Kill him on principle. Hand to wrist. Knee to groin. Knife to throat. But instead I raise my hands in the air, abject surrender. "I get it, Roman! Please!"

The knife hangs there for a second, the tip of the blade a mere centimeter from my skin. Behind it is Roman's twitching, furious face. Then he lets go of my shirt and catches me with a swift slap that sends me crashing with a yelp to the floor.

I feel a droplet of something wet form on my lip, then a drop of blood lands on the marble tile, red on white. It's followed by a second drop and a third, making a tight little grouping on the tile that looks like bloody bullet holes on a target. *Sweep his legs.*

Roman sets the knife on the counter and kneels next to me. "You fooled my father into thinking you're some tough little bitch. But

I wonder, Sofia, I really wonder whether you're hard enough for this business. Hard enough to do what it takes."

I stay that way for a moment, on the floor, and focus on the blood. "I'm hard enough," I say.

"Hard enough for what?"

"Hard enough to do what it takes."

Twenty-Six

I would like to thank Bohdan Kladivo, and his son, Roman. I would like to thank Emil and Libor and the three Brits and the guy on the train from Berlin to Prague. I would like to thank Paulus and Christian, too. And who can forget the pig in the alley behind the bar in Paris? What was it called? Skinny Goat? Fat Goat? Who can remember? In any case, I'd like to thank all these men. For the lessons they taught me. For the practice they gave the thing inside me, the cruelty, which grows larger and stronger and crueler with each passing day.

It's the morning of the auction, a Tuesday. And as it happens, also my birthday. I turn eighteen today—or rather Gwendolyn Bloom, that old, obsolete version of me, who existed before the cruelty ate her, turns eighteen. The eighteenth birthday is the day you become an adult, the day you take everything you learned as a child and apply it to the grown-up world. All that came before today was mere prelude, a rehearsal for the real thing.

Though tonight there will be a celebration, a grand affair with

Roman in a dinner jacket and me in an emerald sequined gown, it will not be a celebration of my birthday. It will be about the men flying in from around the world in their private jets, men who are of such privilege that their money permits them to transcend morality and buy another human being.

And these transcendent transactions are to be accompanied by great ceremony to give them rightness and a civilized hat to wear. Thus, the casino is closed so that the stage set may be dressed with—Roman let me see the list—crudités made that morning by the chef from the Ritz-Carlton and bottles of fifty-five-year-old Macallan scotch and enough Armand de Brignac champagne to drown in. Bohdan and Roman are spending the day schmoozing their clients, while the most senior others are supervising the rented army that takes care of the girls who are already on the casino's private third floor, doing their hair and makeup, altering their gowns.

But the street side isn't involved tonight. Emil and Libor are supposed to be elsewhere, closing another deal. And it's them I'm counting on to help me, even though they don't know it yet.

"Air out my dinner jacket and have it hanging in the bathroom," Roman says before he leaves. "And my bow tie is frayed. Get me a new one from Pařížská—grosgrain, not satin—and see if you can find my cuff links."

"Of course," I say, and watch the door close behind him.

But as busy as they all are, I'm busy, too. So after I take his dinner jacket out of its plastic dry-cleaning bag, dig through drawers to find his cuff links, and stop in at his haberdashery for a new tie, the cruelty and I head off to burn down the world.

Libor's building in a dull neighborhood at the edge of Prague 8 isn't half bad. It's well kept, and there are flowerpots on nearly every balcony. The tiles of the terra-cotta roof seem bright even in the dull midmorning light.

I stand amid the people coming and going from a small grocery store across the street and from here can see that Libor's car is still parked in front of his building. Then I step into an alley, pull out a new burner phone, and dial 1-1-2, the European 9-1-1. The operator answers in Czech, of course, but since I don't speak Czech, I tell her a story in Russian, knowing it's being recorded. At first, I'm afraid because I've never done any acting. Will I be convincing? Do I sound truthful? But the fact is, acting is all I've done since arriving in Europe.

A man named Libor Kren has beaten me, I say. Threatened me with a gun. He's high on methamphetamine, and has a lot of it around the apartment. Five, six kilos maybe. A real drug kingpin, this Libor. Oh, I'm so frightened. I'm hiding in his bathroom as we speak. His address is 556 Na Strázi, Praha 8. Won't you please hurry? I'm afraid for my life. Here he is now at the door—

Then I hang up, pull the SIM card out, and crush it with the heel of my boot. Precisely six minutes, forty-three seconds after I hang up, I watch from across the street as two police cars and a SWAT van arrive simultaneously. Prague cops, in helmets and body armor, submachine guns held tight at their shoulders, race up the steps of the apartment building. Two minutes later, Libor and his junkie brother are frog-marched out of the building. Libor has a fresh black eye and walks with a distinct limp.

It's been less than a week since Libor's last arrest—the night he was supposed to accompany Emil—and I have no doubt they'll be harsher on him this time around. The Russian girl hiding in the bathroom won't pan out, of course, and likely neither will the five or six kilos of meth the caller said was lying around the apartment. But there are certainly some drugs and likely more than a few guns. Even with the best lawyers in Prague, he won't be out for at least a day or two. And that's all I need.

I'm on the next tram to Prague 1 and arrive at the casino half an hour later. Word of Libor's arrest hasn't reached the casino yet, but I hang around, pretending to help the caterers for tonight's auction. When I hear Emil's loud cursing, I know the news has arrived. They were to pick up a shipment of something today, something unrelated to the auction but still very important. Libor's absence creates certain difficulties and the need for improvisation on Emil's part. Lucky thing I'm here.

I pull him aside in a hallway and volunteer reluctantly. How far is it? I ask. Not far, Emil says. Will we be back before evening? I ask. In plenty of time, Emil says. Let's go, I say.

There's no truck or van this time. Only a beat-up Škoda with Emil at the wheel. There are no plates on it, only a temporary registration tag in the rear window issued by the city of Bratislava, Slovakia. I assume we're heading to the *tábor*, but then Emil enters the highway in the direction of Brno, a city about two hours southeast of Prague.

"What's in Brno?" I ask.

"What we're picking up," he says, the tone of his answer making it clear he won't provide details.

"But we're delivering it to the *tábor*, right—whatever it is?"

He eyes me. "Why do you want to know?"

"Just curious."

"Yes," he answers. "Why are you smiling?"

I picture my father in his cell, eyes on the door, hopeless, not knowing the endgame is only hours away.

"Was I?" I say.

It's a straight-up cash deal this time round, Emil tells me later, pulling his knapsack from the backseat. I look inside and find it stuffed with plastic-wrapped bricks of 500-euro notes: 450,000 euros total. It's surprising how small the size and weight of such an amount is.

A half hour outside Brno, we pull off the highway onto a deserted road between two closed factories, smokestacks dead, parking lots empty. We stop along the side of the road and wait. Just as he did on our last pickup, Emil hands me a gun.

"Expecting trouble?"

"You can never tell," he says.

We're there only about five minutes when a small box truck lumbers around the corner at the far end of the road. It looks like the kind people rent when they move, but the sides of it are bare, no logo, no markings other than a registration number. Whatever's inside it weighs the truck down so that it lists and rolls as it crashes through the potholes. It comes to a stop ten meters in front of us.

Emil climbs out. "Stay here and keep your gun ready," he says. "When I wave my arm like so, bring out the knapsack with the money."

Two guys step down from the truck. Their dark hair is meticulously coiffed, and they're wearing bad suits. One carries a stubby Kalashnikov.

Emil approaches, and there's a brief conversation that ends with a broad-shouldered man wearing an orange necktie giving a toothy smile. Emil turns and waves to me, and I walk toward them, knapsack in hand.

Wherever these two are from, they don't share a language other than English with Emil.

"This your girlfriend?" the guy with the orange tie asks.

Emil takes the knapsack from me and tosses it to him. "She's my associate, Nikko."

"Maybe I want her as my associate," he says as he sets the knapsack on the driver's seat of the truck and gives me a leer.

I tense up, wrap my fingers around the gun in my pocket.

"Let's just get this done," Emil says.

Nikko opens the backpack and thumbs through the bricks of cash while the guy with the Kalashnikov stands guard.

"All is good," Nikko says after a moment. "Come, friends, see your purchase."

Emil and I follow him around to the back of the truck while the guy with the Kalashnikov lingers a few paces behind us. He rolls up the door and reveals green crates stenciled with Chinese writing that fill about half the cargo area.

"Twenty crates, PF-89 rocket-propelled grenades, standard eighty-millimeter," he says, running his hand over one of the crates as if it were the hood of a rare car.

"Open them," Emil says.

Nikko takes a crowbar from inside the truck and pries open the lid. Inside, five RPGs are held in place by wooden brackets. They're spindly, cheap-looking things, made of stamped metal parts and plastic, but deadly nonetheless.

While Emil inspects the merchandise, I wade through the math in my head. Five RPGs to a crate times twenty crates equals one hundred RPGs in all. If each one takes out an average of—let's keep the number round—ten victims, then that's a theoretical one thousand dead.

Nice work today, Gwendolyn. Be proud.

"Clean Slovak registration on the truck," Nikko says as he hands Emil the keys. "Should be no problem."

The truck they gave us is slower and shittier than the car we traded them, but by 4:00 p.m., we're just an hour from the *tábor*. Because of our cargo, Emil is taking mainly back roads. "We don't want to be pulled over with shit like this," he explains.

"Who were those guys?"

"Nikko. He gets the RPGs from the Bulgarian defense ministry. The other guy I don't know."

"And who does Pan Kladivo sell them to?"

"Too serious for anyone in Europe." He shrugs. "But as long as it's not aimed at me, who gives a fuck, right?"

I turn back to the paper map spread out on my lap and navigate while Emil tells me he's going to use the money he's making on this deal on a leather couch and hip surgery for his mom.

"Is this truck hard to drive?" I ask.

He shakes his head. "It's not, you know, hard like a big truck is. If you can drive a car, you can drive this."

Since moving to New York, I haven't driven at all. But I took a driver's ed program set up for diplomats' kids at the school I attended in Moscow. Every weekend, my dad and I would drive out to the suburbs and practice in his little Volvo hatchback.

"Can I try?"

"Driving the truck?" Emil says. "Fuck no."

But I talk him into it, and when we finally switch a few kilometers later, Emil grimaces each time I work the clutch wrong and grind the gears. Only after a while does he release his death grip on the handle over the passenger window and calm down. He was right; it's just like driving a car, only bigger and less agile.

"You going to the auction tonight?" he says as the truck trundles down an empty dirt road.

"I don't have a price tag. So, no."

"I'm not going, either," he says bitterly. "Street guys not welcome. Pan Kladivo, he's afraid we'll belch or say the wrong thing in front of his billionaire friends. Fucking racist."

"If the women are already at the casino, who's at the *tábor*?"

"Usual six guards, we still have the—you know."

"No, I don't know."

"That old fag. In the cell. Never mind." He shakes his head. "You do something for me?"

I grip the wheel tightly. "What?"

"Find out from Roman how much the redhead sells for. The one from Petersburg, you know." Emil drums his fingers on the window sill. "Someday I will have a million euros and buy her. Or, you know, not her. One like her. But with bigger tits."

And with that, I decide it's time.

I pull the truck over to the side of the road and open my door. "Something's wrong with the tire," I say as I climb out.

I cross over to the passenger side, stand by the rear wheel, and call Emil's name. He climbs out of the truck. "Look," I say, pointing at the tire.

He squints at it. "It's fine."

"Look closer."

Emil crouches, bangs at the tire with his fist. "Perfect."

But when he turns around, I have the pistol he gave me out of my pocket and trained on the center of his forehead. His mouth flutters, and I shoot him just above the right eye.

A flurry of birds takes flight from the trees around us, and for a moment, they dash through the air like angry angels. Then they disappear, and it's only me and Emil's body.

The guard at the entrance of the *tábor* doesn't hesitate to open the gate. He recognizes me, and with the speed I'm going and the frantic honking of the horn, it's clear there's an emergency.

I pull the truck into the center of the yard, slam the brake into place, and leap to the ground. "Emil's been shot," I scream at the guard at the gate. "Don't just stand there like an idiot, get help!"

The guard bellows at the door, and four more guards from the main building come running toward me. It's the usual crew, the same ones on duty the last time I was here. I roll open the door on the rear of the truck. "He's heavy," I say. "He'll need all of you to carry him."

All five of them climb in and gather around the body, mystified by what to do. Then they crouch down and begin prodding Emil, as if all they needed to do was wake him up. I seize the strap of the door and yank down hard. It crashes into place, and I throw the lever, locking them in.

Their shouts are muffled by the truck's walls, but their meaning is clear enough. Confusion at first, giving way to commands, giving way to rage. Within a few seconds they're hammering on the door to get out, attempting to lift it, the latch rattling loudly.

On the way back from the pickup of the RPGs, locking them inside had been my only plan. But it occurred to me when I was loading Emil's body into the back, why not take the opportunity to make the world a slightly better place?

And so to that end, I reach back into the cab of the truck and pull out an RPG I took from the crates. It's surprisingly light when you consider the damage it's capable of causing, but then again, that's the idea, isn't it? Light and easy enough that even a child can operate it.

I slop through the mud to the far end of the yard, hoist the thing to my shoulder, and align the crude sights on the center of the truck. There's a simple safety switch, no different from the one on my pistol, and I flip it with my thumb.

From the truck I hear more shouting, and the plinking of bullets hitting iron. One of them has thought to bring a pistol and is trying to shoot the lock through the door.

The noise of the grenade launching forward frightens the hell out of me. That something so loud and powerful—it nearly knocks me off my feet—could be achieved with a single, simple pull of a trigger boggles the imagination. And it would be a point worth pondering, had the thought lived more than a half second. But it dies in the roar that follows the whoosh, the white-orange avalanche of fire that slides and rolls and tumbles out from the fractured truck. I feel my body lifting, and it suddenly seems as if I've badly miscalculated how far away I needed to be. I feel my body lifting and moving backward, and I think that death in this manner doesn't really hurt as much as one would expect.

I'm unconscious for a few seconds. Then I open my eyes and see sky above me, a leaden blanket sky, a sunless, lifeless sky. I feel the dull pain of impact, though I don't remember the impact itself.

There's something strange about my vision as I pull myself to my feet, as if the world is sharper than before, as if I can see more clearly. The truck is now a flaming skeleton with only a hint of its former shape, and I think it's beautiful. The men inside it are dead, and my only regret is that they never saw the blade coming. I check my body for wounds, for holes, but aside from the mud, I'm clean.

Dropping the launcher and pulling my pistol from my pocket, I start toward the jail. Five guards climbed into the back of the truck, not the six that Emil said usually manned the place. That means there's one still somewhere in the *tábor*, and I have to be ready for him.

The entrance and hallway are empty, and so is the kitchen. I knock the radio—the sole means of communicating between the camp and Prague—to the ground and pull the wires from the open back in great handfuls. Then I paw through the drawers until I find a ring of heavy iron keys for the cells below. I stuff these in my pocket and help myself to a handsome, nasty-looking Kalashnikov assault rifle someone left on the table. Finally, I rummage through the pockets of the jackets hanging from pegs, pulling out car keys for the vehicles outside.

With the rifle's safety off, I slip from the kitchen to the stairs, descend them quickly, and sweep into the corridor outside the cells.

Again, the sixth guard is nowhere in sight. I open the hatches to all the cells but the last one, my dad's, and find them empty.

I end at my dad's cell and open the hatch slowly, not wanting to see, not wanting to find that after everything I've done, he's been moved, too. But he's there, on his feet, pacing, throwing worried looks at the door. No doubt he heard the explosion and felt it rock the building. At the sounds of the keys in the lock, he backs up to the far wall, terror evident on his face.

I twist the handle of the latch and pull the door back.

He sees only my muddy clothes and the Kalashnikov. Not that he'd recognize me absent these things. The girl he left in New York was soft and lived in fear of the world, and the woman I am now is nothing like her.

He raises his hands in front of him, expecting to be shot. It's the first thing the guards would do if the camp were ever raided. But when the bullets don't come, he peers at me between his fingers. Then his face softens—I see it even through the beard—and he cants his head to the side. My dad squints at me, and I hear a little breath escape his lips.

"Dad," I say.

But this word is a riddle to him, like a word in a foreign language he remembers hearing but has forgotten the meaning of.

"Who are you?" he says quietly.

"Dad, it's me," I say, gently as I can. "It's me. Gwendolyn."

His arms tremble in the air for a moment, then fall to his sides as if whatever held them in place was suddenly snatched away. He shakes his head side to side, refusing to believe that my presence here is anything but a hallucination.

I step forward, just a baby step, and he recoils. "I've told you everything," he pleads. "Where the passcodes were, I told you. I told you."

"It's me," I repeat. "It's Gwendolyn, Dad."

He turns and presses his face into the wall. I hear him sob. "I don't have anything more. I don't. You have it all."

I raise a hand and move it forward tentatively, but when I touch his shoulder, he recoils. Then I touch him again, more forcefully this time, one hand firmly on his shoulder, another on his upper arm. He pulls away, and I feel what little muscle is left on him tremble.

"Dad. Dad, it's me. Listen to my voice, Dad."

His lips—cracked, swollen—begin to move as if he's trying to say something. He closes his eyes, then opens them again, then lifts a hand and presses it to the side of my face. His palm and fingers are wet with sweat.

Now it's my turn to close my eyes, pinching them shut against the tears. He wraps my head in his thin arms, and I can feel his breath against my scalp as he says, "Gwen, it's you. Gwen, my girl."

"I'm here to take you away, Dad."

"How did you—how did you get here?"

"I did terrible things, Dad."

He squeezes me tight, the whole story of what I had to do, the whole everything, no doubt appearing in his imagination in a sudden burst of heat and light.

Twenty-Seven

We have an unspoken truce on questions. He will not ask them of me, and I will not ask them of him until we're away from this prison. The sixth guard may still be around, and we're both smart enough to know this isn't over yet.

He is malnourished but still in good enough shape to move with haste. Thus, he insists on taking the Kalashnikov from me like any good father would, some instinct telling him I might hurt myself with it. Though I shouldn't be shocked by anything anymore, I'm surprised to see that he's clearly handled a weapon like this before. He checks it over, cocks it, and, with the stoic face of an experienced soldier, nods to the open cell door. I follow closely behind him, my pistol out and ready as we ascend the stairs and sweep through the ground floor.

But the stoic face drops away as we exit the building and he catches sight of the still-burning hulk of the truck. He is, I can see, heartbroken. Daughters ought not have to rescue their fathers, and ought not have to become murderers to do it.

Of the cars arrayed in the yard, three were badly damaged by the explosion, and we're missing the keys for two more. From the two remaining options—a Fiat hatchback and a Toyota Land Cruiser—we choose the Toyota.

As I sort through the keys, I hear what sounds like a furious hornet snap through the air beside my neck. I turn to my dad and see a look of surprise suddenly appear on his face as a circle of red expands over his left shoulder. My mind is slow to process what's happening, but his isn't. He raises the Kalashnikov with his right hand and lets off a burst of rounds that hammers at the air with a roar.

My eyes turn to his target, and I see the pudgy guard, the kid who poked at the women as they were herded from the trucks, the one who ordered me to feed them one bar apiece lest they get fat. Recognition comes to me at the precise moment the gun falls from his hands. He staggers forward, mouth agape, hands slack at his sides. Then he collapses to the mud.

By the time I turn my head back to my father, he's leaning on the side of the Land Cruiser, face white, hand pressed to his shoulder. He growls under his breath in pain as I help him into the passenger seat.

"Just a shoulder, Gwen. I've got another one," he says through gritted teeth.

I scramble through the contents of the vehicle looking for a first-aid kit. But all I come up with is a clean, or cleanish, white undershirt. I fold it into a tight square, press it to the wound, and, with a roll of electrical tape from the glove compartment, make a sort of shoulder harness.

"Time to go, Gwen," he says against the pain. "There could be others."

And he's right. The shoulder harness is the best I can do for now, anyway. I put the Land Cruiser in gear and drive through the gates, the truck wallowing like a pig down the gravel path. When we make it onto the main road leading to the highway, I look over and see his face locked in a grimace.

"Where are we going, Gwen?" he says.

"To the embassy. They can help us there."

"No. No embassy."

"But Kladivo—he can't get you there."

He reaches over, squeezes my arm. "Gwen, Bohdan Kladivo is CIA. He's theirs. Their man in Europe."

The words hit me like a hurricane, and it takes me moments to stammer out a response. "He can't be. Kladivo's a monster, dad. He sells people—there were women, girls. . . ."

But he knows this already, has lived it. "And the CIA doesn't care, Gwen."

"But if he's CIA, why was he holding you?"

"Money, Gwen. It's always money. That's the way it works, the whole world. His old boss, Zoric—he left behind anonymous accounts. Kladivo and someone in the CIA were going to steal them. I found out about it." His face pinches with pain, and he leans back in his seat. "*Jesus*, it hurts."

"I have the accounts, Dad," I say. "It was in the book, *1984*. You left it with Bela, and he gave it to me."

He clenches with another kind of pain. "Tell me that's not true, Gwen."

"I found the storage locker in Queens, decoded the cipher, everything."

His face is a mask of sweat. "Fucking Bela," he gasps. "They were never meant for you. Never meant—Gwen, do you have a phone?"

I pull it from my pocket and hand it to him.

He dials a number and presses it to his ear. "Yes, this is Mr. Angler," he says after a moment. "Tell Mr. Martin I'm leaving town today, but I want a grand tour of his apartment before I go."

He's trying to make his voice normal, but it's clear he's in agony. There's a long pause, maybe thirty seconds.

"That's right. The grand tour," he says. "And I'll be bringing a guest. My daughter."

He hangs up and drops the phone to the floor.

"What was that about?" I say. "Who was that?"

"Friends. The only friends I have left," he says, leaning back in his seat, his eyes starting to close. "I'm sorry, sweetheart. For what's about to happen, I'm sorry."

"Dad, wake up. What are you sorry about, Dad? What's about to happen?"

"No embassy, Gwen." His voice is quiet now, and he's drifting into unconsciousness, his last bit of strength used up. "Just drive to Prague."

I check his pulse every two minutes as I drive. It feels weak, and different every time. I pull over somewhere on the outskirts of the city and make sure the bandages are holding—they are—but it's obvious he needs a hospital. With all the guards at the camp dead and the radio destroyed, there's almost no chance Kladivo knows about what happened, but there's no way in hell I'm dropping Dad off at a random hospital and leaving him out in the open.

I find the phone on the floor where my dad dropped it and tap the number of the last call. Three rings, four, then a male voice answers. "Hello again, Mr. Angler," he says. He has a vague, unidentifiable accent—east of France, west of Russia.

"I'm the guest of Mr. Angler, his daughter," I say. "The one he said also wants a grand tour of—I can't remember, someone's new apartment."

"Of course," the voice says. "Has there been trouble?"

"Mr. Angler needs a doctor. He's been shot in the shoulder."

"Is he conscious?"

329

"No."

Silence for a moment. In the background, I hear the clicking of computer keys. "Are you safe at this moment?"

I look around. It's an empty neighborhood of warehouses and industrial shops. "Yes. No. Or, you know, no one's shooting at the moment."

"Stay where you are. Someone will meet you at your location in five minutes," the voice says.

"Do you need an address?"

"We have it, miss. Good-bye."

I have no idea who or what is coming for us, but my father trusted them, and so I have to trust them, too. Still, I keep my pistol out and on my lap and monitor the mirrors for anything heading our way.

Sorry, he'd said, for what's about to happen next. But whatever my father has planned, he'll have to do it without me. I have my own agenda for the day, and it's only half done. What I'll do next is foolish. In fact, it's suicidal. My rational self says to leave it alone, to go and be done with this place. But what my instinct commands, the rest of me must live with. So I decide to do it anyway, or die doing it, or die trying to do it.

I came to Prague out of obligation to my dad, but I'll stay for the obligation I took on when I delivered those women into Bohdan Kladivo's hands. The obligation to free them, no matter the cost.

A large white van rounds the corner. Its windows are tinted dark and the words CITY TOURS are painted on the sides. In Prague 1, these tourist vans are a common sight, but here in the outskirts they're an oddity.

It rolls to a stop directly behind us, and the driver gets out and heads toward me. He's a tall guy, maybe forty, with brown hair turning gray and wearing a blue City Tours jacket. I lower the window.

"Is that Mr. Angler next to you?" the driver says through a smile. His breath smells of spearmint gum, and his accent is pure American.

"He needs a doctor," I say.

"Looks like it," he says. "We'll get him patched up, don't you worry." He motions to the van, and a man and woman climb out. They're dressed in jeans and leather jackets and carry a large canvas pack marked with a red cross. They open the passenger door and begin examining my dad. While the woman presses a stethoscope to his heart, the man probes around the wound with fingers in rubber gloves.

"Let's get him into the van," the woman says.

I start to say something in protest, but the driver places a comforting hand on my shoulder. "They're professionals, and your father's going to be fine," he says. "What's your name, by the way?"

"Sofia—sorry, Gwendolyn."

"Call me Sam," he says. "So, did your father explain what this is?"

"No."

"It's an exfiltration—a big word that means we're getting you and your dad the hell out of here."

"I can't. Not now," I say. "There's something I have to do. It's important. There are— look, people's lives depend on this."

"We leave now or we don't leave at all, you understand? Now turn off the engine." There's no smile on his face anymore. I do as he says and put the keys into his outstretched hand.

He steps back as I open the door and climb down from the Land Cruiser.

"Eight hours," I say.

"What's that?"

"Eight hours," I repeat. "I'll meet you here, at this spot, in exactly eight hours."

Sam shakes his head. "We won't be here, Gwendolyn."

"Find a way," I say.

Roman has been home to change into evening clothes and has already left again by the time I return to the apartment. Thus, my ablutions—the ritual cleansing of the body from the dirt of the tasks behind me and for the tasks ahead—can be conducted in private. I wash away the day's mud and gunpowder with Roman's lavender-scented soap, shave my legs with Roman's razor, and slick my hair to the side with Roman's pomade.

I unwrap the emerald sequined gown from Pařížská Street. My God, is it stunning. I slide into it, somehow manage the zipper in the back, and allow myself to look in the mirror. In the reflection, I don't see my appearance but myself, my self. A woman dressed for battle in emerald mail. A dragon whose scaled skin catches the light and becomes shadow along the contours of my body as the dragon turns and primps and likes what it sees.

Next come the accessories I'll need for this evening at the fancy-dress ball. Dove-gray satin elbow-length gloves made in Paris. Black beaded clutch made in Milan. Brown-yellow capsules of rat poison made in North Korea.

I don't think I'm going to make it to my maybe-on-probably-off appointment with Sam. After careful consideration of all the risks, it's doubtful I'll live that long. But I have sins to make up for. What I delivered those girls into is bad enough, but what happens to them after tonight is even worse. Their fate is my responsibility now—the cost of the sin I committed. If I succeed and free them, then I will deserve to be among the living. If I fail or am captured in my attempt, then I don't deserve to breathe. In that case, I will pop one of the capsules in my mouth and bite down hard. It'll hurt, the next part, but it'll be quick. Faster and less painful than what Bohdan Kladivo would do to me.

There is one final order of business before I leave for the evening.

I settle into the couch in Roman's living room and cross my ankles just so. I can see my reflection in the window, an elegant, featureless silhouette. It takes me a moment to work up the courage, but before I can second-guess my decision, I'm pressing the numbers on my phone and the connection goes through and the other end is ringing.

Two rings. Three. Four. Terrance's voice mail.

I pause stupidly after the tone, unprepared for the possibility that he simply wouldn't pick up. I hear my breath catch in my throat, and now it'll be the first thing he hears, scratchy, panicky unease. "Hey," I say finally. My tone is flat, like a confession. "It's me. I'm—going out. I don't know when I'll be back. Maybe this is the last time I can talk, so—look, I want to thank you for everything." I pause, embarrassed for some reason by what I'm about to say. Once more I hear the static of distance, of satellites and solar flares and the vast, uncrossable space between him and me. I push the embarrassment aside and continue anyway. "I want to say that—I want to tell you that—you know, I've never been in love. Not really. Well, I thought I was once, but—I know this sounds stupid, but . . ."

But then the phone gives three dead-hearted chirps. *Call dropped,* says the screen. When? I wonder. At what point did it drop? What will be the last of my words he hears?

I toss the phone onto the couch beside me. It's probably for the best. Even if he never hears it, at least I said it, or part of it anyway. As to what words would have come out of my mouth next, I don't know. To say I loved him wouldn't have been precisely honest. What I love is the world in which two people are allowed to fall a little in love while sitting on a park bench, afraid only of the dangers presented by sleeping drunks and rain clouds, talking about plans for future lives that now, at least for one of us, will never come true.

Outside on the street below, I hear the high-low siren of an ambulance calling out mournfully that an emergency is at hand. I check the time as I slip my phone into my clutch. Goodness, is it that late already?

I take a cab to the casino, closed for the night to the usual millionaire riffraff. Tonight is all about the billionaires, the ones who sign the paychecks of millionaires and who, for their amusement, have collections of Fabergé eggs and Greek statues and Moldovan teenage girls. The cab eases past the rows of parked limousines to the entryway, where a doorman in a grand cape and hat holds the door for me and greets me by the name of Miss Sofia.

A guard with a handheld magnetometer signals me to raise my hands, then passes the device over my body as another guard inspects my clutch. But of course he finds only my phone and a small bottle labeled ibuprofen, which he does not open.

"You are expected, Miss Sofia?" says a man in a tuxedo with a steely permanent smile.

"I'm invited as a guest of Pan Kladivo," I say.

But he holds up a hand in front of me just as I'm about to start up the grand staircase. "Are you certain it's tonight? Events such as this one are customarily for men only."

I drill my eyes into his. "Then call Pan Kladivo down and ask him," I say. "I'm sure he'd appreciate being pulled away from his clients to repeat what I just told you."

The hand disappears, and my heels click on the marble staircase as I rush to the second floor.

I enter the room through the enormous gilded doors on the mezzanine. Classical music plays over the conversations of twenty or so men in black tie drinking cocktails and chatting and laughing and looking very much forward to testing the additions to their portfolios purchased here tonight.

I am the only woman, and as I cut through the crowd, conversations stop and eyes turn. A few seem to believe I'm one of the objects for sale and brush fingers against my shoulders or lean their heads in for a smell of perfume.

Roman spots me just as I spot him. He pulls away from a conversation and strides toward me. "Sofia!" he exclaims brightly, in absolute contradiction to the murderous expression on his face. He grips me hard by the shoulders.

"Good evening, Roman," I say, not letting him see that it hurts.

He leans in close and hisses, "What in the living hell are you doing here?"

"You asked if I'm hard enough to do what it takes, Roman. Remember? So that's what I'm doing. What it takes."

"This isn't the place for you."

Bohdan appears behind Roman and smiles at me, unfazed and a model of politeness. "Sofia Timurovna, what a delight to see you. And, Roman. I had no idea you invited your girlfriend."

"I didn't," he says. "She was just leaving."

I break away from Roman's grip. "You wanted me to learn the business and help you, Pan Kladivo," I say. "I've already seen one side of it, now I'd like to see the other."

"You know what happens here tonight, yes? Some women might find this business, we may say, *distasteful*. But you do not, Sofia Timurovna?"

"I brought these women to Praha, Pan Kladivo. I would like to see it through," I say evenly. "Besides, a wise man once told me that women who seek to rise in this world must be crueler than even men."

At hearing his own words played back, Bohdan smiles. He exchanges a few words with Roman in Czech and pats me lightly on the cheek. "Then you are welcome to stay," he says.

. . .

335

The young women are introduced to the room through the kitchen doors at eight-thirty sharp, with Miroslav Beran, chin held high like a haughty waiter, leading the parade. Some of the men cackle and elbow one another in the ribs, nodding in the direction of this or that blond- or raven-haired teenager. It's what sharks would do if they had vocal cords and elbows.

Bohdan Kladivo's clients circulate among the newcomers, chatting, studying, and making no effort to hide that they're doing anything other than appraising. A white guy with thin gray hair runs his fingers over the redhead's cheek. An Arab cups a blond's hairdo as if weighing it.

I'd expected the same frightened young women who'd shaken with terror and spat with rage as Emil and I herded them into the truck, but they are not the girls who now parade around the room. They have been transformed into rubber versions of themselves with rubber smiles, who do not flinch when the men touch them. It's only when the men break away and the women believe they are unseen that their expressions change back to stony horror.

The men have been furnished cards with snapshots and a brief biography of each printed in English, Russian, Arabic, French, and Chinese. I find a set of them sitting on a cocktail table.

> Irina, from the city of Vitebsk in Belarus. Irina has fif-
> teen years, and enjoys sport and cinema. She seeks
> a man who is strong both physically and financially,
> and describes herself as a romantic with a ravenous
> appetite for love. Irina has three languages: Belarus-
> sian, Russian, and elementary German, but is willing
> to learn the language preferred by her benefactor.

I find Irina in the crowd. She is thin and flat-chested, dressed tonight in a blue cocktail dress with her white-blond hair arranged elegantly atop her head and makeup applied over a bruise I remember she had on her left eye.

I stay close to Bohdan and Roman, making it clear that I'm with them. Bohdan sees me eyeing Irina's card. "You see the one talking to her now? He's Saudi," Bohdan says. "They always fight for the blonds, easily up to a million euros, sometimes more. Watch."

And, indeed, the Saudi—in a gleaming, ankle-length thawb with a red-checked kaffiyeh on his head—approaches Bohdan moments later. "Seven hundred," he says, waving a glass of scotch in the air.

Bohdan laughs, places a hand on the Saudi's forearm. "I've gotten an offer of nine fifty," he says.

"A million two," says the Saudi.

Bohdan makes a note on a small pad of paper using the pen I gave my father. "I'll let you know at the end of the night, Your Excellency," Bohdan says.

A bear-sized man in a tuxedo charges in, gripping Bohdan's shoulder as the Saudi slips away. His face is red, and he reeks of liquor. "The dark angel," he says in Russian. "Tell me she is not yet taken."

I follow the Russian's extended finger, which points to a woman of about my age with black hair nearly to her waist. Her eyes are dark, too, like two coals that have gone out. She's standing in a corner holding a glass of champagne and trying not to fall over in the high heels they've put her in. I flip through the cards until I find her picture.

> Seventeen-year-old Doina, whose name in her native Romanian means "folk song." She hails from Constanta on the Black Sea, which was occupied for many years by the Ottoman Turks. You can see in her much spicy Turkish blood!

"Rest comfortably, Sergei Mikhailovich, she can still be yours," Bohdan reassures him.

"I offer one fifty," the Russian says as if it were a grave oath.

"You insult me, Sergei Mikhailovich."

The Russian feigns distress, biting his red knuckle. "Two hundred, not a cent more, you old thief."

Bohdan laughs and claps him on the shoulders. "Your bid is noted."

But the smile disappears as soon as the Russian is out of sight. Bohdan leans close to me. "The cheap bastard has been near the top of every Forbes list for the last fifteen years." He nods in Doina's direction. "And you don't see beauty like that every day. It hurts me to see her go for so little."

The parade of bids goes on. Doina from Constanta is followed by Olesya from Chelyabinsk, who is followed by Tamara from Belgrade, who is followed by Endrita from a town in Albania too poor to have a name. I leave after Endrita, excusing myself to a terrace next to the bar. The air is cold tonight and bristles my bare shoulders and arms. I look out at the city, wondering how I'll ever go through with my plan, knowing that it'll never work, knowing that the girls will just head off to Riyadh or Moscow or Macau and I'll die for nothing.

The stars are good tonight, so at least there's that. I look at them, watch them, waiting for a sign I know won't come, waiting for something other than benign indifference. The hardest part about not believing in God isn't knowing there's no heaven. It's knowing there's no hell. People like Bohdan and Roman who sell women into slavery die the same as everyone else. The most you can hope for is that they feel it before they go, pain and terror.

"Not easy, that," says Bohdan Kladivo as he comes up behind me. He drapes his dinner jacket over my shoulders and lights a cigar, puffing it to life like a fish blowing bubbles. The smoke is fragrant and smells expensive.

"What's not easy?"

He gestures with his head to the casino and auction going on inside. "By the third or fourth time you do it, you'll be fine."

"You get used to it?" I ask.

"You get used to the money."

I could flip him over the railing right now. He'd land in the parking lot or on the roof of one of the limousines.

"Life isn't fair, Sofia Timurovna. You know this."

"I do, Pan Kladivo."

"If we didn't do it, someone else would. Pack them up in cargo containers, send them to who knows where. Such a waste that would be. What we do is save, we may say *rescue,* the special ones, the best ones. We rescue them from being fucked by twenty men a night in some shithole roadside brothel. Most of these girls, the girls you see tonight, will eat better than they've ever eaten in their lives. Some will have running water for the first time. Not at all the life of a street whore."

"*Rescue* them?"

"An expression. Perhaps not the right one." He puffs thoughtfully, looks at me from the corners of his eyes. "Are you having second thoughts, Sofia Timurovna? Perhaps you are not the devil I imagined?"

I breathe deeply and turn to him. "I'm every bit the devil you imagined, Pan Kladivo," I say. "Now let us go inside."

Twenty-Eight

For the after-party, the ten winners are gathered on the third floor of the casino, the private floor, the floor onto which I was never permitted as a mere dealer. It's a luxurious place, with leather couches soft as a baby's skin and the heads of dead animals on the walls.

It is filled tonight with the bass-register laughter of men. Their faces glow orange in the light of the stone fireplace. Yet it is also a place of learning, my learning. They are my specimens of *Homo horribilis*, and I take careful notes on their behavior and social interactions. For example, I learn that when one buys something for hundreds of thousands of euros, a certain amount of courtesy is required of the seller, a certain amount of hospitality as one waits for money transfers to clear. I learn that even the pridefully efficient Swiss can take up to two hours to transfer funds between banks, and if one is of the class of lesser moguls or sheiks who banks in the Seychelles or—a sure sign of Russianness—Cyprus, it can take up to four.

I learn also that despite barriers of language and nationality and culture, men who buy women share many other common interests and have no trouble engaging one another in a spirit of comity and even sincere friendliness. The American natural gas magnate who collects antique aircraft finds a new best friend in the Chinese mobile phone king, and the brother-in-law of the cousin of the Saudi king might be said to be developing a man crush on the army general from Gambia. As for the Russian nickel baron, he's teaching both the Indian advertising CEO and the British shipping heir how to dance with a bottle balanced on one's head.

But rich men are impatient men, and all are waiting for the transfers to clear so they can depart to the third floor's other wing, where their purchases await in opulent bedroom suites provided at no additional charge by tonight's hosts.

While the accounts are balanced and travel visas for the women arranged through contacts in ten different foreign ministries, Bohdan and Roman serve cocktails and offer cigars they claim come from the personal stash of the late Saddam Hussein, whose sons were customers before the recent, we may say, *unpleasantness.*

I am at their side playing the role of the learner and eager girlfriend. The American shows me the proper way to clip the end of a cigar and, as he does so, pulls me onto his lap. The Saudi holds his glass of scotch to the light and shows me how to determine its quality by the color alone. The Russian proposes marriage, and I tell him I'll consider it if things don't work out with Roman.

Bohdan takes my upper arm. "You are a charming hostess, Sofia Timurovna," he says under his breath. "You were right to come here tonight." His face is a little redder now than earlier in the evening, and his voice a little less precise.

"Your clients are looking thirsty, Pan Kladivo. Allow me to bring another round of drinks."

"Fine," he says. "But no more for me."

"Ah, but they'll think you rude if you don't join them, Pan Kladivo."
I smile. "One more. Something special."

Bohdan sighs. "One more, but then only water for me."

They are, every one of them, drunk and tired and happy. As I make for the exit, the American takes a slap at my ass. Everyone laughs, even me.

I slip away through the door and down the stairs to the bar, where Rozsa has been kept out of sight, making drinks for the winners. The bored bodyguards for the ten men upstairs are here, too, sentenced to a purgatory of mineral water and chitchat with one another. They spread out at the tables, thick men dressed in cheap black suits. Rozsa is frightened within a centimeter of her wits, frightened of them and the men upstairs. For though no women were permitted even as servers for the auction, she knows quite well why they're here for the after-party.

"A bottle of tequila," I say quietly, standing next to her behind the bar. "Do you have it?"

"Oh, yes," she says. "A very good one, too."

It's not a common drink outside the Western Hemisphere and is therefore exotic and special. Everyone will have a taste. It's the polite thing to do.

"Leave the bottle," I say. "I'll pour."

"Are you sure?"

"Rozsa, do you remember my tarot? From the night I spent at your apartment?"

She pulls a handsome crystal bottle from the very highest shelf, standing on her tiptoes to get it. "Six of cups, the fool, and the death card," she says.

"Rozsa, does anyone know you work here? Close friends in Praha, or family back home you might have told?"

She closes her eyes, ever the Hungarian, knowing somehow what

342

comes next. "Only you are my friend. As for my family, I've been alone since I was twelve."

I place the bottle on the bar and take her hands in mine. "Then you must do two things for me."

"Yes, Sofia."

"The first is, leave here. Leave the country. Now. And don't come back. The second thing you must do, twenty minutes after you're out the door, is call the police."

She takes my hands, closes her eyes. "Another idea. We both leave. You and I. We walk out. France—or England. We could."

When she opens her eyes, I give her a smile and shake my head.

Rozsa inhales, blinks at me. "So it's as I dreamt, before you came. This is the gift."

"I suppose it is."

"And the police. What should I tell them?"

"Tell them—there's been a massacre."

The room has moved on since I slipped away. Some other joke or anecdote has caught their interest. I arrive with the heavy silver tray of thirteen glasses filled to the brim and hold it up in front of me, but there seems little interest.

I sit on the armrest of the chair where the Russian is seated, then lean in close and say, "Sergei Mikhailovich, you are a man who appreciates exotic pleasures, yes?" This gets his attention, so I continue, speaking quietly so only he can hear. "In these glasses, I have tequila that's better than any exotic pleasure you've ever had."

He reaches for a glass, but I pull the tray away. "Not so fast, *gospodin*." Sir. "It is for everyone. We all must share. Will you have the honor of proposing a toast?"

And this is all the nudging he needs, because the next thing

343

I know, bloated Sergei Mikhailovich is on his feet, forcing a glass into everyone's hand.

"Gentlemen!" Sergei Mikhailovich shouts over the din of the conversation. "I wish to make a toast to our excellent friends, Bohdan and Roman Kladivo."

But I interrupt. "Sergei Mikhailovich, we must make it a proper Russian toast. That means one is to drink it all at once. No sipping."

"In the Russian manner!" he bellows. "All at once!"

Everyone raises their glasses.

"To our friends, Bohdan and Roman. We wish you long life!"

And with that, everybody drinks. Everybody but me. As instructed, they down every drop in a single swallow. Only Bohdan disobeys Sergei Mikhailovich's order and drinks only half. He squints at the tequila remaining in his glass, a sour expression on his face.

But Bohdan's expression disappears when Sergei Mikhailovich startles everyone by throwing his glass into the fireplace where it explodes and sends sparks onto the floor. *"Na zdarovye!"* he bellows. To health!

There's an awkward silence for a moment. Then Bohdan steps forward in a spirit of solidarity with his guest and throws his own glass into the fire, too. He's followed by the American, then the Gambian army general, then everyone. They laugh for a good minute.

I know I should leave. But something compels me to stay: If you have the courage for the act, you have the courage to watch the outcome.

And the outcome begins seconds later as the massive dose of cyanide from the rat poison begins to take effect. It starts with the Chinese mobile phone king. He lurches away from the others, hands over his belly, shaking, stance wide as if trying to keep his balance. When he gasps and his body collapses to the floor, throat open, eyes bulging, everyone turns to him and begins to feel it, too.

The Gambian grips the back of a chair and gags. The American sinks to the couch, grabbing at his tie. Even the bear-sized Sergei Mikhailovich taps his chest with a fist before letting out a loud belch and falling to his knees. Bohdan—hands clutching the edge of the desk but otherwise strangely still—looks to Roman, watching as his son doubles over, hands at his throat, mouth agape. Roman looks back at his father, then collapses to the floor where his body thrashes as if electrified. There's a cherry-red cast to Roman's face that grows deeper as the seizure continues.

Bohdan turns to stare at me from across the room. His body may be dying, but his mind isn't, not yet. He's working through the problem—the what and how and finally the who. When the answer comes to him, he forces his fingers into his mouth and vomits on the floor.

I step over the nearly still body of the Gambian general to get to Bohdan. He's reaching into his dinner jacket but having trouble pulling his pistol out. So I take the gun out for him and hold it loosely at my side.

"Sofia Timurovna," he says. "You are a disappointment to me."

I smile gently. "But you've made a mistake, Pan Kladivo," I say. "My name is Gwendolyn Bloom."

Even through the pain, he's able to make the connection. I reach into his dinner jacket, feel around for the inside pocket, and find the fountain pen. Speech is beyond him now as the poison works its way through his body, racing through his veins, seizing every cell it finds and shutting down its flow of oxygen. I hold the pen up so he can see it. Then he convulses and leans forward. I take him in my arms in an embrace and hold him close. His saliva runs warm and slick down my bare shoulder.

"I found him this afternoon, Pan Kladivo," I whisper. "I found my father. He's free now. And the women you sold, they'll be free soon."

I release him, and he folds to the ground. I hear his gasping, and then suddenly I don't. His body quivers on the floor for a moment with a motion that's almost serpentine, then goes still.

Eleven women take the grand staircase down to the first floor where the lobby is illuminated like a disco with spinning blue light. There are cop cars out in front of the casino, a thousand of them, a million, and twice as many officers. A squad of eight, in black helmets and face masks behind a wall of gun barrels, moves toward the entrance in a brilliantly coordinated sixteen-legged trot.

The women push through the doors, raise their hands in the air, and I follow, the last to leave. Officers rush toward us, shouting commands in Czech. I kneel along with the others, the stone hard against my knees. Someone grabs me from behind. Someone forces me to the ground and puts cuffs around my wrists.

For a brief moment, I have the illusion of flying, as if the law of gravity no longer applies to me. It's the feeling I'd get on the balance beam, the very best of the feelings I'd get. Like nothing else, this sensation. But I'm not flying, I'm being carried. There's an officer on each of my limbs, rushing me through the air toward the back of a police car.

Twenty-Nine

I place my hands on the floor and toes on the concrete slab that is my bed and begin the push-ups again. *One. Two. Three. Four.*

There are no windows in the cell other than the one in the door, and that is covered at all times and hasn't been opened once since I got here. There's a camera in the upper corner of the cell under a little black dome of glass. I don't know whether it's always being monitored, but I have to assume it is.

Eighteen. Nineteen. Twenty. Twenty-one.

I sleep only a few minutes at a time. They never turn off the lights, and since there is no blanket, I curl up on the concrete slab, shivering violently in an orange jumpsuit that's thin as paper. I keep track of the time by counting the meals I'm served through a slot at the bottom of the door. Nine meals divided by three per day means I've been here three days.

There's been no contact with anyone since my interrogation the first night. For whatever it's worth, I don't think the guys doing the interrogating were actually Czech cops. Their English was too good, and their suits too expensive. They were government types— specifically, intelligence types. Not that I gave them much by way of new intelligence. I admitted to nothing and told them only my name, my real name, Gwendolyn Bloom. What about the dozen bodies found poisoned? What about the abandoned police station north of Prague with the burnt-out truck? No idea. No clue.

Seventy-two. Seventy-three. Seventy-four. Seventy-five. I collapse to the concrete floor, exhausted but finally warm. There's a noise at the door, and at first I wonder whether it's mealtime already because it seems like I just ate. But then I realize this sound is different. It's the sound of a key in a lock.

There are no windows in the police van, either. I'm alone in the unheated back but grateful they've finally given me cheap felt slippers to go with the jumpsuit. There's not even a guard here, and the wall between me and the front of the van is solid white metal.

We drive for what feels like only twenty minutes or so, first over smooth paved roads, then over cobblestone streets in very slow traffic. Outside, I hear engines and angry horns and distant sirens. We must be back in Prague. The van makes a sharp right turn and almost immediately comes to a stop. I hear voices outside, two women talking to a man, but I can't hear what they're saying or even what language they're saying it in.

The door opens, and I squint at the dull gray sky, the first daylight I've seen in what feels like ages. A female guard motions for me to come out.

It looks and smells like rain today, and there's a biting chill in the air. We're parked in an alley between two very old buildings made of brown stone. A beer bottle rolls along the ground in the wind. The female guard is joined by another, and the two lead me through an unmarked steel door and down a long corridor to a closed elevator.

When the elevator slides open, I'm startled by the sight. It looks like a portal to another, much preferable world. My slippered feet stand in plush red carpet, and I can see my reflection and those of the guards in the mirrors that line the walls. A brass no-smoking sign is mounted over the buttons. The third floor is marked CLUB LEVEL.

Peculiar smells here: disinfectant, nice soap, roasting chicken. Peculiar sounds, too: the chatter of a crowd, a bustling restaurant kitchen, a vacuum cleaner. The elevator climbs up through the floors and as it passes each one lets out not an institutional beep but a well-tuned chime. We stop at the top floor, the fourteenth, and as the doors open, I realize we're in a hotel.

The guards lead me down a hallway and through the open doors of the room at the end of it. Only it's not a room but a suite so large and so nice there's a grand piano in the living room, and a fireplace and two matching couches upholstered in blue silk. A handsome young man with black hair is dressed in a porter's uniform complete with bow tie and white gloves. He bows and smiles pleasantly as if guests show up here all the time in chains and orange jumpsuits.

The guards unshackle me and close the door behind them as they exit, leaving me to blink in confusion at the still-smiling porter.

"Welcome to the Eminence Royale Hotel of Praha, miss. May I familiarize you with your lodgings?"

I stammer that he may, and the porter points out the switch for the fireplace, shows me how to work the tub, and opens the closet in the bedroom to show me where I can find the iron and ironing board. As he does so, I see all my clothing I'd brought to Roman's apartment hanging there, dry-cleaned and pressed.

"Who—who arranged all this?" I ask.

"Friends of yours, miss. That is all I may say because that is all I know."

"And is there a phone? I need to make a call."

"Ah, sadly the phones have been removed. But if you should want for anything, there is an attendant waiting outside the door of the suite twenty-four hours a day."

I see the "attendant" for myself when the porter leaves, a man in his late thirties with the unmoving expression and buzz cut of a soldier. He stands with his back flat against the wall and hands folded over his crotch as if shielding himself from embarrassment. A black suit that's too big for him hangs from his body, and the curly little cord from an earpiece disappears into his jacket.

In other words, he's just another kind of guard, and this is just another kind of jail. I watch the porter go down the hallway and wait for the attendant to say something, but he doesn't, so I close the door. I look for the chain lock, but of course this, like the phone, has been removed.

The room smells pleasantly of vanilla and flowers, in stark contrast to my own smell, which I suddenly notice for the first time. I haven't bathed or combed my hair or so much as brushed my teeth since the day of the auction, and a glance in the gilt mirror above a spray of fresh flowers confirms that I look like a disaster. I head to the bathroom and find that the lock on the door is thankfully still intact.

I strip and climb into the shower. Even the water feels luxurious, softer somehow, hot without scalding. The shampoo lathers perfectly into rich suds, and so does the soap. When I finish, I throw on an enormous white bathrobe as thick and soft as a mink coat. That's when I hear a sound coming from outside the bathroom. It's nothing ominous, just the sound of silverware being set and low conversation. I open the bathroom door and walk through the bedroom to discover a trio of waiters setting up a single but very elaborate place setting on the dining room table. More mysterious gifts.

I look on as one of the bow-tied waiters ladles matzo-ball soup into a bowl, and a second lifts a silver dome over the main course to reveal an enormous and very handsome club sandwich in a nest of french fries. After three days of grayish-pink something that might have been either bland goulash or spicy oatmeal, it's a gorgeous sight, but I know there's no such thing as a free lunch.

I eat it anyway, devouring it all in minutes and washing it down with a bottle of Coke the waiters left chilling in a champagne bucket. I eat too fast and am too full, and finish just in time for the arrival of the bill: a knock at the door that's not really a request because it opens a second later without my saying anything.

It takes me a minute to recognize the figure who walks in as Chase Carlisle, but when it clicks, panic splashes over me like boiling water. Instinctively, I tighten my robe. He's a little heavier and a lot more tired than I remember him looking in New York. Even his perfectly brown hair isn't quite as perfect as it used to be, graying at the temples.

"There's some bullshit Colombian-Asian fusion restaurant down-stairs," he says with the soft Virginia-gentleman lilt. "But I thought after three days of Czech prison food, young Gwendolyn might pre-fer something that sticks to the ribs."

"It was very good, thank you," I say like any nice little girl with good manners would.

Carlisle pulls out a chair and slumps into it. His tie is loosened at his throat and his tweed sport coat looks wrinkled and slept in. "Where is he, Gwendolyn?"

"He?"

"Your father."

My eyes wander to the fork lying next to my plate, and I wonder how fast I can grab it. "I don't know," I say.

"You dropped him off somewhere. After you rescued him. Where was it?"

"Somewhere on the outskirts. We were met by—he used the word *friends*."

"Wouldn't happen to be Russian or Chinese, these friends?"

"They didn't seem Russian or Chinese."

Carlisle lets out a long sigh, slumps his head into his hand, and massages his temples. "It shouldn't have come to this, you know. Those times when we approached you, we were doing it for your own safety."

The words burst out of my mouth angrily, involuntarily: "When the hell did you ever approach me? While you were sitting on your ass in New York, I was here, doing *your* job, trying to find my father."

Carlisle picks up a leftover French fry from my plate as if he's considering eating it. "We tried to rescue you in Berlin, Gwendolyn," he says tiredly. "From that gangster, Christian, remember? Two men approached you on the street. But you pulled a gun and fucked everything up. We tried again on the train to Prague. That time you went through with it—stabbed a man right in the heart."

"He had a pistol," I say.

"After what happened in Berlin, can you blame him?" He shakes his head. "If you had just left it to the professionals, we could have avoided all this."

"Avoided killing your go-to guy for rocket launchers and teenage girls?"

Carlisle's eyebrows arch with mild surprise. Then he rises and walks to the window with hands deep in pockets. "I'm not going to lie, Gwendolyn. This is a filthy, filthy business in a filthy, filthy world.

352

Yes, Bohdan Kladivo was ours. *Was.*" He turns and wags a finger in the air to emphasize the point. "But we put an end to all that once we found out about the human trafficking. Your father, bless him, saw to that."

"Who was it that set my dad up? Who arranged it?"

He runs his fingers over an elegant leather chess board on a table beside the window, then picks up the black queen. "Do you play?"

"Not really."

"It's funny. People are always saying politics is like chess. But it's not. In politics, all the pieces are pawns, and the players aren't even at the table." He tips over the black king and looks at me. "We arrested him in Switzerland, by the way. Getting off a flight in Zurich."

"Arrested who?"

"Joseph Diaz. Diaz and Kladivo were going to split Viktor Zoric's money. Your father was the only one who knew where to find the passcodes." He lets out an exhausted sigh. "As to the accounts those passcodes open, they're the Loch Ness monster of Swiss banking. We still have no idea if they even exist."

I look down, concentrating on the tablecloth, the empty bottle of Coke, anything other than Carlisle. Joey Diaz was always the closest thing I had to family when we lived abroad. We had holidays together, I played with his kids. It was Joey Diaz who told me my dad wasn't a paper-pushing State Department drone but an intelligence operative with the CIA. "Why should I believe you?"

"About?"

"Joey Diaz, any of it. How do I know you're not the one who betrayed my dad?"

A resigned laugh, a sad shake of the head. "I don't know, Gwendolyn. Look around you. Are you in some dungeon? Are there chains on your wrists?"

I see his point and say nothing.

He turns around, hands back in his pockets, just another rumpled, dopey public servant caught up in shit well beyond his pay grade. "Would it help if I showed you the arrest warrant for Joseph Diaz? Or the ten thousand memos that have been back and forth across my desk since your dad disappeared and you decided to go after him?"

"Sure," I say. "Show them to me."

Carlisle arches his eyebrows. "Then you'll have them, I don't know, tonight. Tomorrow morning, latest."

"So what's next? Do I go back to a Czech prison?"

He walks over to me, places a hand on my shoulder. I'm surprised I don't flinch. "No. We take you home. Wait for your father to get in touch. As for the Czechs, we made a deal. It wasn't hard. Half the government wanted to give you a medal for killing Kladivo. We can leave tomorrow, as soon as the debrief is done."

"The debrief?"

Carlisle shrugs. "We ask you what happened, you tell us. A formality. Something to put in the filing cabinet."

She is, I guess, about forty or so, with straight black hair pulled back in a ponytail. She's wearing a navy blue pantsuit and carries a leather case in her hand. Entering the suite, she gives a pleasant, very American inquiry of "Hello?" as if she were just a kindly neighbor looking to borrow the lawn mower. Carlisle introduces her as Dr. Simon, a psychiatrist who will, he says, be helping me through the debrief.

"Just government-speak for a chat," she says, head tilted to the side. "You've been through quite a bit in the last few days, haven't you?"

It's all very chirpy and passive the way she says it. The whole *been through a lot* makes it sound as though it had been a car accident instead of a war of my own making. But maybe that's her point.

"I'm doing fine," I say.

"Gwendolyn, when was the last time you had a tuberculosis shot?"

"No idea."

Dr. Simon holds up the leather case. "Unfortunately, TB is very common in Czech jails, so we strongly recommend a booster shot to anyone in your situation. Do you mind? It'll only hurt for a second."

I'm about to object, but if it moves things along, I'll comply. I sit down on the couch and pull up the sleeve of my robe.

Dr. Simon sits beside me, puts on a pair of translucent rubber gloves, and prepares the injection. Her fingers are cold and sticky on my skin as she squeezes and prods the flesh on my upper arm.

I always had to look away from needles, but for some reason, it doesn't bother me this time. I watch the slender line approach my arm and don't even blink at the pain as it forms a crater in the skin, then slides through it. As she presses the plunger on the syringe, the sensation of being injected with pleasantly cool water spreads from my arm to my chest and into my limbs and head. The doctor places a folded piece of gauze over the hole as she withdraws the needle and tapes it into place.

"Good job," Dr. Simon says as if she were a pediatrician and I were four.

She moves to the armchair, while Carlisle settles into the far end of the couch opposite mine. I can barely see him from where I'm sitting.

"Comfortable?" Dr. Simon asks.

"Sure," I say.

"Then let's talk awhile." She crosses her legs and leans forward, the posture of every shrink I've ever seen in my life. "Let's start with how you rescued your father, your dad. From what I heard, it was quite an adventure."

It's all very annoying, her posture, her tone. And the three days of not knowing whether it's night or day and sleeping in ten-minute increments must be catching up to me. I look over at the grandfather clock in the corner. It's 1:17. I tell myself I'll answer their questions until exactly 1:30, then demand some rest.

I begin with the morning of the auction: the deal for the RPGs, shooting Emil, blowing up the truck, the rescue, the pudgy guard, my dad's wound. It shocks me how much I can remember. I tell her every detail, all of it coming back to me with incredible lucidity as if my memories were an exhibit in a museum I could walk through and describe to a blind companion.

"And tell me about when you left him. Who picked him up, Gwendolyn?"

I describe the City Tours van, the guy named Sam and what he looked like, the two medics and what they looked like. Jesus, how is my memory this good? I tighten the robe and sink deeper into the couch. It's really very cozy here, and maybe I was wrong about this Dr. Simon. She's starting to grow on me. Friendly without being overbearing.

"So, this Sam fellow," she says. "What did he tell you about where they were taking your dad?"

I shake my head. "Nothing at all."

"Nothing? Surely he said something."

"No. I ran away before he had a chance to."

"Did Sam have an accent of any kind?" she says.

"American," I say.

"Interesting," she says.

She follows with questions about what happened later that night. About the poison I used. How I got it. How I slipped it to the men. How I felt about watching them all just collapse and die right there before my eyes. I tell her everything matter-of-factly, describing it as if I were back in the room at the casino, picking my way through the bodies to the exit. When I look up, she's leaning forward, eyebrows arched with concern, a box of tissues in her hand.

I wonder why she's doing this until I feel the tears drying cool on my cheeks and neck. How long have I been crying? I'm embarrassed about weeping in front of her, but only a little. Dr. Simon doesn't seem to mind. She's seen it all before, and she gets it. I can tell.

"Let's go back a little further, Gwendolyn. To New York. Do you remember New York?"

I'm so sleepy. I settle back in the couch. Wriggle down into its corner. Close my eyes.

"Not yet, Gwendolyn," Dr. Simon says. "Just a few more questions, okay?"

"Okay, Dr. Simon."

"We found out about the storage locker in Queens. You went there, didn't you? It's okay. You're not in trouble."

"Yes. I broke a window."

"And what did you find there? In the storage locker?"

My throat feels raw, as if I've been speaking for a long time. Too much to get into. The book cipher. Terrance. "A list of account numbers," I say. "Can I have some water?"

There is a pause, a break in the cadence of the questions as Carlisle slips from sight. He returns a moment later with a glass of water and sets it in front of me.

"And where are those account numbers now, Gwendolyn?" she says as I drink. The water is delicious. Clean and cleansing.

"Destroyed," I say. "Burned."

"Why did you destroy them, Gwendolyn?"

Yael's words from Paris as we watched the paper burning in the wastebasket. *Remember this always: Anyone who asks for these account numbers is your enemy.*

"I—I can't remember. I'm sorry."

"That's all right, Gwendolyn," she says. "Were they the only copy?"

I open my mouth to tell her the answer, to flesh out the story a little. About the copy of *1984*. About the code. How it's no problem to get the account numbers again. But I don't. I don't because I can't. Something won't let the words form. I reach under my robe and scratch at the sore spot on my arm where she gave me the tuberculosis shot. From across the room I see the grandfather clock: 5:58.

I look down, focusing on the fabric of my robe. What's wrong with me? Why can't I answer her? But my mind can focus on nothing but the time on the grandfather clock. There was something I was going to do at a certain time. Some deadline I had set for myself. Now it's passed. Now it's too late.

Then it comes to me. It's almost four and a half hours after I told myself I'd stop answering their questions. Four and a half hours? Jesus Christ, where did the time go? It just disappeared as if I'd fallen asleep. I scratch again at the sore spot on my arm.

I know I should be angry that Dr. Simon betrayed my trust by lying to me. Intellectually, I want to stand up and break her neck. But let's not be rash. Let's not jump to conclusions about her intentions. She'll tell me the truth, Dr. Simon will, all I have to do is ask. She's cool like that. She has the kind of face someone can trust.

"Dr. Simon?" I ask. "That wasn't a TB vaccine you gave me, was it?"

"It was something to help you relax, darling," she says. "And to help you remember."

I retreat back into my head and wonder where the anger is. "Mr. Carlisle?" I say calmly, still not able to muster the anger I know should be there. "It's not true about Joey Diaz, is it?"

Carlisle rises from his seat on the couch and adjusts his pants. Then he steps around the coffee table so he's standing directly in front of me. "Come again?" he asks.

"It wasn't Joey Diaz who betrayed my dad," I say. "It was you."

There's a flash of motion as Carlisle seizes my wrists, but my senses are slow and sloppy, and by the time I realize what's happening, Dr. Simon has another needle in my arm. The sensation of being injected with cool water once again spreads through my body.

Thirty

There are rough hands on my limbs and the sensation of cold night air on my skin. There is the smell of leather and old coffee. There is the sound of distant voices and a motor, big and American, clearing its throat with a chortle as it starts up. Someone buckles me into place with a seat belt, and we begin to move.

There is an emergency of some sort happening, a conclusion my narcotized mind draws from a vague and formless collection of indicators—the way I'm handled, the timbre of men's speech, the tone of the engine. Everything is rushed, urgent. My transport somewhere is to be accomplished quickly, this moment, right now. I try to focus my mind and dissect the collection of indicators, but it's pleasant and warm here in my semiconscious world and something tells me I don't really want to know the answers anyway.

I'm aware of Carlisle sitting next to me. I can tell it's him from the smell. Oaky, rummy cologne, the kind gentlemen with money wear, and the tinge of a certain kind of greedy sweat, the kind that makes dogs growl. He's conversing with someone else, a driver maybe, and I hear the words "wheels-up in forty-five."

Wheels-up. A term relating to flight. They're heading for a flight. *We're* heading for a flight. My eyes flicker open, and I try to pull data in—where I am, who's here—try to assess its meaning. I'm in the back of a large SUV. A Chevy, or so says the emblem on the steering wheel. The vehicle of choice of American embassies everywhere. And I'm not in a robe anymore. Someone dressed me. God, I hope it wasn't Carlisle.

I look outside and see it's already dark as we pass through the outskirts of Prague, outskirts that are quickly giving way to weedy fields and clumps of birch forest visible in the headlamps. The clock on the dashboard says 11:42 p.m.

Carlisle sits beside me, leaning forward, jacket off, no attempt to hide his shoulder holster and pistol any longer. His arm is braced on the driver's headrest, and he's watching the road ahead of us, scanning, searching. He presses a phone to his ear.

"Get ahold of General Aliyev," he shouts, as if the person he was talking to was very far away. "Tell him we're en route to the airstrip. ETA to Ashgabat is seven hours. Got it? Seven hours. Don't disappoint me now."

I try to work out where Ashgabat is. Kazakhstan. Uzbekistan. *Somethingstan*, anyway. What's there? Oil. Dictators. Secret prisons. Turkmenistan—that's it. Run by a man beloved by the US, hated by everyone else, his own citizens most of all. A dictator the US keeps in its pocket for such things as it doesn't have the stomach to do itself.

Carlisle hangs up, slides the phone into his pants pocket.

"What's in Ashgabat?" I say as clearly as the drugs will let me.

He turns to me and seems surprised I can speak. "A charming

coffeehouse. Serves an excellent local cake made with almonds and honey," he says. "It's not too far from a special facility we have there. Someplace you can cool your heels until your father decides he wants you back."

"I've told you everything I know," I say, certain he can hear the fear in my voice.

"And what do you *know* exactly, Gwendolyn?" Carlisle says, turning to me, the broad expanse of his chest and the even broader expanse of his stomach angrily straining at the buttons of his shirt. "That your father's a hero who tried to stop Bohdan Kladivo and a corrupt Agency man from stealing a vast sum of money? Is that what he told you?"

"Something like that," I say.

Carlisle shakes his head, turns back to the road, and sighs. "Isn't there another possible narrative, Gwendolyn? What besides such absolutely *unheard of* integrity makes a man put his life in danger? Hell, put his *daughter's* life in danger?"

He leaves the questions hanging there, supplying no answers as we exit the highway and turn left onto a dirt road. It's rural here. Very empty. Fields, stubbly and recently harvested, shimmer in the moonlight.

What Carlisle's getting at is clear enough. Money. Money would make a man put his life, and even his daughter's life, in danger. I turn away from the idea, actually turn my head away. I know my father to be an honest man who would never lie to me or put me in harm's way. But as soon as this thought crystallizes in my head, my own memory retorts by throwing a brick through it. The lies he told about what he did for a living. The danger he put my mother and me in by accepting a post in Algeria. So if he's a liar and a shitty husband and father, why can't he also be a thief?

"It's not true," I say aloud. But it's reflexive, an automated response.

Like closing your eyes when you sneeze. Like doubling over when you get punched in the stomach.

Carlisle smiles. "So every daughter believes," he says. "But he betrayed himself, Gwendolyn. He tried to steal Zoric's money. Joseph Diaz and Bohdan Kladivo tried to steal it back. Thieves stealing from thieves; that's what the world has come to."

"Stop it," I say, focusing my gaze out the window. We've entered a forest, spooky bare branches desperately clutching at nothing at all. Fuck Carlisle. Fuck Carlisle even if he's right.

"Sad part is, Gwendolyn, you rescued him, then he left you—*again*, a second time." Carlisle's eyes are back and forth from me to the road, but I can tell he's proud of the garden of doubt he's sowing. "You don't have to believe me, of course. But at a certain point, you must decide what you really know to be true."

The SUV rounds a corner, then slows suddenly. Both Carlisle and I look out the windshield and see why. A panel van marked with the words SKUPINA CEZ printed below an orange corporate logo is parked in the middle of the road. Safety cones are standing like sentinels to form a barrier blocking us from going any farther, while a worker in a reflective yellow vest and hard hat is standing in front of us holding a stop sign.

"The hell is this?" Carlisle says.

"No idea," the driver says. "Some power company thing, looks like."

Yellow lights on the roof of the van spin, and two spotlights on stands point downward at a spot in the road where two more workers are standing with shovels in hand. There's machinery of some sort, an air compressor maybe, humming nearby.

The driver lowers the window and gives a shout but the worker with the stop sign points to his ear. The driver shouts again, and this time the man approaches.

"Look, we're trying to get through," the driver says.

The worker shakes his head. "All is," he says, struggling with his English. "Very bad here. No go. No go."

Carlisle leans forward holding an ID card. "This is a diplomatic vehicle, you understand?" he says. "By law, you have to let us pass."

But the man just smiles apologetically and walks back to his post, blocking us with his stop sign.

"For Christ's sake," Carlisle says, slamming the palm of his hand into the driver's headrest. "Go tell them to get out of the way!"

The driver hesitates, then throws the SUV into park and climbs out. I can see him in the headlights, gesturing with his hands, pointing. The man with the stop sign just shakes his head.

It's at this moment that the interior of the SUV is illuminated by blue flashing lights. Both Carlisle and I turn to see a Czech police car pulling up behind us.

"Shit," Carlisle hisses. *"Shit."*

There is something here he recognizes, some pattern he's seen before. My eyes dart back to the driver. The man with the sign and the two other workers are converging around him.

The butt of a flashlight raps against Carlisle's window, not impolite, but leaving no question as to who's now in charge. It's a female cop, dark curly hair jutting out from beneath her hat, leather jacket shiny and new. The flashlight is held in one hand while the other rests on her sidearm.

"Goddammit," Carlisle hisses, and lowers the window halfway.

The cop says something in Czech that is unmistakably an order and shines the flashlight onto Carlisle's face. He produces the magic ID card once again, but the cop waves this away. I have no idea what she's saying, but it's clear she wants him to get out of the car.

Unbidden and out of nowhere, Carlisle's words somehow come back to me: *But at a certain point, you must decide what you really know to be true.*

I return my eyes to the driver and three workers. Something peculiar is happening there, as well. One of the workers, directly behind the driver, has a pistol with a silencer in his hand.

But at a certain point

Carlisle also sees it and reaches for his shoulder holster. The worker beside the driver raises the pistol and points it at the back of the driver's head. The driver is oblivious. Can't see the gun pointed at him. The worker takes his time leveling it, getting it just right, making sure the bullet he's about to fire goes where he wants it to go.

you must decide

The gun slides out of Carlisle's holster, an expert thumb flips the safety, and he's raising it. There's a sound I've heard before, hammer on metal, the sound of a pistol with a silencer firing. It's not Carlisle's. It's the worker's. I catch it just in time to see the aftermath, to see the fan of blood and the body of the driver crumple to the ground.

what you really know

Carlisle raises his pistol and catches the cop by surprise. She's quick, though, and has her own pistol out before Carlisle can fire. Without thought, without being ordered to, my hand travels forward, traversing the space between my side and Carlisle's gun in no measurable time. I twist the pistol, and his wrist gives way like paper. The gun is now in my hand.

to be true.

I fire the pistol into Carlisle's body eight times. I fire the pistol into Carlisle's body until the slide is back and there are no more bullets. I am deaf from the gunshots and do not hear the window break or the voice of the cop as she pulls me from the car.

I am on the ground, semiconscious, staring at the cop's face. She is studying me, checking me for holes, and though I can't hear her words, I recognize her face as Yael's.

The workers pick me up, one on each limb just as the Prague cops did outside the casino. They carry me to the panel van. Doors close. Wheels roll. We're on the move.

Two hours later, just across the German border, Gwendolyn Bloom dies in the living room of a little farmhouse. One of the men from the van hands me the passport I'd abandoned at Yael's studio in Paris. Just as he instructs, I pull it apart, placing each page into the fire burning in the stone hearth. I watch my death, silent and detached, waiting until one page burns up completely before putting the next one in. I save the page with my picture and name on it for last. It takes a long time to catch, but finally the photo of Gwendolyn Bloom blisters and curls and rolls back on itself and becomes black ash.

Just as I finish stirring the remains of the passport with the blackened end of an iron poker, Yael—the woman called Yael—enters through the front door.

She's driven separately, in the police car—to get rid of it, the men told me—and pulled off somewhere a few kilometers before the border. Yael's uniform is gone now, replaced by jeans and a tight sweater.

As she enters, I rush to her, wrapping her in my arms, holding her tightly. She smells of gasoline and fire. Yael gives me a quick squeeze in return, then slips out of the embrace.

"Is he okay? Is my father okay?" I gasp. "Yael, goddammit, tell me."

She says a few words to the men in Hebrew, and they disappear into the kitchen, leaving us alone. She sits on the couch before the fireplace and pats the seat next to her.

"He'll be fine," she says. "Physically, he'll be fine."

I rock forward, let out a relieved gasp. "Is he—in Israel?"

"A private clinic here in Europe. Under a different name. That's all I can say."

"So I can see him. Soon."

Yael shrugs. "A few weeks, I should think. The wound was worse than they thought, but he's doing well."

One of the men comes out of the kitchen carrying two mugs of tea. He sets them on the table in front of us and leaves. Yael reaches for hers and takes a sip. "The boys, they gave you your things, from Carlisle's vehicle? Backpack, clothing?"

"They did."

"And did you do what they said, burn the passport?"

"Yes," I say. "But Sofia's wasn't there."

Yael nods. "That's all right. She's dead anyway."

We watch the fire a moment; I even manage to drink a little of my tea. I could stay like this for a long time. Awash in heat from the fire and my gratitude.

"We worked together once. Your father and I," Yael volunteers suddenly. "He's a good man."

I close my eyes and remember her story from the restaurant in Paris. About the man she fell in love with in Budapest. Married, she'd said. And from the intelligence service of another country. When I open my eyes again, she's looking at me, and I wonder if she knows what I was thinking. "But that's not the only reason you rescued him," I say. "What did you tell me once? About interests being aligned?"

"He got himself in trouble," she says. "So Tel Aviv offered him a trade."

"What trade?"

"Information in exchange for a way out." She pulls the tea bag from the mug, circling the string around her finger. "A new life abroad. All he has to do is tell us what he knows."

"About the accounts?"

"About everything."

Become a spy for Israel, she means. Well, the American government sold him out first, so let the flag-wavers denounce him because I sure as hell won't. But it can't be the only way. "We can go back," I offer. "We can tell the CIA what happened. How it was Carlisle after the money, not my dad."

Yael is quiet for so long I wonder if she heard me. But then she places a hand on my forearm and smiles gently. "Sometimes I forget you're only seventeen," she says.

"Eighteen. I'm eighteen now." I pull my arm away. "You believe that it was Carlisle who set my dad up, don't you? You believe that my dad would never steal, right?"

Her eyes, the cold operative's eyes, are filled with pity. Then she shrugs. "It doesn't really matter what any of us believe, does it?" she says. "The truth is whatever the man holding the gun says it is."

I rise to my feet so quickly my vision goes black for a moment and I think I might faint. Yael leaps up, takes my arm, keeps me upright.

"I have to go back," I say. "There's my aunt Georgina. And Bela and Lili. I need to see them. And someone else. A friend."

"Terrance?" Yael says.

I close my eyes, almost embarrassed. "Yes," I whisper.

She pulls me into a close hug. Once more, gasoline and fire. "It can't happen," she says.

"Just a phone call," I say.

"Not even a phone call," she says. "Nothing. No contact."

"For how long?" I ask.

"For always," she says.

At first, I think Yael is trembling, but then I realize it's me.

There's an inquisitive tap on the door that leads from the kitchen and one of the men enters. He hands Yael an envelope, and she in turn hands it to me.

I know what it is before even opening it. I can tell from the weight. From the shape. I tilt the envelope, and a new passport slides into my hand, still warm.

Acknowledgments

To Jean Feiwel and the entire Feiwel & Friends/Macmillan team: You have brought so many wonderful stories into the world; I'm honored and humbled to be among your authors. To my editor, Liz Szabla: Your elegant ideas, wisdom, and patient guidance keep me on course and straighten the most crooked of narrative paths. To my agent, Tracey Adams: You foretold all that was to come, then made it happen. I could be in no better hands. To Maya Myers: I'm forever grateful, not only for your skill as an editor but for our friendship. To Livy, Julie, and Cassie: You are the best beta readers I could imagine. Thank you for your brutal honesty. To Mom, Dad, Marj, Ali, Achilles, Sam, and Kari: Because we believe in each other, always. To Sonja and Renata: I'm blessed to be your dad. You are why I do this. To Jana: Since that October night in New York so many years ago, you sought only the best from me. Everything I learned about strength and courage and love, I learned from you. To Fred Marfell: You gave that dopey twelve-year-old the F he deserved, then became my friend and mentor. Miss you, dear friend. I wish so badly you were here.

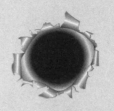

Thank you for reading this FEIWEL AND FRIENDS book.

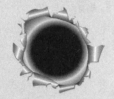

The friends who made

The Cruelty

possible are:

JEAN FEIWEL, Publisher

LIZ SZABLA, Editor in Chief

RICH DEAS, Senior Creative Director

HOLLY WEST, Editor

ALEXEI ESIKOFF, Senior Managing Editor

KIM WAYMER, Production Manager

ANNA ROBERTO, Editor

CHRISTINE BARCELLONA, Associate Editor

EMILY SETTLE, Administrative Assistant

ANNA POON, Editorial Assistant

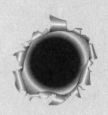

Follow us on Facebook or visit us online at mackids.com.

OUR BOOKS ARE FRIENDS FOR LIFE.